KT-456-921

THE FEMALE QUIXOTE

OR, THE ADVENTURES OF ARABELLA

Mrs Charlotte Lennox

HUGH BAIRD COLLEGE
LIBRARY AND LEARNING CENTRES

NONSUCH

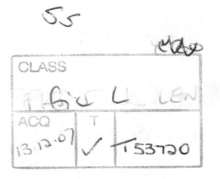

55

MAY

CLASS

F6J L LEN

ACQ   T
13.12.07   ✓   T 53720

First published 1752
Copyright © in this edition Nonsuch Publishing, 2007

Nonsuch Publishing
Cirencester Road, Chalford, Stroud, Gloucestershire, GL6 8PE

Nonsuch Publishing (Ireland)
73 Lower Leeson Street, Dublin 2, Ireland

www.nonsuch-publishing.com

Nonsuch Publishing is an imprint of NPI Media Group

For comments or suggestions, please email the editor of this series at:
classics@tempus-publishing.com

All rights reserved. No part of this book may be reprinted or reproduced or
utilised in any form or by any electronic, mechanical or other means, now known
or hereafter invented, including photocopying and recording, or in any information
storage or retrieval system, without the permission in writing from the Publishers.

British Library Cataloguing in Publication Data.
A catalogue record for this book is available from the British Library.

ISBN 978 1 84588 498 7

Typesetting and origination by NPI Media Group
Printed in Great Britain

Hugh Baird College

T53720

3720

THE FEMALE QUIXOTE

CONTENTS

INTRODUCTION TO THE MODERN EDITION

IN JANUARY 1605 THE FIRST part of Don Miguel de Cervantes y Saavedra's novel *El ingenioso hidalgo don Quixote de la Mancha* was published in Madrid by Francisco de Robles, and became an instant best-seller. The story follows the adventures of Alonso Quixano, a late middle-aged country gentleman in La Mancha (an area of central Spain to the south of Madrid), who spends so much time reading stories of chivalry that he believes them to be true, and that he is the eponymous knight-errant 'Don Quixote.' It is generally regarded as the first modern European novel and is perhaps one of the most important works in the canon of Western literature; its cultural legacy is immense and undoubted.

Alonso Quixano, believing himself to be Don Quixote, decides that he should go in search of adventure: mounted on Rocinante, a rather malnourished horse whose name implies that it has seen better days, and accompanied by Sancho Panza, a rustic neighbour whom he persuades to act as his squire, he rides through La Mancha looking for damsels in distress to rescue, and other suitable deeds of valour to perform. Unsurprisingly, his delusion leads him to regard perfectly ordinary people and events in a totally unrealistic light. The most famous such episode is when, seeing some windmills in the distance, he believes them to be giants and charges towards them, only to be unhorsed by the sails: 'tilting at windmills' has entered the popular imagination as a way of describing attempts to take on phantom adversaries, or indeed almost any futile endeavour in which the protagonist ends up being knocked off his metaphorical horse. Eventually, after many adventures of a similarly ridiculous nature, and thanks to the efforts of his niece, his housekeeper, the curate and the barber, Quixano is disillusioned of his fantasy and renounces knight-errantry and chivalric romances, and the novel ends with his death.

So popular was the first part of *Don Quixote* with contemporary readers that numerous unauthorised editions were soon in print and the original publisher, Robles, found it necessary to issue a third edition himself by 1608. Famously, Alonso Fernández de Avellaneda, whose true identity has never been discovered, wrote a second part (including a preface attacking Cervantes), which appeared in 1614 and capitalised on the success of part one, and spurred Cervantes on to complete his own second part, which was published in the following year. This (authentic) second part is regarded by most scholars as being of superior quality to the first, as the characterisation is deeper and the philosophical discussions between Don Quixote and Sancho Panza more profound. *Don Quixote* has been translated into approximately sixty-five languages and has remained popular throughout the world ever since its first publication.

The cultural legacy of *Don Quixote* can be seen in the literature, art, music, theatre and cinema of most Western European and Northern and South American countries (South America, most of which was then under Spanish dominion, was one of the first places outside Spain itself where it was sold, at least seventy copies reaching Peru in 1605). The novel inspired works of art by Honoré Daumier, Gustave Doré, Pablo Picasso and Salvador Dali; Henry Purcell, Georg Philipp Telemann, Maurice Ravel and Richard Strauss composed music based on it; Jules Massenet and Felix Mendelssohn made it into operas; George Balanchine created a ballet; and there have been numerous adaptations for the theatre and the cinema. However, it is upon other works of literature that *Don Quixote* has had the greatest effect. From *Cardenio*, one of the lost plays by William Shakespeare, to *Asterix in Spain* by René Goscinny and Albert Uderzo, it has influenced authors for more than four centuries.

A number of eighteenth-century English novels drew upon *Don Quixote* to a greater or lesser degree. Henry Fielding noted that he wrote *Joseph Andrews* (1742) 'in Imitation of the Manner of Cervantes'; Laurence Sterne makes numerous references to it in *Tristram Shandy* (1759–1767), including naming Parson Yorrick's horse 'Rocinante;' and *The Spiritual Quixote* (1773) by Richard Graves features a young man who decides to become a preacher-errant, travelling through the countryside looking for people to convert to Methodism, rather than damsels in distress to rescue. Charlotte Lennox's *The Female Quixote; or, the Adventures of Arabella* (1752) is, however, perhaps the closest in spirit to Cervantes' original. Arabella is the daughter of a marquess; when her mother dies shortly after Arabella's birth her father decides to raise her in complete seclusion. Although intelligent and well educated, not to mention beautiful, she grows up without any acquaintance with the real world, and forms her ideas of what it is like based on the 'great store of romances' that had belonged to her mother; 'and, what was more unfortunate, not in the original French, but in very bad translations.' She comes to believe that the outlandish worlds therein portrayed are true reflections of reality: that a single knight should be able to defeat an army of thousands in the service of his lady and that if his lady does not return his love then he will die more or less on the spot. Like Don Quixote, Arabella treats these romances as if they were instruction manuals for life, and holds up the examples of Mandane, Statira and Clelia as he does Amadis de Gaul.

Her insistence on basing her life on what she regards as the laws of romance of course leads to numerous misunderstandings, always to Arabella's disadvantage. When Mr Glanville, a sensible, honourable man who had won her father's approval as a prospective husband before his death, declares his love for Arabella, she sees it as insufferable presumption and banishes him from her presence. When he does not fall down dead as a result it causes her to think that he is not as fervently in love with her as he should be. She expects almost every man she meets to fall madly in love with her, and believes them to do so if they so much as say a kind word to her. She lives in constant fear of being carried off by ravishers, who will take her to a distant castle and force her to marry them, although, naturally, she is confident of being rescued from such a situation by a knight-errant before any real damage is done.

Like Jane Austen's *Northanger Abbey* (1817), which parodied the Gothic novel, *The Female Quixote* is a satirical attack on a particular kind of fiction, without being, by its very nature, in any way against novels *per se*. Charlotte Lennox focused her disapproval upon the kind of lurid French novels that were, during the late eighteenth and early nineteenth centuries, regarded as rather vulgar (although this did nothing to stop them being very popular), and the readers who were in thrall to them. Her portrait of a young woman whose mind is warped by an unvaried diet of unwholesome reading material, and too little knowledge of the real world, remains remarkably fresh and funny more than 250 years after it was written and is an effective warning about the potential dangers of allowing fantasy to overtake reality.

DEDICATION

To the Right Honourable the Earl of Middlesex

My Lord,

Such is the power of interest over almost every mind, that no one is long without arguments to prove any position which is ardently wished to be true, or to justify any measures which are dictated by inclination.

By this subtle sophistry of desire, I have been persuaded to hope that this book may, without impropriety, be inscribed to your lordship; but am not certain that my reasons will have the same force upon other understandings.

The dread which a writer feels of the public censure; the still greater dread of neglect; and the eager wish for support and protection, which is impressed by the consciousness of imbecility; are unknown to those who have never adventured into the world; and, I am afraid, my lord, equally unknown to those who have always found the world ready to applaud them.

It is, therefore, not unlikely, that the design of this address may be mistaken, and the effects of my fear imputed to my vanity: those who see your lordship's name prefixed to my performance, will rather condemn my presumption than compassionate my anxiety.

But, whatever be supposed my motive, the praise of judgment cannot be denied me; for to whom can timidity so properly fly for shelter as

to him who has been so long distinguished for candour and humanity?
How can vanity be so completely gratified, as by the allowed patronage
of him whose judgment has so long given a standard to the national
taste? Or by what other means could I so powerfully suppress all
opposition, but that of envy, as by declaring myself,

My Lord,
Your Lordship's
Obliged and most obedient
Humble Servant,
The Author.

BOOK I

I

Contains a turn at court, neither new nor surprising. Some useless additions to a fine lady's education. The bad effects of a whimsical study, which, some will say, is borrowed from Cervantes

THE MARQUIS OF ——, FOR a long series of years, was the first and most distinguished favourite at court: he held the most honourable employments under the crown, disposed of all places of profit as he pleased, presided at the council, and, in a manner, governed the whole kingdom.

This extensive authority could not fail of making him many enemies: he fell at last a sacrifice to the plots they were continually forming against him: and was not only removed from all his employments, but banished the court for ever.

The pain his undeserved disgrace gave him, he was enabled to conceal by the natural haughtiness of his temper; and, behaving rather like a man who had resigned than been dismissed from his post, he imagined he triumphed sufficiently over the malice of his enemies, while he seemed to be wholly insensible of the effects it produced. His secret discontent, however, was so much augmented by the opportunity he now had of observing the baseness and ingratitude of mankind, which in some degree experienced every day, that he resolved to quit all society whatever, and devote the rest of his life to solitude and privacy. For the place of his retreat, he pitched upon a castle he had in a very remote province of the kingdom, in the neighbourhood of a small village, and several miles distant from any town. The vast extent of ground which surrounded this noble building, he had caused to be laid out in a manner peculiar to his taste: the most laborious endeavours of art had been used to make it appear like the beautiful product of wild uncultivated nature. But if this epitome of Arcadia could boast of only artless and simple beauties, the inside of the castle was adorned with a magnificence suitable to the dignity and immense riches of the owner.

While things were preparing at the castle for his reception, the marquis, though now advanced in years, cast his eyes on a young lady, greatly inferior to himself in quality, but whose beauty and good sense promised him an agreeable companion. After a very short courtship, he married her, and in a few weeks carried his new bride into the country, from whence he absolutely resolved never to return.

The marquis, following the plan of life he had laid down, divided his time between the company of his lady, his library, which was large and well furnished, and his gardens. Sometimes he took the diversion of hunting, but never admitted any company whatever: his pride and extreme reserve rendered him so wholly inaccessible to the country gentry about him, that none ever presumed to solicit his acquaintance.

In the second year of his retirement, the marchioness brought him a daughter, and died in three days after her delivery. The marquis, who had tenderly loved her, was extremely afflicted at her death; but time having produced its usual effects, his great fondness for the little Arabella entirely engrossed his attention, and made up all the happiness of his life. At four years of age, he took her from under the direction of the nurses and women appointed to attend her, and permitted her to receive no part of her education from another which he was capable of giving her himself. He taught her to read and write in a very few months; and, as she grew older, finding in her an uncommon quickness of apprehension, and an understanding capable of great improvements, he resolved to cultivate so promising a genius with the utmost care; and, as he frequently, in the rapture of paternal fondness, expressed himself, render her mind as beautiful as her person was lovely.

Nature had, indeed, given her a most charming face, a shape easy and delicate, a sweet and insinuating voice, and an air so full of dignity and grace, as drew the admiration of all that saw her. These native charms were improved with all the heightenings of art: her dress was perfectly magnificent: the best masters of music and dancing were sent for from London to attend her. She soon became a perfect mistress of the French and Italian languages, under the care of her father; and it is not to be doubted, but she would have made a great proficiency in all useful knowledge, had not her whole time been taken up by another study.

From her earliest youth she had discovered a fondness for reading, which extremely delighted the marquis: he permitted her, therefore, the use of his library, in which, unfortunately for her, were great store of romances, and, what was still more unfortunate, not in the original French, but very bad translations.

The deceased marchioness had purchased these books to soften a solitude which she found very disagreeable; and, after her death, the marquis removed them from her closet into his library, where Arabella found them.

The surprising adventures with which they were filled, proved a most pleasing entertainment to a young lady who was wholly secluded from the world; who had no other diversion but ranging, like a nymph, through gardens; or, to say better, the woods and lawns in which she was enclosed; and who had no other conversation but that of a grave and melancholy father, or her own attendants.

Her ideas, from the manner of her life, and the objects around her, had taken a romantic turn; and, supposing romances were real pictures of life, from them she drew all her notions and expectations. By them she was taught to believe, that love was the ruling principle of the world; that every other passion was subordinate to this; and that it caused all the happiness and miseries of life. Her glass, which she often consulted, always showed her a form so extremely lovely, that, not finding herself engaged in such adventures as were common to the heroines in the romances she read, she often complained of the insensibility of mankind, upon whom her charms seemed to have so little influence.

The perfect retirement she lived in afforded, indeed, no opportunities of making the conquests she desired; but she could not comprehend how any solitude could obscure enough to conceal a beauty like hers from notice: and thought the reputation of her charms sufficient to bring a crowd of adorers to demand her of her father. Her mind being wholly filled with the most extravagant expectations, she was alarmed by every trifling incident: and kept in a continual anxiety by a vicissitude of hopes, fears, wishes, and disappointments.

II

Contains a description of a lady's dress, in fashion not much above two thousand years ago. The beginning of an adventure which seems to promise a great deal

ARABELLA HAD NOW ENTERED INTO her seventeenth year, with the regret of seeing herself the object of admiration to a few rustics only, who happened to see her; when, one Sunday, making use of the permission the marquis sometimes allowed her, to attend Divine service at the church belonging to the village near which they lived, her vanity was flattered with an adorer not altogether unworthy of her notice.

This gentleman was young, gay, handsome, and very elegantly dressed: he was just come from London with an intention to pass some weeks with a friend in that part of the country; and at the time Arabella entered the church, his eyes, which had wandered from one rural fair to another, were in an instant fixed upon her face. She blushed with a very becoming modesty; and, pleased with the unusual appearance of so fine a gentleman, and the particular notice he took of her, passed on to her seat through a double row of country people; who, with a profusion of awkward bows and curtsies, expressed their respect.

Mr Hervey, for that was the stranger's name, was no less surprised at her beauty, than the singularity of her dress; and the odd whim of being followed into the church by three women attendants, who, as soon as she was seated, took their places behind her.

Her dress, though singular, was far from being unbecoming. All the beauties of her neck and shape were set off to the greatest advantage by the fashion of her gown, which, in the manner of a robe, was made to sit tight to her body, and fastened on the breast with a knot of diamonds. Her fine black hair hung upon her neck in curls, which had so much the appearance of being artless, that all but her maid, whose employment it was to give them that form, imagined they were so. Her headdress was only a few knots advantageously disposed, over which she wore a white sarsenet hood, somewhat in the form of a veil, with which she sometimes wholly covered her fair face, when she saw herself beheld with too much attention.

This veil had never appeared to her so necessary before. Mr Hervey's eager glances threw her into so much confusion, that pulling it over her face as much as she was able, she remained invisible to him all the time they afterwards stayed in the church. This action, by which she would have had him understand that she was displeased at his gazing on her with so little respect, only increased his curiosity to know who she was.

When the congregation was dismissed, he hastened to the door, with an intention to offer her his hand to help her to her coach; but seeing the magnificent equipage that waited for her, and the number of servants that attended it, he conceived a much higher idea of her quality than he had at first; and, changing his design, contented himself with only bowing to her as she passed; and as soon as her coach drove away, inquired of some persons nearest him, who she was.

These rustics, highly delighted with the opportunity of talking to the gay Londoner, whom they looked upon as a very extraordinary person, gave him all the intelligence they were able, concerning the lady he inquired after; and filled him with an inconceivable surprise at the strange humour of the marquis, who buried so beautiful a creature in obscurity.

At his return home, he expressed his admiration of her in terms that persuaded his friend she had made some impression on his heart; and, after rallying him a little upon this suspicion, he assumed a more serious air, and told him, if he really liked Lady Bella, he thought it not impossible but he might obtain her. The poor girl, added he, has been kept in confinement so long, that I believe it would not be difficult to persuade her to free herself by marriage. She never had a lover in her life; and therefore the first person who addresses her has the fairest chance for succeeding.

Mr Hervey, though he could not persuade himself his cousin was in earnest when he advised him to court the only daughter of a man of the marquis's quality, and heiress to his vast estates, yet relished the scheme, and resolved to make some attempt upon her before he left the country. However, he concealed his design from his cousin, not being willing to expose himself to be ridiculed, if he did not succeed; and turning the advice he had given him into a jest, left him in the opinion that he thought no more of it.

III

In which the adventure goes on after the accustomed manner

ARABELLA, IN THE MEAN TIME, was wholly taken up with the adventure, as she called it, at church: the person and dress of the gentleman who had so particularly gazed on her there, was so different from what she had been accustomed to see, that she immediately concluded he was of some distinguished rank. It was past a doubt, she thought, that he was excessively in love with her; and, as she soon expected to have some very extraordinary proofs of his passion, her thoughts were wholly employed on the manner in which she should receive them.

As soon as she came home, and had paid her duty to the marquis, she hurried to her chamber, to be at liberty to indulge her agreeable reflections; and, after the example of our heroines, when any thing extraordinary happened to them, called her favourite woman; or, to use her own language, her in whom she confided her most secret thoughts.

Well, Lucy, said she, did you observe that stranger who ey'd *us*[1] so heedfully to-day at church?

This girl, notwithstanding her country simplicity, knew a compliment was expected from her on this occasion; and therefore replied, that she did not wonder at the gentleman's staring at her; for she was sure he had never seen any body so handsome as her ladyship before.

I have not all the beauty you attribute to me, said Arabella, smiling a little; and with a very moderate share of it, I might well fix the attention of a person who seemed not to be over much pleased with the objects about him. However, pursued she, assuming a more serious air, if this stranger be weak enough to entertain any sentiments more than indifferent for me, I charge you upon pain of my displeasure, do not be accessory to the conveying his presumptuous thoughts to me, either

---

1 The heroines always speak of themselves in the plural number.

by letters or messages; nor suffer him to corrupt your fidelity with the presents he will very probably offer you.

Lucy, to whom this speech first gave a hint of what she ought to expect from her lady's lovers, finding herself of more importance than she imagined, was so pleased at the prospect which opened to her, that it was with some hesitation she promised to obey her orders.

Arabella, however, was satisfied with her assurances of observing her directions; and dismissed her from her presence, not without an apprehension of being too well obeyed.

A whole week being elapsed without meeting with the importunities she expected, she could hardly conceal her surprise at so mortifying a disappointment; and frequently interrogated Lucy, concerning any attempts the stranger had made on her fidelity; but the answers she received only increased her discontent, as they convinced her, her charms had not had the effect she imagined. Mr Hervey, however, had been all this time employed in thinking of some means to get acquainted with the marquis; for, being possessed with an extraordinary opinion of his wit, and personal accomplishments, he did not fear making some impression on the heart of the young lady; provided he could have an opportunity of conversing with her.

His cousin's advice was continually in his mind, and flattered his vanity with the most agreeable hopes; but the marquis's fondness for solitude, and that haughtiness which was natural to him, rendered him so difficult of access, that Hervey, from the intelligence he received of his humour, despaired of being able to prosecute his scheme: when meeting with a young farmer in one of his evening walks, and entering into conversation with him upon several country subjects, the discourse at last turned upon the Marquis of ——, whose fine house and gardens were within their view; upon which the young fellow informed him he was brother to a young woman that attended the Lady Arabella; and being fond of lengthening out the conversation with so fine a gentleman, gave him, without being desired, the domestic history of the whole family, as he had received it from Lucy, who was the sister he mentioned.

Hervey, excessively delighted at this accidental meeting with a person so capable of serving his design, affected a great desire of being better acquainted with him; and, under pretence of acquiring some knowledge in rural affairs, accustomed himself to call so often at William's farm, that, at last, he met with the person whom the hopes of seeing had so often carried him thither.

Lucy, the moment she saw him enter, knowing him again, blushed at the remembrance of the discourse which had passed between her lady and herself concerning him; and was not at all surprised at the endeavours he used to speak to her apart: but as soon as he began a conversation concerning Arabella, she interrupted him by saying, I know, sir, that you are distractedly in love with my lady; but she has forbid me to receive any letters or messages from you; and therefore I beg you will not offer to bribe me; for I dare not disobey her.

Mr Hervey was at first so astonished at her speech, that he knew not what to think of it; but after a little reflection, attributing to an excess of awkward cunning what, in reality, was an effect of her simplicity, he resolved to make use of the hint she had given him; and, presenting her with a couple of guineas, entreated her to venture displeasing her lady, by bearing a letter from him; promising to reward her better, if she succeeded.

Lucy made some difficulty to comply; but, not being able absolutely to refuse the first bribe that ever was offered to her, she, after some entreaties, consented to take the letter; and receiving the money he presented her, left him at liberty to write, after she had got her brother to furnish him with materials for that purpose.

IV

A mistake, which produces no great consequences. An extraordinary comment upon a behaviour natural enough. An instance of a lady's compassion for her lover, which the reader may possibly think not very compassionate

HERVEY, WHO WAS MASTER OF no great elegance in letter-writing, was at first at some loss how to address a lady of her quality, to whom he was an absolute stranger, upon the subject of love; but conceiving there was no great occasion for much ceremony in declaring himself to one who had been educated in the country, and who, he believed, could not be displeased with a lover of his figure, he therefore, in plain terms, told her how deeply he was enamoured of her; and conjured her to afford him some opportunity of paying his respects to her.

Lucy received this letter from him with a worse grace than she did the gold; and, though she promised him to deliver it to her lady immediately, yet she kept it a day or two before she had the courage to attempt it; at last, drawing it out of her pocket, with a bashful air, she presented it to her lady, telling her it came from the fine gentleman whom she saw at church.

Arabella blushed at the sight of the letter; and though in reality she was not displeased, yet, being a strict observer of romantic forms, she chid her woman severely for taking it. Carry it back, added she, to the presumptuous writer of it; and let him know how greatly his insolence has offended me.

Lucy, however, suffered the letter to remain on the toilet, expecting some change in her lady's mind: for she traversed the chamber in great seeming irresolution, often stealing a glance to the letter, which she had a strong inclination to open; but searching the records of her memory for a precedent, and not finding that any lady ever opened a letter from an unknown lover, she reiterated her commands to Lucy to carry it back, with a look and accent so very severe, that the girl, extremely apprehensive of having offended her, put the letter again in her pocket, resolving to return it the first opportunity.

Mr Hervey, who had his thoughts wholly taken up with the flattering prospect of success, no sooner saw Lucy, who gave him his letter without speaking a word, than, supposing it had been the answer he expected, he eagerly snatched it out of her hand, and, kissing it first in a rapture of joy, broke it open; but his surprise and confusion, when he saw it was his own letter returned, was inexpressible. For some moments he kept his eyes fastened upon the tender billet, as if he was really reading it. His disappointment, and the ridiculous figure he knew he must make in the eyes of his messenger, filled him with so much confusion, that he did not dare to look up; but recovering himself at last, he affected to turn it into a jest; and, laughing first himself, gave Lucy the liberty of laughing also, who had, with much difficulty, been able to prevent doing it before.

The curiosity he felt to hear how she had acquitted herself of the trust he had reposed in her, made him oblige her to give a truce to her mirth, in order to satisfy him; and Lucy, who was extremely exact in her relations, told him all that had passed, without omitting the smallest circumstance.

Though it was impossible to draw any favourable omen from what he heard, yet he determined to make another effort, before he set out for London; and taking leave of his confidant, after he had appointed her to meet him again the next day, at her brother's, he went home to consider upon means to effect his designs, which the ill success of his first attempt had not forced him to abandon.

Arabella, who expected to hear that the return of his letter would make her lover commit some very extravagant actions; and having impatiently waited for an account of them from Lucy, finding she seemed to have no intention to begin a discourse concerning him, asked her, at last, if she had executed her commission, and returned the letter to the insolent unknown?

The girl answered, Yes.

Which not being all that her lady expected—And how did he receive it? resumed she, peevishly.

Why, madam, replied Lucy, I believe he thought your ladyship had sent him an answer; for he kissed the letter several times.

Foolish wench! replied Arabella, how can you imagine he had the temerity to think I should answer his letter? A favour which, though he had spent years in my service, would have been infinitely greater than he could have expected. No, Lucy, he kissed the letter, either because he thought it had been touched, at least, by my hands, or to show the perfect submission with which he received my commands; and it is not to be doubted but his despair will force him to commit some desperate outrage against himself, which I do not hate him enough to wish, though he has mortally offended me.

Arabella was possessed of great sensibility and softness: and being really persuaded that her lover would entertain some fatal design, seemed so much affected with the thoughts of what might happen, that Lucy, who tenderly loved her, begged her not to be so much concerned for the gentleman: There is no fear, added she, that he will do himself a mischief; for when he discovered his mistake, he laughed heartily, as well as myself.

How! replied Arabella, extremely surprised: did he laugh?

Which Lucy confirming, Doubtless, resumed she, having taken a little time to consider of so strange a phenomenon, he laughed, because his reason was disturbed at the sudden shock he received: unhappy man! his presumption will be severely enough punished, though I do not add anger to the scorn which I have expressed for him; therefore, Lucy, you may tell him, if you please, that, notwithstanding the offence he has been guilty of, I am not cruel enough to wish his death, and that I command him to live, if he can live without hope.

V

In which one would imagine the adventure concluded, but for a promise that something else is to come

LUCY NOW BEGAN TO THINK there was something more than she imagined in this affair. Mr Hervey, indeed, in her opinion, had seemed to be very far from having any design to attempt his own life: but her lady, she thought, could not possibly be mistaken; and therefore she resolved to carry her message to him immediately, though it was then late in the evening.

Accordingly, she went to her brother's, where she had some hope of meeting with him; but not finding him there, she obliged him to go to the house where he lived, and tell him she desired to speak with him.

William, being let into the secret of his sister's frequent meetings with Mr Hervey, imagined she had some agreeable news to acquaint him with; and therefore ran immediately to his relation's house, which was but at a small distance; but he was told Mr Hervey was in bed, very much indisposed, and could not be seen.

This news put Lucy in a terrible fright: she told her apprehensions to her brother; which being such as her lady had put into her head, and were now confirmed by Mr Hervey's illness, the young farmer stood amazed, not being able to comprehend her meaning; and she, without staying to explain herself any farther, went home to the castle, and told her lady, that what she feared was come to pass, the gentleman would certainly die, for he was very ill in bed.

This being no more than what Arabella expected, she discovered no surprise; but only asked Lucy, if she had delivered her message to him.

Would you have me, madam, replied she, go to his house? I am afraid the marquis will hear of it.

My father, replied Arabella, can never be offended with me for doing a charitable action.

Ah! madam, interrupted Lucy, let me go then immediately, for fear the poor gentleman should grow worse.

If he be sick almost to death, resumed Arabella, he will recover, if I command him to do so. When did you hear of a lover dying through despair, when his mistress let him know it was her pleasure he should live? But as it will not be altogether so proper for you to go to his house, as it may be suspected you come from me, I'll write a few lines, which you shall copy, and your brother may carry them to him to-morrow, and I'll engage he shall be well in a few hours.

Saying this, she went into her closet; and, having written a short note, made Lucy write it over again. It was as follows:—

Lucy, to the unfortunate lover of her lady.

My lady, who is the most generous person in the world, has commanded me to tell you, that, presumptuous as you are, she does not desire your death; nay, more, she commands you to live, and permits you, in case you obey her, to hope for her pardon, provided you keep within the bounds she prescribes to you. Adieu.

This letter Lucy copied; and Arabella, examining it again, thought it rather too kind; and, seeming desirous of making some alterations in it, Lucy, who was extremely anxious for Mr Hervey's life, fearing lest she should alter it in such a manner that the gentleman should be at liberty to die if he chose it, conjured her lady in such pressing terms to let it remain as it was, that Arabella suffered herself to be prevailed upon by her entreaties; and, remembering that it was not uncommon for the ladies in romances to relax a little in their severity through the remonstrances of their women, told her, with an enchanting smile, that she would grant her desire; and went to bed with that pleasing satisfaction, which every generous mind experiences at the consciousness of having done some very benevolent action.

In the morning, this life-restoring billet was dispatched by Lucy to her brother, inclosed in one to him, charging him to carry it to the sick gentleman immediately.

William, having a strong curiosity to see what his sister had written, ventured to open it; and, not being able to imagine Lady Bella had really given her orders to write what appeared to him the most unintelligible stuff in the world, resolved to suppress this letter till he had questioned her a little concerning it.

A few hours after, Mr Hervey, who expected to meet Lucy at her brother's, came in. His illness having been only a violent head-ache, to which he was subject, being now quite off, he remembered the appointment he had made; but having waited some time, and she not coming, he returned again to his cousin's, leaving word for her, that he would see her the next day.

Scarce was he gone out, when Lucy, who longed to know what effect her letter had produced on his health, came in; and eagerly inquiring of her brother how Mr Hervey was, received for answer, that he had been there a moment before she came.

Well, cried she, clasping her hands together with surprise, my lady said her letter would cure him, if he was ever so sick; but I did not imagine he would have been well enough to come abroad so soon.

Your lady! interrupted William: why, was it not yourself that wrote the letter you gave to me?

No, truly, brother, resumed she: how was it possible I should write so fine a letter? My lady *made* every word of it, and I only wrote it after her.

William, hearing this, would not own the indiscretion he now thought he had been guilty of, in keeping the letter; but suffered his sister to return to her lady, in the belief that he had delivered it; resolving when he saw her next, to say he had lost it: for he knew not what excuse to make to Mr Hervey for not giving it him when he saw him.

Arabella received the account of her lover's recovery as a thing she was absolutely sure of before; and thinking she had now done all that could be expected from her compassion, resumed her usual severity, and commanded Lucy to mention him no more. If he loves me with that purity he ought to do, pursued she, he will cease to importune me any farther: and though his passion be ever so violent, his respect and submission to my commands will oblige him to silence. The obedience he has already shewn, in recovering at the first intimation I gave, that it was my will he should do so, convinces me I need not apprehend he will renew his follies to displease me.

Lucy, who found by this discourse of her lady's, that her commission was at an end with regard to Mr Hervey, followed her directions so exactly, that she not only spoke no more of him to her; but also, in order to avoid him, neglected to go to her brother's.

His impatience at not seeing her made him prevail upon her brother to go to the castle, and entreat her to give him another interview; but Lucy positively refused; and, to make a merit with her lady of her obedience, informed her of what he had requested.

Arabella, resenting a boldness which argued so little respect to her commands, began now to repent of the compassion she had shewn him; and, commending Lucy for what she had done, bid her tell the insolent unknown, if he ever sent to her again, that she was resolved never to pardon the contempt he had shewn for her orders.

Mr Hervey, finding himself deserted by Lucy, resolved to give over his attempts, congratulating himself for his discretion in not acquainting his cousin with what he had already done: his heart not being very much engaged, he found no great difficulty in consoling himself for his bad success. In a few days he thought of Lady Bella no more than if he had never seen her; but an accident bringing her again in his way, he could not resist the inclination he felt to speak to her; and by that means drew upon himself a very sensible mortification.

VI

In which the adventure is really concluded; though, possibly, not as the reader expected

THE MARQUIS SOMETIMES PERMITTING HIS daughter to ride out, and this being the only diversion she was allowed, or ever experienced, she did not fail to take it as often as she could.

She was returning from one of these airings one day, attended by two servants, when Mr Hervey, who happened to be at some distance, observing a lady on horseback, who made a very graceful figure, he rode up to her, in order to have a nearer view; and knowing Lady Bella again, resolved to speak to her: but while he was considering how he should accost her, Arabella suddenly seeing him, and observing he was making up to her, her imagination immediately suggested to her, that this insolent lover had a design to seize her person; and this thought terrifying her extremely, she gave a loud shriek; which Mr Hervey hearing, rode eagerly up to her to inquire the reason of it, at the same time that her two attendants, as much amazed as himself, came galloping up also.

Arabella, upon his coming close up to her, redoubled her cries. If you have any valour, said she to her servants, defend your unfortunate mistress, and rescue her from this unworthy man.

The servants, believing him to be a highwayman, by this exclamation, and dreading lest he should present his pistol at their heads, if they offered to make any resistance, recoiled a few paces back, expecting he would demand their purses when he had robbed their lady; but the extreme surprise he was in, keeping him motionless; the fellows not seeing any pistols in his hand, and animated by Arabella's cries, who, calling them cowards and traitors, urged them to deliver her; they both, in a moment, laid hold of Mr Hervey, and forced him to alight; which they did also themselves, still keeping fast hold of him, whom surprise, shame, and rage, had hitherto kept silent.

Rascals! cried he, when he was able to speak, what do you mean by using me in this manner? Do you suppose I had any intention to hurt the lady?—What do you take me for?

For a ravisher, interrupted Arabella; an impious ravisher! who, contrary to all laws, both human and divine, endeavour to possess yourself by force of a person whom you are not worthy to serve; and whose charity and compassion you have returned with the utmost ingratitude.

Upon my word, madam, said Mr Hervey, I don't understand one word you say: you either mistake me for some other person, or are pleased to divert yourself with the surprise I am in. But, I beseech you, carry the jest no farther, and order your servants to let me go; or, by Heaven, cried he, struggling to get loose, if I can but free one of my hands, I'll stab the scoundrels before your face.

It is not with threats like these, resumed Arabella, with great calmness, that I can be moved. A little more submission and respect would become you better: you are now wholly in my power: I may, if I please, carry you to my father, and have you severely punished for your attempt; but, to shew you that I am as generous as you are base and designing, I'll give you freedom, provided you promise me never to appear before me again. But, in order to secure my own safety, you must deliver up your arms to my servants, that I may be assured you will not have it in your power to make a second attempt upon my liberty.

Mr Hervey, whose astonishment was increased by every word she spoke, began now to be apprehensive that this might prove a very serious affair, since she seemed resolved to believe he had a design to carry her off; and knowing that an attempt of that nature upon an heiress might have dangerous consequences, he resolved to accept the conditions she offered him: but while he delivered his hanger to the servant, he assured her in the strongest terms, than he had no other design in riding up to her, but to have a nearer view of her person.

Add not falsehood, said Arabella, sternly, to a crime already black enough; for though by an effort of my generosity, I have resolved not to deliver you up to the resentment of my father, yet nothing shall ever be able to make me pardon this outrage. Go, then, pursued she; go, base man, unworthy of the care I took for thy safety; go to some distant country, where I may never hear of thee more, and suffer me, if possible, to lose the remembrance of thy crimes.

Saying this, she ordered her servants, who had got the hanger in their possession, to set him at liberty, and mount their horses; which they did immediately, and followed their lady, who rode with all imaginable speed to the castle.

Mr Hervey, not yet recovered from his surprise, stood some moments considering the strange scene he had been witness to; and in which he had, much against his will, appeared the principal character. As he was not acquainted with Lady Bella's foible, he concluded her fears of him were occasioned by her simplicity, and some misrepresentations that had been made her by Lucy, who he thought had betrayed him; and, fearing this ridiculous adventure would be soon made public, and himself exposed to the sneers of his country acquaintance, he resolved to go back to London as soon as possible.

The next day, pretending he had received a letter which obliged him to set out immediately, he took leave of his cousin, heartily glad at the escape he should make from his raillery; for he did not doubt but the story would very soon be known, and told greatly to his disadvantage.

But Arabella, in order to be completely generous; a quality for which all the heroines are famous, laid a command upon her two attendants not to mention what had passed, giving them at the same time money to secure their secrecy, and threatening them with her displeasure, if they disobeyed.

Arabella, as soon as she had an opportunity, did not fail to acquaint her faithful Lucy with the danger from which she had so happily escaped, thanking Heaven at the same time, with great devotion, for having preserved her from the hands of the ravisher.

Two or three months rolled away, after this accident, without offering any new adventure to our fair visionary; when her imagination, always prepossessed with the same fantastic ideas, made her stumble upon another mistake, equally absurd and ridiculous.

VII

In which some contradictions are very happily reconciled

THE MARQUIS'S HEAD-GARDENER HAD RECEIVED a young fellow into his master's service who had lived in several families of distinction. He had a good face; was tolerably genteel; and having an understanding something above his condition, joined to a great deal of *second-hand* politeness, which he had contracted while he lived in London, he appeared a very extraordinary person among the rustics who were his fellow-servants.

Arabella, when she walked in the garden, had frequent opportunities of seeing this young man, whom she observed with a very particular attention. His person and air had something, she thought, very distinguishing. When she condescended to speak to him about any business he was employed in, she took notice that his answers were framed in a language vastly superior to his condition; and the respect he paid her had quite another air from that of the awkward civility of the other servants.

Having discerned so many marks of a birth far from being mean, she easily passed from an opinion that he was a gentleman, to a belief that he was something more; and every new sight of him adding strength to her suspicions, she remained in a little time perfectly convinced that he was some person of quality, who, disguised in the habit of a gardener, had introduced himself into her father's service, in order to have an opportunity of declaring a passion to her, which must certainly be very great, since it had forced him to assume an appearance so unworthy of his noble extraction.

Wholly possessed with this thought, she set herself to observe him more narrowly, and soon found out that he went very awkwardly about his work; that he sought opportunities of being alone; that he threw himself in her way as often as he could, and gazed on her very attentively. She sometimes fancied she saw him endeavour to smother a sigh when he answered her any question about his work; once saw him leaning against a tree with his hands crossed upon his breast; and, having lost a string of small pearls, which she remembered he had seen her threading as she sat in one of the arbours, was persuaded he had taken it up, and kept it for the object of his secret adoration.

She often wondered, indeed, that she did not find her name carved on the trees, with some mysterious expressions of love; that he was never discovered lying along the side of one of the little rivulets, increasing the stream with his tears; nor, for three months that he had lived there, had ever been sick of a fever caused by his grief and the constraint he put upon himself in not declaring his passion. But she considered again, that his fear of being discovered kept him from amusing himself with making the trees bear the records of his secret thoughts, or of indulging his melancholy in any manner expressive of the condition of his soul; and, as for his not being sick, his youth, and the strength of his constitution, might, even for a longer time, bear him up against the assaults of a fever: but he appeared much thinner and paler than he used to be: and she concluded, therefore, that he must in time sink under the violence of his passion, or else be forced to declare it to her, which she considered as a very great misfortune; for, not finding in herself any disposition to approve his love, she must necessarily banish him from her presence, for fear he should have the presumption to hope that time might do any thing in his favour; and it was possible also, that the sentence she would be obliged to pronounce might either cause his death, or force him to commit some extravagant action, which would discover him to her father, who would, perhaps, think her guilty of holding a secret correspondence with him.

These thoughts perplexed her so much, that, hoping to find some relief by unburdening her mind to Lucy, she told her all her uneasiness. Ah! said she to her, looking upon Edward, who had just passed them, how unfortunate do I think myself in being the cause of that passion which makes this illustrious unknown wear away his days in so shameful an obscurity! Yes, Lucy, pursued she, that Edward, whom you regard as one of my father's menial servants, is a person of sublime quality, who submits to this disguise only to have an opportunity of seeing me every day. But why do you seem so surprised? Is it possible that you have not suspected him to be what he is? Has he never unwittingly made any discovery of himself? Have you not surprised him in discourse with his faithful squire, who certainly lurks hereabouts to receive his commands, and is haply the confidant of his passion? Has he never entertained you with any conversation about me? Or have you never seen any valuable jewels in his possession, by which you suspected him to be not what he appears?

Truly, madam, replied Lucy, I never took him for any body else but a simple gardener: but, now you open my eyes, methinks I can find I have been strangely mistaken; for he does not look like a man of low degree, and he talks quite in another manner from our servants. I never heard him indeed speak of your ladyship, but once; and that was, when he first saw you walking in the garden, he asked our John if you was not the marquis's daughter; and he said you was as beautiful as an angel. As for fine jewels, I never saw any, and I believe he has none; but he has a watch, and that looks as if he was something, madam: nor do I remember to have seen him talk with any stranger that looked like a squire.

Lucy, having thus with her usual punctuality, answered every question her lady put to her, proceeded to ask her, what she should say, if he should beg her to give her a letter as the other gentleman had done.

You must by no means take it, replied Arabella: my compassion had before like to have been fatal to me. If he discovers his quality to me, I shall know in what manner to treat him.

They were in this part of their discourse, when a noise they heard at some distance, made Arabella bend her steps to the place from whence it proceeded; and, to her infinite amazement, saw the head-gardener, with a stick he had in his hand, give several blows to the concealed hero, who suffered the indignity with admirable patience.

Shocked at seeing a person of sublime quality treated so unworthily, she called out to the gardener to hold his hand, who immediately obeyed; and Edward, seeing the young lady advance, sneaked off with an air very different from an Oroondates.

For what crime, pray, said Arabella, with a stern aspect, did you treat the person I saw with you so cruelly? He whom you take such unbecoming liberties with may possibly—But again I ask you, what has he done? You should make some allowance for his want of skill, in the abject employment he is in at present.

It is not for his want of skill, madam, said the gardener, that I corrected him; he knows his business very well, if he would mind it; but, madam, I have discovered him—

Discovered him, do you say? interrupted Arabella: and has the knowledge of his condition not been able to prevent such usage? or rather, has it been the occasion of his receiving it?

His conditions are very bad, madam, returned the gardener; and I am afraid are such as will one day prove the ruin of body and soul too. I have for some time suspected he had evil designs in his head; and just now watched him to the fish-pond, and prevented him from—

O dear! interrupted Lucy, looking pitifully on her lady, whose fair bosom heaved with compassion, I warrant he was going to make away with himself.

No, resumed the gardener, smiling at the mistake, he was only going to make away with some of the carp, which the rogue had caught, and intended, I suppose, to sell: but I threw them into the water again; and if your ladyship had not forbid me, I would have drubbed him soundly for his pains.

Fie! fie! interrupted Arabella, out of breath with shame and vexation: tell me no more of these idle tales.

Then, hastily walking on, to hide the blushes which this strange accusation of her illustrious lover had raised in her face, she continued for some time in the greatest perplexity imaginable.

Lucy, who followed her, and could not possibly reconcile what her lady had been telling her concerning Edward, with the circumstance of his stealing the carp, ardently wished to hear her opinion of this matter; but, seeing her deeply engaged with her own thoughts, she would not venture to disturb her.

Arabella, indeed, had been in such a terrible consternation, that it was some time before she even reconciled appearances to herself; but, as she had a most happy facility in accommodating every incident to her own wishes and conceptions, she examined this matter so many different ways, drew so many conclusions, and fancied so many mysteries in the most indifferent actions of the supposed noble unknown, that she remained at last more than ever confirmed in the opinion that he was some great personage, whom her beauty had forced to assume an appearance unworthy of himself: when Lucy, no longer able to keep silence, drew off her attention from those pleasing images, by speaking of the carp-stealing affair again.

Arabella, whose confusion returned at that disagreeable sound, charged her, in an angry tone, never to mention so injurious a suspicion any more: For, in fine, said she to her, do you imagine a person of his rank could be guilty of stealing carp? Alas! pursued she, sighing, he had, indeed, some fatal design; and, doubtless, would have executed it, had not this fellow so luckily prevented him.

But Mr Woodbind, madam, said Lucy, saw the carp in his hand: I wonder what he was going to do with them.

Still, resumed Arabella, extremely chagrined, still will you wound my ears with that horrid sound? I tell you, obstinate and foolish wench, that this unhappy man went thither to die; and if he really caught the fish, it was to conceal his design from Woodbind: his great mind could not suggest to him, that it was possible he might be suspected of a baseness like that this ignorant fellow accused him of; therefore he took no care about it, being wholly possessed by his despairing thoughts.

However, madam, said Lucy, your ladyship may prevent his going to the fish-pond again, by laying your commands upon him to live.

I shall do all that I ought, answered Arabella; but my care for the safety of other persons must not make me forget what I owe to my own.

As she had always imputed Mr Hervey's fancied attempt to carry her away to the letter she had written to him, upon which he had probably founded his hopes of being pardoned for it, she resolved to be more cautious for the future in giving such instances of her compassion; and was at a great loss in what manner to comfort her despairing lover, without raising expectations she had no inclination to confirm: but she was delivered from her perplexity a few days after, by the news of his having left the marquis's service; which she attributed to some new design he had formed to obtain her: and Lucy, who always thought as her lady did, was of the same opinion; though it was talked among the servants, that Edward feared a discovery of more tricks, and resolved not to stay till he was disgracefully dismissed.

VIII

In which a mistake, in point of ceremony, is rectified

ARABELLA HAD SCARCE DONE THINKING of this last adventure, when the marquis communicated a piece of intelligence to her, which opened a prospect of an infinite number of new ones.

His nephew, having just returned from his travels was preparing to come and pay him a visit in his retreat, and, as he always designed to marry Arabella to this youth, of whom he was extremely fond, he told his daughter of the intended visit of her cousin, whom she had not seen since she was eight years old; and, for the first time, insinuated his design of giving him to her for an husband.

Arabella, whose delicacy was extremely shocked at this abrupt declaration of her father, could hardly hide her chagrin; for, though she always intended to marry some time or other, as all the heroines had done, yet she thought such an event ought to be brought about with an infinite deal of trouble; and that it was necessary she should pass to this state through a great number of cares, disappointments, and distresses of various kinds, like them; that her lover should purchase her with his sword from a crowd of rivals, and arrive to the possession of her heart by many years of service and fidelity.

The impropriety of receiving a lover of her father's recommending appeared in its strongest light. What lady in romance ever married the man that was chosen for her? In those cases, the remonstrances of a parent are called persecutions; obstinate resistance, constancy, and courage; and an aptitude to dislike the person proposed to them, a noble freedom of mind which disdains to love or hate by the caprice of others.

Arabella, strengthening her own resolutions by those examples of heroic disobedience, told her father, with great solemnity of accent, that she would always obey him in all just and reasonable things; and, being persuaded that he would never attempt to lay any force upon her inclinations, she would endeavour to make them conformable to his, and receive her cousin with that civility and friendship due to so near a relation, and a person whom he honoured with his esteem.

The marquis, having had frequent occasions of admiring his daughter's eloquence, did not draw any unpleasing conclusion from the nice distinctions she made; and, being perfectly assured of her consent whenever he demanded it, expected the arrival of his nephew with great impatience.

Arabella, whose thoughts had been fully employed since this conversation with her father, was indulging her meditations in one of the most retired walks in the garden; when she was informed by Lucy, that her cousin was come, and that the marquis had brought him into the garden to look for her.

That instant they both entered the walk; when Arabella, prepossessed as she was against any favourable thoughts of the young Glanville, could not help betraying some surprise at the gracefulness of his figure.

It must be confessed, said she to her attendant, with a smile, that this lover my father has brought us, is no contemptible person: nevertheless, I feel an invincible repugnance in myself against receiving him in that character.

As she finished these words, the marquis came up, and presented Mr Glanville to her; who, saluting her with the freedom of a relation, gave her a disgust that abused itself immediately in her fair face, which was overspread with such a gloom, that the marquis was quite astonished at it. Indeed, Arabella, who expected he would hardly have presumed to kiss her hand, was so surprised at his freedom, in attempting her lips, that she not only expressed her indignation by frowns, but gave him to understand he had mortally offended her.

Mr Glanville, however, was neither surprised nor angry at her resentment; but, imputing it to her country education, endeavoured to rally her out of her ill-humour; and the marquis, being glad to find a behaviour, which he thought proceeded from her dislike of her cousin, was only an effect of an over-scrupulous modesty, told her that Mr Glanville had committed no offence by saluting her, since that was a civility which was granted to all strangers at the first interview, and therefore could not be refused to a relation.

Since the world is so degenerated in its customs from what it was formerly, said Arabella, with a smile full of contempt upon her cousin, I am extremely happy in having lived in a solitude which has not yet exposed me to the mortification of being a witness to manners I cannot approve; for if every person I shall meet with for the future be so deficient in their respect to ladies as my cousin is, I shall not care how much I am secluded from society.

But, dear Lady Bella, interrupted Mr Glanville gaily, tell me, I beseech you, how I must behave to please you; for I should be extremely glad to be honoured with your good opinion.

The person, resumed she, whom I must teach how to acquire my good opinion, will, I am afraid, hardly recompense me, by his docility in learning, for the pains I should be at in instructing him.

But, resumed Glanville, that I may avoid any more occasions of offending you, only let me know how you would be approached for the future.

Since, answered she, there is no necessity to renew the ceremony of introducing you again to me, I have not a second affront of that kind to apprehend; but I pray tell me if all cavaliers are as presuming as yourself; and if a relation of your sex does not think a modest embrace from a lady a welcome sufficiently tender?[1]

Nay, cousin, cried Glanville, eagerly, I am now persuaded you are in the right; an embrace is certainly to be preferred to a cold salute. What would I give, that the marquis would introduce me a second time, that I might be received with so delightful a welcome?

The vivacity with which he spoke this, was so extremely disagreeable to Arabella, that she turned from him abruptly, and, striking into another walk, ordered Lucy to tell him she commanded him not to follow her.

---

1 The heroines, though they think a kiss of the hand a great condescension to a lover, and never grant it without blushes and confusion, yet make no scruple to embrace him upon every short absence.

Mr Glanville, however, who had no notion of the exact obedience which was expected from him, would have gone after her, notwith-standing this prohibition, which Lucy delivered in a most peremptory manner, after her lady's example; but the marquis, who had left the young people at liberty to discourse, and had walked on, that he might not interrupt them, turning about, and seeing Glanville alone, called him to have some private discourse with him; and, for that time, spared Arabella the mortification of seeing her commands disobeyed.

IX

In which a lover is severely punished for faults which the reader never would have discovered, if he had not been told

THE MARQUIS, THOUGH HE HAD resolved to give Arabella to his nephew, was desirous he should first receive some impressions of tenderness for her, before he absolutely declared his resolution; and ardently wished he might be able to overcome that reluctance which she seemed to have for marriage; but, though Glanville in a very few days became passionately in love with his charming cousin, yet she discovered so strong a dislike to him, that he marquis feared it would be difficult to make her receive him for an husband: he observed she took all opportunities of avoiding his conversation; and seemed always out of temper when he addressed any thing to her; but was well enough pleased when he discoursed with him; and would listen to the long conversations they had together with great attention.

The truth is, she had too much discernment not to see Mr Glanville had a great deal of merit: his person was perfectly handsome; he possessed a great share of understanding, an easy temper, and a vivacity which charmed every one but the insensible Arabella.

She often wondered, that a man, who, as she told her confidant, was master of so many fine qualities, should have a disposition so little capable of feeling the passion of love with a delicacy and fervour she expected to inspire, or that he, whose conversation was so pleasing on every other subject, should make so poor a figure when he entertained her with matters of gallantry. However, added she, I should be to blame to desire to be beloved by Mr Glanville; for I am persuaded that passion would cause no reformation in the coarseness of his manners to ladies, which makes him so disagreeable to me, and might possibly increase my aversion.

The marquis, having studied his nephew's looks for several days, thought he saw inclination enough in them for Arabella, to make him receive the knowledge of his intention with joy: he, therefore, called him into his closet, and told him in few words, that, if his heart was not pre-engaged, and his daughter capable of making him happy, he resolved to bestow her upon him, together with all his estates.

Mr Glanville received this agreeable news with the strongest expressions of gratitude; assuring his uncle, that Lady Bella, of all the women he had ever seen, was most agreeable to his taste; and that he felt for her all the tenderness and affection his soul was capable of.

I am glad of it, my dear nephew, said the marquis, embracing him: I will allow you, added he, smiling, but a few weeks to court her: gain her heart as soon as you can, and when you bring me her consent your marriage shall be solemnized immediately.

Mr Glanville needed not a repetition of so agreeable a command: he left his uncle's closet, with his heart filled with the expectation of his approaching happiness; and, understanding Arabella was in the garden, he went to her with the resolution to acquaint her with the permission her father had given him to make his addresses to her.

He found his fair cousin, as usual, accompanied with her women; and, seeing that, notwithstanding his approach, they still continued to walk with her; and impatient of the restraint they laid him under, I beseech you, cousin, said he, let me have the pleasure of walking with you alone: what necessity is there for always having so many witnesses of our conversation?—You may retire, said he, speaking to Lucy and the other woman: I have something to say to your lady in private.

Stay, I command you, said Arabella, blushing at an insolence so uncommon, and take orders from no one but myself. I pray you, sir, pursued she, frowning, what intercourse of secrets is there between you and me, that you expect I should favour you with a private conversation; an advantage which none of your sex ever boasted to have gained from me, and which, haply, you should he the last upon whom I should bestow it?

You have the strangest notions, answered Glanville, smiling at the pretty anger she discovered; certainly you may hold a private conversation with any gentleman, without giving offence to decorum and I may plead a right to this happiness above any other, since I have the honour to be your relation.

It is not at all surprising, resumed Arabella, gravely, that you and I should differ in opinion upon this occasion: I don't remember that ever we agreed in any thing; and I am apt to believe we never shall.

Ah! don't say so, Lady Bella, interrupted he: what a prospect of misery you lay before me! for, if we are always to be opposite to each other, it is necessary you must hate me as much as I admire and love you.

These words, which he accompanied with a gentle pressure of her hand, threw the astonished Arabella into such an excess of anger and shame, that, for a few moments, she was unable to utter a word.

What a horrid violation this, of all the laws of gallantry and respect, which decree a lover to suffer whole years in silence before he declares his flame to the divine object that causes it; and then with awful tremblings and submissive prostrations at the feet of the offended fair!

Arabella could hardly believe her senses when she heard a declaration, not only made without the usual forms, but also, that the presumptuous criminal waited for an answer without seeming to have any apprehension of the punishment to which he was to be doomed; and that, instead of deprecating her wrath, he looked with a smiling wonder upon her eyes, as if he did not fear their lightning would strike him dead.

Indeed, it was scarce possible for him to help smiling and wondering too, at the extraordinary action of Arabella; for, as soon as he had pronounced those fatal words, she started back two or three steps; cast a look at him full of the highest indignation: and, lifting up her fine eyes to heaven, seemed, in the language of romance, to accuse the gods for subjecting her to so cruel an indignity.

The tumult of her thoughts being a little settled, she turned again towards Glanville, whose countenance expressing nothing of that confusion and anxiety common to an adorer in so critical a circumstance, her rage returned with greater violence than ever.

If I do not express all the resentment your insolence has filled me with, said she to him, affecting more scorn than anger, 'tis because I hold you too mean for my resentment; but never hope for my pardon for your presumptuous confession of a passion I could almost despise myself for inspiring. If it be true that you love me, go and find your punishment in that absence to which I doom you; and never hope I will suffer a person in my presence, who has affronted me in the manner you have done.

Saying this, she walked away, making a sign to him not to follow her.

Mr Glanville, who was at first disposed to laugh at the strange manner in which she received his expressions of esteem for her, found something so extremely haughty and contemptuous in the speech she had made, that he was almost mad with vexation.

As he had no notion of his cousin's heroic sentiments, and had never read romances, he was quite ignorant of the nature of his offence; and supposing the scorn she had expressed for him was founded upon the difference of their rank and fortune, his pride was so sensibly mortified at that thought, and at her so insolently forbidding him her presence, that he was once inclined to shew his resentment of such ungenteel usage, by quitting the castle without taking leave even of the marquis, who, he thought, could not be ignorant of the reception he was likely to meet with from his daughter, and ought to have guarded him against it, if he really meant him so well as he seemed to do.

As he was extremely violent and hasty in his resolutions, and nicely sensible of the least affront, he was not in a condition to reason justly upon the marquis's conduct in this affair; and while he was fluctuating with a thousand different resolutions, Lucy came to him with a billet from her lady, which she delivered without staying till he opened it, and was superscribed in this manner:

Arabella to the Most Presumptuous Man in the World

You seem to acknowledge so little respect and deference for the commands of a lady, that I am afraid it will be but too necessary to reiterate that which, at parting, I laid upon you: know, then, that I absolutely insist upon your repairing, in the only manner you are able, the affront you have put upon me; which is, by never

appearing before me again. If you think proper to confine me to my
chamber, by continuing here any longer, you will add disobedience
to the crime by which you have already mortally offended

Arabella.

The superscription of this letter, and the uncommon style of it,
persuaded Mr Glanville that, what he had been foolish enough to
resent as an affront, was designed as a jest, and meant to divert him
as well as herself: he examined her behaviour again, and wondered
at his stupidity in not discovering it before. His resentment vanishing
immediately, he returned to the house; and went, without ceremony, to
Arabella's apartment, which he entered before she perceived him, being
in a profound musing.at one of the windows: the noise he made in
approaching her, obliged her at last to look up; when starting, as if she
had seen a basilisk, she flew to her closet, and shutting the door with
great violence, commanded him to leave her chamber immediately.

Mr Glanville, still supposing her in jest, entreated her to open the
door; but, finding she continued obstinate, Well, said he, going away, I
shall be revenged on you some time hence, and make you repent the
tricks you play me now.

Arabella not being able to imagine any thing by these words he
spoke in raillery, but that he really, in the spite and anguish of his
heart, threatened her with executing some terrible enterprise; she did
not doubt but he either intended to carry her away, or, thinking her
aversion to him proceeded from his having a rival happy enough to be
esteemed by her, those mysterious words he had uttered related to his
design of killing him; so that as she knew he could discover no rival to
wreak his revenge upon, she feared that, at once to satisfy that passion, as
well as his love, he would make himself master of her liberty: For, in fine,
said she to Lucy, to whom she communicated all her thoughts, have I
not every thing to apprehend from a man who knows so little how to
treat my sex with the respect which is our due; and who, after having,
contrary to the timorous nature of that passion, insulted me with a free

declaration of love, treats my commands with the utmost contempt by appearing before me again; and even threatens me with the revenge he is meditating at this moment.

Had Mr Glanville been present, and heard the terrible misfortunes which she presaged from the few words he had jestingly spoke, he would certainly have made her quite furious, by the diversion her mistake would have afforded him. But the more she reflected on his words, the more she was persuaded of the terrible purpose of them.

It was in vain to acquaint her father with the reasons she had for disliking his choice: his resolution was fixed; and if she did not voluntarily conform to it, she exposed herself to the attempts of a violent and unjust lover, who would either prevail upon the marquis to lay a force upon her inclinations, or to make himself master of her person, and never cease persecuting her till he had obliged her to give him her hand.

Having reasoned herself into a perfect conviction that all these things must necessarily happen, she thought it both just and reasonable to provide for her own security by a speedy flight. The want of a precedent, indeed, for an action of this nature, held her a few moments in suspense; for she did not remember to have read of any heroine that voluntarily left her father's house, however persecuted she might be: but she considered, that there was not any of the ladies in romances, in the same circumstances with herself, who was without a favoured lover, for whose sake it might have been believed she had made an elopement, which would have been highly prejudicial to her glory; and as there was no foundation for any suspicion of that kind in her case, she thought there was nothing to hinder her from withdrawing from a tyrannical exertion of parental authority, and the secret machinations of a lover, whose aim was to take away her liberty, either by obliging her to marry him or by making her a prisoner.

X

Contains several incidents, in which the reader is expected to be extremely interested

ARABELLA HAD SPENT SOME HOURS in her closet, revolving a thousand different stratagems to escape from the misfortune that threatened her, when she was interrupted by Lucy; who, after desiring admittance, informed her, that the marquis, having rode out to take the air that evening, had fallen from his horse and received some hurt; that he was gone to bed, and desired to see her.

Arabella, hearing her father was indisposed, ran to him, excessively alarmed; and reflecting on the resolution she had just before taken, of leaving him, which aggravated her concern, she came to his bedside with her eyes swimming in tears. Mr Glanville was sitting near him: but rising at her appearance to give her his chair, which she accepted without taking any notice of him, he stood at some distance contemplating her face, to which sorrow had given so many charms, that he gazed on her with an eagerness and delight that could not escape her observation.

She blushed excessively at the passionate looks he gave her; and finding the marquis's indisposition not considerable enough to oblige her to a constant attendance at his bed-side, she took the first opportunity of returning to her chamber: but as she was going out, Glanville presented his hand to lead her up stairs, which she scornfully refusing—

Sure, cousin, said he, a little piqued, you are not disposed to carry on your ill-natured jest any farther.

If you imagined I jested with you, said Arabella, I am rather to accuse the slowness of your understanding, for your persisting in treating me thus freely, than the insolence I first imputed it to: but, whatever is the cause of it, I now tell you again, that you have extremely offended me; and if my father's illness did not set bounds to my resentment at present, I would make you know, that I would not suffer the injury you do me so patiently.

Since you would have me to believe you are serious, replied Glanville, be pleased to let me know what offence it is you complain of; for I protest I am quite at a loss to understand you.

Was it not enough, resumed Arabella, to affront me with an insolent declaration of your passion, but you must also, in contempt of my commands to the contrary, appear before me again, pursue me to my chamber, and use the most brutal menaces to me?

Hold, pray, madam, interrupted Glanville, and suffer me to ask you; if it is my presumption in declaring myself your admirer that you are so extremely offended at?

Doubtless it is, sir, answered Arabella; and such a presumption as, without the aggravating circumstances you have since added to it, is sufficient to make me always your enemy.

I beg pardon, returned Mr Glanville, gravely, for that offence; and also for staying any longer in a house which you have so genteelly turned me out of.

My pardon, Mr Glanville, resumed she, is not so easily gained: time, and your repentance, may, indeed, do much towards obtaining it.

Saying this, she made a sign to him to retire, for he had walked up with her to her chamber; but finding he did not obey her, for, really, he was quite unacquainted with these sorts of dumb commands, she hastily retired to her closet, lest he should attempt to move her pity by any expressions of despair for the cruel banishment she had doomed him to.

Mr Glanville, seeing she had shut herself up in her closet, left her chamber, and retired to his own, more confounded than ever at the behaviour of his cousin.

Her bidding him so peremptorily to leave the house, would have equally persuaded him of her ignorance and ill-breeding, had not the elegance of her manners, in every other respect, proved the contrary; nor was it possible to doubt she had a great share of understanding, since her conversation, singular as some of her sentiments seemed to him, was far superior to most other ladies. Therefore, he concluded the affront he had received proceeded from her disdain to admit the addresses of any person whose quality was inferior to hers; which, probably, was increased by some particular dislike she had to his person.

His honour would not permit him to make use of that advantage her father's authority could give him and, wholly engrossed by his resentment of the usage he had received from her, he resolved to set out for London the next day without seeing the marquis, from whom he was apprehensive of some endeavours to detain him.

Having taken this resolution, he ordered his servant to have the horses ready early in the morning; and without taking any notice of his intention, he left the castle, riding as fast as possible to the next stage, from whence he wrote to his uncle; and, dispatching a messenger with his letter, held on his way to London.

The marquis, being pretty well recovered from his indisposition by a good night's rest, sent for Mr Glanville in the morning, to walk with him, as was his custom, in the garden; but hearing he had rode out, though he imagined it was only to take the air, yet he could not help accusing him, in his own thoughts, of a little neglect, for which he resolved to chide him when he returned: but his long stay filling him with some surprise, he was beginning to express his fears that something had befallen him, to Arabella, who was then with him, when a servant presented him the letter which Mr Glanville's messenger had that moment brought.

The marquis, casting his eyes on the direction, and knowing his nephew's hand, Bless me! cried he, extremely surprised, What can this mean? Bella, added he, here's a letter from your cousin.

Arabella, at these words, started up; and preventing her father, with a respectful action, from opening it, I beseech you, my lord, said she, before you read this letter, suffer me to assure you, that if it contains any thing fatal, I am not at all accessary to it: it is true, I have banished my cousin as a punishment for the offence he was guilty of towards me; but, Heaven is my witness, I did not desire his death ; and if he has taken any violent resolution against himself, he has greatly exceeded my commands.

The marquis, whose surprise was considerably increased by these words, hastily broke open the letter, which she perceiving, hurried out of the room; and, locking herself up in her closet, began to bewail the effect of her charms, as if she was perfectly assured of her cousin's death.

The marquis, however, who, from Lady Bella's exclamation, had prepared himself for the knowledge of some very extraordinary accident, was less surprised than he would otherwise have been at the contents; which were as follows:—

My Lord,

   As my leaving your house so abruptly will certainly make me appear guilty of a most unpardonable rudeness, I cannot dispense with myself from acquainting your lordship with the cause; though, to spare the reproaches Lady Bella will probably cast on me for doing so, I could wish you knew it by any other means.

   But, my lord, I value your esteem too much to hazard the loss of it by suffering you to imagine that I am capable of doing any thing to displease you. Lady Bella was pleased to order me to stay no longer in the house, and menaced me with some very terrible usage, if I disobeyed her: she used so many other contemptuous expressions to me, that, I am persuaded, I shall never be so happy as to possess the honour you designed for, my lord, your most obedient, &c.

                                        Charles Glanville.

When the marquis had read this letter, he went to his daughter's apartment with an intention to chide her severely for the usage of his nephew; but seeing her come to meet him with her eyes bathed in tears, he insensibly lost some part of his resentment.

Alas! my lord, said she, I know you come prepared to load me with reproaches upon my cousin's account; but I beseech your lordship, do not aggravate my sorrows: though I banished Mr Glanville, I did not desire his death; and, questionless, if he knew how I resent it, his ghost would be satisfied with the sacrifice I make him.

The marquis not being able to help smiling at this conceit, which he saw had so strongly possessed her imagination that she had no sort of doubt but that her cousin was dead, asked her, if she really believed Mr Glanville loved her well enough to die with grief at her ill usage of him.

If, said she, he loves me not well enough to die for me, he certainly loves me but little; and I am the less obliged to him.

But I desire to know, interrupted the marquis, for what crime it was you took the liberty to banish him from my house?

I banished him, my lord, resumed she, for his presumption in telling me he loved me.

That presumption, as you call it, though I know not for what reason, said the marquis, was authorised by me: therefore know, Bella, that I not only permit him to love you, but I also expect you should endeavour to return his affection, and look upon him as the man whom I design for your husband: there's his letter, pursued he, putting it into her hand. I blush for the rudeness you have been guilty of; but endeavour to repair it by a more obliging behaviour for the future: I am going to send after him immediately to prevail upon him to return; therefore write him an apology, I charge you, and have it done by the time my messenger is ready to set out.

Saying this, he went out of the room: Arabella eagerly opened the letter, and finding it in a style so different from what she expected, her dislike of him returned with more violence than ever.

Ah! the traitor! said she aloud; is it thus that he endeavours to move my compassion? How greatly did I over-rate his affection, when I imagined his despair was capable of killing him? Disloyal man! pursued she, walking about, is it by complaints to my father that thou expectest to succeed? And dost thou imagine the heart of Arabella is to be won by violence and injustice?

In this manner she wasted the time allotted for her to write; and when the marquis sent for her letter, having no intention to comply, she went to his chamber, conjuring him not to oblige her to a condescension so unworthy of her.

The marquis, being now excessively angry with her, rose up in a fury, and, leading her to his writing-desk, ordered her instantly to write to her cousin.

If I must write, my lord, said she, sobbing, pray be so good as to dictate what I must say.

Apologize for your rude behaviour, said the marquis; and desire him, in the most obliging manner you can, to return.

Arabella, seeing there was a necessity for obeying, took up the pen, and wrote the following billet:—

The Unfortunate Arabella to the Most Ungenerous Glanville

It is not by the power I have over you, that I command you to return, for I disclaim any empire over so unworthy a subject; but, since it is my father's pleasure I should invite you back, I must let you know that I repeal your banishment, and expect you will immediately return with the messenger who brings this. However, to spare your acknowledgments, know, that it is in obedience to my father's absolute commands, that you receive this mandate from

Arabella.

Having finished this billet, she gave it to the marquis to read; who, finding a great deal of his own haughtiness of temper in it, could not resolve to check her for a disposition so like his own; yet he told her her style was very uncommon. And pray, added he, smiling, who taught you to superscribe your letters thus? 'The unfortunate Arabella to the most ungenerous Glanville.' Why, Bella, this superscription is wholly calculated for the bearer's information: but come, alter it immediately; for I do not choose my messenger should know that you are unfortunate, or that my nephew is ungenerous.

Pray, my lord, replied Arabella, content yourself with what I have already done in obedience to your commands, and suffer my letter to remain as it is: methinks it is but reasonable I should express some little resentment at the complaint my cousin has been pleased to make to you against me; nor can I possibly make any letter more obliging, without being guilty of an unpardonable meanness.

You are a strange girl, replied the marquis, taking the letter, and enclosing it in one from himself; in which he earnestly entreated his nephew to return, threatening him with his displeasure if he disobeyed, and assuring him that his daughter would receive him as well as he could possibly desire.

The messenger being dispatched, with orders to ride post, and overtake the young gentleman, he obeyed his orders so well that he came up with him at ——; where he intended to lodge that night.

Mr Glanville, who expected his uncle would make use of some methods to recall him, opened his letter without any great emotion; but seeing another inclosed, his heart leaped to his mouth, not doubting but it was a letter from Arabella; but the contents surprised him so much, that he hardly knew whether he ought to look upon them as an invitation to return, or a new affront, her words were so distant and haughty. The superscription being much the same with a billet he had received from her in the garden, which had made him conclude her in jest, he knew not what to think of it. One would swear this dear girl's head is turned, said he to himself, if she had not more *wit* than her whole sex besides.

After reading Arabella's letter several times, he at last opened his uncle's; and seeing the pressing instances he made him to return, he resolved to obey; and the next morning he set out for the castle.

Arabella, during the time her cousin was expected, appeared so melancholy and reserved, that the marquis was extremely uneasy. You have never, said he to her, disobeyed me in any one action of your life; and I may with reason expect you will conform to my will in the choice I have made of a husband for you, since it is impossible to make any objection either to his person or mind; and being the son of my sister, he is certainly not unworthy of you, though he has not a title.

My first wish, my lord, replied Arabella, is to live single, not being desirous of entering into any engagement which may hinder my solicitude and cares, and lessen my attendance upon the best of fathers, who, till now, has always most tenderly complied with my inclinations in every thing: but if it is your absolute command that I should marry, give me not to one, who, though he has the honour to be allied to you, has neither merited your esteem, nor my favour, by any action worthy of his birth, or the passion he pretends to have for me; for in fine, my lord, by what services has he deserved the distinction with which you honour him? Has he ever delivered you from any considerable danger? Has he saved your life, and hazarded his own for you, upon any occasion whatever? Has he merited my esteem by his sufferings, fidelity, and respect? or by any great and generous action, given me a testimony of his love, which should oblige me to reward him with my affection? Ah! my lord, I beseech you, think not so unworthily of your daughter, as to bestow her upon one who has done so little to deserve her: if my happiness be dear to you, do not precipitate me into a state from whence you cannot recal me, with a person whom I can never affect.

She would have gone on, but the marquis interrupted her sternly. I'll hear no more, said he, of your foolish and ridiculous objections. What stuff is this you talk of? What service am I to expect from my nephew? And by what sufferings is he to merit your esteem? Assure yourself, Arabella, continued he, that I will never pardon you, if you presume to treat my nephew in the manner you have done. I perceive you have no real objection to make to him: therefore I expect you will endeavour to obey me without reluctance; for, since you seem to be so little acquainted with what will most conduce to your own happiness, you must not think it strange if I insist upon directing your choice in the most important business of your life.

Arabella was going to reply, but the marquis ordered her to be silent; and she went to her own apartment in so much affliction, that she thought her misfortunes were not exceeded by any she had ever read.

XI

In which a logical argument is unseasonably interrupted

THE MARQUIS WAS ALSO EXTREMELY uneasy at her obstinacy: he desired nothing more ardently than to marry her to his nephew; but he could not resolve to force her consent; and, however determined he appeared to her, yet, in reality, he intended only to use persuasions to effect what he desired; and, from the natural sweetness of her temper, he was sometimes not without hopes that she might at last be prevailed upon to comply.

His nephew's return restored him to part of his usual tranquillity: after he had gently chid him for suffering himself to be so far transported with his resentment at the little humours of a lady, as to leave his house without acquainting him, he bade him go to Arabella, and endeavour to make his peace with her.

Mr Glanville accordingly went to her apartment, resolving to oblige her to come to some explanation with him concerning the offence she complained of; but that fair incensed lady, who had taken shelter in her closet, ordered Lucy to tell him she was indisposed, and could not see him.

Glanville, however, comforted himself for this disappointment by the hopes of seeing her at supper; and accordingly she came when the supper bell rung, and, making a very cool compliment to her cousin, placed herself at table. The soft languor that appeared in her eyes, gave such an additional charm to one of the loveliest faces in the world, that Glanville, who sat opposite to her, could not help gazing on her with a very particular attention; he often spoke to her, and asked her trifling questions, for the sake of hearing the sound of her voice, which sorrow had made enchantingly sweet.

When supper was over, she would have retired; but the marquis desired her to stay and entertain her cousin, while he went to look over some dispatches he had received from London.

Arabella blushed with anger at this command; but not daring to disobey, she kept her eyes fixed on the ground, as if she dreaded to hear something that would displease her.

Well, cousin, said Glanville, though you desire to have no empire over so unworthy a subject as myself, yet I hope you are not displeased at my returning, in obedience to your commands.

Since I am not allowed any will of my own, said she, sighing, it matters not whether I am pleased or displeased; nor is it of any consequence to you to know.

Indeed but it is, Lady Bella, interrupted he; for if I knew how to please you, I would never, if I could help it, offend: therefore, I beg you, tell me how I have disobliged you; for certainly you have treated me as harshly as if I had been guilty of some very terrible offence.

You had the boldness, said she, to talk to me of love; and you well know that persons of my sex and quality are not permitted to listen to such discourses; and if for that offence I banished you my presence, I did no more than decency required of me, and which I would yet do, were I mistress of my own actions.

But is it possible, cousin, said Glanville, that you can be angry with any one for loving you? Is that a crime of so high a nature as to merit an eternal banishment from your presence?

Without telling you, said Arabella, blushing, whether I am angry at being loved, it is sufficient, you know, that I will not pardon the man who shall have the presumption to tell me he loves me.

But, madam, interrupted Glanville, if the person who tells you he loves you, be of a rank not beneath you, I conceive you are not at all injured by the favourable sentiments he feels for you; and though you are not disposed to make any returns to his passion, yet you are certainly obliged to him for his good opinion.

Since love is not voluntary, replied Arabella, I am not obliged to any person for loving me; for, questionless, if he could help it, he would.

If it is not a voluntary favour, interrupted Glanville, it is not a voluntary offence; and if you do not think yourself obliged by one, neither are you at liberty to be offended with the other.

The question, said Arabella, is not whether I ought to be offended at being loved, but whether it is not an offence to be told I am so.

If there is nothing criminal in the passion itself, madam, resumed Glanville, certainly there can be no crime in declaring it.

However specious your arguments may appear, interrupted Arabella, I am persuaded it is an unpardonable crime to tell a lady you love her; and though I had nothing else to plead, yet the authority of custom is sufficient to prove it.

Custom, Lady Bella, said Glanville, smiling, is wholly on my side; for the ladies are so far from being displeased at the addresses of their lovers, that their chiefest care is to gain them, and their greatest triumph to hear them talk of their passion: so, madam, I hope you will allow that argument has no force.

I do not know, answered Arabella, what sort of ladies they are who allow such unbecoming liberties; but I am certain that Statira, Parisatis, Clelia, Mandane, and all the illustrious heroines of antiquity, whom it is a glory to resemble, would never admit of such discourses.

Ah! for Heaven's sake, cousin, interrupted Glanville, endeavouring to stifle a laugh, do not suffer yourself to be governed by such antiquated maxims! The world is quite different to what it was in those days; and the ladies in this age would as soon follow the fashions of the Greek and Roman ladies, as mimic their manners; and, I believe, they would become one as well as the other.

I am sure, replied Arabella, the world is not more virtuous now than it was in their days: and there is good reason to believe it is not much wiser: and I do not see why the manners of this age are to be preferred to those of former ones, unless they are wiser and better: however, I cannot be persuaded that things are as you say; but that when I am a little better acquainted with the world, I shall find as many persons who resemble Oroondates, Artaxerxes, and the illustrious lover of Clelia, as those who are like Teribases, Artaxes, and the presuming and insolent Glanville.

By the epithets you give me, madam, said Glanville, I find you have placed me in very bad company: but pray, madam, if the illustrious lover of Clelia had never discovered his passion, how would the world have come to the knowledge of it?

He did not discover his passion, sir, resumed Arabella, till by the services he did the noble Clelius, and his incomparable daughter, he could plead some title to their esteem: he several times preserved the life of that renowned Roman; delivered the beautiful Clelia when she was a captive; and, in time, conferred so many obligations upon them, and all their friends, that he might well expect to be pardoned by the divine Clelia for daring to love her. Nevertheless, she used him very harshly when he first declared his passion, and banished him also from her presence; and it was a long time before she could prevail upon herself to compassionate his sufferings.

The marquis, coming in, interrupted Arabella; upon which she took occasion to retire, leaving Glanville more captivated with her than ever.

He found her usage of him was grounded upon examples she thought it her duty to follow; and, strange as her notions of life appeared, yet they were supported with so much wit and delicacy, that he could not help admiring her, while he foresaw the oddity of her humour would throw innumerable difficulties in his way before he should be able to obtain her.

However, as he was really passionately in love with her, he resolved to accommodate himself, as much as possible, to her taste, and endeavour to gain her heart by a behaviour most agreeable to her: he therefore assumed an air of great distance and respect; never mentioned his affections, nor the intentions of her father in his favour; and the marquis observing his daughter conversed with him with less reluctance than usual, leaving to time, and the merit of his nephew, to dispose her to comply with his desires, resolved not to interpose his authority in an affair upon which her own happiness so much depended.

XII

In which the reader will find a specimen of the true pathetic, in a speech of Oroondates. The adventure of the books

ARABELLA SAW THE CHANGE IN her cousin's behaviour with a great deal of satisfaction; for she did not doubt but his passion was as strong as ever, but that he forbore, through respect, from entertaining her with any expressions of it: therefore she now conversed with him with the greatest sweetness and complaisance; she would walk with him for several hours in the garden, leaning upon his arm, and charmed him to the last degree of admiration by the agreeable sallies of her wit, and her fine reasoning upon every subject he proposed.

It was with the greatest difficulty he restrained himself from telling her a thousand times a day that he loved her to excess, and conjuring her to give her consent to her father's designs in his favour: but, though he could get over his fears of offending her, yet it was impossible to express any sentiments of this nature to her, without having her women witnesses of his discourse; for when he walked with her in the garden, Lucy and another attendant always followed her; if he sat with her in her own chamber, her women were always at one end of it; and when they were both in the marquis's apartment, where her women did not follow her, poor Glanville found himself embarrassed by his presence; for, conceiving his nephew had opportunities enough of talking to his daughter in private, he always partook of their conversation.

He passed some weeks in this manner, extremely chagrined at the little progress he made; and was beginning to be heartily weary of the constraint he laid upon himself, when Arabella one day furnished him, without designing it, with an opportunity of talking to her on the subject he wished for.

When I reflect, said she, laughing, upon the difference there was between us some days ago, and the familiarity in which we live at

present, I cannot imagine by what means you have arrived to a good
fortune you had so little reason to expect; for, in fine, you have given me
no signs of repentance for the fault you committed, which moved me to
banish you; and I am not certain whether, in conversing with you in the
manner I do, I give you not as much reason to find fault with my too
great easiness, as you did me to be displeased with your presumption.

Since, returned Glanville, I have not persisted in the commission of
those faults which displeased you, what greater signs of repentance can
you desire, than this reformation in my behaviour.

But repentance ought to precede reformation, replied Arabella,
otherwise there is great room to suspect it is only feigned; and a
sincere repentance shews itself in such visible marks, that one can
hardly be deceived in that which is genuine. I have read of many
indiscreet lovers, who, not succeeding in their addresses, have
pretended to repent, and acted as you do; that is, without giving any
signs of contrition for the fault they had committed, have eat and slept
well, never lost their colour, or grew one bit thinner by their sorrow;
but contented themselves with saying they repented; and, without
changing their disposition to renew their fault, only concealed their
intention for fear of losing any favourable opportunity of committing
it again: but true repentance, as I was saying, not only produces
reformation, but the person who is possessed of it voluntarily punishes
himself for the faults he has been guilty of. Thus Mazares, deeply
repenting of the crime his passion for the divine Mandane had forced
him to commit; as a punishment, obliged himself to follow the fortune
of his glorious rival, obey all his commands, and fighting under his
banners, assist him to gain the possession of his adored mistress. Such
a glorious instance of self-denial was, indeed, a sufficient proof of
his repentance; and infinitely more convincing than the silence he
imposed upon himself with respect to his passion.

Oroondates, to punish himself for his presumption, in daring to tell
the admirable Statira that he loved her, resolved to die, to expiate his
crime: and, doubtless, would have done so, if his fair mistress, at the
entreaty of her brother, had not commanded him to live.

But pray, Lady Bella, interrupted Glanville, were not these gentlemen happy at last in the possession of their mistresses?

Doubtless they were, sir, resumed she; but it was not till after numberless misfortunes, infinite services, and many dangerous adventures, in which their fidelity was put to the strongest trials imaginable.

I am glad, however, said Glanville, that the ladies were not insensible; for, since you do not disapprove of their compassion for their lovers, it is to be hoped you will not be always as inexorable as you are now.

When I shall be so fortunate, interrupted she, to meet with a lover who shall have as pure and perfect a passion for me as Oroondates had for Statira, and give me as many glorious proofs of his constancy and affection, doubtless I shall not be ungrateful; but, since I have not the merits of Statira, I ought not to pretend to her good fortune; and shall be very well contented if I escape the persecutions which persons of my sex, who are not frightfully ugly, are always exposed to, without hoping to inspire such a passion as that of Oroondates.

I should be glad to be better acquainted with the actions of this happy lover, madam, said Glanville; that, forming myself upon his example, I may hope to please a lady as worthy of my regard as Statira was of his.

For heaven's sake, cousin, replied Arabella, laughing, how have you spent your time; and to what studies have you devoted your hours, that you could find none to spare for the perusal of books from which all useful knowledge may be drawn which gives us the most shining examples of generosity, courage, virtue, and love; which regulate our actions, form our manners, and inspire us with a noble desire of emulating those great, heroic, and virtuous actions, which made those persons so glorious in their age, and so worthy imitation in ours? However, as it is never too late to improve, suffer me to recommend to you the reading of these books, which will soon make you discover the improprieties you have been guilty of; and will, probably, induce you to avoid them for the future.

I shall certainly read them, if you desire it, said Glanville: and I have so great an inclination to be agreeable to you, that I shall embrace every opportunity of becoming so; and will therefore take my instructions from these books, if you think proper, or from yourself; which, indeed, will be the quickest method of teaching me.

Arabella having ordered one of her women to bring Cleopatra, Cassandra, Clelia, and the grand Cyrus from her library, Glanville no sooner saw the girl return, sinking under the weight of those voluminous romances, than he began to tremble at the apprehension of his cousin laying her commands upon him to read them; and repeated of his complaisance, which exposed him to the cruel necessity of performing what to him appeared an Herculean labour, or else incurring her anger by his refusal.

Arabella, making her women place the books upon a table before her, opened them, one after another, with eyes sparkling with delight; while Glanville sat wrapt in admiration at the sight of so many huge folios written, as he conceived, upon the most trifling subjects imaginable.

I have chosen out these few, said Arabella (not observing his consternation), from a great many others, which compose the most valuable part of my library; and by that time you have gone through these, I imagine you will be considerably improved.

Certainly, madam, replied Glanville, turning over the leaves in great confusion, one may, as you say, be greatly improved; for these books contain a great deal: and looking over a page of Cassandra, without any design, read these words, which were part of Oroondate's soliloquy when he received a cruel sentence from Statira:—

Ah, cruel! (says this miserable lover) and what have I done to merit it? Examine the nature of my offence, and you will see I am not so guilty, but that my death may free me from part of that severity. Shall your hatred last longer than my life? and can you detest a soul that forsakes its body only to obey that you? No, no, you are not so hard-hearted: that satisfaction will, doubtless, content you: and when I shall cease to be, doubtless I shall cease to be odious to you.

Upon my soul, said Glanville, stifling a laugh with great difficulty, I cannot help blaming the lady this sorrowful lover complains of, for her great cruelty; for here he gives one reason to suspect, that she will not even be contented with his dying in obedience to her commands, but will hate him after death; an impiety quite inexcusable in a Christian!

You condemn this illustrious princess with very little reason, interrupted Arabella, smiling at his mistake; for, besides that she was not a Christian, and ignorant of those divine maxims of charity and forgiveness, which Christians, by their profession, are obliged to practise, she was very far from desiring the death of Oroondates; for, if you will take the pains to read the succeeding passages, you will find that she expresses herself in the most obliging manner in the world; for when Oroondates tells her he would live, if she would consent he should, the princess most sweetly replies, I not only consent, but also entreat it! and, if I have any power, command it. However, lest you should fall into the other extreme, and blame this great princess for her easiness, (as you before condemned her for her cruelty) it is necessary you should know how she was induced to this favourable behaviour to her lover: therefore pray read the whole transaction. Stay! here it begins, continued she, turning over a good many pages, and marking where he should begin to read.

Glanville, having no great stomach to the task, endeavoured to evade it, by entreating his cousin to relate the passages she desired he should be acquainted with: but she declining it, he was obliged to obey, and began to read where she directed him: and, to leave him at liberty to read with greater attention, she left him, and went to a window at the other end of the chamber.

Mr Glanville, who was not willing to displease her, examined the task she had set him, resolving, if it was not a very hard one, to comply; but counting the pages, he was quite terrified at the number, and could not prevail upon himself to read them: therefore, glancing them over, he pretended to be deeply engaged in reading, when, in reality, he was contemplating the surprising effect these books had produced in the mind of his cousin; who, had she been untainted with the ridiculous whims they created in her imagination, was, in his opinion, one of the most accomplished ladies in the world.

When he had sat long enough to make her believe he had read what she had desired, he rose up, and joining her at the window, began to talk of the pleasantness of the evening, instead of the rigour of Statira.

Arabella coloured with vexation at his extreme indifference in a matter which was of such prodigious consequence in her opinion; but disdaining to put him in mind of his rudeness, in quitting a subject they had not thoroughly discussed, and which she had taken so much pains to make him comprehend, she continued silent, and would not condescend to afford him an answer to any thing he said.

Glanville, by her silence and frowns, was made sensible of his fault; and, to repair it, began to talk of the inexorable Statira, though, indeed, he did not well know what to say.

Arabella, clearing up a little, did not disdain to answer him upon her favourite topic: I knew, said she, you would be ready to blame this princess equally for her rigour and her kindness; but it must be remembered, that what she did in favour of Oroondates was wholly owing to the generosity of Artaxerxes.

Here she stopped, expecting Glanville to give his opinion; who, strangely puzzled, replied at random, To be sure madam, he was a very generous rival.

Rival! cried Arabella: Artaxerxes the rival of Oroondates! Why certainly you have lost your wits: he was Statira's brother; and it was to his mediation that Oroondates, or Orontes, owed his happiness.

Certainly, madam, replied Glanville, it was very generous in Artaxerxes, as he was brother to Statira to interpose in behalf of an unfortunate lover; and both Oroondates and Orontes were extremely obliged to him.

Orontes, replied Arabella, was more obliged to him than Oroondates: since the quality of Orontes was infinitely below that of Oroondates.

But, madam, interrupted Glanville, (extremely pleased at his having so well got over the difficulty he had been in,) which of these two lovers did Statira make happy?

This unlucky question immediately informed Arabella, that she had been all this time the dupe of her cousin; who, if he had read a single page, would have known that Orontes and Oroondates was the same person; the name of Orontes being assumed by Oroondates to conceal his real name and quality.

The shame and rage she conceived at so glaring a proof of his disrespect, and the ridicule to which she had exposed herself; were so great, that she could not find words severe enough to express her resentment; but protesting that no consideration whatever should oblige her to converse with him again, she ordered him instantly to quit her chamber; and assured him, if he ever attempted to approach her again, she would submit to the most terrible effects of her father's resentment, rather than be obliged to see a person who had, by his unworthy behaviour, made himself her scorn and aversion.

Glanville, who saw himself going to be discarded a second time, attempted with great submission, to move her to recall her cruel sentence; but Arabella, bursting into tears, complained so pathetically of the cruelty of her destiny, in exposing her to the hated importunities of a man she despised, and whose presence was so insupportable, that Glanville, thinking it best to let her rage evaporate a little before he attempted to pacify her, quitted her chamber; cursing Statira and Orontes a thousand times, and loading the authors of those books with all the imprecations his rage could suggest.

XIII

The adventure of the books continued

IN THIS TEMPER HE WENT to the garden to pass over the chagrin this unfortunate accident had given him; when, meeting the marquis, who insisted upon knowing the cause of that ill-humour so visible in his countenance, Glanville related all that had passed; but, in spite of his anger, it was impossible for him to repeat the circumstances of his disgrace without laughing, as well as the marquis; who thought the story so extremely diverting, that he would needs hear it over again.

However, Charles, said he, though I shall do what I can to gain your pardon from Bella, yet I shall not scruple to own you acted extremely wrong, in not reading what she desired you; for, besides losing an opportunity of obliging her, you drew yourself into a terrible dilemma; for how was it possible for you to evade a discovery of the cheat you put upon her, when she began to talk with you upon those passages she had desired you to read?

I acknowledge my error, my lord, answered Glanville; but if you restore me to my cousin's favour again, I promise you to repair it by a different behaviour for the future.

I will see what I can do for you, said the marquis, leaving him, to go to Arabella's apartment, who had retired to her closet, extremely afflicted at this new insult she had received from her cousin: her grief was the more poignant, as she was beginning to imagine, by the alteration in his behaviour, that he would prove such a lover as she wished for. Mr Glanville's person and qualifications had attracted her particular notice: and, to speak in the language of romance, she did not hate him; but, on the contrary, was very much disposed to wish him well: therefore it was no wonder she extremely resented the affront she had received from him.

The marquis, not finding her in her chamber, proceeded to her closet, where her women informed him she was retired; and, knocking gently at the door, was admitted by Arabella, whom he immediately discerned to have been weeping very much, for her fine eyes were red and swelled, and the traces of her tears might still be observed on her fair face, which, at the sight of the marquis, was overspread with a blush, as if she was conscious of her weakness in lamenting the crime her cousin had been guilty of.

The marquis drew a favourable omen for his nephew from her tears and confusion; but, not willing to increase it by acknowledging he had observed it, he told her he was come, at Mr Glanville's request, to make up the quarrel between them.

Ah! my lord, interrupted Arabella, speak no more to me of that unworthy man, who has so grossly abused my favour, and the privilege I allowed him: his baseness and ingratitude are but too manifest; and there is nothing I so much regret as my weakness in restoring him to part of my good opinion, after he had once forfeited it, by an insolence not to be paralleled.

Indeed, Bella, said the marquis, smiling, you resent too deeply these slight matters: I cannot think my nephew so guilty as you would have me believe he is: and you ought neither to be angry nor surprised, that he preferred your conversation before reading in a foolish old-fashioned book that you put in his hands.

If your lordship had ever read these books, replied Arabella, reddening with vexation, it is probable you would have another opinion of them: but, however that may be, my cousin is not to be excused for the contempt he showed to my commands; and for daring, by the cheat he put on me, to expose me to the shame of seeing myself so ridiculously imposed upon.

However, you must forgive him, said the marquis; and I insist upon it, before I quit your apartment, that you receive him into favour.

Pardon me, my lord, replied Arabella: this is what I neither can nor ought to do; and I hope you will not wrong me so much as to continue to desire it.

Nay, Bella, said he, this is carrying things too far, and making trifling disputes of too great consequence: I am surprised at your treatment of a man whom, after all, if ever you did intend to obey me, you must consent to marry.

There is no question, my lord, replied she, but it would be my glory to obey you in whatever is possible: but this you command me now to do not being so, I conceive you will rather impute my refusal to necessity than choice.

How! returned the marquis, will you endeavour to persuade me, that it is not possible Mr Glanville should be your husband?

It is impossible he should be so with my consent, resumed Arabella: and I cannot give it without wounding my own quiet in a most sensible manner.

Come, come, Bella, said the marquis, (fretting at her extreme obstinacy), this is too much: I am to blame to indulge your foibles in this manner: your cousin is worthy of your affection, and you cannot refuse it to him without incurring my displeasure.

Since my affection is not in my own power to bestow, said Arabella, weeping, I know not how to remove your displeasure; but, questionless, I know how to die, to avoid the effects of what would be to me the most terrible misfortune in the world.

Foolish girl! interrupted the marquis, how strangely do you talk? Are the thoughts of death become so familiar to you, that you speak of dying with so little concern?

Since, my lord, resumed she, in an exalted tone, I do not yield, either in virtue or courage, to many others of my sex, who, when persecuted like me, have fled to death for relief, I know not why I should be thought less capable of it than they; and if Artemisa, Candace, and the beautiful daughter of Cleopatra, could brave the terrors of death for the sake of the men they loved, there is no question but I also could imitate their courage, to avoid the man I have so much reason to hate.

The girl is certainly distracted, interrupted the marquis, excessively enraged at the strange speech she had uttered: these foolish books my nephew talks of have turned her brain! Where are they? pursued he, going into her chamber: I'll burn all I can lay my hands upon.

Arabella, trembling for the fate of her books, followed her father into the room; who, seeing the books which had caused this woeful adventure lying upon the table, he ordered one of her women to carry them into his apartment, vowing he would commit them all to the flames.

Arabella not daring, in the fury he was in, to interpose, he went out of the room, leaving her to bewail the fate of so many illustrious heroes and heroines, who, by an effect of a more cruel tyranny than any they had ever experienced before, were going to be cast into the merciless flames: which would, doubtless, pay very little regard to the divine beauties of the admirable Clelia, or the heroic valour of the brave Orontes; and the rest of those great princes and princesses, whose actions Arabella proposed for the model of hers.

Fortune, however, which never wholly forsook these illustrious personages, rescued them from so unworthy a fate, and brought Mr Glanville into the marquis's chamber just as he was giving orders to have them destroyed.

END OF THE FIRST BOOK

BOOK II

I

In which the adventure of the books is happily concluded

THE MARQUIS, AS SOON AS he saw Mr Glanville, told him he was resolved to cure Arabella of her whims, by burning the books that had put them into her head: I have seized upon some of them, pursued he, smiling; and you may, if you please, wreak your spite upon these authors of your disgrace, by burning them yourself.

Though I have all the reason in the world to be enraged with that incendiary Statira, said Glanville, laughing, for the mischief she has done me; yet I cannot consent to put such an affront upon my cousin, as to burn her favourite books: and now I think of it, my lord, pursued he, I will endeavour to make a merit with Lady Bella by saving them; therefore spare them, at my request, and let me carry them to her. I shall be quite unhappy till we are friends again.

You may do as you will, said the marquis; but I think it is encouraging her in her follies to give them to her again.

Glanville, without replying, eagerly took up the books, for fear the marquis should change his mind; and, highly delighted with the opportunity he had got of making his peace with Lady Bella, ran to her apartments, loaded with these kind intercessors; and, making his way by Lucy, who would have opposed him, penetrated even into the closet of the melancholy fair-one, who was making bitter reflections on the cruelty of her destiny, and bewailing her loss with a deluge of tears.

As ridiculous as the occasion of these tears was, yet Glanville could not behold them without being affected: assuming, therefore, a countenance as sad as he was able, he laid the books before her, and told her, he hoped she would excuse his coming into her presence without her permission, since it was only to restore her those books, whose loss she seemed so greatly to lament; and added, that it was with much difficulty he prevailed upon the marquis not to burn them immediately;

and his fears, that he might really do as he threatened, made him snatch them up, and bring them, with so little ceremony, into her closet.

Arabella, whose countenance brightened into a smile of pleasing surprise at the sight of her recovered treasure, turned her bright eyes upon Glanville with a look of complacency that went to his heart.

I well perceive, said she, that in exaggerating the merit of this little service you have done me, you expect I should suffer it to cancel your past offences. I am not ungrateful enough to be insensible of any kindness that is shown me; and, though I might be excused for suspecting it was rather policy than friendship, that induced you to seek my father's satisfaction, by saving these innocent victims of my father's displeasure, nevertheless I pardon you upon the supposition, that you will, for the future, avoid all occasion of offending me.

At these words she made a sign to him to be gone, fearing the extravagance of his joy would make him throw himself at her feet to thank her for the infinite favour she had conferred upon him: but, finding he seemed disposed to stay longer, she called one of her women into the closet; and, by some very significant frowns, gave Glanville to understand his stay was displeasing; so that he left her, with a very low bow, highly pleased at her having repealed his banishment, and assured the marquis that nothing could have happened more fortunate for him, than this intended disposal of his daughter's books, since it had proved the means of restoring him to her favour.

II

Which contains a very natural incident

FROM THIS TIME MR GLANVILLE, though he was far from coming up to Lady Bella's idea of a lover, yet, by the pains he apparently seemed to be at in obliging her, made every day some progress in her esteem. The marquis was extremely pleased at the harmony which subsisted between them; though he could have wished to have seen their marriage advance a little faster; but Glanville, who was better acquainted with Arabella's foible than the marquis, assured him, he would ruin all his hopes if he pressed her to marry; and entreated him to leave it entirely to him, to dispose her to consent to both their wishes.

The marquis was satisfied with his reasons, and resolving not to importune his daughter upon that subject any more, they lived for some months in a perfect tranquillity; to which an illness the marquis was seized with, and which was from the first thought to be dangerous, gave a sad interruption.

Arabella's extreme tenderness upon this occasion, her anxious solicitude, her pious cares, and never-ceasing attendance at the bed-side of her sick father, were so many new charms that engaged the affection of Glanville more strongly. As the marquis's indisposition increased, so did her care and assiduity: she would not allow any one to give him any thing but herself; bore all the pettish humours of a sick man with a surprising sweetness and patience; watched whole nights successively by his bed-side; and when, at his importunity, she consented to take any rest, it was only on a couch in his chamber, from whence no entreaties could make her remove. Mr Glanville partook with her in these fatigues; and, by his care of her father, and tenderness for her, confirmed her in the esteem she had entertained of him.

The marquis, who had struggled with the violence of his distemper for a fortnight, died on the fifteenth day in the arms of Arabella, who received his last looks; his eyes never removing themselves from her face, till they were closed by death. Her spirits, which the desire she had of being useful to him, had alone supported, now failed her at once; and she fell upon the bed, without sense or motion, as soon as she saw him expire.

Mr Glanville, who was kneeling on the other side, and had been holding one of his uncle's hands, started up in the most terrible consternation, and, seeing the condition she was in, flew to her relief; her women, while he supported her, used all the endeavours they could think of to recover her; but she continued so long in her swoon, that they apprehended she was dead; and. Glanville was resigning himself up to the most bitter sorrow, when she opened her eyes; but it was only to close them again. Her faintings continued the whole day; and the physicians declaring she was in great danger, from her extreme weakness, she was carried to bed in a condition that seemed to promise very little hopes of her life.

The care of the marquis's funeral devolving upon Mr Glanville, he sent a messenger express for his father, who was appointed guardian to Lady Bella, the marquis having first asked her if she was willing it should be so. This gentleman arrived time enough to be witness of that sad ceremony, which was performed with a magnificence suitable to the birth and fortune of the marquis.

Lady Bella kept her bed several days, and her life was thought to be in danger; but her youth, and the strength of her constitution, overcame her disease: and, when she was so well recovered as to be able to admit of a visit from her uncle, Mr Glanville sent for permission to introduce him. The afflicted Arabella granted his request; but, being then more indisposed than usual, she entreated they would defer their visit for an hour or two, which they complied with; and, returning at the appointed time, were conducted into her dressing-room by Lucy, who informed them her lady was just fallen into a slumber.

Mr Glanville, who had not seen her for some days, expected her waking with great impatience; and pleased himself with describing her, with a lover's fondness, to his father, when the sound of her voice in the next room interrupted him.

III

Which treats of a consolatory visit, and other grave matters

ARABELLA, BEING THEN AWAKENED FROM her slumber, was indulging her grief by complaints, which her women were so used to hear, that they never offered to disturb her. Merciless fate! said she, in the most moving tone imaginable; cruel destiny! that, not contented with having deprived my infancy of the soft cares and tender indulgences of a mother's fondness, has robbed me of the only parent I had left, and exposed me, at these early years, to the grief of losing him who was not only my father, but my friend, and protector of my youth!

Then, pausing a moment, she renewed her complaints with a deep sigh: Dear relics of the best of fathers! pursued she, why was it not permitted me to bathe you with my tears? Why were those sacred remains of him, from whom I drew my life, snatched from my eyes, ere they had poured their tribute of sorrow over them? Ah, pitiless women! said she to her attendants, you prevented me from performing the last pious rites to my dear father! You, by your cruel care, hindered me from easing my sad heart, by paying him the last duties he could receive from me? Pardon, O dear and sacred shade of my loved father! pardon this unwilling neglect of thy afflicted child, who, to the last moment of her wretched life, will bewail thy loss!

Here she ceased speaking; and Mr Glanville, whom this soliloquy had much less confounded than his father, was preparing to go in, and comfort her: when the old gentleman stopping him with a look of great concern, My niece is certainly much worse than we apprehend, said he. She is in a delirium: our presence may, perhaps, discompose her too much.

No, sir, replied Glanville, extremely confused at this suspicion: my cousin is not so bad as you suppose: it is common enough for people in any great affliction to ease themselves by complaints.

But these, replied the knight, are the strangest complaints I ever heard, and savour so much of phrenzy, that I am persuaded her head is not quite right.

Glanville was going to reply, when Lucy, entering, told him her lady had ordered their admission; upon which they followed her into Arabella's chamber, who was lying negligently upon her bed.

Her deep mourning, and the black gauze, which covered part of her fair face, was so advantageous to her shape and complexion, that Sir Charles, who had not seen her since she grew up, was struck with an extreme surprise at her beauty, while his son was gazing on her so passionately, that he never thought of introducing his father to her, who contemplated her with as much admiration as his son, though with less passion.

Arabella, rising from her bed, saluted her uncle with a grace that wholly charmed him; and turning to receive Mr Glanville, she burst into tears at the remembrance of his having assisted her in her last attendance upon her father. Alas, sir! said she, when we saw each other last, we were both engaged in a very melancholy office: had it pleased Heaven to have spared my father, he would, doubtless, have been extremely sensible of your generous cares; nor shall you have any reason to accuse me of ingratitude, since I shall always acknowledge your kindness as I ought.

If you think you owe me any obligation, returned Glanville, pay me, dearest cousin, by moderating your sorrow: indeed, you suffer yourself to sink too much under an affliction which is impossible to be remedied.

Alas! answered Arabella, my grief is very slight, compared to that of many others upon the death of their relations. The great Sisygambis, who, questionless, wanted neither fortitude nor courage, upon the news of her grand-daughter's death, wrapt herself up in her veil; and, resolving never more to behold the light, waited for death in that posture. Menecrates, upon the loss of his wife, built a magnificent tomb for her; and, shutting himself up in it, resolved to pass away the remainder of his life with her ashes. These, indeed, were glorious effects of piety and affection, and unfeigned signs of an excessive sorrow:

what are the few tears I shed, to such illustrious instances of grief and affection as these?

Glanville, finding his cousin upon this strain, blushed extremely, and would have changed the subject; but the old gentleman, who had never heard of these two persons she mentioned, who expressed their sorrow for their losses in so strange a manner, was surprised at it, and was resolved to know more about them.

Pray, niece, said he, were you acquainted with these people, who could not submit to the dispensation of Providence, but, as one may say, flew in the face of Heaven by their impatience?

I am very well acquainted with their history, resumed Arabella; and I can assure you, they were both very admirable persons.

Oh! Oh! their history! interrupted the knight. What, I warrant you, they are to be found in the Fairy Tales, and those sort of books! Well, I never could like such romances, not I; for they only spoil youth, and put strange notions into their heads.

I am sorry, resumed Arabella, blushing with anger, that we are like to differ in opinion upon so important a point.

Truly, niece, said Sir Charles, if we never differ in any thing else, I shall he very easy about this slight matter; though I think a young lady of your fine sense (for my son praises you to the skies for your *wit*) should not be so fond of such ridiculous nonsense as these story-books are filled with.

Upon my word, sir, resumed Arabella, all the respect I owe you cannot hinder me from telling you that I take it extremely ill you should, in my presence, rail at the finest productions in the world. I think we are infinitely obliged to these authors, who have, in so sublime a style, delivered down to posterity heroic actions of the bravest men, and most virtuous of women. But for the inimitable pen of the famous Scudery, we had been ignorant of the lives of many great and illustrious persons: the warlike actions of Oroondates, Aronces, Juba, and the renowned Artaban, had, haply, never been talked of in our age; and those fair and chaste ladies, who were the objects of their pure and constant passions, had still been buried in obscurity; and neither their divine beauties, or singular virtue, been the subject of our admiration and praise. But for the famous Scudery, we had not known the true cause of that action of Clelia's, for which the senate decreed her a statue; namely, her casting herself, with an unparalleled courage, into the Tyber, a deep and rapid river, as you must certainly know, and swimming to the other side. It was not, as the Roman historians falsely report, a stratagem to recover herself, and the other hostages, from the power of Porsenna; it was to preserve her honour from violation by the impious Sextus, who was in the camp. But for Scudery, we had still thought the inimitable poetess Sappho to be a loose wanton, whose verses breathed nothing but unchaste and irregular fires: on the contrary, she was so remarkably chaste, that she would never even consent to marry; but, loving Phaon, only with a Platonic passion, obliged him to restrain his desires within the compass of a brother's affections. Numberless are the mistakes he has cleared up of this kind; and I question, if any other historian but himself knew that Cleopatra was really married to Julius Caesar; or that Caesario, her son by this marriage, was not murdered, as was supposed, by the order of Augustus, but married the fair Queen of Ethiopia, in whose dominions he took refuge. The prodigious acts of valour, which he has recounted of those accomplished princes, have never been equalled by the heroes of either the Greek or Roman historians. How poor and insignificant are the actions of their warriors to Scudery's, where one of those admirable heroes would put whole armies into terror, and with his single arm oppose a legion!

Indeed, niece, said Sir Charles, no longer able to forbear interrupting her, these are all very improbable tales. I remember, when I was a boy, I was very fond of reading the history of Jack the Giant Killer, and Tom Thumb; and these stories so filled my head, that I really thought one of those little fellows killed men an hundred feet high; and that the other, after a great many surprising exploits, was swallowed up by a cow.

You was very young, sir, you say, interrupted Arabella, tartly, when those stories gained your belief: however, your judgment was certainly younger, if you ever believed them at all; for as credulous as you are pleased to think me, I should never, at any age, have been persuaded such things could have happened.

My father, madam, said Glanville, who was strangely confused all this time, bore arms in his youth; and soldiers, you know, never trouble themselves much with reading.

Has my uncle been a soldier, said Arabella, and does he hold in contempt the actions of the bravest soldiers in the world?

The soldiers you speak of, niece, said Sir Charles, were, indeed, the bravest soldiers in the world; for I don't believe they ever had their equals.

And yet, sir, said Arabella, there are a great number of such soldiers to be found in Scudery.

Indeed, my dear niece, interrupted Sir Charles, they are to be found no where else, except in your imagination, which, I am sorry to see, is filled with such *whimsies*.

If you mean this to affront me, sir, resumed Arabella, hardly able to forbear tears, I know how far, as my uncle, I ought to bear with you: but methinks it is highly unkind to aggravate my sorrows by such cruel jests; and since I am not in an humour to suffer them, don't take it ill, if I entreat you to leave me to myself.

Mr Glanville, who knew nothing pleased his cousin so much as paying an exact obedience to her commands, rose up immediately; and, bowing respectfully to her, asked his father if he should attend him into the gardens.

The baronet, who thought Arabella's behaviour bordered a good deal upon rudeness, took his leave with some signs of displeasure upon his countenance; and, notwithstanding all his son could say in excuse for her, he was extremely offended.

What! said he to Mr Glanville, does she so little understand the respect that is due to me as her uncle, that she so peremptorily desired me to leave her room? My brother was to blame to take so little care of her education: she is quite a rustic!

Ah! don't wrong your judgment so much, sir, said Glanville: my cousin has as little of the rustic as if she had passed all her life in court: her fine sense, and the native elegance of her manners, give an inimitable grace to her behaviour; and as much exceed the studied politeness of other ladies I have conversed with, as the beauties of her person do all I have ever seen.

She is very handsome, I confess, returned Sir Charles: but I cannot think so well of her *wit* as you do; for methinks she talks very oddly, and has the strangest conceits! Who, but herself, would think it probable that one man could put a whole army to flight; or commend a foolish fellow for living in a tomb, because his wife was buried in it? Fie, fie! these are silly and extravagant notions, and will make her appear very ridiculous.

Mr Glanville was so sensible of the justness of this remark, that he could not help sighing; which his father observing, told him, that since she was to be his wife, it was his business to produce a reformation in her; for, added he, notwithstanding the immense fortune she will bring you, I should be sorry to have a daughter-in-law for whom I should blush as often as she opened her mouth.

I assure you, sir, said Mr Glanville, I have but very little hopes that I shall be so happy as to have my cousin for a wife; for though it was my uncle's command I should make my addresses to her, she received me so ill, as a lover, that I have never dared to talk to her upon that subject since.

And pray, resumed Sir Charles, upon what terms are you at present?

While I seem to pretend nothing to her as a lover, replied Mr Glanville, she is very obliging, and we live in great harmony together; but, I am persuaded, if I exceed the bounds of friendship in my professions, she will treat me extremely ill.

But, interrupted Sir Charles, when she shall know that her father has bequeathed you one-third of his estate, provided she don't marry you, 'tis probable her mind may change; and you may depend upon it, since your heart is so much set upon her, that, as I am her guardian, I shall press her to perform the marquis's will.

Ah! sir, resumed Mr Glanville, never attempt to lay any constraint upon my cousin in an affair of this nature: permit me to tell you, it would be an abuse of the marquis's generous confidence, and what I would never submit to.

Nay, nay, said the old gentleman, you have no reason to fear any compulsion from me: though her father has left me her guardian till she is of age, yet it is with such restriction, that my niece is quite her own mistress in that respect; for though she is directed to consult me in her choice of an husband, yet my consent is not absolutely necessary. The marquis has certainly had a great opinion of his daughter's prudence; and I hope she will prove herself worthy of it by her conduct.

Mr Glanville was so taken up with his reflections upon the state of his affairs, that he made but little reply; and, as soon as he had disengaged himself, retired to his chamber, to be at more liberty to indulge his meditations. As he could not flatter himself with having made any impression upon the heart of Arabella, he foresaw a thousand inconveniencies from the death of the marquis; for, besides that he lost a powerful mediator with his cousin, he feared that, when she appeared in the world, her beauty and fortune would attract a crowd of admirers, among whom, it was probable, she would find some one more agreeable to her taste than himself. As he loved her with great tenderness, this thought made him extremely uneasy; and he would sometimes wish the marquis had laid a stronger injunction upon her in his will to marry him; and regretted the little power his father had over her: but he was too generous to dwell long upon these thoughts, and contented himself with resolving to do all that was honourable to obtain her, without seeking for any assistance from unjustifiable methods.

IV

Which contains some common occurrences, but placed in a new light

ARABELLA, IN A FEW DAYS, leaving her chamber, had so many opportunities of charming her uncle by her conversation, which, when it did not turn upon any incident in her romances, was perfectly fine, easy, and entertaining, that he declared he should quit the castle with great regret, and endeavoured to persuade her to accompany him to town: but Arabella, who was determined to pass the year of her mourning in the retirement she had always lived in, absolutely refused, strong as her curiosity was to see London.

Mr Glanville secretly rejoiced at this resolution, though he seemed desirous of making her change it; but she was unalterable; and, therefore, the baronet did not think proper to press her any more.

Her father's will being read to her, she seemed extremely pleased with the article in favour of Mr Glanville, wishing him joy of the estate that was bequeathed to him with a most enchanting sweetness.

Mr Glanville sighed, and cast his eyes on the ground, as he returned her compliment, with a very low bow: and Sir Charles, observing his confusion, told Arabella, that he thought it was a very bad omen for his son, to wish him joy of an estate which he could not come to the possession of but by a very great misfortune.

Arabella, understanding his meaning, blushed; and, willing to change the discourse, proceeded to consult her uncle upon the regulation of her house. Besides the legacies her father had bequeathed to his servants, those who were more immediately about his person she desired might have their salaries continued to them: she made no other alteration, than discharging these attendants; retaining all the others, and submitting to her uncle the management of her estates; receiving the allowance he thought proper to assign her, till she was of age, of which she wanted three years.

Every thing being settled, Sir Charles prepared to return to town. Mr Glanville, who desired nothing so much as to stay some time longer

with his cousin in her solitude, got his father to entreat that favour
for him of Arabella: but she represented to her uncle the impropriety
of a young gentleman's staying with her in her house, now her father
was dead, in a manner so genteel and convincing, that Sir Charles
could press it no farther; and all that Mr Glanville could obtain, was a
permission to visit her some time after, provided he could prevail upon
his sister, Miss Charlotte Glanville, to accompany him.

The day of their departure being come, Sir Charles took his leave
of his charming niece, with many expressions of esteem and affection;
and Mr Glanville appeared so concerned, that Arabella could not help
observing it, and bade him *adieu* with great sweetness.

When they were gone, she found her time hung heavy upon her hands:
her father was continually in her thoughts, and made her extremely
melancholy: she recollected the many agreeable conversations she had
had with Glanville, and wished it had been consistent with decency
to have detained him. Her books being the only amusement she had
left, she applied herself to reading with more eagerness than ever: but,
notwithstanding the delight she took in this employment, she had so
many hours of solitude and melancholy to indulge the remembrance of
her father in, that she was very far from being happy.

As she wished for nothing more passionately than an agreeable
companion of her own sex and rank, an accident threw a person in her
way, who, for some days, afforded her a little amusement. Stepping one
day out of her coach, to go into church, she saw a young lady enter,
accompanied by a middle-aged woman, who seemed to be an attendant.
As Arabella had never seen any one above the rank of a gentleman farmer's
daughter in this church, her attention was immediately engaged by the
appearance of this stranger, who was very magnificently dressed. Though
she did not seem to be more than eighteen years of age, her stature was
above the ordinary size of women; and, being rather too plump to be
delicate, her *mien* was so majestic, and such an air of grandeur was diffused
over her whole person, joined to the charms of a very lovely face, that
Arabella could hardly help thinking she saw the beautiful Candace before
her, who, by Scudery's, description, very much resembled this fair one.

Arabella, having heedfully observed her looks, thought she saw a great appearance of melancholy in her eyes, which filled her with a generous concern for the misfortunes of so admirable a person: but the service beginning, she was not at liberty to indulge her reflections upon this occasion, as she never suffered any thoughts, but those of religion, to intrude upon her mind during these pious rites.

As she was going out of church, she observed the young lady, attended only by the woman who came with her, preparing to walk home, and therefore stept forward, and saluted her with a grace peculiar to herself, entreated her to come into her coach, and give her the pleasure of setting her down at her own house. So obliging an offer, from a person of Arabella's rank, could not fail of being received with great respect by the young lady, who was not ignorant of all the forms of good breeding, and, accepting her invitation, she stepped into the coach; Arabella obliging her woman to come in also, for whom, as she had that day only Lucy along with her, there was room enough.

As they were going home, Arabella, who longed to be better acquainted, entreated the fair stranger, as she called her, to go to the castle, and spend the day with her: and she consenting, they passed by the house where she lodged, and alighted at the castle, where Arabella welcomed her with the most obliging expressions of civility and respect. The young lady, though perfectly versed in the modes of town-breeding, and nothing-meaning ceremony, was at a loss how to make proper returns to the civilities of Arabella. The native elegance and simplicity of her manners were accompanied with so much real benevolence of heart, such insinuating tenderness, and graces so irresistible, that she was quite oppressed with them; and having spent most of her time between her toilet and quadrille, was so little qualified for partaking a conversation so refined as Arabella's, that her discourse appeared quite tedious to her, since it was neither upon fashions, assemblies, cards, nor scandal.

Her silence, and that absence of mind which she betrayed, made Arabella conclude she was under some very great affliction: and to amuse her, after dinner, led her into the gardens, supposing a person whose uneasiness, as she did not doubt, proceeded from love, would be pleased with the sight of groves and streams, and be tempted to disclose her misfortunes while they wandered in that agreeable privacy. In this, however, she was deceived: for though the young lady sighed several times, yet, when she did speak, it was only of indifferent things, and not at all in the manner of an afflicted heroine.

After observing upon a thousand trifles, she told Arabella, at last, to whom she was desirous of making known her alliance to quality, that these gardens were extremely like those of her father's-in-law, the Duke of ——, at——.

At this intimation, she expected Arabella would be extremely surprised; but that lady, whose thoughts were always familiarized to objects of grandeur, and would not have been astonished if she had understood her guest was the daughter of a king, appeared so little moved, that the lady was piqued by her indifference: and, after a few moment's silence, began to mention going away.

Arabella, who was desirous of retaining her a few days, entreated her so obligingly to favour her with her company for some time in her solitude, that the other could not refuse: and dispatching her woman to the house where she lodged, to inform them of her stay at the castle, would have dispensed with her coming again to attend her, had not Arabella insisted upon the contrary.

The reserve which the daughter-in-law of the Duke of —— still continued to maintain, notwithstanding the repeated expressions of friendship Arabella used to her, increased her curiosity to know her adventures, which she was extremely surprised she had never offered to relate; but attributing her silence upon this head to her modesty, she was resolved, as was the custom in those cases, to oblige her woman, who, she presumed, was her confidante, to relate her lady's history to her, and sending for this person one day, when she was alone, to attend her in her closet, she gave orders to her women, if the fair stranger came to inquire for her, to say she was then busy, but would wait on her as soon as possible.

After this caution, she ordered Mrs Morris to be admitted: and, obliging her to sit down, told her she sent for her in order to hear from her the history of her lady's life, which she was extremely desirous of knowing.

Mrs Morris, who was a person of sense, and had seen the world, was extremely surprised at this request of Arabella, which was quite contrary to the laws of good-breeding, and, as she thought, betrayed a great deal of impertinent curiosity: she could not tell how to account for the free manner in which she desired her to give up her lady's secrets, which, indeed, were not of a nature to be told; and appeared so much confused, that Arabella took notice of it: and supposing it was her bashfulness which caused her embarrassment, she endeavoured to re-assure her by the most affable behaviour imaginable.

Mrs Morris, who was not capable of much fidelity for her lady, being but lately taken into her service, and not extremely fond of her, thought she had now a fine opportunity of recommending herself to Arabella, by telling her all she knew of Miss Groves, for that was her name; and therefore told her, since she was pleased to command it, she would give her what account she was able of her lady: but entreated her to be secret, because it was of great consequence to her, that her affairs should not be known.

I always imagined, said Arabella, that your beautiful mistress had some particular reason for not making herself known, and for coming in this private manner into this part of the country: you may assure yourself, therefore, that I will protect her as far as I am able, and offer her all the assistance in my power to give her; therefore you may acquaint me with her adventures, without being apprehensive of a discovery that would be prejudicial to her.

Mrs Morris, who had been much better pleased with the assurances of a reward for the intelligence she was going to give her, looked a little foolish at these fine promises, in which she had no share; and Arabella, supposing she was endeavouring to recollect all the passages of her lady's life, told her she need not give herself the trouble to acquaint her with any thing that passed during the infancy of her lady, but proceed to acquaint her with matters of greater importance: And since, said she, you have, no doubt, been most favoured with her confidence, you will do me a pleasure to describe to me, exactly all the thoughts of her soul, as she has communicated then to you, that I may the better comprehend her history.

V

The history of Miss Groves, interspersed with some very curious observations

THOUGH, MADAM, SAID MRS MORRIS, I have not been long in Miss Groves's service, yet I know a great many things by means of her former woman, who told them to me, though my lady thinks I am ignorant of them; and I know that this is her second trip into the country.

Pray, interrupted Arabella, do me the favour to relate things methodically: of what use is it to me to know that this is your lady's second trip, as you call it, into the country, if I know not the occasion of it? Therefore begin with informing me, who were the parents of this admirable young person.

Her father, madam, said Mrs Morris, was a merchant; and at his death left her a large fortune, and so considerable a jointure to his wife, that the Duke of ——, being then a widower, was tempted to make his addresses to her. Mrs Groves was one of the proudest women in the world; and this offer flattering her ambition more than ever she had reason to expect, she married the duke after a very short courtship, and carried Miss Groves down with her to ——, where the duke had a fine seat, and where she was received by his grace's daughters, who were much about her own age, with great civility. Miss Groves, madam, was then about twelve years old, and was educated with the duke's daughters, who in a little time became quite disgusted with their new sister; for Miss Groves, who inherited her mother's pride, though not her understanding, in all things affected an equality with those young ladies, who, conscious of the superiority of their birth, could but ill bear with her insolence and presumption. As they grew older, difference of their inclinations caused perpetual quarrels amongst them; for his grace's daughters were serious, reserved, and pious. Miss Groves affected noisy mirth, was a great romp, and delighted in masculine exercises.

The duchess was often reflected on for suffering her daughter, without any other company than two or three servants, to spend great part of the day in riding about the country, leaping over hedges, and ditches, exposing her fair face to the injuries of the sun and wind; and, by those coarse exercises, contracting a masculine and robust air not becoming her sex and tender years; yet she could not be prevailed upon to restrain her from this diversion, till it was reported, she had listened to the addresses of a young sportsman who used to mix in the train when she went upon those rambles, and procured frequent opportunities of conversing with her.

There is a great difference, interrupted Arabella, in suffering addresses, and being betrayed into an involuntary hearing of them, and this last I conceive to have been the case of your lady; for it is not very probable she would so far forget what she owed to her own glory, as to be induced to listen quietly to discourses like those you mention.

However, madam, resumed Mrs Morris, the duchess thought it necessary to keep her more at home; but even here she was not without meeting adventures, and found a lover in the person who taught her to write.

That, indeed, was a very notable adventure, said Arabella; but it is not strange that love should produce such metamorphoses: it is not very long ago that I heard of a man of quality who disguised himself in a poor habit, and worked in the gardens of a certain nobleman, whose daughter he was enamoured with: these things happen every day.

The person I speak of, madam, said Mrs Morris, was never discovered to be any thing better than a writing master; and yet, for all that, Miss was *smitten* with his fine person, and was taking measures to run away with him, when the intrigue was discovered, the lover dismissed, and the young lady, whose faulty conduct had drawn upon her her mother's dislike, was sent up to London, and allowed to be her own mistress at sixteen; to which unpardonable neglect of her mother she owes the misfortunes that have since befallen her.

Whatever may be the common opinion of this matter, interrupted Arabella, again, I am persuaded the writing-master, as you call him, was some person of quality, who made use of that device to get access to his beautiful mistress. Love is ingenious in artifices: who would have thought, that, under the name of Alcippus, a simple attendant of the fair Artemisa, princess of Armenia, the gallant Alexander, son of the great and unfortunate Antony, by Queen Cleopatra, was concealed, who took upon himself that mean condition for the sake of seeing his adored princess? Yet the contrivance of Orontes, prince of the Massagetes, was far more ingenious, and even dangerous; for this valiant and young prince happening to see the picture of the beautiful Thalestris, daughter of the queen of the Amazons, he fell passionately in love with her: and, knowing that the entrance into that country was forbid to men, he dressed himself in women's apparel; and, finding means to be introduced to the queen and her fair daughter, whose amity he gained by some very singular services in the wars, he lived several years undiscovered in their court. I see, therefore, no reason to the contrary, but that this writing-master might have been some illustrious person, whom love had disguised; and I am persuaded, added she, smiling, that I shall hear more of him anon, in a very different character.

Indeed, madam, said Mrs Morris, whom this speech of Arabella had extremely surprised, I never heard any thing more about him than what I have related: and, for what I know, he continues still to teach writing; for I do not suppose the duchess's displeasure could affect him.

How is it possible, said Arabella, that you can suppose such an offence to probability? In my opinion, it is much more likely that this unfortunate lover is dead through despair; or, perhaps, wandering over the world in search of that fair one who was snatched from his hopes.

If it was his design to seek for her, madam, resumed Mrs Morris, he need not have gone far, since she was only sent to London, whither he might easily have followed her.

There is no accounting for these things, said Arabella: perhaps he has been imposed upon, and made to believe, that it was she herself that banished him from her presence: it is probable, too, that he was jealous, and thought she preferred some one of his rivals to him. Jealousy is inseparable from true love; and the slightest matters imaginable will occasion it; and what is still more wonderful, this passion creates the greatest disorders in the most sensible and delicate hearts. Never was there a more refined and faithful passion than that of the renowned Artamenes for Mendane; and yet this prince was almost driven to distraction by a smile, which he fancied he saw in the face of his divine mistress, at a time when she had some reason to believe he was dead; and he was so transported with grief and rage, that though he was a prisoner in his enemy's camp, where the knowledge of his quality would have procured him certain death, yet he determined to hazard all things for the sake of presenting himself before Mandane and upbraiding her with her infidelity; when, in reality, nothing was farther from the thoughts of that fair and virtuous princess, than the lightness he accused her of; so that, as I said before, it is not at all to be wondered at, if this disguised lover of your lady was driven to despair by suspicions as groundless, perhaps, as those of Artamenes, yet not the less cruel and tormenting.

Mrs Morris, finding Arabella held her peace at these words, went on with her history in this manner:—Miss Groves, madam, being directed by her woman in all things, took up her lodgings in her father's house, who was a broken tradesman, and obliged to keep himself concealed for fear of his creditors; here she formed her equipage, which consisted of a chair, one footman, a cook, and her woman. As she was indulged with the command of what money she pleased, her extravagance was boundless: she lavished away large sums at gaming which was her favourite diversion; kept such a number of different animals for favourites, that their maintenance amounted to a considerable sum every year. Her woman's whole family were supported at her expense; and, as she frequented all public places, and surpassed ladies of the first quality in finery, her dress alone consumed great part of her income. I need not tell you, madam, that my lady was a celebrated beauty: you have yourself been pleased to say, that she is very handsome. When she first appeared at court, her beauty and the uncommon dignity of her person, at such early years, made her the object of general admiration. The king was particularly struck with her; and declared to those about him, that Miss Groves was the finest woman at court. The ladies, however, found means to explain away all that was flattering in this distinction: they said Miss Groves was clumsy; and it was her resemblance to the *unwieldy German* ladies that made her so much admired by his majesty. Her pride, and the quality airs she affected, were the subject of great ridicule to those that envied her charms: some censures were maliciously cast on her birth; for, as she was always styled the Duchess of ———'s daughter, a custom she introduced herself, she seemed to disclaim all title to a legal father. Miss Groves, as universally admired as she was, yet made but very few particular conquests. Her fortune was known to be very considerable, and her mother's jointure was to descend to her after her death: yet there was no gentleman who would venture upon a wife of Miss Groves's taste for expense, as very few estates to which she could pretend, would support her extravagance. The Honourable Mr L———, brother to the Earl of ———, was the only one amidst a crowd of admirers, who made any particular address to her. This gentleman was tolerably handsome, and had the art of making himself agreeable to the ladies by a certain air of softness and tenderness which never failed to make some impression upon those he desired to deceive.

Miss Groves was ravished with her conquest; and boasted of it so openly, that people who were acquainted with this gentleman's character, foreseeing her fate, could not help pitying her.

A very few month's courtship completed the ruin of poor Miss Groves; she fell a sacrifice to oaths which had been often prostituted for the same inhuman purposes; and became so fond of her betrayer, that it was with great difficulty he could persuade her not to give him, even in public, the most ridiculous proofs of her tenderness. Her woman pretends she was ignorant of this intrigue, till, Miss Groves growing big with child, it could no longer be concealed: it was at length agreed she should lie in at her own lodgings, to prevent any suspicions from her retreating into the country; but that scheme was over-ruled by her woman's mother, who advised her to conceal herself in some village, not far from town, till the affair was over.

Miss Groves approved of this second proposal, but took advantage of her shape, which, being far from delicate, would not easily discover any growing bigness, to stay in town as long as she possibly could. When her removal was necessary, she went to the lodgings provided for her, a few miles distant from London: and, notwithstanding the excuses which were framed for this sudden absence, the true cause was more than suspected by some busy people, who industriously inquired into her affairs.

Mr L—— saw her but seldom during her illness: the fear of being discovered was his pretence but her friends easily saw through this disguise, and were persuaded Miss Groves was waning in his affections.

As she had a very strong constitution, she returned to town at the end of three weeks: the child was dead, and she looked handsomer than ever. Mr L—— continued his visits; and the town to make remarks of them. All this time the duchess never troubled herself about the conduct of this unfortunate young creature; and the people she was with had not the goodness to give her the least hint of her misconduct, and the waste of her fortune: on the contrary, they almost turned her head with their flatteries, preyed upon her fortune, and winked at her irregularities.

She was now a second time with child: her character was pretty severely handled by her enemies; Mr L—— began openly to slight her; and she was several thousand pounds in debt. The mother and sisters of her woman, in whose house she still was, were base enough to whisper the fault she had been guilty of to all their acquaintances. Her story became generally known: she was shunned and neglected by every body; and even Mr L——, who had been the cause of her ruin, entirely abandoned her, and boasted openly of the favours he had received from her.

Miss Groves protested to her friends, that he had promised her marriage: but Mr L—— constantly denied it; and never scrupled to say, when he was questioned about it, that he found Miss Groves too easy a conquest to make any perjury necessary. Her tenderness, however, for this base man was so great, that she could never hear to bear him railed at in her presence; but would quarrel with the only friends she had left, if they said any thing to his disadvantage. As she was now pretty far advanced with child, she would have retired into the country; but the bad condition of her affairs made her removal impossible: in this extremity she had recourse to her uncle, a rich merchant in the city, who, having taking all the necessary precautions for his own security, paid Miss Groves's debts, carrying on, in her name, a law-suit with the duchess, for some lands which were to be put into her hands when she was of age, and which that great lady detained. Miss Groves being reduced to live upon something less than an hundred a year, quitted London, and came into this part of the country, where she was received by Mrs Barnet, one of her woman's sisters, who is married to a country gentleman of some fortune. In her house she lay in of a girl, which Mr L—— sent to demand, and will not be persuaded to inform her how, or in what manner, he has disposed of the child.

Her former woman leaving her, I was received in her place, from whom I learnt all these particulars: and Miss Groves having gained the affections of Mr Barnet's brother, her beauty, and the large fortune which she has in reversion, has induced him, notwithstanding the knowledge of her past unhappy conduct, to marry her. But their marriage is yet a secret, Miss Groves being apprehensive of her uncle's displeasure for not consulting him in her choice.

Her husband is gone to London, with an intention to acquaint him with it: and when he returns, their marriage will be publicly owned.

VI

Containing what a judicious reader will hardly approve

MRS MORRIS ENDING HER NARRATION, Arabella, who had not been able to restrain her tears at some parts of it, thanked her for the trouble had had been at; and assured her of her secrecy. Your lady's case, said she, is much to be lamented; and greatly resembles the unfortunate Cleopatra's, whom Julius Caesar privately marrying, with a promise to own her for his wife when he should be peaceable master of the Roman empire, left that great queen big with child: and, never intending to perform his promise, suffered her to be exposed to the censures the world has so freely cast upon her, and which she so little deserved.

Mrs Morris seeing the favourable light in which Arabella viewed the actions of her lady, did not think proper to say any thing to undeceive her; but went out of the closet, not a little mortified at her disappointment: for she saw she was likely to receive nothing for betraying her lady's secrets, from Arabella; who seemed so little sensible of the pleasure of scandal as to be wholly ignorant of its nature, and not to know it when it was told her.

Miss Groves, who was just come to Lady Bella's chamber-door, to inquire for her, was surprised to see her woman come out of it; and who, upon meeting her, expressed great confusion. As she was going to ask her some questions concerning her business there, Arabella, came out of the closet, and seeing Miss Groves in her chamber, asked her pardon for staying so long from her.

I have been listening to your history, said she, with great frankness, which your woman has been relating; and I assure you I am extremely sensible of your misfortunes.

Miss Groves, at these words, blushed with extreme confusion, and Mrs Morris turned pale with astonishment and fear. Arabella, not sensible that she had been guilty of any indiscretion, proceeded to make reflections upon some part of her story, which, though they were not at all disadvantageous to that young lady, she received as so many insults; and asked Lady Bella if she was not ashamed to tamper with a servant to betray the secrets of her mistress.

Arabella, a little surprised at so rude a question, answered with great sweetness; and protested to her, that she would make no use of what she had learned of her affairs: For, in fine, madam, said she, do you think I am less fit to be trusted with your secrets, than the princess of the Leontines was with those of Clelia, between whom there was no greater amity and acquaintance than with us? And you must certainly know, that the secrets which that admirable person entrusted with Lysimena, were of a nature to be more dangerous, if revealed, than yours. The happiness of Clelia depended upon Lysimena's fidelity; and the liberty, nay, haply, the life of Aronces, would have been in danger, if she had betrayed them. Though I do not intend to arrogate to myself the possession of those admirable qualities which adorned the princess of the Leontines, yet I will not yield to her, or any one else, in generosity and fidelity; and if you will be pleased to repose as much confidence in me, as those illustrious lovers did in her, you shall be convinced I will labour as earnestly for your interest, as that fair princess did for those of Aronces and Clelia.

Miss Groves was so busied in reflecting upon the baseness of her woman in exposing her, that she heard not a word of this fine harangue (at which Mrs Morris, notwithstanding the cause she had for uneasiness, could hardly help laughing): but, assuming some of that haughtiness in her looks, for which she used to be remarkable, she told Lady Bella, that she imputed her impertinent curiosity to her country ignorance and ill-breeding; and she did not doubt but she would be served in her own kind, and meet with as bad fortune as she had done; and, perhaps, deserve it worse than she did; for there are more false men in the world besides Mr L——; and she was no handsomer than other people.

Saying this, she flung out of the room, her woman following, leaving Arabella in such confusion at a behaviour of which she had never before had an idea, that for some moments she remained immoveable.

Recollecting herself, at last, and conceiving that civility required she should endeavour to appease this incensed lady, she went down stairs after her; and, stopping her just as she was going out of the house, entreated her to be calm, and suffer her to vindicate herself from the imputation of being impertinently curious to know her affairs.

Miss Groves, quite transported with shame and anger, refused absolutely to stay.

At least, madam, said Arabella, stay till my coach can be got ready, and don't think of walking home so slightly attended.

This offer was as sullenly answered as the other; and Arabella, finding she was determined to venture home, with no other guard than her woman, who silently followed her, ordered two of her footmen to attend her at a small distance; and to defend her, if there should be occasion.

For who knows, says she to Lucy, what accident may happen? Some one or other of her insolent lovers may take this opportunity to carry her away; and I should never forgive myself for being the cause of such a misfortune to her.

Mrs Morris having found it easy to reconcile herself to her lady, by assuring her, that Lady Bella was acquainted with great part of her story before; and that what she told her, tended only to justify her conduct, as she might have been convinced by what Lady Bella said; they both went home with a resolution to say nothing of what had passed with relation to the cause of the disgust Miss Groves had received; but only said, in general, that Lady Bella was the most ridiculous creature in the world, and was so totally ignorant of good-breeding that it was impossible to converse with her.

VII

Which treats of the Olympic Games

WHILE ARABELLA WAS RUMINATING ON the unaccountable behaviour of her new acquaintance, she received a letter from her uncle, informing her (for she had expressly forbid Mr Glanville to write to her), that his son and daughter intended to set out for her seat in a few days.

This news was received with great satisfaction by Arabella, who hoped to find an agreeable companion in her cousin; and was not so insensible of Mr Glanville's merit, as not to feel some kind of pleasure at the thought of seeing him again.

This letter was soon followed by the arrival of Mr Glanville and his sister, who, upon the sight of Arabella, discovered some appearance of astonishment and chagrin; for, notwithstanding all her brother had told her of her accomplishments, she could not conceive it possible for a young lady, bred up in the country, to be so perfectly elegant and genteel as she found her cousin.

As Miss Charlotte had a large share of coquetry in her composition, and was fond of beauty in none of her own sex but herself, she was sorry to see Lady Bella possessed of so great a share; and, being in hopes her brother had drawn a flattering figure of her cousin, she was extremely disappointed at finding the original so handsome.

Arabella, on the contrary, was highly pleased with Miss Glanville; and, finding her person very agreeable, did not fail to commend her beauty; a sort of complaisance mightily in use among the heroines, who knew not what envy or emulation meant. Miss Glanville received her praises with great politeness, but could not find in her heart to return them: and, as soon as these compliments were over, Mr Glanville told Lady Bella how tedious he had found the short absence she had forced him to, and how great was his satisfaction at seeing her again.

I shall not dispute the truth of your last assertion, replied Arabella, smiling, since I verily believe you are mighty well satisfied at present; but I know not how you will make it appear that an absence, which you allow to be short, has seemed so tedious to you; for this is a manifest contradiction. However, pursued she, preventing his reply, you look so well, and so much at ease, that I am apt to believe absence has agreed very well with you.

And yet I assure you, madam, said Mr Glanville, interrupting her, that I have suffered more uneasiness, during this absence, than I fear you will permit me to tell you.

Since, replied Arabella, that uneasiness has neither made you thinner nor paler, I don't think you ought to be pitied; for, to say the truth, in these sort of matters, a person's bare testimony has but little weight.

Mr Glanville was going to make her some answer, when Miss Glanville, who, while they had been speaking, was adjusting her dress at the glass, came up to them, and made the conversation more general.

After dinner, they adjourned to the gardens, where the gay Miss Glanville, running eagerly from one walk to another, gave her brother as many opportunities of talking to Lady Bella as he could wish. However, he stood in such awe of her, and dreaded so much another banishment, that he did not dare, otherwise than by distant hints, to mention his passion: and Arabella, well enough pleased with a respect that in some measure came up to her expectation, discovered no resentment at insinuations she was at liberty to dissemble the knowledge of; and if he could not, by her behaviour, flatter himself with any great hopes, yet he found as little reason, in Arabella's language, to despair.

Miss Glanville, at the end of a few weeks, was so tired of the magnificent solitude she lived in, that she heartily repented her journey; and insinuated to her brother her inclination to return to town.

Mr Glanville, knowing his stay was regulated by his sister's, entreated her not to expose him to the mortification of leaving Arabella so soon; and promised her he would contrive some amusements for her, which should make her relish the country better than she had yet done.

Accordingly, he proposed to Arabella to go to the races, which were to be held at ——, a few miles from the castle. She would have excused herself, upon account of her mourning; but Miss Glanville discovered so great an inclination to be present at this diversion, that Arabella could no longer refuse to accompany her.

Since, said she to Miss Glanville, you are fond of public diversions, it happens very luckily, that these races are to be held at the time you are here. I never heard of them before, and I presume it is a good many years since they were last celebrated.—Pray, sir, pursued she, turning to Glanville, do not these races, in some degree, resemble the Olympic games? Do the candidates ride in chariots?

No, madam, replied Glanville: the jockeys are mounted upon the fleetest coursers they can procure; and he who first reaches the goal obtains the prize.

And who is the fair lady that is to bestow it? resumed Arabella. I dare engage one of her lovers will enter the lists: she will, doubtless, be in no less anxiety than he; and the shame of being overcome will hardly affect him with more concern than herself; that is, provided he be so happy as to have gained her affections. I cannot help thinking the fair Elismonda was extremely happy in this particular: for she had the satisfaction to see her secret admirer victor in all the exercises at the Olympic games, and carry away the prize from many princes and persons of rare quality, who were candidates with him; and he had also the glory to receive three crowns, in one day, from the hands of his adored princess; who, questionless, bestowed them upon him with an infinite deal of joy.

What sort of races were these, madam? said Miss Glanville, whose reading had been very confined.

The Olympic games, miss, said Arabella, so called from Olympia, a city near which they were performed, in the plains of Elis, consisted of foot and chariot-races, combats with the cestus, wrestling, and other sports. They were instituted in honour of the gods and heroes; and were therefore termed sacred, and were considered as a part of religion.

They were a kind of school, or military apprenticeship; in which the courage of the youth found constant employment: and the reason why victory in those games was attended with, such extraordinary applause, was, that their minds might be quickened with great and noble prospects, when, in this image of war, they arrived to a pitch of glory, approaching, in some respects, to that of the most famous conquerors. They thought this sort of triumph one of the greatest parts of happiness of which human nature was capable: so that when Diagoras had seen his sons crowned in the Olympic games, one of his friends made him this compliment: 'Now, Diagoras, you may die satisfied; since you can't be a god.' It would tire you, perhaps, was I to describe all the exercises performed there: but you may form a general notion of them, from what you have doubtless read of justs and tournaments.

Really, said Miss Glanville, I never read about any such things.

No! replied Arabella, surprised. Well, then, I must tell you, that they hold a middle place, between a diversion and a combat; but the Olympic games were attended with a much greater pomp and variety: and not only all Greece, but other neighbouring nations, were in a manner drained, to furnish out the appearance.

Well, for my part, said Miss Glanville, I never before heard of these sort of races. Those I have been at were quite different. I know the prizes and bets are sometimes very considerable.

And, doubtless, interrupted Arabella, there are a great many heroes who signalize themselves at these races; not for the sake of the prize, which would be unworthy of great souls, but to satisfy that burning desire of glory, which spurs them on to every occasion of gaining it.

As for the heroes, or jockeys, said Miss Glanville, call them what you please, I believe they have very little share, either of the profit or glory; for their masters have the one, and the horses the other.

The masters! Interrupted Arabella: what, I suppose a great many foreign princes send their favourites to combat in their name? I remember to have read, that Alcibiades triumphed three times successively at the Olympic games, by means of one of his domestics, who, in his master's name, entered the lists.

Mr Glanville, fearing his sister would make some absurd answer, and thereby disoblige his cousin, took up the discourse; and turning it upon the Grecian history, engrossed her conversation for two hours, wholly to himself; while Miss Glanville (to whom all they said was quite unintelligible) diverted herself with humming a tune, and tinkling her cousin's harpsichord; which proved no interruption to the more rational entertainment of her brother and Arabella.

VIII

Which concludes with an excellent moral sentence

THE DAY BEING COME ON which they designed to be present at the races (or, as Arabella called them, the games), Miss Glanville, having spent four long hours in dressing herself to the greatest advantage, in order, if possible, to eclipse her lovely cousin, whose mourning, being much deeper, was less capable of ornaments, came into her chamber; and, finding her still in her morning-dress, For Heaven's sake, Lady Bella, said she, when do you propose to be ready? Why, it is almost time to be gone, my brother says, and here you are not dressed.—Don't be uneasy, said Arabella, smiling, and going to her toilet. I shall not make you wait long.

Miss Glanville seating herself near the table, resolved to be present while her cousin was dressing, that she might have an opportunity to make some remarks to her disadvantage: but she was extremely mortified to observe the haste and negligence she made her women use in this important employment: and that, notwithstanding her indifference, nothing could appear more lovely and genteel.

Miss Glanville, however, pleased herself with the certainty of seeing her cousin's dress extremely ridiculed, for the peculiar fashion of her gown, and the veil, which, as becoming as it was, would, by its novelty, occasion great diversion among the ladies, helped to comfort her for the superiority of her charms, which, partial as she was to her own, she could not help secretly confessing.

Arabella being dressed in much less time than her cousin, Mr Glanville was admitted, who led her down stairs to her coach. His sister (secretly repining at the advantage Arabella had over her, in having so respectful an adorer) followed; and, being placed in the coach, they set out with great appearance of good-humour on all sides.

They got to —— but just time enough to see the beginning of the first course. Arabella, who fancied the jockeys were persons of great distinction, soon became interested in the fate of one of them, whose appearance pleased her more than the others. Accordingly, she made vows for his success, and appeared so extremely rejoiced at the advantage he had gained, that Miss Glanville maliciously told her, people would make remarks at the joy she expressed, and fancy she had a more than ordinary interest in that jockey who had first reached the goal.

Mr Glanville, whom this impertinent insinuation of his sister had filled with confusion and spite, sat biting his lips, trembling for the effect it would produce on Arabella: but she, giving quite another turn to her cousin's words, I assure you, said she with a smile, I am not any farther interested in the fate of this person, who has hitherto been successful, than what the handsomeness of his garb, and the superiority of his skill, may demand from an unprejudiced spectator; and though I perceive you imagine he is some concealed lover of mine, yet I don't remember to have ever seen him; and I am confident it is not for my sake that he entered the lists; nor is it my presence which animates him.

Lord bless me, madam! replied Miss Glanville, who would ever think of such strange things as these you talk of? Nobody will pretend to deny that you are very handsome, to be sure but yet, thank Heaven, the sight of you is not so dangerous, but that such sort of people as these are may escape your chains.

Arabella was so wholly taken up with the event of the races, that she gave very little heed to this sarcastic answer of Miss Glanville, whose brother, taking advantage of an opportunity which Arabella gave him by putting her head quite out of the coach, chid her very severely for the liberty she took with her cousin. Arabella, by looking earnestly out of the window, had given so full a view of her fine person to a young baronet, who was not many paces from the coach, that, being struck with admiration at the sight of so lovely a creature, he was going up to some of her attendants to ask who she was, when he perceived Mr Glanville, with whom he was intimately acquainted, in the coach with her: immediately he made himself known to his friend, being excessively rejoiced at having got an opportunity of beginning an acquaintance with a lady whose sight had so charmed him.

Mr Glanville, who had observed the profound bow he made to Arabella, accompanied with a glance that showed an extreme admiration of her, was very little pleased at this meeting; yet he dissembled his thoughts well enough in his reception of him. But Miss Glanville was quite overjoyed, hoping she would now have her turn of gallantry and compliment: therefore, accosting him in her free manner, Dear Sir George, said she, you come in a lucky time to brighten up the conversation: relations are such dull company for one another, 'tis half a minute since we have exchanged a word.

My cousin, said Arabella, smiling, has so strange a disposition for mirth, that she thinks all her moments are lost, in which she finds nothing to laugh at: for my part, I do so earnestly long to know to which of these pretenders fortune will give the victory, than I can suffer my cares for them to receive no interruption from my cousin's agreeable gaiety. Mr Glanville, observing the baronet gazed upon Arabella earnestly while she was speaking those few words, resolved to hinder him from making any reply, by asking him several questions concerning the racers, their owners, and the bets which were laid; to which Arabella added, And pray, sir, said she, do me the favour to tell me, if you know who that gallant man is who has already won the first course.

I don't know really, madam, said Sir George, what his name is! extremely surprised at her manner of asking.

The jockey had now gained the goal a second time; and Arabella could not conceal her satisfaction. Questionless, said she, he is a very extraordinary person: but I am afraid we shall not have the pleasure of knowing who he is; for it he has any reason for keeping himself concealed, he will evade any inquiries after him, by slipping out of the lists while this hurry and tumult lasts, as Hortensius did at the Olympic games; yet, notwithstanding all his care, he was discovered by being obliged to fight a single combat with one of the persons whom he had worsted at those games.

Mr Glanville, who saw his sister, by her little coquetries with Sir George, had prevented him from hearing great part of this odd speech, proposed returning to the castle, to which Arabella agreed; but conceiving civility obliged her to offer the convenience of a lodging to a stranger of Sir George's appearance, and who was an acquaintance of her cousin's, You must permit me, said she to Mr Glanville, to entreat your noble friend will accompany us to the castle, where he will meet with better accommodations than at any inn he can find; for I conceive, that coming only to be a spectator of these games, he is wholly unprovided with a lodging.

The baronet, surprised at so uncommon a civility, was at a loss what answer to make her at first; but, recollecting himself, he told her that he would, if she pleased, do himself the honour to attend her home; but as his house was at no great distance from ——, he should be put to no inconveniency for a lodging.

Miss Glanville, who was not willing to part so soon with the baronet, insisted, with her cousin's leave, upon his coming into the coach; which he accordingly did, giving his horse to the care of his servant: and they proceeded together to the castle; Arabella still continuing to talk of the games, as she called them, while poor Glanville, who was excessively confused, endeavoured to change the discourse, not without an apprehension, that every subject he could think of would afford Arabella an occasion of spewing her foible, which, notwithstanding the pain it gave him, could not lessen his love.

Sir George, whose admiration of Lady Bella increased the longer he saw her, was extremely pleased with the opportunity she had given him of cultivating an acquaintance with her: he therefore lengthened out his visit, in hopes of being able to say some fine things to her before he went away; but Miss Glanville, who strove by all the little arts she was mistress of, to engage his conversation wholly to herself, put it absolutely out of his power; so that he was obliged to take his leave without having the satisfaction of even pressing the fair hand of Arabella, so closely was he observed by her cousin. Happy was it for him, that he was prevented by her vigilance from attempting a piece of gallantry which would undoubtedly have procured him a banishment from her presence; but, ignorant how kind fortune was to him in baulking his designs, he was ungrateful enough to go away in a mighty ill-humour with this fickle goddess; so little capable are poor mortals of knowing what is best for them.

IX

Containing some curious anecdotes

L ADY BELLA, FROM THE FAMILIARITY with which Miss Glanville
treated this gay gentleman, concluding him her lover, and one who
was apparently well received by her, had a strong curiosity to know her
adventures; and as they were walking the next morning in the garden,
she told her, that she thought it was very strange they had hitherto
observed such a reserve to each other, as to banish mutual trust and
confidence from their conversation. Whence comes it, cousin, added
she, being so young and lovely as you are, that you, questionless, have
been engaged in many adventures, you have never reposed trust enough
in me to favour me with a recital of them?

Engaged in many adventures, madam! returned Miss Glanville, not
liking the phrase: I believe I have been engaged in as few as your
ladyship.

You are too obliging, returned Arabella, who mistook what she said
for a compliment; for, since you have more beauty than I, and have also
had more opportunities of making yourself beloved, questionless you
have a greater number of admirers.

As for admirers, said Miss Charlotte, bridling, I fancy I have had my
share! Thank God, I never found myself neglected; but, I assure you,
madam, I have had no adventures, as you call them, with any of them

No, really! interrupted Arabella., innocently. No, really, madam!
retorted Miss Glanville; and I am surprised you should think so.

Indeed, my dear, said Arabella, you are very happy in this respect, and
also very singular; for I believe there are few young ladies in the world,
who have any pretensions to beauty, that have not given rise to a great
many adventures; and some of them, haply, very fatal.

If you knew more of the world, Lady Bella, said Miss Glanville, pertly,
you would not be so apt to think that young ladies engaged themselves

in troublesome adventures. Truly, the ladies that are brought up in town are not so ready to run away with every man they see.

No, certainly, interrupted Arabella: they do not give their consent to such proceedings; but, for all that, they are doubtless run away with many times; for truly there are some men, whose passions are so unbridled, that they will have recourse to the most violent methods to possess themselves of the objects they love. Pray do you remember how often Mandane was run away with?

Not I, indeed, madam, replied Miss Glanville: I know nothing about her: but I suppose she is a Jew, by her outlandish name.

She was no Jew, said Arabella, though she favoured that people very much; for she obtained the liberty of great numbers of them from Cyrus, who had taken them captives, and could deny her nothing she asked.

Well, said Miss Glanville, and I suppose she denied *him* nothing he asked; and so they were even.

Indeed but she did though, resumed Arabella for she refused to give him a glorious scarf which she wore, though he begged it on his knees.

And she was very much in the right, said Miss Glanville; for I see no reason why a lover should expect a gift of any value from his mistress.

Doubtless, said Arabella, such a gift was worth a million of services; and had he obtained it, it would have been a glorious distinction for him: however, Madane refused it; and, severely virtuous as you are, I am persuaded you can't help thinking she was a little too rigorous in denying a favour to a lover like him.

Severely virtuous, Lady Bella! said Miss Glanville, reddening with anger. Pray what do you mean by that? Have you any reason to imagine I would grant any favour to a lover? Why, if I did, cousin, said Arabella, would it derogate so much from your glory, think you, to bestow a favour upon a lover worthy your esteem, and from whom you had received a thousand marks of a most pure and faithful passion, and also a great number of very singular services?

I hope, madam, said Miss Glanville, it will never be my fate to be so much obliged to any lover, as to be under the necessity of granting him favours in requital.

I vow, cousin, interrupted Arabella, you put me in mind of the fair and virtuous Antonia, who was so rigid and austere, that she thought all expressions of love were criminal; and was so far from granting any person permission to love her, that she thought it a mortal offence to be adored even in private.

Miss Glanville, who could not imagine Arabella spoke this seriously, but that it was designed to sneer at her great eagerness to make conquests, and the liberties she allowed herself in, which had probably come to her knowledge, was so extremely vexed at the malicious jest, as she thought it, that, not being able to revenge herself, she burst into tears.

Arabella's good-nature, made her greatly affected at this sight; and, asking her pardon for having undesignedly occasioned her so much uneasiness, begged her to be composed, and tell her in what she had offended her, that she might be able to justify herself in her apprehensions!

You have made no scruple to own, madam, said she, that you think me capable of granting favours to lovers; when, Heaven knows, I never granted a kiss without a great deal of confusion!

And you had certainly much reason for confusion, said Arabella, excessively surprised at such a confession: I can assure you I never injured you so much in my thoughts, as to suppose you ever granted a favour of so criminal a nature.

Look you there, now! said Miss Glanville, weeping more violently than before. I knew what all your round-about speeches would come to. All you have said in vindication of granting favours, was only to draw we into a confession of what I have done: how ungenerous was that!

The favours I spoke of, madam, said Arabella, were quite of another nature, than those it seems you have so liberally granted: such as giving a scarf, a bracelet, or some such thing, to a lover, who haply sighed whole years in silence, and did not presume to declare his passion, till he had lost best part of his blood in defence of the fair-one he loved. It was when you maintained that Mandane was in the right to refuse her magnificent scarf to the illustrious Cyrus, that I took upon me to oppose your rigidness; and so much mistaken was I in your temper, that I foolishly compared you to the fair and wise Antonia, whose severity was so remarkable; but really, by what I understand from your own confession, your disposition resembles that of the inconsiderate Julia, who would receive a declaration of love without anger from any one; and was not over-shy, any more than yourself, of granting favours almost as considerable as that you have mentioned.

While Arabella was speaking, Miss Glanville, having dried up her tears, sat silently swelling with rage, not knowing whether she should openly avow her resentment for the injurious language her cousin had used to her, by going away immediately, or, by making up the matter, appear still to be her friend, that she might have the opportunities of revenging herself. The impetuosity of her temper made her most inclined to the former; but the knowledge that Sir George was to stay yet some months in the country, made her unwilling to leave a place, where she might often see a man whose fine person had made some impression upon her heart; and, not enduring to leave such a charming conquest to Arabella, she resolved to suppress her resentment for the present; and listened, without any appearance of discomposure, to a fine harangue of her cousin upon the necessity of reserve, and distant behaviour, to men who presumed to declare themselves lovers, enforcing her precepts with examples drawn from all the romances she had ever read; at the end of which she embraced her, and assured her, if she had said any thing harsh, it proceeded from her great regard to her glory, of which she ardently wished to see her as fond as herself.

Miss Glanville constrained herself to make a reply that might not appear disagreeable: and they were upon these terms when Mr Glanville came up to them, and told Lady Bella Sir George had sent to entreat their company at his house that day. But, added he, as I presume you will not think proper to go, on account of your mourning, neither my sister nor I will accept the invitation.

I dare say, interrupted Miss Glanville, hastily, Lady Bella will not expect such a needless piece of ceremony from us; and if she don't think proper to go, she won't confine *us*.

By no means, cousin, said Arabella, smiling; and being persuaded Sir George makes the entertainment purely for your sake, it would not be kind in me to deprive him of your company.

Mr Glanville being pleased to find his cousin discovered no inclination to go, would have persuaded his sister not to leave Lady Bella; but Miss Glanville looked so much displeased at his request, that he was obliged to insist upon it no more; and both retiring to dress, Lady Bella went up to her apartment, and betook herself to her books, which supplied the place of all company to her.

Miss Glanville, having taken more than ordinary pains in dressing herself, in order to appear charming in the eyes of Sir George, came in to pay her compliments to Lady Bella before she went, not doubting but she would be chagrined to see her look so well: but Lady Bella, on the contrary, praised the clearness of her complexion, and the sparkling of her eyes.

I question not, said she, but you will give fetters to more persons than one to-day; but remember, I charge you, added she, smiling, while you are taking away the liberty of others, to have a special care of your own.

Miss Glanville, who could not think it possible one woman could praise another with any sincerity, cast a glance at the glass, fearing it was rather because she looked but indifferently that her cousin was so lavish in her praises; and while she was settling her features in a mirror which every day represented a face infinitely more lovely than her own, Mr Glanville came in, who, after having very respectfully taken leave of Lady Bella, led his sister to the coach.

Sir George, who was extremely mortified to find Lady Bella not in it, handed Miss Glanville out with an air so reserved, that she rallied him upon it; and gave her brother a very unpleasing emotion, by telling Sir George she hoped Lady Bella's not coming along with them would not make him bad company.

As he was too gallant to suffer an handsome young lady, who spread all her attractions for him, to believe he regretted the absence of another when she was present, he coquetted with her so much, that Mr Glanville was in hopes his sister would wholly engage him from Lady Bella.

X

In which our heroine is engaged in a very perilous adventure

IN THE MEAN TIME, THAT solitary fair one was alarmed by a fear of a very unaccountable nature; for being in the evening in her closet, the windows of which had a prospect of the gardens, she saw her illustrious concealed lover, who went by the name of Edward, while he was in her father's service, talking with great emotion to her house-steward, who seemed earnestly to listen to some propositions he was making to him. Her surprise at this sight was so great, that she had not power to observe them any longer: but, seating herself in her chair, she had just spirits enough to call Lucy to her assistance; who, extremely frighted at the pale looks of her lady, gave her a smelling bottle, and was preparing to cut her lace, when Arabella, preventing her, told her, in a low voice, that she feared she should be betrayed into the hands of an insolent lover, who was come to steal her away. Yes, added she, with great emotion, I have seen this presumptuous man holding a conversation with one of my servants; and though I could not possibly, at this distance, hear their discourse, yet the gestures they used in speaking explained it too well to me: and I have reason to expect, I shall suffer the same violence that many illustrious ladies have done before me; and be carried away by force from my own house, as they were.

Alas! madam! said Lucy, terrified at this discourse, who is it that intends to carry your ladyship away? Sure no robbers will attempt any mischief at such a time as this!

Yes, Lucy, replied Arabella, with great gravity, the worst kind of robbers; robbers who do not prey upon gold and jewels, but, what is infinitely more precious, liberty and honour. Do you know, that person who called himself Edward, and worked in these gardens like a common gardener, is now in the house, corrupting my servants, and, questionless, preparing to force open my chamber, and carry me away? And Heaven knows when I shall be delivered from his chains!

God forbid! said Lucy, sobbing, that ever such a lady should have such hard hap? What crime, I wonder, can you be guilty of, to deserve to be in chains?

My crime, resumed Arabella, is to have attractions which expose me to these inevitable misfortunes, which even the greatest princesses have not escaped. But, dear Lucy, can you not think of some methods by which I may avoid the evil which waits me? Who knows but that he may, within these few moments, force a passage into my apartment? These slight locks can make but a poor resistance to the violence he will he capable of using.

Oh, dear madam! cried Lucy, trembling, and pressing near her, what shall we do?

I asked your advice, said she; but I perceive you are less able than myself to think of any thing to save me.—Ah! Glanville! pursued she, sighing, would to Heaven thou wert here now!

Yes, madam, said Lucy, Mr Glanville, I am sure, would not suffer any one to hurt your ladyship.

As thou valuest my friendship, said Arabella, with great earnestness, never acquaint him with what has just now escaped my lips. True, I did call upon him in this perplexity; I did pronounce his name; and that, haply, with a sigh, which involuntarily forced its way: and, questionless, if he knew his good fortune, even amidst the danger of losing me for ever, he would resent some emotions of joy; but I should die with shame at having so indiscreetly contributed to his satisfaction; and, therefore, again I charge you, conceal, with the utmost care, what I have said.

Indeed, madam, said Lucy, I shall tell him nothing but what your ladyship bids me; and I am so frighted, that I can think of nothing but that terrible man that wants to carry you away. Mercy on us! added she, starting, I think I hear somebody on the stairs!

Do not be alarmed, said Arabella, in a majestic tone: it is I who have most reason to fear: nevertheless, I hope the grandeur of my courage will not sink under this accident. Hark! somebody knocks at the door of my anti-chamber—My own virtue shall support me—Go, Lucy, and ask who it is.

Indeed I can't, madam, said she, clinging to her. Pray, pardon me: indeed I am so afraid, I cannot stir.

Weak-souled wench! said Arabella, how unfit art thou for accidents like these! Ah, had Cylenia and Martesia been like thee, the fair Berenice, and the divine princess of Media, had not so eagerly entreated their ravishers to afford them their company in their captivity! But go, I order you, and ask who it is that is at the door of my apartment: they knock again: offer at no excuses, but do your duty.

Lucy, seeing her lady was really angry, went trembling out of the closet; but would go no farther than her bed-chamber, from whence she called out to know who was at the door.

I have some business with your lady, said the house-steward (for it was he that knocked): can I speak with her at present?

Lucy, a little re-assured by his voice, made no answer; but, creeping softly to the door of the anti-chamber, double locked it; and then cried out in a transport, No, I will take care you shall not come to my lady.

And why, pray, Mrs Lucy? said the steward: What have I done, that you are so much my enemy?

You are a rogue, said Lucy, growing very courageous, because the door was locked between them.

A rogue! said he: What reason have you for calling me a rogue? I assure you I will acquaint my lady with your insolence. I came to speak to her ladyship about Edward; who prayed me to intercede for him, that he may be taken again into her service; for he says my lady never believed any thing against him; and that was my business; but when I see her, I'll know whether you are allowed to abuse me in this manner.

Arabella, by this time, was advanced as far as the bed-chamber, longing to know what sort of conference Lucy was holding with her intended ravisher; when that faithful confidant, seeing her, came running to her, and whispered her, that the house-steward was at the door, and said he wanted to intercede for Edward.

Ah! the traitor! said Arabella, retiring again: has he, then, really bargained with that disloyal man, to deliver up his mistress?—I am undone, Lucy, said she, unless I can find a way to escape out of the house. They will, questionless, soon force the door of my apartments.

Suppose, said Lucy, your ladyship went down the stairs that leads from your dressing-room into the garden; and you may hide yourself in the gardener's house till Mr Glanville come.

I approve, said Arabella, of one part of your proposal: but I shall not trust myself in the gardener's house; who, questionless, is in the plot with the rest of my perfidious servants, since none of them have endeavoured to advertise me of my danger. If we can gain the gardens undiscovered, we may get out by that door at the foot of the terrace, which leads into the fields; for you know I always keep the key of that private door: so Lucy, let us commend ourselves to the direction of Providence, and be gone immediately.

But what shall we do, madam, said Lucy, when we are got out?

Why, said Arabella, you shall conduct me to your brother's; and, probably, we may meet with some generous cavalier by the way, who will protect us till we get thither: however, as I have as great a danger to fear within doors as without, I will venture to make my escape, though I should not be so fortunate as to meet with any knight who will undertake to protect me from the danger which I may apprehend in the fields.

Saying this, she gave the key of the door to Lucy, whose heart beat violently with fear; and, covering herself with some black cypress, which she wore in the nature of a veil, went softly down the little staircase to the terrace, followed by Lucy, (who looked eagerly about her every step that she went;) and having gained the garden-door, hastily unlocked it, and fled as fast as possible across the fields, in order to procure a sanctuary at William's house; Arabella begging Heaven to throw some generous cavalier in her way, whose protection she might implore, and taking every tree at a distance for a horse and knight, hastened her steps to meet her approaching succour; which as soon as she came near, miserably baulked her expectations.

Though William's farm was not more than two miles from the castle; yet Arabella, unused to such a rude way of travelling, began to be greatly fatigued: the fear she was in of being pursued by her apprehended ravisher, had so violent an effect upon her spirits, that she was hardly able to prosecute her flight and to complete her misfortunes, happening to stumble over a stump of a tree that lay in her way, she strained her ancle, and the violent anguish she felt threw her into a swoon.

Lucy, upon whose arm she leaned, perceiving her fainting, screamed out aloud, not knowing what to do with her in that condition: she placed her upon the ground, and supporting her head against the fatal stump, began to rub her temples, weeping excessively all the time. Her swoon still continuing, the poor girl was in inconceivable terror: her brother's house was now but a little way off; but it being impossible for her to carry her lady thither without some help, she knew not what to resolve upon.

At length, thinking it better to leave her for a few moments to run for assistance, than to sit by her and see her perish for want of it, she left her, though not without extreme agony, and flew with the utmost eagerness to her brother's. She was lucky enough to meet him just coming out of his door: and telling him the condition in which she left her lady, he, without asking any questions about the occasion of so strange an accident, notwithstanding his amazement, ran with all speed to the place where Lucy had left her: but to their astonishment and sorrow, she was not to be found: they walked a long time in search of her; and Lucy being almost distracted with fear, lest she had been carried away, made complaints, that so puzzled her brother, he knew not what to say to her: but finding their search fruitless, they agreed to go home to the castle, supposing, with some appearance of reason, that they might hear of her there.

Here they found nothing but grief and confusion. Mr Glanville and his sister were just returned, and had been at Lady Bella's apartment; but, not finding her there, they asked her women where she was, who, not knowing any thing of her flight, concluded she was in the garden with Lucy. Mr Glanville, surprised at her being at that hour in the garden, ran eagerly to engage her to come in, being apprehensive she would take cold, by staying so late in the air: but not finding her in any of her usual walks, he ordered several of the servants to assist in searching the whole garden, sending them to different places: but they all returned without success, which filled him with the utmost consternation.

He was returning excessively uneasy to the house, when he saw Lucy, who had been just told, in answer to her inquiries about her lady, that they were gone to look for her in the garden; and running up to Mr Glanville, who hoped to hear news of Lady Bella, from her, Oh, sir! said she, is my lady found?

What, Lucy! said Mr Glanville (more alarmed than before) do not you know where she is? I thought you had been with her.

Oh, dear! cried Lucy, wringing her hands: for certain my poor lady was stolen away while she was in that fainting fit—Sir, said she to Glanville, I know who the person is that my lady said (and almost broke my heart) would keep her in chains: he was in the house not many hours ago.

Mr Glanville, suspecting this was some new whim of Arabella's, would not suffer Lucy to say any more before the servants, who stood gaping with astonishment at the strange things she uttered; but had her follow him to his apartment, and he would hear what she could inform him concerning this accident. He would, if possible, have prevented his sister from being present at the story; but, not being able to form any excuse for not suffering her to hear every thing that related to her cousin, they all three went into his chamber: where he desired Lucy to tell him what she knew about her lady.

You must know, sir, said Lucy, sobbing, that there came a man here to take away my lady; a great man he is, though he worked in the gardens for he was in love with her: and so he would not own who he was.

And pray, interrupted Miss Glanville, who told you he was a great man, as you say?

My lady told me, said Lucy: but howsomever, he was turned away; for the gardener says he catched him stealing carp.

A very great man, indeed, said Miss Glanville, that would steal carp!

You must know, madam, said she, that was only a pretence; for he went there, my lady says, to drown himself.

Bless me! cried Miss Glanville, laughing; the girl's distracted, sure.—
Lord! brother, don't listen to her nonsensical tales: we shall never find
my cousin by her.

Leave her to me, said Mr Glanville, whispering: perhaps I may discover
something by her discourse, that will give us some light into this affair.

Nay, I'll stay, I am resolved, answered she: for I long to know where
my cousin is: though, do you think what the girl says is true, about a
great man disguised in the gardens? Sure my cousin could never tell
her such stuff: but, now I think of it, added she, Lady Bella, when we
were speaking about the jockey, talked something about a lover: I vow
I believe it is as the girl says. Pray let's hear her out.

Mr Glanville was ready to die with vexation, at the charmer of his
soul being thus exposed: but there was no help for it.

Pray, said he to Lucy, tell us no more about this man: but if you can
guess where your lady is, let me know.

Indeed I can't, sir, said she; for my lady and I both stole out of the
house, for fear Edward should break open the doors of her apartment;
and we were running as fast as possible to my brother's house, (where
she said she would hide herself till you came): but my poor dear lady
fell down, and hurt herself so much, that she fainted away: I tried what
I could to fetch her again: but she did not open her eyes; so I ran like
lightning to my brother, to come and help me to carry her to the farm;
but, when we came back, she was gone.

What do you say, cried Mr Glanville, with a distracted look: did you
leave her in that condition in the fields? And was she not to be found
when you came back?

No, indeed, sir, said Lucy, weeping; we could not find her, though we
wandered about: a long time.

Oh, Heavens! said he, walking about the room in a violent emotion,
where can she be? What is become of her?—Dear sister, pursued he,
order somebody to saddle my horse: I'll traverse the country all night
in quest of her.

You had best inquire, sir, said Lucy, if Edward is in the house: he
knows, may be, where my lady is.

Who is he? cried Glanville.

Why the great man, sir, said Lucy, whom we thought to be a gardener, who came to carry my lady away, which made her get out of the house as last as she could.

This is the strangest story, said Miss Glanville, that ever I heard: sure nobody would be so mad to attempt such an action; my cousin has the oddest whims—

Mr Glanville, not able to listen any longer, charged Lucy to say nothing of this matter to any one: and then ran eagerly out of the room, ordering two or three of the servants to go in search of their lady: he then mounted his horse in great anguish of mind, not knowing whither to direct his course.

XI

In which the lady is wonderfully delivered

Bᴜʀ ᴛᴏ ʀᴇᴛᴜʀɴ ᴛᴏ Aʀᴀʙᴇʟʟᴀ, whom we left in a very melancholy situation—Lucy had not been gone long from her before she opened her eyes: and, begining to come perfectly to herself, was surprised to find her woman not near her: the moon shining very bright, she looked round her, and called Lucy as loud as she was able: but not seeing her, or hearing any answer, her fears became so powerful; that she had like to have relapsed into her swoon.

Alas! unfortunate maid that I am! cried she, weeping excessively, questionless I am betrayed by her on whose fidelity I relied, and who was acquainted with my most secret thoughts: she is now with my ravisher, directing his pursuit, and I have no means of escaping from his hands! Cruel and ungrateful wench, thy unparalleled treachery grieves me no less than all my other misfortunes: but why do I say her treachery is unparalleled? Did not the wicked Arianta betray her mistress into the power of her insolent lover? Ah! Arabella, thou art not single in thy misery, since the divine Mandane was, like thyself, the dupe of a mercenary servant.

Having given a moment or two to these sad reflections, she rose from the ground with an intention to walk on; but her ancle was so painful, that she could hardly move: her tears began now to flow with greater violence; she expected every moment to see Edward approach her, and was resigning herself up to despair, when a chaise, driven by a young gentleman, passed by her. Arabella, thanking Heaven for sending this relief, called out as loud as she could, conjuring him to stay.

The gentleman, hearing a woman's voice, stopped immediately, and asked what she wanted.

Generous stranger, said Arabella, advancing as well as she was able, do not refuse your assistance to save me from a most terrible danger:

I am pursued by a person whom, for very urgent reasons, I desire to avoid. I conjure you, therefore, in the name of her you love best, to protect me: and may you be crowned with the enjoyment of all your wishes, for so charitable an action!

If the gentleman was surprised at this address, he was much more astonished at the beauty of her who made it: her stature, her shape, her inimitable complexion, the lustre of her fine eyes, and the thousand charms that adorned her whole person, kept him a minute silently gazing upon her, without having the power to make her an answer.

Arabella, finding he did not speak, was extremely disappointed. Ah, sir! said she, what do you deliberate upon? Is it possible you can deny so reasonable a request, to a lady in my circumstances?

For God's sake, madam, said the gentleman, alighting, and approaching her, let me know who you are, and how I can be of any service to you.

As for my quality, said Arabella, be assured it is not mean: and let this knowledge suffice at present. The service I desire of you is to convey me to some place where I may be in safety for this night. To-morrow I will entreat you to let some persons, whom I shall name to you, know where I am: to the end they may take proper measures to secure me from the attempts of an insolent man, who has driven me from my own house, by the designs he was going to execute.

The gentleman saw there was some mystery in her case, which she did not choose to explain: and being extremely glad at having so beautiful a creature in his power, told her she might command him in all she pleased; and helping her into the chaise, drove off as fast as he could: Arabella suffering no apprehensions from being alone with a stranger, since nothing was more common to heroines than such adventures; all her fears being of Edward, whom she fancied every moment she saw pursuing them; and, being extremely anxious to be in some place of safety, she urged her protector to drive as fast as possible; who, willing to have her at his own house, complied with her request; but was so unlucky in his haste, as to overturn the chaise. Though neither Arabella nor himself were hurt by the fall, yet the necessity there was to stay some time to put the chaise in a condition to carry them

any farther, filled her with a thousand apprehensions, lest they should
be overtaken.

In the mean time, the servants of Arabella, among whom Edward,
not knowing how much he was concerned in her flight, was
resolved to distinguish himself by his zeal in searching for her, had
dispersed themselves about in different places: chance conducted
Edward to the very spot where she was; when Arabella, perceiving
him while he was two or three paces off, Oh, sir! cried she, behold
my persecutor! Can you resolve to defend me against the violence
he comes to offer me?

The gentleman, looking up, and seeing a man in livery approaching
them, asked her if that was the person she complained of? and if it was
her servant?

If he is my servant, sir, replied she, blushing, he never had my
permission to be so: and, indeed, no one else can boast of my having
granted them such a liberty.

Do you know whose servant he is, then, madam? replied the
gentleman, a little surprised at her answer, which he could not well
understand.

You throw me into a great embarrassment, sir, resumed Arabella,
blushing more than before: questionless, he appears to be mine; but,
since, as I told you before, he never discovered himself to me, and I
never permitted him to assume that title, his services, if ever I received
any from him, were not at all considered by me as things for which I
was obliged to him.

The gentleman, still more amazed at answers so little to the purpose,
was going to desire her to explain herself upon this strange affair,
when Edward coming up close to Arabella, cried out, in a transport, O,
madam! thank God you are found.

Hold, impious man! said Arabella, and do not give thanks for that
which, haply, may prove thy punishment. If I am found, thou wilt be
no better for it; and if thou continuest to persecute me, thou wilt
probably meet with thy death where thou thinkest thou hast found
thy happiness.

The poor fellow, who understood not a word of this discourse, stared upon her like one that had lost his wits; when the protector of Arabella approaching him, asked him, with a stern look, what he had to say to that lady, and why he presumed to follow her?

As the man was going to answer him, Mr Glanville came galloping up; and Edward seeing him, ran up to him, and informed him that he had met with Lady Bella, and a gentleman, who seemed to have been overturned in a chaise, which he was endeavouring to refit, and that her ladyship was offended with him for coming up to her; and also, that the gentleman had used some threatening language to him upon that account.

Mr Glanville, excessively surprised at what he heard, stopped; and ordering a servant who came along with him to run back to the castle, and bring a chaise thither to carry Lady Bella home, he asked Edward several more questions relating to what she and the gentleman had said to him: and, notwithstanding his knowledge of her ridiculous humour, he could not help being alarmed by her behaviour, nor concluding that there was something very mysterious in the affair.

While he was thus conversing with Edward, Arabella, who had spied him almost as soon, was filled with apprehension to see him hold so quiet a parly with her ravisher: the more she reflected upon this accident, the more her suspicions increased; and persuading herself at last that Mr Glanville was privy to his designs, this belief, however improbable, wrought so powerfully upon her imagination, that she could not restrain her tears.

Doubtless, said she, I am betrayed, and the perjured Glanville is no longer either my friend or lover: he is this moment concerting measures with my ravisher how to deliver me into his power; and, like Philadaspes, is glad of an opportunity, by his treachery, to be rid of a woman whom his parents and hers had destined for his wife.

Mr Glanville having learned all he could from Edward, alighted; and giving him his horse to hold, came up to Arabella: and, after expressing his joy at meeting with her, begged her to let him know what accident had brought her, unattended, from the castle, at that time of night.

If by this question, said the incensed Arabella, you would persuade me you are ignorant of the cause of my flight, know, your dissimulation will not succeed; and that, having reason to believe you are equally guilty with him from whose intended violence I fled, I shall have recourse to the valour of this knight you see with me to defend me, as well against you. as that ravisher, with whom I see you leagued, —Ah, unworthy cousin! pursued she, what dost thou propose to thyself by so black a treachery? What is to be the price of my liberty, which thou so freely disposest of? Has thy friend there, says she (pointing to Edward), a sister, or any relation, for whom thou barterest by delivering me up to him? But assure thyself, this stratagem shall be of no use to thee; for if thou art base enough to oppress my valiant deliverer with numbers, and thinkest by violence to get me into thy power, my cries shall arm heaven and earth in my defence. Providence may, haply, send some generous cavaliers to my rescue; and, if Providence fails me, my own hand shall give me freedom: for that moment thou offerest to seize me, that moment shall be the last of my life.

While Arabella was speaking, the young gentleman and Edward, who listened to her eagerly, thought her brain was disturbed: but Mr Glanville was in a terrible confusion, and silently cursed his ill fate, to make him in love with a woman so ridiculous.

For Heaven's sake, cousin, said he, striving to repress some part of his disorder, do not give way to these extravagant notions! There is nobody intends to do you any wrong.

What! interrupted she, would you persuade me that that impostor there, pointing to Edward, has not a design to carry me away, which you, by supporting him, are not equally guilty of?

Who? I madam! cried out Edward: sure your ladyship does not suspect me of such a strange design! God knows I never thought of such a thing!

Ah, dissembler! interrupted Arabella, do not make use of that sacred name to mask thy impious falsehoods: confess with what intent you came into my father's service disguised?

I never came disguised, madam, returned Edward.

No! said Arabella. What means that dress in which I see you, then?

It is the marquis's livery, madam, said Edward, which he did not order to be taken from me when I left his service.

And with what purpose didst thou wear it? said she. Do not your thoughts accuse you of your crime?

I always hoped, madam—said he.

You hoped! interrupted Arabella, frowning. Did I ever give you reason to hope? I will not deny but I had compassion on you: but even that you was ignorant of.

I know, madam, you had compassion on me, said Edward; for your ladyship, I always thought, did not believe me guilty.

I was weak enough, said she, to have compassion on you, though I did believe you guilty.

Indeed, madam, returned Edward, I always hoped, as I said before, (but your ladyship would not hear me out), that you did not believe any malicious reports; and therefore you had compassion on me.

I had no reports of you, said she, but what my own observation gave me; and that was sufficient to convince me of your fault.

Why, madam, said Edward, did your ladyship see me steal the carp, then, which was the fault unjustly laid to my charge?

Mr Glanville, as much cause as he had for uneasiness, could with great difficulty restrain laughter at this ludicrous circumstance; for he guessed what crime Arabella was accusing him of. As for the young gentleman, he could not conceive what she meant, and longed to hear what would be the end of such a strange conference. But poor Arabella was prodigiously confounded at his mentioning so low an affair; not being able to endure that Glanville and her protector should know a lover of hers could be suspected of so base a theft.

The shame she conceived at it, kept her silent for a moment: but recovering herself at last, No, said she, I knew you better than to give any credit to such an idle report: persons of your condition do not commit such paltry crimes.

Upon my soul, madam, said the young gentleman, persons of his condition often do worse.

I don't deny it, sir, said Arabella; and the design he meditated of carrying me away was infinitely worse.

Really, madam, returned the gentleman, if you are such a person as I apprehend, I don't see how he durst make such an attempt.

It is very possible, sir, said she, that I might be carried away, though I was of greater quality than I am: were not Mandane, Candace, and Clelia, and many other ladies who underwent the same fate, of a quality more illustrious than mine?

Really, madam, said he, I know none of these ladies.

No, sir! said Arabella, extremely mortified.

Let me entreat you, cousin, interrupted Glanville, who feared this conversation would be very tedious, to expose yourself no longer to the air at this time of night: suffer me to conduct you home.

It concerns my honour, said she, that this generous stranger should not think I am the only one that was ever exposed to these insolent attempts.—You say, sir, pursued she, that you don't know any of these ladies I mentioned before: let me ask you, then, if you are acquainted with Parthenissa, or Cleopatra, who were both for some months in the hands of their ravishers?

As for Parthenissa, madam, said he, neither have I heard of her: nor do I remember to have heard of any more than one Cleopatra; but she was never ravished, I am certain, for she was too willing.

How, sir? said Arabella: was Cleopatra ever willing to run away with her ravisher?

Cleopatra was a whore: was she not, madam? said he.

Hold thy peace, unworthy man, said Arabella, and profane not the memory of that fair and glorious queen by such injurious language; that queen, I say, whose courage was equal to her beauty, and her virtue surpassed by neither. Good heavens! what a black defamer have I chosen for my protector!

Mr Glanville, rejoicing to see Arabella in a disposition to be offended with her new acquaintance, resolved to sooth her a little, in hopes of prevailing upon her to return home. Sir, said he to the gentleman, who could not conceive why the lady should so warmly defend Cleopatra, you were in the wrong to cast such reflections upon that great queen, (repeating what he had heard his cousin say before); for all the world, pursued he, knows she was married to Julius Caesar.

Though I commend you, said Arabella, for taking the part of a lady so basely vilified; yet let not your zeal for her honour induce you to say more than is true for its justification; for thereby you weaken, instead of strengthening, what may be said in her defence. One falsehood always supposes another, and renders all you can say suspected; whereas pure, unmixed truth, carries conviction along with it, and never fails to produce its desired effect.

Suffer me, cousin, interrupted Glanville, again to represent to you, the inconveniency you will certainly feel, by staying so late in the air; leave the justification of Cleopatra to some other opportunity, and take care of your own preservation.

What is it you require of me? said Arabella. Only, resumed Glanville, that you would be pleased to return to the castle, where my sister, and all your servants, are inconsolable for your absence,

But who can assure me, answered she, that I shall not, by returning home, enter voluntarily into my prison? The same treachery which made the palace of Candace the place of her confinement, may turn the castle of Arabella into her goal. For, to say the truth, I still more than suspect you abet the designs of this man: since I behold you in his party, and ready, no doubt, to draw your sword in his defence; how will you be able to clear yourself of this crime? Yet I will venture to return to my house, provided you will swear to me you will offer me no violence, with regard to your friend there: and also I insist, that he, from this moment, disclaim all intentions of persecuting me, and banish himself from my presence for ever. Upon this condition I pardon him, and will likewise pray to Heaven to pardon him also.—Speak, presumptuous unknown, said she to Edward, wilt thou accept of my pardon upon the terms I offer it thee? And wilt thou take thyself to some place where I may never behold thee again?

Since your ladyship, said Edward, is resolved not to receive me into your service, I sha'n't trouble you any more; but I think it hard to be punished for a crime I was not guilty of.

It is better, said Arabella, turning from him, that thou shouldest complain of my rigour, than the world tax me with lightness and indiscretion.—And now, sir, said she to Glanville, I must trust myself to your honour, which I confess I do a little suspect; but, however, it is possible you have repented, like the poor prince Thrasybulus, when he submitted to the suggestions of a wicked friend, to carry away the fair Alcionida, whom he afterwards restored. Speak, Glanville, pursued she, are you desirous of imitating that virtuous prince, or do you still retain your former sentiments?

Upon my word, madam, said Glanville, you will make me quite mad, if you go on in this manner: pray let me see you safe home; and then, if you please, you may forbid my entrance into the castle, if you suspect me of any bad intentions towards you.

It is enough, said she, I will trust you.—As for you, sir, speaking to the young gentleman, you are so unworthy, in my apprehensions, by the calumnies you have uttered against a person of that sex which merits all your admiration and reverence, that I hold you very unfit to be a protector of any of it: therefore I dispense with your services upon this occasion; and think it better to trust myself to the conduct of a person, who, like Thrasybulus, by his repentance, has restored himself to my confidence, than to one, who, though indeed he has never betrayed me, yet seems very capable of doing so, if he had the power.

Saying this, she gave her hand to Glanville, who helped her into the chaise that was come from the castle; and the servant who brought it, mounting his horse, Mr Glanville drove her home, leaving the gentleman, who by this time had refitted his chaise, in the greatest astonishment imaginable at her unaccountable behaviour.

END OF THE SECOND BOOK

BOOK III

I

Two conversations, out of which the reader may pick up a great deal

ARABELLA, CONTINUING TO RUMINATE UPON her adventure during their little journey, appeared so low-spirited and reserved, that Mr Glanville, though he ardently wished to know all the particulars of her flight and meeting with that gentleman, whose company he found her in, was obliged to suppress his curiosity for the present, out of a fear of displeasing her. As soon as they alighted at the castle, her servants ran to receive her at the gates, expressing their joy to see her again, by a thousand confused exclamations.

Miss Glanville being at her toilet when she heard of her arrival, ran down to welcome her; in her hurry forgetting, that as her woman had been curling her hair, she had no cap on.

Arabella received her compliments with a little coolness; for, observing that her grief for her absence had not made her neglect any of her usual solicitude about her person, she could not conceive it had been very great: therefore, when she made some slight answer to the hundred questions she asked in a breath, she went up to her apartment; and, calling Lucy, who was crying with joy for her return, she questioned her strictly concerning her leaving her in the fields, acknowledging to her that she suspected her fidelity, though she wished at the same time she might be able to clear herself.

Lucy, in her justification, related, after her punctual way, all that had happened; by which Arabella was convinced she had not betrayed her, and was also in some doubt whether Mr Glanville was guilty of any design against her.

Since, said she to Lucy, thou art restored to my good opinion, I will, as I have always done, unmask my thoughts to thee. I confess, then, with shame and confusion, that I cannot think of Mr Glanville's assisting the unknown to carry me away, without *resenting* a most poignant grief:

questionless, my weakness will surprise thee; and could I conceal it from myself, I would from thee: but, alas! it is certain that I do not hate him; and I believe I never shall, guilty as he may be in my apprehensions.

Hate him! madam, said Lucy: God forbid you should ever hate Mr Glanville, who, I am sure, loves your ladyship as well as he does his own sister!

You are very confident, Lucy, said Arabella, blushing, to mention the word *love* to me: if I thought my cousin had bribed thee to it, I should be greatly incensed: however, though I forbid you to talk of his passion, yet I permit you to tell me the violence of his transports when I was missing; the threats he uttered against my ravishers; the complaints he made against fortune; the vows he offered for my preservation; and, in fine, whatever extravagances the excess of his sorrow forced him to commit.

I assure you, madam, said Lucy, I did not hear him say any of all this.

What! interrupted Arabella: and didst thou not observe the tears trickle from his eyes, which, haply, he strove to conceal? Did he not strike his bosom with the vehemence of his grief; and cast his accusing and despairing eyes to Heaven, which had permitted such a misfortune to befall me?

Indeed, madam, I did not, resumed Lucy, but he seemed to be very sorry, and said he would go and look for your ladyship.

Ah, the traitor! interrupted Arabella, in a rage: fain would I have found out some excuse for him, and justified him in my apprehensions; but he is unworthy of these favourable thoughts. Speak of him no more, I command you: he is guilty of assisting my ravisher to carry me away, and therefore merits my eternal displeasure. But though I could find reasons to clear him even of that crime, yet he is guilty of indifference and insensibility for my loss, since he neither died with grief at the news of it, nor needed the interposition of his sister, or the desire of delivering me, to make him live.

Arabella, when she had said this, was silent; but could not prevent some tears stealing down her fair face: therefore, to conceal her uneasiness, or to be more at liberty to indulge it, she ordered Lucy to make haste and undress her; and, going to bed, passed the small remainder of the night, not in rest, which she very much needed, but in reflections on all the passages of the preceding day; and finding, or imagining she found, new reasons for condemning Mr Glanville, her mind was very far from being at ease.

In the morning lying later than usual, she received a message from Mr Glanville, inquiring after her health; to which she answered, that he was too little concerned in the preservation of it, to make it necessary to acquaint him.

Miss Glanville soon after sent to desire permission to drink her chocolate by her bedside; which, as she could not in civility refuse, she was very much perplexed how to hide her melancholy from the eyes of that discerning lady, who, she questioned not, would interpret it in favour of her brother.

Upon Miss Glanville's appearance, she forced herself to assume a cheerful look, asking her pardon for receiving her in bed; and complaining of bad rest, which had occasioned her lying late.

Miss Glanville, after answering her compliments with almost equal politeness, proceeded to ask her an hundred questions concerning the cause of her absence from the castle: Your woman, pursued she, laughing, told us a strange medley of stuff about a great man, who was a gardener, and wanted to carry you away. Sure there was nothing in it! Was there?

You must excuse me, cousin, said Arabella, if I do not answer your questions precisely now: it is sufficient that I tell you, certain reasons obliged me to act in the manner I did, for my own preservation; and that, another time, you shall know my history which will explain many things you seem to be surprised at, at present.

Your history! said Miss Glanville. Why, will you write your own history then?

I shall not write it, said Arabella; though, questionless, it will be written after my death.

And must I wait till then for it? resumed Miss Glanville, gaily.

No, no, interrupted Arabella: I mean to gratify your curiosity sooner; but it will not be yet a good time; and, haply, not till you have acquainted me with yours.

Mine! said Miss Glanville: it would not be worth your hearing; for really I have nothing to tell that would make an history.

You have, questionless, returned Arabella, gained many victories over hearts; have occasioned many quarrels between your servants, by favouring some one more than the others; probably you have caused some bloodshed; and have not escaped being carried away once or twice: you have also, I suppose, undergone some persecution from those who have the disposal of you, in favour of a lover whom you have an aversion to; and lastly, there is, haply, some one among your admirers who is happy enough not to be hated by you.

I assure you, interrupted Miss Glanville, I hate none of my admirers; and I can't help thinking you very unkind to use my brother as you do: I am sure, there is not one man in an hundred that would take so much from your hands as he does.

Then there is not one man in an hundred, resumed Arabella, whom I should think worthy to serve me. But pray, madam, what ill usage is it your brother complains of? I have treated him with much less severity than he had reason to expect; and, notwithstanding he had the presumption to talk to me of love, I have endured him in my sight; an indulgence for which I may haply be blamed in after-ages.

Why sure, Lady Bella, said Miss Glanville, it would be no such crime for my brother to love you!

But it was a mortal crime to tell me so, interrupted Arabella.

And why was it such a mortal crime to tell you so? said Miss Glanville, Are you the first woman, by millions, that has been told so?—Doubtless, returned Arabella, I am the first woman of my quality, that ever was told so by any man, till after an infinite number of services, and secret sufferings: and truly I am of the illustrious Mandane's mind; for she said, that she should think it an unpardonable presumption, for the greatest king on earth to tell her he loved her, though after ten years of the most faithful services, and concealed torments.

Ten years! cried out Miss Glanville, in amazement: did she consider what alterations ten years would make in her face, and how much older she would be at the end of ten years, than she was before?

Truly, said Arabella, it is not usual to consider such little matters so nicely; one never has the idea of an heroine older than eighteen, though her history begins at that age, and the events which compose it contain the space of twenty more.

But, dear cousin, resumed Miss Glanville, do you resolve to be ten years a-courting? Or rather, will you be loved in silence ten years, and be courted the other ten; and so marry when you are an old woman?

Pardon me, cousin, resumed Arabella: I must really find fault with the coarseness of your language. Courting, and old woman! What strange terms! Let us, I beseech you, end this dispute: if you have any thing to say in justification of your brother, which, I suppose, was the chief intention of your visit, I shall not be rude enough to restrain you; though I could wish you would not lay me under the necessity of hearing what I cannot persuade myself to believe.

Since, returned Miss Glanville, I know of no crime my brother has been guilty of, I have nothing to say in his justification: I only know, that he is very much mortified at the message you sent him this morning; for I was with him when he received it. But pray, what has he done to offend you?

If Mr Glanville, interrupted Arabella, hopes for my pardon, he must purchase it by his repentance, and a sincere confession of his fault; which you may much better understand from himself, than from me; and, for this purpose, I will condescend to grant him a private audience, at which I desire you would be present; and also, I should take it well, if you would let him know, that he owes this favour wholly to your interposition.

Miss Glanville, who knew her brother was extremely desirous of seeing Arabella, was glad to accept of these strange terms; and left her chamber, in order to acquaint him with that lady's intentions.

II

A solemn interview

IN THE MEAN TIME, THAT fair-one being risen, and negligently dressed, as was her custom, went into her closet, sending to give Miss Glanville notice that she was ready to see her. This message immediately brought both the brother and sister to her apartment: and Miss Glanville, at her brother's request, staying in the chamber, where she busied herself in looking at her cousin's jewels, which lay upon the toilet, he came alone into the closet, in so much confusion at the thoughts of the ridiculous figure he had made in complying with Arabella's fantastical humours, that his looks persuading her there was some great agitation in his mind, she expected to see him fall at her feet, and endeavour to deprecate her wrath by a deluge of tears.

Mr Glanville, however, disappointed her in that respect; for, taking a seat near her, he began to entreat her, with a smiling countenance, to tell him in what he had offended her; protesting, that he was not conscious of doing or saying any thing to displease her.

Arabella was greatly confused at this question, which she thought she had no reason to expect; it not being possible for her to tell him she was offended, that he was not in absolute despair for her absence, without, at the same time, confessing she looked upon him in the light of a lover whose expressions of a violent passion would not have displeased her: therefore, to disengage herself from the perplexity his question threw her into, she was obliged to offer some violence to her ingenuousness; and, contrary to her real belief, tax him again with a design of betraying her into the power of the unknown.

Mr Glanville, though excessively vexed at her persisting in so ridiculous an error, could hardly help smiling at the stern manner in which she spoke: but knowing of what fatal consequence it would be to him, if he indulged any gaiety in so solemn a conference, he composed his looks to a gravity suitable to the occasion; and asked her, in a very submissive tone, what motive she was pleased to assign for so extraordinary a piece of villainy, as that she supposed him guilty of.

Truly, answered she, blushing, I do not pretend to account for the actions of wicked and ungenerous persons.

But, madam, resumed Glanville, if I must needs be suspected of a design to seize upon your person, methinks it would have been more reasonable to suppose I would rather use that violence in favour of my own pretensions, than those of any other whatever; for, though you have expressly forbid me to tell you I love you, yet I hope you still continue to think I do.

I assure you, returned Arabella, assuming a severe look, I never gave myself the trouble to examine your behaviour with care enough to be sensible if you still were guilty of the weakness which displeased me; but, upon a supposition that you repented of your fault, I was willing to live with you upon terms of civility and friendship, as became persons in that degree of relationship in which we are: therefore, if you are wise, you will not renew the remembrance of those follies I have long since pardoned; nor seek occasions of offending me by new ones of the same kind, lest it produce a more severe sentence than that I formerly laid upon you.

However, madam, replied Glanville, you must suffer me to assure you, that my own interest, which was greatly concerned in your safety, and my principles of honour, would never allow me to engage in so villainous an enterprise, as that of abetting any person in stealing you away: nor can I conceive how you possibly could imagine a fellow who was your menial servant could form so presumptuous and dangerous a design.

By your manner of speaking, resumed Arabella, one would imagine you were really ignorant, both of the quality of that presumptuous man, as well as his designed offence: but yet, it is certain, I saw you in his company; and saw you ready to draw your sword in his defence, against my deliverer. Had I not the evidence of my own senses for your guilt, I must confess I could not be persuaded of it by any other means: therefore, since appearances are certainly against you, it is not strange if I cannot consent to acquit you in my apprehensions, till I have more certain confirmation of your innocence, than your bare testimony only; which, at present, has not all the weight with me it had some time ago.

I protest, madam, said Mr Glanville, who was strangely perplexed, I have reason to think my case extremely hard, since I have brought myself to be suspected by you, only through my eagerness to find you, and solicitude for your welfare.

Doubtless, interrupted Arabella, if you are innocent, your case is extremely hard; yet it is not singular: and therefore you have less reason to complain: the valiant Coriolanus, who was the most passionate and faithful lover imaginable, having, by his admirable valour, assisted the ravishers of his adored Cleopatra, against those who came to rescue her, and by his arm alone, opposed to great numbers of their enemies, facilitated the execution of their design, had the mortification afterwards to know, that he had all that time been fighting against that divine princess, who loaded him with the most cruel reproaches for the injury he had done her: yet fortune was so kind as to give him the means of repairing his fault, and restoring him to some part of her good opinion: for, covered with wounds as he was, and fatigued with fighting before, yet he undertook, in that condition, to prevent her ravishers from carrying her off: and, for several hours, continued fighting alone with near two hundred men, who were not able to overcome him, notwithstanding his extreme weariness, and the multitude of blows which they aimed at him: therefore, Glanville, considering you, as Cleopatra did that unfortunate prince, who was before suspected by her, as neither guilty nor innocent, I can only, like her, wish you may find some occasion of justifying yourself from the crime laid to your charge. Till then, I must be under a necessity of banishing you from my presence, with the same consolatory speech she used to that unfortunate prince—Go, therefore, Glanville, go, and endeavour your own justification: I desire you should effect it no less than you do yourself: and if my prayers can obtain from Heaven this favour for you, I shall not scruple to offer some *in your behalf.*

III

In which the interview is ended, not much to the lover's satisfaction, but exactly conformable to the rules of romance

ARABELLA WHEN SHE HAD PRONOUNCED these words, blushed excessively, thinking she had said too much: but, not seeing any signs of extreme joy in the face of Glanville, who was silently cursing Cleopatra, and the authors of those romances that had ruined so noble a mind, and exposed him to perpetual vexations, by the unaccountable whims they had raised—Why are you not gone, said she, while I am in an humour not to repent of the favour I have shown you ?

You must excuse me, cousin, said Mr Glanville, peevishly, if I do not think so highly as you do of the favour. Pray how am I obliged to you for depriving me of the pleasure of seeing you, and sending me on a wild-goose chase, after occasions to justify myself of a crime I am wholly innocent of, and would scorn to commit?

Though, resumed Arabella, with great calmness, I have reason to be dissatisfied with the cool and unthankful manner, in which you receive my indulgence, yet I shall not change the favourable disposition I am in towards you, unless you provoke me to it by new acts of disobedience: therefore, in the language of Cleopatra, I shall tell you—

Upon my soul, madam, interrupted Glanville, I have no patience with that rigorous gipsey, whose example you follow so exactly, to my sorrow: speak in your own language, I beseech you; for I am sure neither her's nor any one's upon earth can excel it.

Yes, said Arabella, striving to repress some inclination to smile at this sally, notwithstanding your unjust prohibitions, I shall make use of the language of that incomparable lady, to tell you my thoughts: which are, that it is possible you might be sufficiently justified in my apprehensions, by the anxiety it now appears you had for my safety, by the probability which I find in your discourse, and the good opinion I have of you, were it not requisite to make your innocence apparent to the world, that so it might be lawful for Arabella to re-admit you, with honour, into her former esteem and friendship.

Mr Glanville, seeing that it would be in vain to attempt to make her alter her fantastical determination at this time, went out of the closet without deigning to make any reply to his sentence, though delivered in the language of the admirable Cleopatra: but his ill-humour was so visible in his face, that Arabella, who mistook it for an excess of despair, could not help feeling some kind of pity for the rigour which the laws of honour and romance obliged her to use him with. And while she sat meditating upon the scene which had just passed, Mr Glanville returned to his own room, glad that his sister, not being in Arabella's chamber, where he had left her, had no opportunity of observing his discontent, of which she would not fail to inquire the cause.

Here he sat, ruminating upon the follies of Arabella, which he found grew more glaring every day: every thing furnished matter for some new extravagance; her character was so ridiculous, that he could propose nothing to himself but eternal shame and disquiet, in the possession of a woman for whom he must always blush and be in pain. But her beauty had made a deep impression on his heart: he admired the strength of her understanding, her lively wit, the sweetness of her temper, and a thousand amiable qualities which distinguished her from the rest of her sex: her follies, when opposed to all those charms of mind and person, seemed inconsiderable and weak; and though they were capable of giving him great uneasiness, yet they could not lessen a passion which every sight of her so much the more confirmed.

As he feared it was impossible to help loving her, his happiness depended upon curing her of her romantic notions; and though he knew not how to effect such a change in her as was necessary to complete it, yet he would not despair, but comforted himself with hopes of what he had not courage to attempt. Sometimes he fancied company, and an acquaintance with the world, would produce the alteration he wished: yet he dreaded to see her exposed to ridicule by her fantastical behaviour, and become the jest of persons who were not possessed of half her understanding.

While he traversed his chamber, wholly engrossed by these reflections, Miss Glanville was entertaining Sir George, of whose coming she was informed while she was in Arabella's chamber.

IV

In which our heroine is greatly disappointed

MISS GLANVILLE, SUPPOSING HER BROTHER would be glad not to be interrupted in his conference with Lady Bella, did not allow any one to acquaint them with Sir George's visit; and telling the baronet her cousin was indisposed, had by these means all his conversation to herself.

Sir George, who ardently wished to see Lady Bella, protracted his visit, in hopes that he should have that satisfaction before he went away. And that fair lady, whose thoughts were a little discomposed by the despair she apprehended Mr Glanville was in, and fearful of the consequences, when she had sat some time after he left her, ruminating upon what had happened, quitted her closet, to go and inquire of Miss Glanville in what condition his mind seemed to be when he went away; for she never doubted but that he was gone, like Coriolanus, to seek out for some occasion to manifest his innocence.

Hearing, therefore, the voice of that lady, who was talking and laughing very loud in one of the summer parlours; and being terrified with the apprehension that it was her brother with whom she was thus diverting herself, she opened the door of the room precipitately, and by her entrance filled Sir George with extreme pleasure; while her unexpected sight produced a quite contrary effect on Miss Glanville.

Arabella, eased of her fear that it was Mr Glanville, who, instead of dying with despair, was giving occasion for that noisy laugh of his sister, saluted the baronet with great civility: and, turning to Miss Glanville, I must needs chide you, said she, for the insensibility with which it appears you have parted with your brother.

Bless me, madam! interrupted Miss Glanville, what do you mean? Whither is my brother gone?

That, indeed, I am quite ignorant of, resumed Arabella: and I suppose he himself hardly knows what course he shall take: but he has been with you, doubtless, to take his leave.

Take his leave! repeated Miss Glanville: has he left the castle so suddenly then, and gone away without me?

The enterprise upon which he is gone, said Arabella, would not admit of a lady's company: and, since he has left so considerable an hostage with me as yourself, I expect he will not be long before he return, and, I hope, to the satisfaction of us both.

Miss Glanville, who could not penetrate into the meaning of her cousin's words, began to be strangely alarmed: but presently supposing she had a mind to divert herself with her fears, she recovered herself, and told her she would go up to her brother's chamber, and look for him.

Arabella did not offer to prevent her, being very desirous of knowing whether he had not left a letter for her upon his table, as was the custom in those cases; and, while she was gone, Sir George seized the opportunity of saying an hundred gallant things to her, which she received with great indifference; the most extravagant compliments being what she expected from all men: and provided they did not directly presume to tell her they loved her, no sort of flattery or adulation could displease her.

In the mean time, Miss Glanville having found her brother in his chamber, repeated to him what Lady Bella had said, as she supposed, to fright her.

Mr Glanville hearing this, and that Sir George was with her, hastened to them as fast as possible, that he might interrupt the foolish stories he did not doubt she was telling.

Upon Miss Glanville's appearance with her brother, Arabella was astonished.

I apprehended, sir, said she, that you were some miles from the castle by this time; but your delay and indifference convince me you neither expect nor wish to find the means of being justified in my opinion.

Pray, cousin, interrupted Glanville, speaking softly to her, let us leave this dispute to some other time.

No, sir, resumed she, aloud; my honour is concerned in your justification: nor is it fit I should submit to have the appearance of amity for a person who has not yet sufficiently cleared himself of a crime, with too much reason, laid to his charge. Did Coriolanus, think you, act in this manner? Ah! if he had, doubtless Cleopatra would never have pardoned him: nor will I any longer suffer you to give me repeated causes of discontent.

Sir George, seeing confusion in Mr Glanville's countenance, and rage in Arabella, began to think that what he had at first taken for a jest, was a serious quarrel between them, at which it was not proper he should be present; and was preparing to go, when Arabella, stopping him with a graceful action—

If, noble stranger, said she, you are so partial to the failings of a friend, that you will undertake to defend any unjustifiable action he may be guilty of, you are at liberty to depart: but if you will promise to be an unprejudiced hearer of the dispute between Mr Glanville and myself, you shall know the adventure which has given rise to it; and will be judge of the reasonableness of the commands I have laid on him.

Though, madam, said Sir George, bowing very low to her, Mr Glanville is my friend, yet there is no likelihood I shall espouse his interest against yours: and a very strong prepossession I feel in favour of you, already persuades me that I shall give sentence on your side, since, you have honoured me so far as to constitute me judge of this difference.

The solemn manner in which Sir George (who began to suspect Lady Bella's peculiar turn) spoke this, pleased her infinitely; while Mr Glanville, vexed as he was, could hardly forbear laughing: when Arabella, after a look of approbation to Sir George, replied—

I find I have unwillingly engaged myself to more than I first intended: for, to enable you to judge clearly of the matter in dispute, it is necessary you should know my whole history.

Mr Glanville, at this word, not being able to constrain himself, uttered a groan of the same nature with those which are often heard in the pit at the representation of a new play. Sir George understood him perfectly well, yet seemed surprised; and Arabella, starting up—

Since, said she, I have given you no new cause of complaint, pray from whence proceeds this increase of affliction?

I assure you, cousin, answered he, my affliction, if you please to term it so, increases every day, and I believe will make me mad at last; for this unaccountable humour of yours is not to be borne.

You do not seem, replied Arabella, to be far from madness already; and if your friend here, upon hearing the passages between us, should pronounce you guilty, I shall be at a loss whether I ought to treat you as a madman or a criminal. Sir, added she, turning to Sir George, you will excuse me, if, for certain reasons, I can neither give you my history myself; nor be present at the relation of it. One of my women, who is most in my confidence, shall acquaint you with all the particulars of my life; after which I expect Mr Glanville will abide by your decision, as, I assure myself, I shall be contented to do.

Saying this she went out of the parlour, in order to prepare Lucy for the recital she was to make.

Mr Glanville, resolving not to be present at this new absurdity, ran out after her, and went into the garden, with a strong inclination to hate the lovely visionary who gave him such perpetual uneasiness; leaving his sister alone with the baronet, who diverted herself extremely with the thoughts of hearing her cousin's history, assuring the baronet that he might expect something very curious in it, and find matter sufficient to laugh at; for she was the most whimsical woman in the world.

Sir George, who resolved to profit by the knowledge of her foible, made very little reply to Miss Glanville's sneers; but waited patiently for the promised history, which was much longer in coming than he imagined.

V

Some curious instructions for relating an history

ARABELLA, AS SOON AS SHE left them, went up to her apartment; and
calling Lucy into her closet, told her, that she had made choice
of her, since she was best acquainted with her thoughts, to relate her
history to her cousins, and a person of quality who was with them.

Sure your ladyship jests with me, said Lucy. How can I make a history
about your ladyship?

There is no occasion, replied Arabella, for you to make a history:
there are accidents enough in my life to afford matter for a long one:
all you have to do is to relate them as exactly as possible. You have lived
with me from my childhood, and are instructed in all my adventures;
so that you must be certainly very capable of executing the task I have
honoured you with.

Indeed, said Lucy, I must beg your ladyship will excuse me. I never
could tell how to repeat a story when I have read it; and I know it is
not such simple girls as I can tell histories: it is only fit for clerks, and
such sort of people, that are very learned.

You are learned enough for that purpose, said Arabella; and if you
make so much difficulty in performing this part of your duty, pray how
came you to imagine you were fit for my service, and the distinction I
have favoured you with? Did you ever hear of any woman that refused
to relate her lady's story when desired? Therefore, if you hope to possess
my favour and confidence any longer, acquit yourself handsomely of
this task to which I have preferred you.

Lucy, terrified at the displeasure she saw in her lady's countenance,
begged her to tell her what she must say.

Well! exclaimed Arabella; I am certainly the most unfortunate woman
in the world! Every thing happens to me in a contrary manner from
any other person! Here, instead of my desiring you to soften those parts

of my history where you have greatest room to flatter, and to conceal, if possible, some of those disorders my beauty has occasioned, you ask me to tell you what you must say, as if it was not necessary you should know as well as myself, and be able not only to recount all my words and actions, even the smallest and most inconsiderable, but also all my thoughts, however instantaneous: relate exactly every change of my countenance, number all my smiles, half-smiles, blushes, turnings pale, glances, pauses, full-stops, interruptions; the rise and falling of my voice, every motion of my eyes, and every gesture which I have used for these ten years past; nor omit the smallest circumstance that relates to me.

Lord bless me, madam! said Lucy, excessively astonished: I never, till this moment, it seems, knew the hundredth thousandth part of what was expected from me. I am sure, if I had, I would never have gone to service; for I might well know I was not fit for such slavery.

There is no such great slavery in doing all I have mentioned to you, interrupted Arabella: it requires, indeed, a good memory, in which I never thought you deficient; for you are punctual to the greatest degree of exactness in recounting every thing one desires to hear from you.

Lucy, whom this praise soothed into good-humour, and flattered with a belief that she was able, with a little instruction, to perform what her lady required, told her if she pleased only to put her in a way how to tell her history, she would engage, after doing it once, to tell it again whenever she was desired.

Arabella being obliged to comply with this odd request, for which there was no precedent in all the romances her library was stuffed with, began to inform her in this manner—

First, said she, you must relate my birth, which you know is very illustrious; and because I am willing to spare you the trouble of repeating things that are not absolutely necessary, you must apologize to your hearers for slipping over what passed in my infancy, and the first eight or ten years of my life; not failing, however, to remark, that, from some sprightly sallies of imagination, at those early years, those about me conceived marvellous hopes of my future understanding: from thence you must proceed to an accurate description of my person.

What, madam! interrupted Lucy, must I tell what sort of person you have, to people who have seen you but a moment ago?

Questionless you must, replied Arabella; and herein you follow the examples of all the squires and maids who relate their masters' and ladies' histories; for though it be a brother, or near relation, who has seen them a thousand times, yet they never omit an exact account of their persons.

Very well, madam, said Lucy; I shall be sure not to forget that part of my story. I wish I was as perfect in all the rest.

Then, Lucy, you must repeat all the conversations I ever held with you upon the subjects of love and gallantry, that your audience may be so well acquainted with my humour as to know exactly, before they are told, how I shall behave in whatever adventures befall me. After that, you may proceed to tell them how a noble unknown saw me at church: how prodigiously he was struck with my appearance; the tumultuous thoughts that this first view of me occasioned in his mind.

Indeed, madam, interrupted Lucy again, I can't pretend to tell his thoughts; for how should I know what they were? None but himself can tell that.

However that may be, said Arabella, I expect that you should decipher all his thoughts as plainly as he himself could do; otherwise my history will be very imperfect. Well, I suppose you are at no loss about that whole adventure, in which you yourself bore so great a share; so I need not give you any farther instructions concerning it: only you must be sure, as I said before, not to omit the least circumstance in my behaviour, but relate every thing I did, said, and thought, upon that occasion. The disguised gardener must appear next in your story: here you will of necessity be a little deficient, since you are not able to acquaint your hearers with his true name and quality; which, questionless, is very illustrious. However, above all, I must charge you not to mention that egregious mistake about the carp; for you know how—

Here Miss Glanville's entrance put a stop to the instructions Lucy was receiving; for she told Arabella that Sir George was gone.

How! returned she: is he gone? Truly I am not much obliged to him for the indifference he has shewed to hear my story.

Why, really, madam, said Miss Glanville, neither of us expected you would be as good as your word, you were so long in sending your woman down; and my brother persuaded Sir George you were only in jest; and Sir George has carried him home to dinner.

And is it at Sir George's, replied Arabella, that your brother hopes to meet with an occasion of clearing himself? He is either very insensible of my anger, or very conscious of his own innocence.

Miss Glanville, having nothing to say in answer to an accusation she did not understand, changed the discourse; and the two ladies passed the rest of the day together with tolerable good humour on Miss Glanville's side; who was in great hopes of making a conquest of the baronet, before whom Arabella had made herself ridiculous enough. But that lady was far from being at ease: she had laid herself under a necessity of banishing Mr Glanville, if he did not give her some convincing proof of his innocence; which, as matters stood, she thought would be very hard for him to procure; and, as she could not absolutely believe him guilty, she was concerned she had gone so far.

VI

A very heroic chapter

M R GLANVILLE, COMING HOME IN the evening, a little elevated with the wine of which he had drank too freely at Sir George's, being told the ladies were together, entered the room where they were sitting; and, beholding Arabella, whose pensiveness had given an enchanting softness to her face, with a look of extreme admiration—

Upon my soul, cousin, said he, if you continue to treat me so cruelly, you'll drive me mad. How I could adore you this moment, added he, gazing passionately at her, if I might but hope you did not hate me!

Arabella, who did not perceive the condition he was in, was better pleased with this address than any he had ever used; and, therefore, instead of chiding him as she was wont, for the freedom of his expressions, she cast her bright eyes upon the ground with so charming a confusion, that Glanville, quite transported, threw himself on his knees before her; and, taking her hand, attempted to press it to his lips: but she, hastily withdrawing it—

From whence is this new boldness? said she. And what is it you would implore by that prostrate posture? I have told you already upon what conditions I will grant you my pardon. Clear yourself of being an accomplice with my designed ravisher, and I am ready to restore you to my esteem.

Let me perish, madam, returned Glanville, if I would not die to please you, this moment.

It is not your death that I require, said she: and though you should never be able to justify yourself in my opinion, yet you might, haply, expiate your crime by a less punishment than death.

What shall I do, then, my angelic cousin? resumed he.

Truly, said she, the sense of your offence ought so mortally to afflict you, that you should invent some strange kind of penance for yourself, severe enough to prove your penitence sincere. You know, I suppose, what the unfortunate Orontes did, when he found he had wronged his adored Thalestris by an injurious suspicion.

I wish he had hanged himself! said Mr Glanville, rising up in a passion, at seeing her again in her attitudes.

And why, pray, sir, said Arabella, are you so severe upon that poor prince; who was, haply, infinitely more innocent than yourself?

Severe, madam! said Glanville, fearing he had offended her. Why, to be sure, he was a sad scoundrel to use his adored Thalestris as he did: and I think one cannot he too severe upon him.

But, returned Arabella, appearances were against her; and he had some shadow of reason for his jealousy and rage: then, you know, amidst all his transports, he could not be prevailed upon to draw his word against her.

What did that signify? said Glanville. I suppose he scorned to draw his sword upon a woman: that would have been a shame indeed.

That woman, sir, resumed Arabella, was not such a contemptible antagonist as you think her: and men as valiant, possibly, as Orontes, (though, questionless, he was one of the most valiant men in the world) have been cut in pieces by the sword of that brave Amazon.

Lord bless me! said Miss Glanville, I should be afraid to look at such a terrible woman: I am sure she must be a very masculine sort of creature.

You are much mistaken, miss, said Arabella: for Thalestris, though the most stout and courageous of her sex, was, nevertheless, a perfect beauty; and had as much harmony and softness in her looks and person, as she had courage in her heart and strength in her blows.

Indeed, madam, resumed Miss Glanville, you can never persuade me, that a woman who can fight, and cut people to pieces with her blows, can have any softness in her person: she must needs have very masculine hands, that could give such terrible blows: and I can have no notion of the harmony of a person's looks, who, by what you say, must have the heart of a tiger. But, indeed, I don't think there ever could be such a woman.

What, miss! interrupted Arabella; do you pretend to doubt that there ever was such a person as Thalestris, queen of the Amazons? Does not all the world know the adventures of that illustrious princess; her affection for the unjust Orontes, who accused her of having a scandalous intrigue with Alexander, whom she went to meet with a very different design, upon the borders of her kingdom? The injurious letter he wrote her, upon this suspicion, made her resolve to seek for him all over the world, to give him that death he had merited, by her own hand: and it was in those encounters that he had with her, while she was thus incensed, that he forbore to defend himself against her, though her sword was often pointed to his breast.

But, madam, interrupted Mr Glanville, pray what became of this queen of the Amazons? Was she not killed at the siege of Troy?—She never was at the siege of Troy, returned Arabella: but she assisted the princes who besieged Babylon, to recover the liberty of Statira and Parisatis; and it was in the opposite party that she met with her faithless lover.

If he was faithless, madam, said Mr Glanville, he deserved to die: and I wish, with all my soul, she had cut him in pieces with that famous sword of her's that had done such wonders.

Yet this faithless man, resumed Arabella, whom you seem to have such an aversion to, gave so glorious a proof of his repentance and sorrow, that the fair queen restored him to her favour, and held him in much dearer affection than ever: for, after he was convinced of her innocence, he was resolved to punish himself with a rigour equal to the fault he had been guilty of; and, retiring to the woods, abandoned for ever the society of men; dwelling in a cave, and living upon bitter herbs, passing the days and nights in continual tears and sorrow for his crime. And here he proposed to end his life, had not the fair Thalestris found him out in this solitude; and, struck with the sincerity of his repentance, pardoned him; and, as I have said before, restored him to her favour.

And to shew you, said Glanville, that I am capable of doing as much for you, I will, if you insist upon it, seek out for some cave, and do penance in it, like that Orontes, provided you will come and fetch me out of it, as that same fair queen did him.

I do not require so much of you, said Arabella; for I told you before, that, haply, you are justified already in my opinion: but yet it is necessary you should find out some method of convincing the world of your innocence; otherwise it is not fit, I should live with you upon terms of friendship and civility.

Well, well, madam, said Glanville, I'll convince you of my innocence, by bringing that rascal's head to you, whom you suspect I was inclined to assist in stealing you away.

If you do that, resumed Arabella, doubtless you will be justified in my opinion, and the world's also; and I shall have no scruple to treat you with as much friendship as I did before.

My brother is much obliged to you, madam, interrupted Miss Glanville, for putting him upon an action that would cost him his life!

I have so good an opinion of your brother's valour, said Arabella, that I am persuaded he will find no difficulty in performing his promise; and I make no question but I shall see him covered with the spoils of that impostor, who would have betrayed me; and, I flatter myself, he will be in a condition to bring me his head, as he bravely promises, without endangering his own life.

Does your ladyship consider, said Miss Glanville, that my brother can take away no person's life whatever, without endangering his own?

I consider, madam, said Arabella, your brother as a man possessed of virtue and courage enough to undertake to kill all my enemies and persecutors, though I had ever so many; and I presume he would be able to perform as many glorious actions for my service, as either Juba, Cæsario, Artamenes, or Artaban, who, though not a prince, was greater than any of them.

If those persons you have named, said Miss Glanville, were murderers, and made a practice of killing people, I hope my brother will be too wise to follow their examples: a strange kind of virtue and courage, indeed, to take away the lives of one's fellow-creatures! How did such wretches escape the gallows, I wonder?

I perceive, interrupted Arabella, what kind of apprehensions you have: I suppose you think, if your brother was to kill my enemy, the law would punish him for it; but pray undeceive yourself, miss. The law has no power over heroes: they may kill as many men as they please, without being called to any account for it; and the more lives they take away, the greater is their reputation for virtue and glory. The illustrious Artaban, from the condition of a private man, raised himself to the sublimest pitch of glory by his valour; for he not only would win half a dozen battles in a day; but, to show that victory followed him wherever he went, he would change parties, and immediately the vanquished became conquerors; then, returning to the side he had quitted, changed the laurels of his former friends into chains. He made nothing of tumbling kings from their thrones, and giving away half a dozen crowns in a morning; for his generosity was equal to his courage; and to this height of power did he raise himself by his sword. Beginning at first with petty conquests, and not disdaining to oppose his glorious arm to sometimes less than a score of his enemies; so, by degrees, inuring himself to conquer inconsiderable numbers, he came at last to be the terror of whole armies, who would fly at the sight of his single sword.

This is all very astonishing, indeed, said Miss Glanville. However, I must entreat you not to insist upon my brother's quarrelling and fighting with people, since it will be neither for your honour nor his safety: for I am afraid, if he was to commit murder to please you, the laws would make him suffer for it; and the world would be very free with its censures on your ladyship's reputation, for putting him upon such shocking crimes.

By your discourse, miss, replied Arabella, one would imagine you knew as little in what the good reputation of a lady consists, as the safety of a man; for certainly the one depends entirely upon his sword, and the other upon the noise and bustle she makes in the world. The blood that is shed for a lady enhances the value of her charms: and the more men a hero kills, the greater his glory; and, by consequence, the more secure he is. If to be the cause of a great many deaths can make a lady infamous, certainly none were ever more so than Mandane, Cleopatra, and Statira, the most illustrious names in antiquity; for each of whom, haply, an hundred thousand men were killed; yet none were ever so unjust as to profane the virtue of those divine beauties, by casting any censures upon them for these glorious effects of their charms, and the heroic valour of their admirers.

I must confess, interrupted Miss Glanville, I should not be sorry to have a duel or two fought for me in Hyde-Park; but then I would not have any blood shed for the world.

Glanville here interrupting his sister with a laugh, Arabella also could not forbear smiling at the harmless kind of combats her cousin was fond of.

But to put an end to the conversation, and the dispute which gave rise to it, she obliged Mr Glanville to promise to fight with the impostor Edward, whenever he found him; and either to take away his life, or force him to confess he had no part in the design he had meditated against her.

This being agreed upon, Arabella, conducting Miss Glanville to her chamber, retired to her own, and passed the night with much greater tranquillity than she had done the preceding; being satisfied with the care she had taken of her own glory, and persuaded that Glanville was not unfaithful—a circumstance that was of more consequence to her happiness than she was yet aware of.

VII

In which our heroine is suspected of insensibility

WHILE THESE THINGS PASSED AT the castle, Sir George was meditating on the means he should use to acquire the esteem of Lady Bella, of whose person he was a little enamoured, but of her fortune a great deal more.

By the observations he had made on her behaviour, he discovered her peculiar turn: he was well read in romances himself, and had actually employed himself some weeks in giving a new version of the Grand Cyrus; but the prodigious length of the task he had undertaken terrified him so much that he gave it over: nevertheless, he was perfectly well acquainted with the chief characters in most of the French romances; could tell every thing that was borrowed from them in all the new novels that came out; and, being a very accurate critic, and a mortal hater of Dryden, ridiculed him for want of invention, as it appeared by his having recourse to these books for the most shining characters and incidents in his plays. Almanzor, he would say, was the copy of the famous Artaban in Cleopatra, whose exploits Arabella had expatiated upon to Miss Glanville and her brother; his admired character of Melantha in Marriage à-la-Mode, was drawn from Berissa in the Grand Cyrus; and the story of Osmyn and Bensayda, in his Conquest of Grenada, taken from Sesostris and Timerilla in that romance.

Fraught, therefore, with the knowledge of all the extravagancies and peculiarities in those books, he resolved to make his addresses to Arabella in the form they prescribed; and, not having delicacy enough to be disgusted with the ridicule in her character, served himself with her foible, to effect his designs.

It being necessary, in order to his better acquaintance with Arabella, to be upon very friendly terms with Miss Glanville and her brother, he said a thousand gallant things to the one, and seemed so little offended with the gloom he observed upon the countenance of the other, who positively assured him, that Arabella meant only to laugh at him, when she promised him her history, that he entreated him, with the most obliging earnestness, to favour him with his company at his house, where he omitted no sort of civility, to confirm their friendship and intimacy; and persuaded him, by several little and seemingly unguarded expressions, that he was not so great an admirer of Lady Bella, as of her agreeable cousin Miss Glanville.

Having thus secured a footing in the castle, he furnished his memory with all the necessary rules of making love in Arabella's taste, and deferred his next visit no longer than till the following day; but Mr Glanville being indisposed, and not able to see company, he knew that it would be in vain to expect to see Arabella, since it was not to be imagined Miss Glanville could admit of a visit, her brother being ill; and Lady Bella must be also necessarily engaged with her.

Contenting himself, therefore, with having inquired after the health of the two ladies, he returned home, not a little vexed at his disappointment.

Mr Glanville's indisposition increasing every day, grew at last dangerous enough to fill his sister with extreme apprehensions. Arabella, keeping up to her forms, sent regularly every day to inquire after his health; but did not offer to go into his chamber, though Miss Glanville was almost always there.

As she conceived his sickness to be occasioned by the violence of his passion for her, she expected some overture should be made her by his sister, to engage her to make him a visit; such a favour being never granted by any lady to a sick lover, till she was previously informed her presence was necessary to hinder the increase of his distemper.

Miss Glanville would not have failed to represent to her cousin the incivility and carelessness of her behaviour, in not deigning to come and see her brother in his indisposition, had not Mr Glanville, imputing this neglect to the nicety of her notions, which he had upon other occasions experienced, absolutely forbid her to say any thing to her cousin upon this subject.

Miss Glanville being thus forced to silence, by the fear of giving her brother uneasiness, Arabella was extremely disappointed to find, that, in five days illness, no application had been made to her, either by the sick lover, or his sister, who she thought interested herself too little in his recovery; so that her glory obliging her to lay some constraint upon herself, she behaved with a coolness and insensibility that increased Miss Glanville's aversion to her, while, in reality, she was extremely concerned for her cousin's illness; but not supposing it dangerous, since they had not recourse to the usual remedy of beseeching a visit from the person whose presence was alone able to work a cure, she resolved to wait patiently the event.

However, she never failed in her respect to Miss Glanville, whom she visited every morning before she went to her brother; and also constantly dined with her in her own apartment, inquiring always, with great sweetness, concerning her brother's health; when perceiving her in tears one day as she came in, as usual, to dine with her, she was extremely alarmed; and asked with great precipitation if Mr Glanville was worse.

He is so bad, madam, returned Miss Glanville, that I believe it will be necessary to send for my papa, for fear he should die, and he not see him.

Die, miss! interrupted Arabella eagerly: No, he must not die; and shall not, if the pity of Arabella is powerful enough to make him live. Let us go then cousin, said she, her eyes streaming with tears; let us go and visit this dear brother, whom you lament: haply the sight of me may repair the evils my rigour has caused him; and since, as I imagine, he has forborne, through the profound respect he has for me, to request the favour of a visit, I will voluntarily bestow it on him, as well for the affection I bear you, as because I do not wish his death.

You do not wish his death, madam! said Miss Glanville, excessively angry at a speech, in her opinion, extremely insolent. Is it such a mighty favour, pray, not to wish the death of my brother, who never injured you? I am sure your behaviour has been so extremely inhuman, that I have repented a thousand times we ever came to the castle.

Let us not waste the time in idle reproaches, said Arabella. If my rigour has brought your brother into this condition, my compassion can draw him out of it: it is no more than what all do suffer, who are possessed of a violent passion; and few lovers ever arrive to the possession of their mistresses, without being several times brought almost to their graves, either by their severity or some other cause. But nothing is more easy than to work a cure in these cases; for the very sight of the person beloved sometimes does it, as it happened to Artamenes, when the divine Mandane condescended to visit him: a few kind words spoken by the fair princess of Persia to Oroondates, recalled him from the gates of death; and one line from Parisatis's hand, which brought a command to Lysimachus to live, made him not only resolve, but even able to obey her.

Miss Glanville, quite out of patience at this tedious harangue, without any regard to ceremony, flounced out of the room, and ran to her brother's chamber, followed by Arabella, who imputed her rude haste to a suspicion that her brother was worse.

VIII

In which we hope the reader will be differently affected

AT THEIR ENTRANCE INTO THE room, Miss Glanville inquired of the physician, just going out, how he found her brother; who replied, that his fever was increased since last night, and that it would not (seeing Arabella preparing to go to his bedside) be proper to disturb him.

Saying this, he bowed, and went out; and Miss Glanville repeating what the physician had said, begged her to defer speaking to him till another time.

I know, said she, that he apprehends the sight of me will cause so many tumultuous motions in the soul of his patient, as may prove prejudicial to him: nevertheless, since his disorder is, questionless, more in his mind than body, I may prove, haply, a better physician than he; since I am more likely than he to cure an illness I have caused.

Saying this, she walked up to Mr Glanville's bed-side, who, seeing her, thanked her in a weak voice, for coming to see him, assuring her, he was very sensible of the favour she did him

You must not, said she, blushing, thank me too much, lest I think the favour I have done you is really of more consequence than I imagined, since it merits so many acknowledgments. Your physician tells us, pursued she, that your life is in danger, but I persuade myself you will value it so much from this moment, that you will not protract your cure any longer.

Are you mad, madam, whispered Miss Glanville, who stood behind her, to tell my brother that the physician says he is in danger? I suppose you really wish he may die, or you would not talk so.

If, answered she, whispering again to Miss Glanville, you are not satisfied with what I have already done for your brother, I will go as far as modesty will permit me; and gently pulling open the curtains—

Glanville, said she, with a voice too much raised for a sick person's ear, I grant to your sister's solicitations, what the fair Statira did to an interest yet more powerful; since, as you know it was her own brother who pleaded in favour of the dying Orontes: therefore, considering you in a condition haply no less dangerous than that of that passionate prince, I condescend, like her, to tell you that I do not wish your death; that I entreat you to live; and, lastly, by all the power I have over you, I command you to recover.

Ending these words, she closed the curtain, that her transported lover might not see her blushes and confusion, which were so great, that, to conceal them, even from Miss Glanville, she hurried out of the room, and retired to her own apartment, expecting in a little time, to receive a billet, under the sick man's hand, importing, that in obedience to her commands, he was recovered, and ready to throw himself at her feet, to thank her for that life she had bestowed upon him, and to dedicate the remains of it to her service.

Miss Glanville, who staid behind her in a strange surprise at her ridiculous behaviour, though she longed to know what her brother thought of it, finding he continued silent, would not disturb him. The shame he conceived at hearing so absurd a speech from a woman he passionately loved, and the desire he had not to hear his sister's sentiments upon it, made him counterfeit sleep, to avoid any discourse with her upon so disagreeable a subject.

That day his fever increased; and the next, the physician pronouncing him in great danger, a messenger was dispatched to town, to hasten the coming of Sir Charles; and poor Miss Glanville was quite inconsolable under the apprehensions of losing him.

Arabella, not to derogate from her character, affected great firmness of mind upon this occasion; she used the most persuasive eloquence to moderate her cousin's affliction, and caused all imaginable care to be taken of Mr Glanville. While any one was present, her looks discovered only a calm and decent sorrow; yet when she was alone, or had only her dear Lucy with her, she gave free vent to her tears, and discovered a grief for Mr Glanville's illness little different from that she had felt for her father's.

As she now visited him constantly every day, she took an opportunity, when she was alone by his bed-side, to chide him for his disobedience, in not recovering, as she had commanded him.

Dear cousin, answered he, faintly, can you imagine health is not my choice? And do you think I would suffer these pains if I could possibly ease myself of them?

Those pains, replied Arabella, mistaking his complaint, ought to have ceased when the cause of them did; and when I was no longer rigorous, you ought no longer to have suffered. But tell me, since you are, questionless, one of the strangest men in the world, and the hardest to be comforted; nay, and I may add, the most disobedient of all that ever wore the fetters of love; tell me, I say, what I must do to content you?

If I live, cousin, said Glanville—

Nay, interrupted Arabella, since my empire over you is not so absolute as I thought; and since you think fit to reserve to yourself the liberty of dying, contrary to my desire; I think I had better resolve not to make any treaty with you. However, as I have gone thus far, I will do something more; and tell you, since I have commanded you to live, I will also permit you to love me, in order to make the life I have bestowed on you, worthy your acceptance. Make me no reply, said she, putting her hand on his mouth; but begin from this moment to obey me.

Saying this, she went out of the room.

A few hours after, his fever being come to a height, he grew delirious, and talked very wildly; but a favourable crisis ensuing, he fell into a sound and quiet sleep, and continued in it for several hours; upon his waking, his physician declared his fever was greatly abated, and the next morning pronounced him out of danger.

Miss Glanville, transported with joy, ran to Lady Bella, and informed her of this good news; but as she did not make her the acknowledgments she expected, for being the cause of his recovery, she behaved with more reserve than Miss Glanville thought was necessary, which renewed her former disgusts; yet, dreading to displease her brother, she concealed it from the observation of her cousin.

Arabella being desirous of completing her lover's cure by some more favourable expressions, went to his chamber, accompanied by Miss Glanville.

I see, said she, approaching to his bed-side, with an enchanting smile, that you know how to be obedient, when you please; and I begin to know, by the price you set upon your obedience, that small favours will not content you.

Indeed, my dearest cousin, said Glanville, who had found her more interested in his recovery than he expected, you have been very obliging, and I will always most gratefully own it.

I am glad, interrupted Arabella, that gratitude is not banished from all your family; and that that person in it for whom I have the most sensibility is not entirely divested of it.

I hope, said Mr Glanville, my sister has given you no cause to complain of her.

Indeed but she has, replied Arabella: for notwithstanding she is obliged to me for the life of a brother, whom questionless she loves very well; nevertheless, she did not deign to make me the least acknowledgment for what I have done in your favour. However, Glanville, provided you continue to observe that respect and fidelity towards me, which I have reason to hope for from you, your condition shall be never the worse for Miss Glanville's unacknowledging temper; and I now confirm the grant I yesterday made you, and repeat it again; that I permit you to love me, and promise you not to be displeased at any testimonies you will give me of your passion, provided you serve me with an inviolable fidelity.

But, madam, returned Mr Glanville, to make my happiness complete, you must also promise to love me; or else what signifies the permission you give me to love you?

You are almost as unacknowledging as your sister, resumed Arabella, blushing; and if your health was perfectly re-established, questionless, I should chide you for your presumption: but since something must be allowed for sick persons, whose reason one may suppose is weakened by their indisposition, I will pardon your indiscretion at this time, and counsel you to wait patiently for what Heaven will determine in your favour. Therefore endeavour to merit my affection by your respect, fidelity, and services; and hope from my justice whatever it ought to bestow.

Ending this speech with a solemnity of accent that gave Mr Glanville to understand any reply would offend her, he silently kissed her fair hand, which she held out to him; a favour, his sickness, and the terms upon which they now were, gave him a right to expect; and, finishing her visit for that time, left him to his repose;—being extremely pleased at the prospect of his recovery, and very well satisfied at having so gracefully got over so great a difficulty, as that of giving him permission to love her; for, by the laws of romance, when a lady has once given her lover that permission, she may lawfully allow him to talk to her upon the subject of his passion, accept all his gallantries, and claim an absolute empire over all his actions; reserving to herself the right of fixing the time when she may own her affection: and when that important step is taken and his constancy put to a few years more trial; when he has killed all his rivals, and rescued her from a thousand dangers; she at last condescends to reward him with her hand; and all her adventures are at an end for the future.

END OF THE THIRD BOOK

BOOK IV

I

In which our heroine discovers her knowledge in astronomy

SIR GEORGE, WHO HAD NEVER missed a day, during Mr Glanville's illness, in sending to the castle, now he was able to see company, visited him very frequently, and sometimes had the happiness to meet with Arabella in his chamber; but knowing the conditions of her father's will, and Mr Glanville's pretensions, he was obliged to lay so much constraint upon himself, in the presence of Miss Glanville, and her brother, that he hardly durst trust his eyes, to express his admiration of her, for fear of alarming them with any suspicion of his designs. However, he did not fail to recommend himself to her esteem, by a behaviour to her full of the most perfect respect; and very often, ere he was aware, uttered some of the extravagant compliments that the gallants in the French romances use to their mistresses.

If he walked with her in the gardens, he would observe that the flowers, which were before languishing and pale, bloomed with fresh beauty at her approach; that the sun shone out with double brightness, to exceed, if possible, the lustre of her eyes and that the wind, fond of kissing her celestial countenance, played with her fair hair and, by gentle murmurs, declared its happiness.

If Miss Glanville happened to be present, when he talked to her in this strain, she would suppose he was ridiculing her cousin's fantastical turn, and, when she had an opportunity of speaking to him alone, would chide him with a great deal of good humour, for giving her so much diversion at her cousin's expense.

Sir George, improving this hint, persuaded Miss Glanville, by his answers, that he really laughed at Arabella; and being now less fearful of giving any suspicion to the gay coquette, since she assisted him to deceive her, he applied himself with more assiduity than ever, to insinuate himself into Arabella's favour.

However, the necessity he was under of being always of Arabella's opinion sometimes drew him into little difficulties with Miss Glanville. Knowing that young lady was extremely fond of scandal, he told her, as a most agreeable piece of news, one afternoon, when he was there, that he had seen Miss Groves, who, he supposed, had come into the country upon the same account as she had done a twelvemonth before. Her marriage being yet a secret, the complaisant baronet threw out an hint or two concerning the familiarity and correspondence there was between her and the gentleman to whom she was really secretly married.

Miss Glanville, making the most of this intelligence, said a thousand severe things against the unfortunate Miss Groves; which Arabella, always benevolent and kind, could not bear.

I persuade myself, said she to her cousin, that you have been misinformed concerning this beauty, whose misfortunes you aggravate by your cruel censures; and whoever, has given you the history of her life has, haply, done it with great injustice.

Why, madam, interrupted Miss Glanville, do you think you are better acquainted with her history, as you call it, who have never been in town, where her follies made her so remarkable, than persons who were eye-witnesses to all her ridiculous actions.

I apprehend, said Arabella, that I who have had a relation made to me of all the passages of her life, and have been told all her most secret thoughts, may know as much, if not more, than persons who have lived in the same place with her, and have not had that advantage; and I think I know enough to vindicate her from many cruel aspersions.

Pray, madam, returned Miss Glanville, will your ladyship pretend to defend her scandalous commerce with Mr L——?

I know not, miss, said Arabella, why you call her intercourse with that perjured man by so unjust an epithet. If Miss Groves be unchaste, so was the renowned Cleopatra, whose marriage with Julius Caesar is controverted to this day!

And what reasons, madam, said Miss Glanville, have you for supposing Miss Groves was married to Mr L——, since all the world knows to the contrary?

Very sufficient ones, said Arabella; since it is hardly possible to suppose a young lady of Miss Groves's quality would stain the lustre of her descent by so shameful an intrigue; and also since there are examples enough to be found of persons who suffered under the same unhappy circumstances as herself, yet were perfectly innocent, as was that great queen I have mentioned—who, questionless, you, sir, are sufficiently convinced, was married to that illustrious conqueror; who, by betraying so great and so fair a queen, in a great measure tarnished the glory of his laurels.

Married, madam! replied Sir George. Who presumes to say, that fair queen was not married to that illustrious conqueror!

Nay, you know, sir, interrupted Arabella, many people did say, even while she was living, that she was not married; and have branded her memory with infamous calumnies, upon account of the son she had by Caesar, the brave Czœsario, who, under the name of Cleomedon, performed such miracles of valour in Ethiopia.

I assure you, madam, said Sir George, I was always a great admirer of the famous Cleomedon, who was certainly the greatest hero in the world.

Pardon me, sir, said Arabella, Cleomedon was, questionless, a very valiant man; but he, and all the heroes that ever were, must give place to the unequalled prince of Mauritania; that illustrious, and for a long time unfortunate, lover of the divine Cleopatra, who was daughter, as you questionless know, of the great queen we have been speaking of.

Dear heart! said Miss Glanville, what is all this to the purpose? I would fain know, whether Sir George believes Miss Groves was ever married to Mr L——.

Doubtless, I do, said he; for, as Lady Bella says, she is in the same unhappy circumstance with the great Cleopatra; and if Julius Caesar could be guilty of denying his marriage with that queen, I see no reason to suppose, why Mr L—— might not be guilty of the same kind of injustice.

So then, interrupted Miss Glanville, reddening with spite, you will really offer to maintain, that Miss Groves was married? Ridiculous! How such a report would he laughed at in London!

I assure you, replied Arabella, if ever I go to London, I shall not scruple to maintain that opinion to every one, who will mention that fair one to me; and use all my endeavours to confirm them in it.

Your ladyship would do well, said Miss Glanville, to persuade people that Miss Groves, at fifteen, did not want to run away with her writing-master.

As I am persuaded myself, said Arabella, that writing-master was some noble stranger in disguise, who was passionately in love with her, I shall not suffer any body in my hearing to propagate such an unlikely story; but since he was a person worthy of her affection, if she had run away with him, her fault was not without example, or even excuse.—You know what the fair Artemisa did for Alexander, sir, pursued she, turning to Sir George: I would fain know your sentiments upon the action of that princess, which some have not scrupled to condemn.

Whoever they are, madam, said Sir George, who condemn the fair Artemisa for what she did for Alexander, they are miscreants and slanderers; and though that beautiful princess has been dead more than two thousand years, I would draw my sword in defence of her character, against all who should presume, in my presence, to cast any censures upon it.

Since you are so courageous, said Miss Glanville, laughing excessively at this sally, which she thought was to ridicule her cousin, it is to be hoped you will defend a living lady's character, who may thank you for it, and make the world believe that her correspondence with Mr L—— was entirely innocent, and that she never had any design to run away with her writing-master.

Are you resolved, cousin, said Lady Bella, to persist in that ridiculous mistake, and take a nobleman for a writing-master, only because his love put him upon such a stratagem to obtain his mistress?

Indeed, Lady Bella, said Miss Glanville, smiling, you may as well persuade me the moon is made of a cream cheese, as that any nobleman turned himself into a writing-master to obtain Miss Groves.

Is it possible, miss, said Arabella, that you can offer such an affront to my understanding, as to suppose I would argue upon such a ridiculous system, and compare the second glorious luminary of the heavens to so unworthy a resemblance? I have taken some pains to contemplate the heavenly bodies; and, by reading and observation, am able to comprehend some part of their excellence: therefore it is not probable I should descend to such trivial comparisons, and liken a planet, which haply is not much less than our earth, to a thing so inconsiderable as that you name.

Pardon me, dear cousin, interrupted Miss Glanville, laughing louder than before, if I divert myself a little with the extravagance of your notions. Really, I think you have no reason to be angry if I supposed you might make a comparison between the moon and a cream cheese, since you say that same moon, which don't appear broader than your gardener's face, is not much less than the whole world. Why, certainly, I have more reason to trust my own eyes than such whimsical notions as these.

Arabella, unwilling to expose her cousin's ignorance by a longer dispute upon this subject, begged her to let it drop for the present; and, turning to Sir George, I am very glad, said she, that having always had some inclination to excuse, and even to defend, the flight of Artemisa, with Alexander, my opinion is warranted by that of a person so generous as yourself. Indeed, when we consider that this princess forsook her brother's dominions, and fled away with a lover whom she did not hate, questionless her enemies accuse her, with some appearance of reason, of too great imbecility.

But, madam, replied Sir George, her enemies will not take the pains to examine her reasons for this conduct.

True, sir, resumed Arabella; for she was in danger of seeing a prince, who loved her, put to a cruel and infamous death upon a public scaffold; and she did not resolve to fly with him, till all her tears and prayers were found ineffectual to move the king her brother to mercy.

Though, replied Sir George, I am extremely angry with the indiscreet Cepio, who discovered Alexander to the Armenian king; yet what does your ladyship think of that gallant action of his, when he saw him upon the scaffold, and the executioner ready to cut off his head? How brave it was of him to pass undauntedly through the prodigious number of guards that environed the scaffold; and, with his drawn sword, run the executioner through the body, in the sight of them all! Then, giving the prince another sword, engaged more than two thousand men in his defence.

Questionless, replied Arabella, it was a glorious action; and when I think how the king of Armenia was enraged to see such a multitude of soldiers fly from the swords of two men, I cannot choose but divert myself with the consternation he was in: yet that was nothing to the horrible despair which tormented him afterwards, when he found that Alexander, after being again taken and imprisoned, had broken his chains, and carried away with him the princess Artemisa his sister.

II

In which a very pleasing conversation is left unfinished

As ARABELLA WAS IN THIS part of her discourse, a servant came to inform her that Sir Charles Glanville was just alighted. Upon which Miss Glanville flew to receive her father; and Arabella, walking a little slower after her, gave Sir George an opportunity of holding a little longer conversation with her.

I dare believe, madam, said he, when you read the story of the unfortunate Alexander, your fair eyes did not refuse to shed some tears at the barbarous and shameful death he was going to suffer: yet I assure you, melancholy as his situation was, it was also very glorious for him, since he had the sublime satisfaction of dying for the person he adored; and had the ravishing pleasure to know, that his fate would draw tears from that lovely princess for whom he sacrificed his life. Such a condition, madam, ought to be envied rather than pitied; for, next to the happiness of possessing the person one adores, certainly the glory of dying for her is most to be coveted.

Arabella, pleasingly surprised to hear language so conformable to her own ideas, looked for a moment upon the baronet with a most enchanting complacency in her eyes.

It must be confessed, sir, says she, that you speak very rationally upon these matters; and by the tenderness and generosity of your sentiments, you give me cause to believe that your heart is prepossessed with some object worthy of inspiring them.

Sir George, seeming as if he struggled to suppress a sigh, You are in the right, madam, said he, to suppose, that if my heart be prepossessed with any object, it is with one who is capable of inspiring a very sublime passion; and I assure you, if ever it submits to any fetters, they shall be imposed on me by the fairest person in the world.

Since love is not voluntary, replied Arabella, smiling, it may happen that your heart may be surprised by a meaner beauty than such a one as you describe: however, as a lover has always an extraordinary partiality for the beloved object, it is probable what you say may come to pass; and you may be in love with the fairest person in the world, in your own opinion.

They were now so near the house, that Sir George could reply no otherways than by a very passionate glance, which Arabella did not observe, being in haste to pay her respects to her uncle, whom she met just going to Mr Glanville. Her looks were directed to him. Sir Charles saluting her with great affection, they all went into Mr Glanville's chamber, who received his father with the utmost respect and tenderness; extremely regretting the trouble he had been at in taking a journey to the castle upon his account, and gently blaming his sister for her precipitancy in alarming him so soon.

Sir Charles, extremely overjoyed to find him so well recovered, would not allow him to blame Miss Glanville for what she had done; but addressing himself to his niece, he thanked her for the care she had taken of Mr Glanville, in very obliging terms.

Arabella could not help blushing at her uncle's compliment, supposing he thanked her for having restored her cousin to his health.

I assure you, sir, said she, Mr Glanville is less obliged to my commands, than to the goodness of his constitution, for his recovery; and herein he was not so obedient as many persons I could name to him.

Mr Glanville, unwilling to permit the company's observation upon this speech, began to acquaint his father with the rise and progress of his distemper: but though the old gentleman listened with great attention to his son while he was speaking, yet, not having lost a word of what Arabella had said, as soon as he was done he turned to his niece, and asked her how she could be so unjust as to accuse his son of disobedience, because he did not recover when she commanded him. Why, madam, added he, you want to carry your power farther than ever any beauty did before you; since you pretend to make people sick and well whenever you please.

Really, sir, replied Arabella, I pretend to no more power than what I presume all others of my sex have upon the like occasions and since nothing is more common than for a gentleman, though ever so sick, to recover in obedience to the commands of that person who has an absolute power over his life, I conceive I have a right to think myself injured, if Mr Glanville, contrary to mine, had thought proper to die.

Since, said the old gentleman, smiling, my son has so well obeyed your commands in recovering his health, I shall tremble, lest, in obedience to a contrary command of yours, he should die, and deprive me of an heir; a misfortune which, if it should happen, I should place to your account.

I assure you, said Arabella, very gravely, I have too great an esteem for Mr Glanville, to condemn him to so severe a punishment as death for light offences; and since it is not very probable that he will ever commit such crimes against me, as can be only expiated by his death, such as infidelity, disobedience, and the like, you have no reason to fear such a misfortune by my means.

Alas! replied Sir George, you beauties make very nice distinctions in these cases; and think, if you do not directly command your lovers to die, you are no ways accountable for their death. And when a lover, as it often happens, dies through despair of ever being able to make himself beloved; or, being doomed to banishment, or silence, falls into a fever, from which nothing but kindness can recover him; and that being denied, he patiently expires; I say, when these things happen, as they certainly do every day, how can you hold yourselves guiltless of their deaths, which are apparently occasioned either by your scorn or insensibility?

Sir Charles and Miss Glanville were extremely diverted at this speech of Sir George's; and Mr Glanville, though he would have wished he had been rallying any other person's follies than his cousin's, yet could not help smiling at the solemn accent in which he delivered himself.

Arabella, mightily pleased with his manner of talking, was resolved to furnish him with more occasions of diverting the company at her expense.

I see, answered she, you are one of those persons who call a just decorum, which all ladies, who love glory as they ought to do, are obliged to preserve, by the name of severity; but, pray, what would you have a lady do, whom an importunate lover presumes to declare his passion to? You know it is not permitted us to listen to such discourses; and you know also, whoever is guilty of such an offence, merits a most rigorous punishment: moreover, you find, that when a sentence of banishment or silence is pronounced upon them, these unhappy criminals are so conscious of the justice of their doom, that they never murmur against their judge who condemns them; and therefore, whatever are their fates in consequence of that anger they have incurred, the ladies, thus offended, ought not to be charged with it as any cruel exertion of their power.

Such eloquence as yours, madam, replied Sir George, might defend things yet more unjustifiable. However, you must give me leave, as being interested in the safety of my sex, still to be of opinion, that no man ought to be hated because he adores a beautiful object, and consecrates all his moments to her service.

Questionless, resumed Arabella, he will not be hated, while, out of the respect and reverence he bears her, he carefully conceals his passion from her knowledge; but as soon as ever he breaks through the bounds which that respect prescribes him, and lets her understand his true sentiments, he has reason to expect a most rigorous sentence, since he certainly, by that presumption, has greatly deserved it.

If the ladies, replied Sir George, were more equitable, and would make some distinction between those who really love them in a passionate and respectful silence, and others who do not feel the power of their charms, they might spare themselves the trouble of hearing what so mortally offends them: but when a lady sees a man every day, who, by his looks, sighs, and solicitude to please her, by his numberless services, and constant attendance on her, makes it evident that his soul is possessed with a violent passion for her; I say, when a lady sees, and yet will not see, all this, and persists in using a passionate adorer with all the indifference due to a man wholly insensible of the power of her charms; what must he do in such a mortifying situation, but make known his torments to her that occasions them, in order to prevail upon her, to have some sense of what he does and feels hourly for her sake.

But since he gains nothing by the discovery of his passion, resumed Arabella, but, on the contrary, loses the advantages he was before possessed of, which were very great; since he might see and discourse with his mistress every day, and haply have the hour to do her a great many petty services, and receive some of her commands; all these advantages he loses when he declares he loves: and, truly, I think a man who is so unwise as to hazard a certain happiness for a very improbable hope, deserves to be punished, as well for his folly as presumption; and, upon both these accounts, banishment is not too rigorous a sentence.

III

Definition of love and beauty. The necessary qualities of a hero and heroine

Though, replied Mr Glanville, you are very severe in the treatment you think it necessary our sex should receive from yours, yet I wish some of our town-beauties were, if not altogether of your opinion, yet sufficiently so as to make it not a slavery for a man to be in their company; for unless one talks of love to these fair coquettes the whole time one is with them, they are quite displeased, and look upon a man who can think any thing, but themselves, worthy his thoughts or observation, with the utmost contempt.—How often have you and I, Sir George, pursued he, pitied the condition of the few men of sense, who are sometimes among the crowd of beaux who attend the two celebrated beauties to all places of polite diversion in town? For those ladies think it a mortal injury done to their charms, if the men about them have eyes or ears for any object but their faces, or any sound but that of their voices: so that the connoisseurs in music, who attend them to Ranelagh, must stop their ears, like Ulysses, when the syren Frasi sings; and the wits who gallant them to the side-box, must lay a much greater constraint upon themselves, in order to resist the soul-moving Garrick, and appear insensible while he is upon the stage.

Upon my soul, added Sir George (forgetting the character he assumed), when I have seen some persons of my acquaintance talking to the eldest of these ladies, while one of Congreve's comedies has been acting; his face quite turned from the stage, and hers overspread with an eternal smile; her fine eyes sometimes lifted up in a beautiful surprise, and a little enchanting giggle half hid with her fan; in spite of their inattention, I have been ready to imagine, he was entertaining her with remarks upon the play, which she was judicious enough to understand. And yet I have afterwards been informed by himself, that nothing was less in their thoughts; and all that variety in her face, and that extreme seeming earnestness in his discourse, was occasioned by the most trifling subjects imaginable: he perhaps had been telling her, how the sight of her squirrel, which peeped out of her pocket, surprised some ladies she was visiting; and what they said upon her fondness for it, when she was gone; blaming them at the same time for their want of delicacy, in not knowing how to set a right value upon such pleasing animals. Hence proceeded her smiles, the lifting up of her eyes, the half-stifled laugh, and all the pretty gestures that appeared so wonderfully charming to all those who did not hear their discourse; and it is upon such trifles as these, or else on the inexhaustible subjects of their charms, that all who are ambitious of being near these miracles, are under a necessity of talking.

And pray, interrupted Arabella, what subjects afford a more pleasing variety of conversation, than those of beauty and love? Can we speak of any object so capable of delighting as beauty, or of any passion of the mind more sublime and pleasing than love?

With submission, madam, said Glanville, I conceive, all that can be said either of beauty, or of love, may be comprised in a very few words. All who have eyes, and behold true beauty, will be ready to confess it is a very pleasing object: and all that can be said of it may be said in a very few words; for when we have run over the catalogue of charms, and mentioned fine eyes, fine hair, delicate complexion, regular features, and an elegant shape, we can only add a few epithets more, such as lovely, dangerous, enchanting, irresistible, and the like; and every thing that can be said of beauty is exhausted. So likewise it is with love: we know that Admiration precedes it, that Beauty kindles it, Hope keeps it alive, and Despair puts an end to it: and that subject may be as soon discussed as the other, by the judicious use of proper words; such as wounds, darts, fires, languishings, dyings, torture, rack, jealousy, and a few more of no signification but upon this subject.

Certainly, sir, said Arabella, you have not well considered what you say, since you maintain that love and beauty are subjects easily and quickly discussed. Take the pains, I beseech you, to reflect a little upon those numerous and long conversations, which the subjects have given rise to in Clelia, and the Grand Cyrus, where the most illustrious and greatest personages in the world manage the disputes; and the agreeable diversity of their sentiments on those heads affords a most pleasing and rational entertainment. You will there find, that the greatest conquerors, and heroes of invincible valour, reason with the most exact and scrupulous nicety upon love and beauty; the superiority of fair and brown hair controverted by warriors with as much eagerness as they dispute for the victory in the field: and the different effects of that passion upon different hearts defined with the utmost accuracy and eloquence.

I must own, interrupted Sir Charles, I should have but a mean opinion of those warriors, as you call them, who could busy themselves in talking of such trifles; and be apt to imagine such insignificant fellows, who could wrangle about the colour of their mistress's hair, would be the first to turn their backs upon the enemy in battle.

Is it possible, sir, resumed Arabella, glowing with indignation, that you can entertain such unworthy thoughts of heroes, who merit the admiration and praise of all ages for their inestimable valour, whom the spears of a whole army opposed to each of their single swords would not oblige to fly?—What think you, sir, pursued she, looking at Sir George, of the injurious words which my uncle has uttered against those heroic princes, whose courage, I believe, you are as well acquainted with as myself? The great Oroondates, the invincible Artaban, the valiant and fortunate Artamenes, the irresistible Juba, the incomparable Cleomedon, and an hundred other heroes I could name, are all injured by this unjust assertion of my uncle: since certainly they were not more famous for their noble and wonderful actions in war, than for the sublimity and constancy of their affections in love.

Some of these heroes you have named, replied Sir George, had the misfortune, even in their lives, to be very cruelly vilified. The great Oroondates was a long time accused of treachery to his divine princess; the valiant and unfortunate Artamenes was suspected of inconstancy; and the irresistible Juba reproached with infidelity and baseness, by both his mistress and friend.

I never knew you was so well acquainted with these persons, interrupted Mr Glanville, and I fancy it is but very lately that you have given yourself the trouble to read romances.

I am not of your opinion, said Arabella. Sir George, questionless, has appropriated great part of his time to the perusal of those books, so capable of improving him in all useful knowledge; the sublimity of love and the quintessence of valour; which two qualities, if possessed in a superlative degree, form a true and perfect hero, as the perfection of beauty, wit, and virtue, make a heroine worthy to be served by such an illustrious personage. And I dare say Sir George has profited so much by the great examples of fidelity and courage he has placed before his eyes, that no consideration whatever could make him for one moment fail in his constancy to the divine beauty he adores; and, inspired by her charms, he would scorn to turn his back, as my uncle phrases it, upon an army of an hundred thousand men.

I am extremely obliged to you, madam, said Sir George, bowing his head to the ground to hide a smile he could not possibly restrain, for the good opinion you have of my courage and fidelity.

As for Sir George's courage, cousin, said Mr Glanville, laughing, I never disputed it: and though it be, indeed, a very extraordinary exertion of it, to fight singly against an army of an hundred thousand men; yet since you are pleased to think it probable, I am as willing to believe Sir George may do it, as any other man: but, as for his fidelity, in matters of love, I greatly suspect it, since he has been charged with some very flagrant crimes of that nature.

How, sir! resumed Arabella. Have you ever been faithless, then? and, after having sworn, haply, to devote your whole life to the service of some beauty, have you ever violated your oaths, and been base enough to forsake her?

I have too much complaisance, madam, said Sir George, to contradict Mr Glanville, who has been pleased positively to assert, that I have been faithless, as you most unkindly phrase it.

Nay, sir, replied Arabella, this accusation is not of a nature to be neglected; and though a king should say it, I conceive, if you are innocent, you have a right to contradict him, and clear yourself. Do you consider how deeply this assertion wounds your honour and happiness for the future? What lady, think you, will receive your services, loaded, as you are, with the terrible imputation of inconstancy?

Oh! as for that, madam, said Miss Glanville, I believe no lady will think the worse of Sir George for being faithless. For my part, I declare nothing pleases me so much, as gaining a lover from another lady; which is a greater compliment to one's beauty, than the addresses of a man that never was in love before.

You may remember, cousin, replied Arabella, that I said once before, your spirit and humour resembled a certain great princess very much; and I repeat it again, never was there a greater conformity in tempers and inclinations.

My daughter, said Sir Charles, is mightily obliged to you, Lady Bella, for comparing her to a great princess: undoubtedly you mean it as a compliment.

If you think, said Arabella, that barely comparing her to a princess be a compliment, I must take the liberty to differ from you. My cousin is not so many degrees below a princess, as that such a comparison should be thought extraordinary: for if her ancestors did not wear a crown, they might, haply, have deserved it; and her beauty may one day procure her a servant, whose sword, like that of the great Artaban, may win her a sceptre; who, with a noble confidence, told his princess, when the want of a crown was objected to him, 'I wear a sword, madam, that can perform things more difficult than what you require: and if a crown be all that I want to make me worthy of you, tell me what kingdom in the world you choose to reign in, and I will lay it at your feet.'

That was a promise, replied Sir George, fit only for the great Artaban to make: but, madam, if you will permit me to make any comparison between that renowned warrior and myself, I would venture to tell you, that even the great Artaban was not exempted from the character of inconstancy any more than myself, since, as you certainly know, he was in love with three great princesses successively.

I grant you, replied Arabella, that Artaban did wear the chains of three princesses successively; but it must also be remembered, in his justification, that the two first of these beauties refused his adorations, and treated him with contempt, because he was not a prince: therefore, recovering his liberty, by those disdains they cast on him, he preserved that illustrious heart from despair, to tender it with more passionate fidelity to the divine princess of the Parthians; who, though greatly their superior in quality and beauty, did permit him to love her. However, I must confess, I found something like levity in the facility he found in breaking his fetters so often; and when I consider, that among all those great heroes, whose histories I have read, none but himself ever bore, without dying, the cruelties he experienced from those princesses, I am sometimes tempted to accuse him myself of inconstancy: but indeed every thing we read of that prodigy of valour is wholly miraculous; and since the performance of impossibilities was reserved for him, I conclude this miracle also, among many others, was possible to him, whom nothing was ever able to resist upon earth. However, pursued she, rising, I shall not absolutely condemn you, till I have heard your adventures from your own mouth, at a convenient time, when I shall be able to judge how far you merit the odious appellation of inconstancy.

Saying this, she saluted her uncle, who had for some time been conversing in a low voice with his son, with a grace wholly charming, and retired to her apartment. Miss Glanville following her a few moments after, (the compliment, extravagant as it was, which she had paid her, having procured her some good will from the vain and interested Miss Glanville,) they conversed together with a great deal of good humour till dinner-time, which, because Mr Glanville was not absolutely recovered, was served in his chamber.

IV

In which our heroine is engaged in a new adventure

As Mr Glanville took a great deal of pains to turn the discourse upon subjects on which the charming Arabella could expatiate, without any mixture of that absurdity which mingled itself in a great many others, the rest of that day, and several others, were passed very agreeably: at the end of which, Mr Glanville being perfectly recovered, and able to go abroad, the baronet proposed to take the diversion of hunting; which Arabella, who was used to it, consented to partake of; but being informed that Miss Glanville could not ride, and chose to stay at home, she would have kept her company, had not Sir Charles insisted upon the contrary.

As Sir George, and some other gentlemen, had invited themselves to be of the party, Arabella, on her coming down to mount her horse, found a great many young gallants ready to offer her their assistance upon this occasion: accepting, therefore, with great politeness, this help from a stranger, who was nearest her, she mounted her horse, giving occasion to every one that was present, to admire the grace with which she sat and managed him. Her shape being as perfect as any shape could possibly be, her riding-habit discovered all its beauties: her hat, and the white feather waving over part of her fine black hair, gave a peculiar charm to her lovely face; and she appeared with so many advantages in this dress and posture, that Mr Glanville, forgetting all her absurdities, was wholly lost in the contemplation of so many charms, as her whole person was adorned with.

Sir George, though he really admired Arabella,, was not so passionately in love as Mr Glanville; and, being a keen sportsman, eagerly pursued the game, with the rest of the hunters: but Mr Glanville minded nothing but his cousin, and kept close by her.

After having rode a long time, Arabella—conceiving it a piece of cruelty not to give her lover an opportunity of talking to her, as, by his extreme solicitude, he seemed ardently to desire—coming to a delightful valley, she stopped, and told Mr Glanville, that being weary of the chase she should alight, and repose herself a little under the shade of those trees.

Mr Glanville, extremely pleased at this proposition, dismounted; and, having helped her to alight, seated himself by her on the grass.

Arabella, expecting he would begin to talk to her of his passion, could not help blushing at the thoughts of having given him such an opportunity; and Mr Glanville endeavouring to accommodate himself to her ideas of a lover, expressed himself in terms extravagant enough to have made a reasonable woman think he was making a jest of her: all which, however, Arabella was extremely pleased with; and she observed such a just decorum in her answers, that, as the writers of romance phrase it, if she did not give him any absolute hopes of being beloved, yet she said enough to make him conclude she did not hate him.

They had conversed in this manner near a quarter of an hour, when Arabella, perceiving a man at a little distance, walking very composedly, shrieked out aloud; and, rising with the utmost precipitation, flew from Mr Glanville, and went to untie her horse; while his astonishment being so great at her behaviour, that he could not, for a moment or two, ask her the cause of her fear.

Do you not see, said she, out of breath with the violence of her apprehensions, the person who is coming towards us? It is the same, who, some months ago, attempted to carry me away, when I was riding out with only two attendants: I escaped for that time the danger that threatened me; but, questionless, he comes now to renew his attempts: therefore can you wonder at my fear?

If it should be as you say, madam, interrupted Glanville, what reason have you to fear? Do you not think I am able to defend you?

Ah! without doubt, you are able to defend me, answered she: and though, if you offer to resist the violence he comes to use against me, he will, haply, call two or three dozen armed men to his assistance, who are, I suppose, concealed hereabouts, yet I am not apprehensive, that you will be worsted by them. But as it happened to the brave Juba, and Cleomedon, while they were fighting with some hundred men, who wanted to carry away their princesses before their faces, and were giving death at every blow, in order to preserve them, the commander of these ravishers seeing the two princesses sitting, as I was, under a tree, ordered them to be seized by two of his men, and carried away, while the two princes were losing best part of their blood in their defence: therefore, to prevent such an accident happening, while you are fighting for my rescue, I think it will be the safest way for me to get on horse-back, that I may be in a condition to escape; and that you may not employ your valour to no purpose.

Saying this, having, with Mr Glanville's assistance, loosed her horse from the tree, he helped her to mount, and then remounted his own.

Your antagonist, said Arabella, is on foot; and therefore, though I prize your life extremely, yet I cannot dispense with myself from telling you, that it is against the law of knighthood to take any advantage of that kind over your enemy: nor will I permit your concern for my safety to make you forget what you owe to your own reputation.

Mr Glanville, fretting excessively at her folly, begged her not to make herself uneasy about things that were never likely to happen.

The gentleman yonder, added he, seems to have no designs to make any attempt against you: if he should, I shall know how to deal with him; but, since he neither offers to assault me nor affront you, I think we ought not to give him any reason to imagine we suspect him, by gazing on him thus, and letting him understand, by your manner, that he is the subject of our conversation. If you please, madam, we will endeavour to join our company.

Arabella, while he was speaking, kept her eyes fixed upon his face, with looks which expressed her thoughts were labouring upon some very important point; and, after a pause of some moments, Is it possible, said she, with a tone of extreme surprise, that I should be so mistaken in you? Do you really want courage enough to defend me against that ravisher?

Oh, heavens! madam, interrupted Glanville, try not my temper thus: courage enough to defend you! 'Sdeath! you will make me mad! Who, in the name of wonder, is going to molest you?

He whom you see there, replied Arabella, pointing to him with her finger: for know, cold and insensible as thou art to the danger which threatens me, yonder knight is thy rival, and a rival, haply, who deserves my esteem better than thou dost; since, if he has courage enough to get me by violence into his power, that same courage would make him defend me against any injuries I might be offered from another. And since nothing is so contemptible in the eyes of a woman, as a lover who wants spirit to die in her defence, know, I can sooner pardon him, whom thou wouldst cowardly fly from, for the violence which he meditates against me, than thyself for the pusillanimity thou hast betrayed in my sight.

With these words she galloped away from her astonished lover; who, not daring to follow her, for fear of increasing her suspicions of his cowardice, flung himself off his horse in a violent rage; and, forgetting that the stranger was observing, and now within hearing, he fell a cursing and exclaiming against the books that had turned his cousin's brain, and railing at his own ill fate that condemned him to the punishment of loving her. Mr Hervey (for it really was he), whom an affair of consequence had brought again into the country, hearing some of Mr Glanville's last words, and observing the gestures he used, concluded that he had been treated like himself by Arabella, whom he knew again at a distance: therefore coming up to Mr Glanville, laughing—

Though I have not the honour of knowing you, sir, said he, I must beg the favour you will inform me, if you are not disturbed at the ridiculous folly of the lady I saw with you just now? She is the most fantastical creature that every lived, and, in my opinion, fit for a mad-house. Pray, are you acquainted with her?

Mr Glanville, being in a very ill humour, could not brook the freedom of this language against his cousin, whose follies he could not bear any one should rail at but himself; and being provoked at his sneers, and the interruption he had given to their conversation, he looked upon him with a disdainful frown, and told him in a haughty tone, that he was very impertinent to speak of a lady of her quality and merit so rudely.

Oh! sir, I beg your pardon, replied Mr Hervey, laughing more than before. What, I suppose you are the champion of this fair lady! But, I assure myself, if you intend to quarrel with every one that will laugh at her, you will have more business upon your hands than you can well manage.

Mr Glanville, transported with rage at this insolence, hit him such a blow with the butt-end of his whip, that it stunned him for a moment; but, recovering himself, he drew his sword, and, mad with the affront he had received, made a push at Glanville; who, avoiding it with great dexterity, had recourse to his hanger for his defence.

Arabella, in the mean time, who had not rid far, concealing herself behind some trees, saw all the actions of her lover, and intended ravisher; and being possessed with an opinion of her cousin's cowardice, was extremely rejoiced to see him fall upon his enemy first, and that with so much fury, that she had no longer any reason to doubt his courage. Her suspicions therefore being removed, her tenderness for him returned; and when she saw them engaged with their swords (for, at that distance, she did not plainly perceive the difference of their weapons) her apprehensions for her cousin were so strong, that though she did not doubt his valour, she could not bear to see him expose his life for her; and without making any reflections upon the singularity of her design, she was going to ride up to them, and endeavour to part them; when she saw several men come towards them, whom she took to be the assistants of her ravisher, though they were, in reality, hay-makers; who, at a distance, having seen the beginning of their quarrel, had hastened to part them.

Terrified, therefore, at this reinforcement, which she thought would expose her cousin to great danger, she galloped with all speed after the hunters, being directed by the sound of the horn. Her anxiety for her cousin made her regardless of her own danger, so that she rode with a surprising swiftness; and, overtaking the company, she would have spoken to tell them of her cousin's situation: when her spirits failing her, she could only make a sign with her hand, and sunk down in a swoon, in the arms of Sir George, who eagerly galloped up to her, and supporting her as well as he was able till some others came to her relief, they took her off her horse, and placed her upon the ground; when by the help of some water they brought from a spring near them, in a little time she came to herself.

Sir Charles, who seeing her come up to them without his son, and by her fainting concluded some misfortune had happened to him, the moment she opened her eyes, asked her eagerly where he was.

Your son, said Arabella, sighing, with a valour equal to that of the brave Cleomedon, is this moment fighting in my defence against a crowd of enemies; and is, haply, shedding the last drop of his blood in my quarrel.

Shedding the last drop of his blood, *haply*! repeated Sir Charles, excessively grieved, and not a little enraged at Arabella, supposing she had introduced him into some quarrel: it may be happy for you, madam; but I am sure it will make me very miserable, if my son comes to any harm.

If it be the will of Heaven he should fall in this combat, resumed Arabella, he can never have a more glorious destiny; and as that consideration will, doubtless, sweeten his last moments, so it ought to be your consolation. However, I beg you'll lose no time, but haste to his assistance; for since he has a considerable number of enemies to deal with, it is not improbable but he may be overpowered at last.

Where did you leave my son, madam? cried Sir Charles, eagerly.

He is not far off, replied Arabella: and you will doubtless be directed to the place, by the sight of the blood of his enemies which he has spilt.—Go that way, pursued she, pointing with her finger towards the place where she had left her cousin: there you will meet with him, amidst a crowd of foes, whom he is sacrificing to my safety, and his just resentment.

Sir Charles, not knowing what to think, galloped away, followed by most part of the company; Sir George telling Lady Bella that he would stay to defend her against any attempts that might be made on her liberty, by any of her ravisher's servants, who were, probably, straggling about. Arabella, however, being perfectly recovered, insisted upon following her uncle.

There is no question, said she, but Mr Glanville is victorious. I am only apprehensive from the dangerous wounds he may have received in the combat, which will require all our care and assistance.

Sir George, who wanted to engross her company a little to himself, in vain represented to her, that, amidst the horrors of a fight so bloody as that must certainly be, in which Mr Glanville and his friends would be now engaged, it would be dangerous for her to venture her person; yet she would not be persuaded; but, having mounted her horse, with his assistance, she rode as fast as she was able after the rest of the company.

V

Being a chapter of mistakes

S IR CHARLES, WHO, BY THIS time, had got to the place she had directed him to, but saw no appearance of lighting, and only a few haymakers in discourse together, inquired if there had been any quarrel between two gentlemen in that place.

One of them, at this question, advancing, told Sir Charles, that two gentlemen had quarrelled there, and were fighting with swords; but that they had parted them: and that one of them, having an horse tied to a tree, mounted him and rode away: that the other, they believed, was not far off; and that there had been no blood shed, they having come time enough to prevent it.

Sir Charles was extremely satisfied with this account; and giving the haymakers some money for the good office they did in parting the two combatants, rode up to Lady Bella, and informed her that his son was safe.

I cannot imagine he is safe, replied she, when I see some of his enemies (pointing to the haymakers) still alive. It is not customary, in those cases, to suffer any to escape; and, questionless, my cousin is either dead, or a prisoner, since all his adversaries are not vanquished.

Why, you dream, madam, replied Sir Charles: those fellows yonder are haymakers. What should make them enemies to my son? They were lucky enough to come in time to prevent him and another gentleman from doing each other a mischief. I cannot imagine for what reason my son quarrelled with that person they speak of: perhaps you can inform me?

Certainly, sir, said Arabella, I can inform you, since I was the cause of their quarrel. The story is too long to tell you now; and, besides, it is so connected with the other accidents of my life, that it is necessary you should be acquainted with my whole history, in order to comprehend it. But if those persons are what you say, and did really part my cousin and his antagonist, truly I believe they have done him a very ill office; for,

I am persuaded, my cousin will never be at rest, till, by his rival's death, he has freed himself from one capable of the most daring enterprises to get me into his power: and since I cannot be in security, while he lives, and persists in the resolution he has taken to persecute me, it had been better if he had suffered all the effects of my cousin's resentment at that time, than to give him the trouble to hunt him through the world, in order to sacrifice him to the interest of his love and vengeance.

Sir Charles, no less astonished than alarmed at this discovery of his niece's sanguinary sentiments told her, he was sorry to see a lady so far forget the gentleness of her sex, as to encourage and incite men to such extremities upon her account. And for the future, added he, I must entreat you, niece, to spare me the affliction of seeing my son exposed to these dangerous quarrels; for, though his life is so little regarded by you, yet it is of the utmost consequence to me.

Arabella, who found matter sufficient in the beginning of this speech, to be offended with her uncle, yet, mistaking the latter part of it for a pathetic complaint of her cruelty, replied, very gravely, that her cousin's safety was not so indifferent to her as he imagined; and that she did not hate him so much but that his death would affect her very sensibly.

Arabella, in speaking these words, blushed with shame, as thinking they were rather too tender and Sir Charles, who coloured likewise, from a very different motive, was opening his mouth to tell her, that he did not think his son was much obliged to her for not hating him; when Arabella, supposing he designed to press her to a farther explanation of the favourable sentiments she felt for Mr Glanville, stopped him with precipitation. Press me no more, said she, upon this subject and, as I have already spoken too much, haply, before so many witnesses, seek not to enhance my confusion, by prolonging a discourse that at present must needs be disagreeable to me.

I shall readily agree with you, madam, replied Sir Charles, that you have spoken too much; and if I had thought you capable of speaking in the manner you have done, I would have been more cautious in giving you an occasion for it.

I should imagine, sir, said Arabella, blushing with anger, as she before did with shame, that you would be the last person in the world who could think I had spoken too much upon this occasion and since you are pleased to tell me so, I think it fit to let you know, that I have not, in my opinion, transgressed the laws of decency and decorum, in what I have said in my cousin's favour; and I can produce many examples of greater freedom of speech, in princesses, and ladies of the highest quality. However, I shall learn such a lesson of moderation in this respect, from your reproof, that I promise you, neither yourself nor Mr Glanville shall have any cause, for the future, to complain of my want of discretion.

Sir Charles, who was very polite and good-natured, was half angry with himself, for having obliged his niece to such a submission, as he thought it; and, apologizing for the rudeness of his reprehension, assured her that he was perfectly convinced of her discretion in all things, and did not doubt but her conduct would be always agreeable to him.

Arabella, who, from what her uncle had said, began to entertain suspicions that would never have entered any imagination but hers, looked earnestly upon him for half a moment, as if she wished to penetrate into the most secret recesses of his heart: but, fancying she saw something in his looks that confirmed her apprehensions, she removed her eyes from his face, and fastening them on the ground, remained for some moments in confusion.—Sir Charles, whom her apparent disturbance made very uneasy, proposed returning to the castle: telling Lady Bella he expected to find his son already there.

It is more than probable, said she, turning to Sir George, that my cousin is gone in pursuit of my ravisher; and the interruption that has been given to his designed vengeance, making him more furious than before, it is not likely he will return till he has punished his insolence by that death he so justly merits. Mr Glanville is already so happy in your opinion, said Sir George, with a very profound sigh, that there is no need of his rendering you this small service to increase your esteem: but, if my prayers are heard, the punishment of your ravisher will be reserved for a person less fortunate, indeed, than Mr Glanville, though not less devoted to your interest, and concerned in your preservation.

Sir George, counterfeiting a look of extreme confusion and fear, as he ended these words—

Arabella, who perfectly comprehended the meaning they were designed to convey, thought herself obliged to take no notice of them: and, therefore, without making any reply to the young baronet, who ventured slowly to lift his eyes to her face, in order to discover if there were any signs of anger in it, she told Sir Charles she inclined to go home; and Sir George, with the rest of the company, attended them to the castle; where, as soon as they arrived, they took their leave.

Sir George, notwithstanding Arabella's care to deprive him of an opportunity of speaking to her, told her, in a whisper, having eagerly alighted to help her off her horse, I am going, madam, to find out that insolent man, who has dared to offer violence to the fairest person in the world: and, if I am so happy as to meet with him, he shall either take my life, or I will put him into a condition never to commit any more offences of that nature.

Saying this, he made a low bow; and, being desirous to prevent her answer, remounted his horse, and went away with the rest of the company.

Arabella, who, upon this occasion, was all confusion, mixed with some little resentment, discovered so much emotion in her looks, while Sir George was whispering to her, that her uncle, as he was handing her into the house, asked her, if she was offended at any thing Sir George had said to her.

Arabella, construing this question as she had done some other things her uncle had said to her, replied, in a reserved manner; Since my looks, contrary to my intention, have betrayed my thoughts to you, I will not scruple to confess, that I have some cause to be offended with Sir George; and that, in two instances to-day, he has seemed to forget the respect he owes me.

Sir Charles was fired at this account, Is it possible, said he, that Sir George has had the assurance to say any thing to offend you, and that before my face too? This affront is not to be borne.

I am sorry, replied Arabella, eyeing him heedfully, to see you so much concerned at it.

Don't be uneasy, interrupted Sir Charles: there will be no bad consequences happen from it; but he shall hear of it, added he, raising his voice with passion: I'll force him this night to explain himself.

You must pardon me, sir, said Arabella, more and more confirmed in her notions, if I tell you, that I am extremely offended at your uncommon zeal upon this occasion; and also I must assure you, that a little more calmness would be less liable to suspicion.

Miss Glanville coming to meet them, Sir Charles, who did not take much notice of what Arabella said, eagerly inquired for his son; and, hearing he was not come home, was apprehensive of his meeting again with the person he had quarrelled with: but his fears did not last long; for Mr Glanville came in, having purposely avoided the company, to hide the uneasiness Lady Bella's tormenting folly had given him.

VI

In which the mistakes are continued

As soon as Mr Glanville appeared, the two ladies retired; Miss Glanville asking Arabella a hundred questions concerning their diversion, the drift of which was, to know how Sir George behaved to her, but that fair lady, whose thoughts were wholly employed on the strange accidents that had happened to her on that day, longed to be at liberty to indulge her reflections; and, complaining of extreme weariness, under pretence of reposing herself till dinner, got quit of Miss Glanville's company, which, at that time, she thought very tedious.

As soon as she was left to herself, her imagination running over all that had happened, she could not help confessing, that few women ever met with such a variety of adventures in one day: in danger of being carried off by violence by one lover; delivered by another; insinuations of love from a third, who, she thought, was enamoured of her cousin; and what was still more surprising a discovery, that her uncle was not insensible of her charms, but was become the rival of his own son.

As extravagant as this notion was, Arabella found precedents in her romances of passions full as strange and unjustifiable; and confirmed herself in that opinion, by recollecting several examples of unlawful love. Why should I not believe, said she, that my charms can work as powerful effects as those of Olympia, princess of Thrace, whose brother was passionately enamoured of her.

Did not the divine Clelia inspire Maherbal with a violent passion for her; who, though discovered to be her brother, did not, nevertheless, cease to adore her? And, to bring an instance still nearer to my own case, was not the uncle of the fair Alcyone in love with her? And did he not endeavour to win her heart by all the methods in his power?

Ah! then, pursued she, let us doubt no more of our misfortune; and, since our fatal beauty has raised this impious flame, let us stifle it with our rigour, and not allow an ill-timed pity, or respect, to encourage a passion which may, one day, cast a blemish upon our glory.

Arabella, having settled this point, proceeded to reflect on the conquest she had made of Sir George: she examined his words over and over, and found them so exactly conformable to the language of an Oroondates or Orontes that she could not choose but be pleased but: recollecting that it behoved her, like all other heroines, to be extremely troubled and perplexed at an insinuation of love, she began to lament the cruel necessity of parting with an agreeable friend; who, if he persisted in making her acquainted with his thoughts, would expose himself to the treatment persons so indiscreet always meet with: nor was she less concerned, lest, if Mr Glanville had not already dispatched her ravisher, Sir George, by wandering in search of him, and, haply, sacrificing him to his eager desire of serving her, should by that means lay her under an obligation to him, which, considering him as a lover, would be a great mortification.

Sir George, however, was gone home to his own house, with no thoughts of pursuing Arabella's ravisher: and Mr Glanville, being questioned by his father concerning his quarrel, invented some trifling excuse for it; which not agreeing with the account the baronet had received from Arabella, he told his son, that he had concealed the truth from him, and that there was more in that affair than he had owned. You quarrelled, added he, upon Arabella's account and she did not scruple to affirm it before all the company.

Mr Glanville, who had vainly flattered himself with an hope that his cousin had not acquainted the company with her whimsical apprehensions, was extremely vexed when he found she had exposed herself to their ridicule, and that it was probable even he had not escaped: but willing to know from her own mouth how far she had carried her folly, he went up to her chamber; and, being immediately admitted, she began to congratulate him upon the conquest he had gained, as she supposed, over his enemy, and thanked him very solemnly for the security he had procured for her.

Mr Glanville, after assuring her that she was in no danger of ever being carried away by that person whom she feared, proceeded to inquire into all that had passed between her and the company whom she had joined when she left him: and Arabella, relating every particular, gave him the mortification to know that her folly had been sufficiently exposed. But she touched upon her fears for him with so much delicacy, and mentioned her fainting in such a manner, as insinuated a much greater tenderness than he before had reason to hope for; and this knowledge destroying all his intentions to quarrel with her for what she had said, he appeared so easy and satisfied that Arabella, reflecting upon the misfortune his father's new-born passion would probably be the occasion of to him, could not help sighing at the apprehension; looking on him, at the same time, with a kind of pitying complacency, which did not escape Mr Glanville's notice.

I must know the reason of that sigh, cousin, said he, smiling, and taking her hand.

If you are wise, replied Arabella, gravely, you will be contented to remain in the pleasing ignorance you are at present; and not seek to know a thing which will, haply, afford you but little satisfaction.

You have increased my curiosity so much by this advice, resumed he, accommodating his looks to Arabella's, that I shall not be at rest till I know what it is you conceal from me: and since I am so much concerned in it, even by your own confession, I have a right to press you to explain yourself.

Since you are so importunate, replied Arabella, I must tell you that I will not do you so great a diskindness as to explain myself; nor will I be the first who shall acquaint you with your misfortune, since you will, haply, too soon arrive at the knowledge of it by other means.

Glanville, who imagined this was some new whim that had got into her head, was but little perplexed at an insinuation, which, had he been ignorant of her foible, would have given him great uneasiness: but, being sensible that she expected he would press her to disclose herself, and appear extremely concerned at her refusing him that satisfaction, he counterfeited so well, that she was at a loss how to evade the arguments he used to make her unfold the terrible mystery; when the dinner-bell ringing, and relieving her for the present, Mr Glanville led her down to the parlour, where Sir Charles and his daughter attended their coming.

VII

In which the mistakes are not yet cleared up

THE BARONET, WHO HAD BEEN put into a bad humour by Arabella's insinuations that Sir George had affronted her, appeared reserved and uneasy; and, being resolved to question her about it, was willing first to know exactly what it was his niece had been offended at: but as he feared, if it came to his son's knowledge, it would produce a quarrel between the young gentlemen that might have dangerous consequences, he was desirous of speaking to her alone; and, as soon as dinner was over, asked her to take a walk with him upon the terrace, telling her he had something to say to her in private. Arabella, whose fears had been considerably increased by the pensiveness which appeared in her uncle's looks during dinner, and supposed he wanted a private conversation only to explain himself more clearly to her than he had yet done, was excessively alarmed at this request; and casting her eyes down to the ground, blushed in such a manner, as betrayed her confusion, and made Miss Glanville and her brother believe that she suspected her uncle had a design to press her soon to give her hand to Mr Glanville, which occasioned her apparent disorder.

Sir Charles, however, who had not so heedfully observed her behaviour, repeated his request; adding, with a smile, upon her giving him no answer, Sure, Lady Bella, you are not afraid to be alone with your uncle.

No, sir, replied Arabella, giving him a piercing look: I am not afraid of being alone with my uncle, and, as long as he pretends to be no more than my uncle, I shall not scruple to hear what he has to say to me.

Sir Charles, a little vexed at an answer which insinuated, as he thought, a complaint of his having pretended to more authority over her than he ought, told her, he hoped she had no cause to believe he would displease her by any improper exertion of that power over her with which her father had entrusted him: For I assure you, added he, I would rather you should follow my advice as an uncle, than obey me as a guardian and, since my affection for you is, perhaps, greater than what many people have for a niece, my solicitude ought to be imputed to that motive.

I have all the sense I ought to have of that affection you honour me with, replied Arabella; and since I hope it will be always what it should be, without wishing for its increase, I am contented with those testimonies I have already received of it, and do not desire any other.

Sir Charles, a little puzzled to understand the meaning of these words, which the grave looks of Arabella made yet more mysterious, rose from his seat with an air of discontent. I should have been glad to have spoken a word in private with you, niece, said he; but since you think proper to make so much ceremony in such a trifle, I'll defer it till you are in a better humour.

Miss Glanville, seeing her father going out of the room, stepped before him: Nay, papa, said she, if you want to speak with my cousin, my brother and I will go out, and leave you to yourselves.

You will do me a very great displeasure, said Arabella; for I am sure my uncle has not any thing of consequence to say to me. However, added she, seeing Miss Glanville go away, I am resolved I will not be left alone; and therefore, Mr Glanville, since I can pretend to some power over you, I command you to stay.

You may remember, madam, said Mr Glanville, with a smile, you refused to gratify my curiosity with regard to something you hinted to me some time ago: and to punish you, added he, going out of the room, I am resolved you shall listen to what my father has to say to you; for, by your unwillingness to hear it, I imagine you suspect already what it is.

Arabella, finding she had no way to avoid hearing what she dreaded so much, and observing her uncle had resumed his chair, prepared to give him audience; but, in order to deprive him of all hope that she would receive his discourse favourably, she assumed the severest look she was capable of; and, casting her eyes on the ground, with a mixture of anger and shame, waited with a kind of fear and impatience for what he had to say.

I see, madam, said the baronet, observing her confusion, that you apprehend what I am going to say to you; but I beseech you, do not fear I have any intentions but such as you will approve.

You are certainly in the right, sir, said Arabella, in the interpretation you have put on my looks: I am really in pain about the purport of your discourse; and you would particularly oblige me, if you would dispense with me from hearing it.

I see, replied Sir Charles, that, out of a mistaken fear, you are unwilling to hear me, in order to avoid coming to the explanation I desire: but I tell you, once again, you have nothing to apprehend.

I have every thing to apprehend, sir, resumed Arabella, tartly, while you persist, in your design of disobliging me; and you cannot give me a greater proof of the badness of your intentions, than by thus forcing me to listen to discourses I ought to avoid.

Since my word has no weight with you, replied Sir Charles, I'll condescend to assure you, by the most sacred oath, that I do not mean to come to any extremities with Sir George concerning what you already told me: all I desire to know is, if you think you had any reason to be offended with him for any thing he said. And, in that case, I cannot dispense with myself from expostulating with him about it,

You would do me a favour, sir, resumed Arabella, if you would interest yourself a little less in what Sir George said to me. The offence was committed against me only; and none but myself has any right to resent it.

It is enough, niece, said Sir Charles, rising. You acknowledge sufficient to make me resolve to oblige him to ask pardon for the affront you have received. However, I beg you may make yourself easy: no ill consequences will happen from this affair, provided my son does not know it; and I know you have too much discretion to acquaint him with it.

Saying this, he went out of the room, leaving Arabella in great confusion at what he had said; which, in her opinion, had amounted almost to a plain declaration of his passion; and his design of putting an end to Sir George's pretensions, whom, it was probable, he looked upon as a more dangerous rival than his son, confirmed her in the opinion of his resolution to persecute her.

Full of the reflections this accident had occasioned, she went to walk in the garden, where Mr Glanville, his sister having just left him, joined her.

As he imagined his father's design, in speaking to her alone, was to prevail upon her to consent to marry him before he left the country, which was what he most earnestly wished, he drew a bad omen from the discontent which appeared in her eyes.

Is it with me, cousin, said he, or with what my father has been saying to you, that you are angry?

With both, replied Arabella, hastily; for if you had staid in the room, as I commanded you, I should not have been exposed to the pain of hearing things so disagreeable.

Since I knew what would be the purport of my father's discourse, said Mr Glanville, you ought not to be surprised I could not resolve to give any interruption to it by my presence; and being so much interested in the success of his solicitations, I could not choose but give him an opportunity of speaking to you alone, as he desired.

It seems, then, resumed Arabella, you know what was the subject of his conversation.

I believe I can guess, interrupted Mr Glanville, smiling.

Is it possible, cried Arabella, starting back in great surprise, that, knowing, as you say you do, your father's intentions, you would resolve to furnish him with an opportunity of disclosing them?

Can you blame me, said Mr Glanville, for suffering him to undertake what I durst not myself? I know your delicacy, or rather your severity, so well, that I am sensible, if I had taken the liberty to say, what my father has said, you would have been extremely offended, and punished me as you have often done, with a banishment from your presence. Nay, pursued he, seeing astonishment and anger in her countenance, I perceive you are, at this moment, going to pronounce some terrible sentence against me.

You are deceived, said Arabella, with a forced calmness: I am so far from being offended with you, that I am ready to acknowledge, you merit very extraordinary praises for the perfect resignation you show to the will, and for your credit, I will suppose, the commands of your father: but I would advise you to be contented with the reputation of being a dutiful son; and, for the future, never aspire to that of being a faithful lover.

Speaking these words, which were wholly unintelligible to her amazed admirer, she left him, and went to her own apartment, strangely surprised at the indifference of Mr Glanville; who, as she understood what he had said, was not only willing to resign her to his father, but also took upon him to mediate in his behalf.

As she was unwilling to acknowledge, even to herself, that the grief she felt at this discovery proceeded from any affection for her cousin, she imputed it to the shame of seeing herself so basely forsaken and neglected; and, not being able to find a precedent for such an indignity offered to the charms of any lady in her romances, the singularity of her fate, in this respect, seemed to demand all her uneasiness.

VIII

Which contains some necessary consequences of the foregoing mistakes. A soliloquy on a love-letter

WHILE ARABELLA PASSED HER TIME in her closet, in the most disagreeable reflections, Glanville was racking his brain to find out the meaning of those mysterious words she had uttered at leaving him. He examined them twenty times over, but could not possibly penetrate into their sense;. but supposing, at last, that they really meant nothing at all, or were occasioned by some new flight of her imagination, he went to find out his father, in order to know what had passed between him and Arabella.

Sir Charles, however, was not to be found: he had ordered his horse to be made ready, under pretence of taking a little ride after dinner; and, passing by Sir George's house, alighted to pay him a visit.

The young baronet, being at home, received him with great politeness; and Sir Charles, whose peculiar disposition was to be nicely tenacious of every thing which he imagined had any relation to the honour of his family, took the first opportunity to question him concerning the confusion his whisper had occasioned in Lady Bella; adding, that she had confessed he had given her reason to take ill what he had said to her.

Sir George, who was by no means willing to quarrel with the uncle of Arabella, received the old gentleman's remonstrances with a great deal of calmness; and, finding Arabella had not discovered the purport of that whisper which had offended her, he told Sir Charles that the confusion he saw in her countenance was occasioned by his rallying her upon the fright she had been in upon Mr Glanville's account. He added some other particulars, that, entirely taking away all inclination in Sir Charles to pursue the matter any further, they parted upon very good terms; Sir George promising, very soon, to return his visit at the castle.

Mr Glanville, upon his father's return, being impatient to know what he had said to Arabella, inquired with so much precipitation, concerning the conversation they had had together, that Sir Charles, unwilling to tell him the truth, and not having time to consider of an answer, evaded his question in such a manner, that Mr Glanville could not help making some observation upon it; and, comparing this circumstance with what Arabella had said, though he could not comprehend the meaning that seemed to be concealed under their behaviour, he immediately concluded, there was some mystery which it concerned him to find out.

Possessed with this opinion, he longed for an opportunity to talk with Arabella alone. But he was not so happy to obtain one; for, though that fair one presided at the tea-table, as usual, and also appeared at supper, yet she so industriously avoided all occasions of being alone with him, though but for a moment, and appeared so reserved and uneasy, that it was impossible for him to speak to her upon that subject.

As soon as it was time to retire, he resolved to request the favour of a few moments' conversation with her, in her own apartment; and when he had, as was his custom, handed her up stairs, instead of wishing her a good night at her chamber door, he was going to desire permission to enter it with her; when Lucy, coming to meet her lady, whispered her in the ear; upon which Arabella, turning towards him, gave him a hasty salute, and hurried into her apartment.

Glanville, no less vexed at this disappointment, than perplexed at that whisper, which had caused such a visible emotion in Arabella, retired to his own room, tormented with a thousand uneasy suspicions, for which he could not exactly assign a cause; and wishing impatiently for the next day, in which he hoped to procure some explanation of what at present greatly perplexed him.

In the mean time, Arabella, who had been informed by Lucy, in that whisper, who was eager to let her know it, that a messenger had brought a letter from Sir George, and, late as it was at night, waited for an answer, was debating with herself, whether she would open this billet or not. She had a strong inclination to see what it contained; but, fearful of transgressing the laws of romance, by indulging a curiosity not justifiable by example, she resolved to return this letter unopened.

Here, said she to Lucy, give this letter to the messenger that brought it; and tell him, I was excessively offended with you for receiving it from his hands.

Lucy, taking the letter, was going to obey her orders; when, recollecting herself, she bid her stay.

Since Sir George, said she to herself, is no declared lover of mine, I may, without any offence to decorum, see what this letter contains. To refuse receiving it, will be to acknowledge that his sentiments are not unknown to me; and, by consequence, to lay myself under a necessity of banishing him: nor is it fit that I should allow him to believe I am so ready to apprehend the meaning of every gallant speech which is used to me; and to construe such insinuations as he took the liberty to make me, into declarations of love.

Allowing, therefore, the justness of these reasons, she took the letter out of Lucy's hand; and, being upon the point of opening it, a sudden thought controlled her designs: she threw it suddenly upon her toilet; and, looking very earnestly upon it

Presumptuous paper! said she, speaking with great emotion to the letter. Bold repository of thy master's daring thoughts! Shall I not be blamed by all who hereafter will hear or read my history, if, contrary to the apprehensions I have, that thou containest a confession that will displease me, I open thy seal, and become accessory to thy writer's guilt, by deigning to make myself acquainted with it? And thou, too indiscreet and unwary friend, whose folds contain the acknowledgment of his crime! what will it advantage thee or him, if, torn by my resenting hand, I make thee suffer for the part though bearest in thy master's fault; and teach him, by thy fate, how little kindness he has to expect from me! Yes, to spare myself the trouble of reading what will, questionless, greatly displease me, I will return thee, uninjured, into thy master's hands; and, by that moderation, make him repent the presumption he has been guilty of.

IX

Containing a love-letter in the heroic style; with some occasional reasonings by Lucy, full of wit and simplicity

OUR FAIR HEROINE HAVING ENDED the foregoing soliloquy, took up the letter and gave it to Lucy, who had, all the time she was speaking, observed a profound silence, mixed with a most eager attention:

Here, pursued she, carry it to the person who brought it, and bid him tell his master, that, lest I should find any thing in it which may offend me, I have chosen not to read it; and, if he is wise, he will profit by my concern for him, and take care how he hazards displeasing me a second time by an importunity of this kind, which I shall not so easily pardon him.

Lucy, who had taken particular notice of this speech, in order to remember every word of it when she repeated it again, went conning her lesson to the place where she had desired the servant to wait her coming: but he was gone; such being indeed his master's orders; for he was apprehensive that, following the custom of the ladies in romances, Arabella would return his letter: and therefore, to deprive her of an opportunity of sending it back that night, he ordered his man to say he waited for an answer; but, as soon as he conveniently could, to come away without one.

Lucy, in a great surprise at the servant's going away, returned to her lady with the letter in her hand, telling her she must needs read it now, since the person who brought it was gone.

It must be confessed, said Arabella, taking the letter from her, with a smile, he has fallen upon an ingenious device to make me keep it for this night; and since, haply, I may be mistaken in the contents, I have a mind to open it.

Lucy did not fail to confirm her lady in this design: and Arabella, making as if she yielded to the importunities of her confidante, opened the letter; which she found as follows:—

The Unfortunate and Despairing Bellmour to the Divine Arabella

Madam,

Since it is, doubtless, not only with your permission, but even by
your commands, that your uncle, Sir Charles Glanville, comes to
pronounce the sentence of my death, in the denunciation of your
anger, I submit, madam, without repining at the rigour of that
doom you have inflicted on me. Yes, madam, this criminal, who has
dared to adore you with the most sublime and perfect passion that
ever was, acknowledges the justice of his punishment; and, since it
is impossible to cease loving you, or to live without telling you he
does so, he is going voluntarily to run upon that death your severity
makes him wish for, and the greatness of his crime demands. Let
my death, then, O divine Arabella, expiate the offence I have been
guilty of! And let me hope those fair eyes, that have beheld me with
scorn when alive, will not refuse to shed some tears upon my tomb!
and that when you remember my crime of loving you, you will also
be pleased to remember that I died for that crime; and wish for no
other comfort in death, but the hope of your not hating when he
is no more, the unhappy

Bellmour.

Arabella, who had read this letter aloud, sighed gently at the
conclusion of it: but poor Lucy, who was greatly affected at so dolorous
an epistle, could not restrain her tears; but sobbed so often, and with
so much violence, as at length recalled her lady from the reverie into
which she was plunged.

What ails you? said she to her confidante, greatly surprised. What is
the cause of this unseemly sorrow?

Oh, madam! cried Lucy, her sobs making a frequent and
unpleasing interruption in her words; I shall break my heart to be
sure. Never was such sad mournful letter in the world: I could cry

my eyes out for the poor gentleman. Pray excuse me, madam; but, indeed, I can't help saying you are the most hard-heartedest lady I ever knew in my born days. Why, to be sure, you don't care if an hundred fine gentlemen should die for you, though their spirits were to haunt you every night. Well, I would not have what your ladyship has to answer for, for all the world!

You are a foolish wench! replied Arabella, smiling at her simplicity. Do you think I have any cause to accuse myself, though five thousand men were to die for me! It is very certain my beauty has produced very deplorable effects: the unhappy Harvey has expiated, by his death, the violence his too-desperate passion forced him to meditate against me: the no less guilty, the noble unknown Edward, is wandering about the world, in a tormenting despair, and stands exposed to the vengeance of my cousin, who has vowed his death. My charms have made another person, whose character ought to be sacred to me, forget all the ties of consanguinity, and become the rival of his son, whose interest he once endeavoured to support: and lastly, the unfortunate Bellmour consumes away in an hopeless passion; and, conscious of his crime, dooms himself, haply, with more severity than I desire, to a voluntary death, in hopes thereby of procuring my pardon and compassion when he is no more. All these, Lucy, as I said before, are very deplorable effects of my beauty; but you must observe, that my will has no part in the miseries that unfortunate beauty occasions; and that, though I could even wish myself less fair, in order to avoid giving so much unhappiness to others, yet these wishes would not avail; and since, by a fatal necessity, all these things will happen, whether I would or no, I must comfort myself under the uneasiness which the sensibility of my temper makes me feel, by the reflection, that, with my own consent, I contribute nothing to the misfortune of those who love me.

Will your ladyship, then, let poor Sir George die? said Lucy, who had listened very attentively to this fine harangue without understanding what it meant.

Questionless, he must die, replied Arabella, if he persists in his design of loving me.

But pray, madam, resumed Lucy, cannot your ladyship command him to live, as you did Mr Harvey and Mr Glanville, who both did as you had them?

I may command him to live, said Arabella; and there is no question but he would obey me, if I likewise permit him to love me: but this last not being fit for me to do, I see no way to prevent the sad resolution he has taken.

To be sure, madam, returned Lucy, your ladyship knows what you ought to do better than I can advise your ladyship, being that you are more learned than me: but, for all that, I think it's better to save life than to kill, as the Bible book says: and since I am sure your ladyship is a good Christian, if the gentleman dies for the want of a few kind words, or so, I am sure you will be troubled in mind about it.

It must be confessed, said Arabella, smiling, that though your solicitations are not very eloquent, they are very earnest and affecting; and I promise you I will think about it: and, if I can persuade myself I am doing no wrong thing by concerning myself about his preservation, I will dispatch you to-morrow morning with my orders to him to live, or at least to proceed no farther in his design of dying, till he has farther cause.

Lucy being extremely glad she had gained her point, called in her lady's other woman, who, having assisted her to undress, left her in her closet, to which she always retired for an hour before she went to bed.

END OF THE FOURTH BOOK

BOOK V

I

A dispute very learnedly handled by two ladies, in which the reader may take what part he pleases

Mr Glanville, who was too much in love to pass the night with any great degree of tranquillity, under the apprehensions he felt; it being the nature of that passion to magnify the most inconsiderable trifles into things of the greatest importance, when they concern the beloved object; did not fail to torment himself with a thousand different fears, which the mysterious behaviour of his father, and the more mysterious words of his mistress, gave rise to. Among many various conjectures, all equally unreasonable, he fixed upon one no way advantageous to Sir Charles; for, supposing that the folly of Arabella had really disgusted him, and made him desirous of breaking off the designed match between them, he was, as he thought, taking measures to bring this about, knowing, that if Lady Bella refused to fulfil her father's desire in this particular, a very considerable estate would descend to him.

Upon any other occasion, Mr Glanville would not have suspected his father of so ungenerous an action; but lovers think every thing possible which they fear; and being prepossessed with this opinion, he resolved the next morning to sound his father's inclinations by entreating him to endeavour to prevail upon Lady Bella to marry him before her year of mourning for the marquis was expired.

Attending him, therefore, at breakfast, in his own chamber, he made his designed request, not without heedfully observing his countenance at the same time, and trembling lest he should make him an answer that might confirm his uneasy suspicion.

Sir Charles, however, agreeably surprised him, by promising to comply with his desire that day: for, added he, though my niece has some odd ways, yet, upon the whole, she is a very accomplished woman: and, when you are her husband, you may probably find the means of curing her of those little follies, which at present are conspicuous enough; but being occasioned by a country education, and a perfect ignorance of the world, the instruction which then you will not scruple to give her, and which, from a husband, without any offence to her delicacy she may receive, may reform her conduct, and make her behaviour as complete as, it must be confessed, both her person and mind now are.

Mr Glanville, having acquiesced in the justice of this remark, as soon as breakfast was over, went to visit the two ladies, who generally drank their chocolate together.

Miss Glanville being then in Lady Bella's apartment, he was immediately admitted, where he found them engaged in a high dispute; and, much against his will, was obliged to be arbitrator in the affair, they having, upon his entrance, both appealed to him.

But, in order to place this momentous affair in a true light, it is necessary to go back a little, and acquaint the reader with what had passed in the apartment; and also, following the custom of the romance and novel-writers, in the heart of our heroine.

No sooner were her fair eyes open in the morning, than the unfortunate Sir George presenting himself to her imagination, her thoughts, to use Scudery's phrase, were at a cruel war with each other: she wished to prevent the death of this obsequious lover; but she could not resolve to preserve his life, by giving him that hope he required; and without which, she feared, it would be impossible for him to live.

After pondering a few hours upon the necessity of his case, and what a just regard to her own honour required of her, decorum prevailed so much over compassion, that she resolved to abandon the miserable Sir George to all the rigour of his destiny; when, happily for the disconsolate lover, the history of the fair Amalazontha coming into her mind, she remembered, that this haughty princess, having refused to marry the person her father recommended to her, because he had not a crown upon his head; nevertheless, when he was dying for love of her, condescended to visit him, and even to give him a little hope, in order to preserve his life: she conceived it could be no blemish to her character, if she followed the example of this most glorious princess, and suffered herself to relax a little in her severity, to prevent the effect of her lover's despair.

Fear not, Arabella, said she to herself; fear not to obey the dictates of thy compassion, since the glorious Amalazontha justifies, by her example, the means thou wilt use to preserve a noble life, which depends upon a few words thou shalt utter.

When she had taken this resolution, she rung her bell for her women; and as soon as she was dressed, she dismissed them all but Lucy, whom she ordered to bring her paper and pens, telling her she would write an answer to Sir George's letter.

Lucy obeyed with great joy: but by that time she had brought her lady all the materials for writing, her mind was changed; she having reflected, that Amalazontha, whose example, in order to avoid the censure of future ages, she was resolved exactly to follow, did not write to Ambiomer, but paid him a visit, she resolved to do the like; and therefore bad Lucy take them away again, telling her she had thought better of it, and would not write to him.

Lucy, extremely concerned at this resolution, obeyed her very slowly, and with great seeming regret.

I perceive, said Arabella, you are afraid I shall abandon the unfortunate man you solicit for, to the violence of his despair: but though I do not intend to write to him, yet I will make use of a method, perhaps as effectual; for, to speak truly, I mean to make him a visit; his fever, I suppose. being violent enough by this time to make him keep his bed.

And will you be so good, madam, said Lucy, to go and see the poor gentleman? I'll warrant you, he will be ready to die with joy when he sees you.

It is probable what you say may happen, replied Arabella; but there must be proper precautions used to prevent those consequences which the sudden and unexpected sight of me may produce. Those about him, I suppose, will have discretion enough for that; therefore give orders for the coach to be made ready, and tell my women they must attend me; and be sure you give them directions, when I enter Sir George's chamber, to stay at a convenient distance, in order to leave me an opportunity of speaking to him, without being heard. As for you, you may approach the bed-side with me; since, being my confidante, you may hear all we have to say.

Arabella having thus settled the ceremonial of her visit, according to the rules prescribed by romances, sat down to her tea-table, having sent to know if Miss Glanville was up, and received for answer, that she would attend her at breakfast.

Arabella, who had at first determined to say nothing of this affair to her cousin, could not resist the desire she had of talking upon a subject so interesting; and, telling her with a smile, that she was about to make a very charitable visit that morning, asked her, if she was disposed to bear her company in it.

I know you country ladies, said Miss Glanville, are very fond of visiting your sick neighbours: for my part, I do not love such a grave kind of amusement; yet, for the sake of the airing, I shall be very willing to attend you.

I think, said Arabella, with a more serious air than before, it behoves every generous person to compassionate the misfortunes of their acquaintance and friends, and to relieve them as far as lies in their power; but those miseries we ourselves occasion to others, demand, in a more particular manner, our pity: and, if consistent with honour, our relief.

And pray, returned Miss Glanville, who is it you have done any mischief to, which you are to repair by this charitable visit, as you call it?

The mischief I have done, replied Arabella, blushing, and casting down her eyes, was not voluntary. I assure you: yet I will not scruple to repair it, if I can; though, since my power is confined by certain unavoidable laws, my endeavours may not haply have all the success I could wish.

Well, but, dear cousin, interrupted Miss Glanville, tell me, in plain English, what this mischief is, which you have done; and to what purpose you are going out this morning?

I am going to pay a visit to Sir George Bellmour, replied Arabella; and I entreat you, fair cousin, to pardon me for robbing you of so accomplished a lover. I really always thought he was in love with you, till I was undeceived by some words he spoke yesterday, and a letter I received from him last night, in which he has been bold enough to declare his passion to me, and, through the apprehensions of my anger, is this moment dying with grief: and it is to reconcile him to life, that I have prevailed upon myself to make him a visit; in which charitable design, as I said before, I should be glad of your company.

Miss Glanville, who believed not a word Lady Bella had said, burst out a laughing at a speech that appeared to her so extremely false and ridiculous.

I see, said Arabella, you are of a humour to divert yourself with the miseries of a despairing lover; and in this particular you greatly resemble the fair and witty Doralisa, who always jested at such maladies as are occasioned by love. However, this insensibility does not become you so well as her, since all her conduct was conformable to it, no man in the world being bold enough to talk to her of love; but you, cousin, are ready, even by your own confession, to listen to such discourses from anybody; and therefore this behaviour in you may be with more justice termed levity, than indifference.

I perceive, cousin, said Miss Glanville, I have always the worst of those comparisons you are pleased to make between me and other people; but, I assure you, as free and indiscreet as you think me, should very much scruple to visit a man upon any occasion whatever.

I am quite astonished, Miss Glanville, resumed Arabella, to hear you assume a character of so much severity; you who have granted favours of a kind in a very great degree criminal.

Favours! interrupted Miss Glanville; criminal favours! Pray explain yourself, madam.

Yes, cousin, said Arabella, I repeat it again; criminal favours, such as allowing persons to talk to you of love; not forbidding them to write to you; giving them opportunities of being alone with you for several moments together; and several other civilities of the like nature, which no man can possibly merit, under many years' services, fidelity, and pains. All these are criminal favours, and highly blameable in a lady who has any regard for her reputation.

All these, replied Miss Glanville, are nothing in comparison of making them visits; and no woman, who has any reputation at all, will be guilty of taking such liberties.

What, miss! replied Arabella, will you dare, by this insinuation, to cast any censures upon the virtue of the divine Mandane, the haughty Amalazontha, the fair Statira, the cold and rigid Parisatis, and many other illustrious ladies, who did not scruple to visit their lovers, when confined to their beds, either by the wounds they received in battle, or the more cruel and dangerous ones they suffered from their eyes? These chaste ladies, who never granted a kiss of their hand to a lover, till he was upon the point of being their husband, would, nevertheless, most chairitably condescend to approach their bedside, and speak some compassionate words to them, in order to promote their cure, and make them submit to live; nay, these divine beauties would not refuse to grant the same favour to persons whom they did not love, to prevent the fatal consequences of their despair.

Lord, madam! interrupted Miss Glanville, I wonder you can talk so blasphemously, to call a parcel of confident creatures divine, and such terrible words.

Do you know, miss, said Arabella, with a stern look, that it is of the greatest princesses that ever were whom you speak in this irreverent manner! Is it possible that you can be ignorant of the sublime quality of Mandane, who was the heiress of two powerful kingdoms? Are you not sensible, that Amalazontha was queen of Turringia? And will you pretend to deny the glorious extraction of Statira and Parisatis, princesses of Persia?

I shall not trouble myself to deny any thing about them, madam, said Miss Glanville; for I never heard of them before; and, really, I do not choose to be always talking of queens and princesses, as if I thought none but such great people were worthy my notice: it looks so affected, I should imagine every one laughed at me that heard me.

Since you are so very scrupulous, returned Arabella, that you dare not imitate the sublimest among mortals, I can furnish you with many examples, from the conduct of persons whose quality was not much superior to yours, which may reconcile you to an action, you at present, with so little reason, condemn; and to name but one among some thousands, the fair Cleonice, the most rigid and austere beauty in all Sardis, paid several visits to the passionate Ligdainis, when his melancholy, at the ill success of his passion, threw him into a fever, that confined him to his bed.

And pray, madam, who was that Cleonice? said Miss Glanville: and where did she live?

In Sardis I tell you, said Arabella, in the kingdom of Lydia.

Oh! then it is not in our kingdom, said Miss Glanville: what signifies what foreigners do? I shall never form my conduct upon the example of outlandish people; what is common enough in their countries would be very particular here; and you can never persuade me, that it is seemly for ladies to pay visits to men in their beds.

A lady, said Arabella, extremely angry at her cousin's obstinacy, who will suffer men to press her hand, write to her, and talk to her of love, ought to be ashamed of such an affected niceness as that you pretend to.

I insist upon it, madam, said Miss Glanville, that all those innocent liberties you rail at may be taken by any woman without giving the world room to censure her: but, without being very bold and impudent, she cannot go to see men in their beds; a freedom that only becomes a sister or near relation.

So, then, replied Arabella, reddening with vexation, you will persist in affirming the divine Mandane was impudent.

If she made such indiscreet visits as those, she was, said Miss Glanville.

Oh, heavens! cried Arabella, have I lived to hear the most illustrious princess that ever was in the world so shamefully reflected on?

Bless me, madam! said Miss Glanville, what reason have you to defend the character of this princess so much? She will hardly thank you for your pains, I fancy!

Were you acquainted with the character of that most generous princess, said Arabella, you would be convinced that she was sensible of the smallest benefits; but it is not with a view of acquiring her favour, that I defend her against your inhuman aspersions, since it is more than two thousand years since she died; yet common justice obliges me to vindicate a person so illustrious for her birth and virtue; and were you not my cousin, I should express my resentment in another manner, for the injury you do her.

Truly, said Miss Glanville, I am not much obliged to you, madam, for not downright quarrelling with me for one that has been in her grave two thousand years. However, nothing shall make me change my opinion, and I am sure most people will be of my side of the argument.

That moment Mr Glanville sending for permission to wait upon Arabella, she ordered him to be admitted, telling Miss Glanville she would acquaint her brother with the dispute; to which she consented.

II

Which inculcates, by a very good example, that a person ought not to be too hasty in deciding a question he does not perfectly understand

YOU ARE COME VERY OPPORTUNELY, sir, said Arabella, when he entered the room, to be judge of a great controversy between Miss Glanville and myself. I beseech you, therefore, let us have your opinion upon the matter.

Miss Glanville maintains, that it is less criminal in a lady to hear persons talk to her of love, allow them to kiss her hand, and permit them to write to her, than to make a charitable visit to a man who is confined to his bed through the violence of his passion and despair; the intent of this visit being only to prevent the death of an unfortunate lover, and, if necessary, to lay her commands upon him to live.

And this latter is your opinion, is it not, madam? said Mr Glanville.

Certainly, sir, replied Arabella; and in this I am justified by all the heroines of antiquity.

Then you must be in the right, madam, returned Mr Glanville, both because your own judgment tells you so, and also the example of these heroines you mention.

Well, madam, interrupted Miss Glanville, hastily, since my brother has given sentence on your side, I hope you will not delay your visit to Sir George any longer.

How! said Mr Glanville, surprised: is Lady Bella going to visit Sir George? Pray, madam, may I presume to inquire the reason for your doing him this extraordinary favour?

You are not very wise, said Arabella, looking gravely upon Miss Glanville, to discover a thing which may haply create a quarrel between your brother and the unfortunate person you speak of: yet since this indiscretion cannot be recalled, we must endeavour to prevent the consequences of it.

I assure you, madam, interrupted Mr Glanville, extremely impatient to know the meaning of these hints, you have nothing to fear from me: therefore you need not think yourself under the necessity of concealing this affair from me.

You are not, haply, so moderate as you pretend, said Arabella, (who would not have been displeased to have seen him in all the jealous transports of an enraged Orontes); but, whatever ensues, I can no longer keep from your knowledge a truth your sister has begun to discover; but, in telling you what you desire to know, I expect you will suppress all inclinations to revenge, and trust the care of your interest to my generosity.

You are to know, then, that in the person of your friend Sir George, you have a rival, haply the more to be feared, as his passion is no less respectful than violent. I possibly tell you more than I ought, pursued she, blushing, and casting down her eyes, when I confess, that for certain considerations, wherein perhaps you are concerned, I have received the first insinuation of this passion with disdain enough; and I assure myself that you are too generous to desire any revenge upon a miserable rival, of whom death is going to free you.

Then, taking Sir George's letter out of her cabinet, she presented it to Mr Glanville.

Read this, added she; but read it without suffering yourself to be transported with any violent motions of anger: and as in fight I am persuaded you would not oppress a fallen and vanquished foe, so in love I may hope an unfortunate rival will merit your compassion.

Never doubt it, madam, replied Mr Glanville, receiving the letter which Miss Glanville, with a beating heart, earnestly desired to hear read. Her brother, after asking permission of Arabella, prepared to gratify her curiosity; but he no sooner read the first sentence, than, notwithstanding all his endeavours, a smile appeared in his face; and Miss Glanville, less able, and indeed less concerned to restrain her mirth at the uncommon style, burst out a laughing, with so much violence, as obliged her brother to stop, and counterfeit a terrible fit of coughing, in order to avoid giving Arabella the like offence.

The astonishment of this lady, at the surprising and unexpected effect her lover's letter produced on Miss Glanville, kept her in a profound silence, her eyes wandering from the sister to the brother; who, continuing his cough, was not able for some moments to go on with his reading.

Arabella, during this interval, having recovered herself a little, asked Miss Glanville if she found any thing in a lover's despair capable of diverting her so much as she seemed to be with that of the unfortunate Sir George.

My sister, madam, said Mr Glanville, preventing her reply, knows so many of Sir George's infidelities, that she cannot persuade herself he is really in such a dangerous way as he insinuates: therefore you ought not to be surprised, if she is rather disposed to laugh at this epistle, than to be moved with any concern for the writer, who, though he is my rival, I must say, appears to be in a deplorable condition.

Pray, sir, resumed Arabella, a little composed by those words, finish the letter: your sister may possibly find more cause for pity than contempt, in the latter part of it.

Mr Glanville, giving a look to his sister sufficient to make her comprehend that he would have her restrain her mirth for the future, proceeded in his reading; but every line increasing his strong inclination to laugh, when he came to the pathetic wish, that her fair eyes might shed some tears upon his tomb, no longer able to keep his assumed gravity, he threw down the letter in a counterfeited rage.

Curse the stupid fellow! cried he: is he mad, to call the finest black eyes in the universe fair?—Ah! cousin, said he to Arabella, he must be little acquainted with the influence of your eyes, since he can so egregiously mistake their colour.

And it is very plain, replied Arabella, that you are little acquainted with the sublime language in which he writes, since you find fault with an epithet which marks the beauty, not the colour of those eyes he praises; for, in fine, fair is indifferently applied, as well to black and brown eyes, as to light and blue ones, when they are either really lovely in themselves, or by the lover's imagination created so; and therefore, since Sir George's prepossession has made him see charms in my eyes, which, questionless, are not there, by calling them fair he has very happily expressed himself, since therein he has the sanction of those great historians who wrote the histories of lovers he seems to imitate, as well in his actions as style.

I find my rival is very happy in your opinion, madam, said Mr Glanville; and I am apt to believe, I shall have more reason to envy than pity his situation.

If you keep within the bounds I prescribe you, replied Arabella, you shall have no reason to envy his situation; but, considering the condition to which his despair has by this time certainly reduced him, humanity requires we should take some care of him; and to show how great my opinion of your generosity is, I will even entreat you to accompany me in the visit I am going to make him.

Mr Glanville being determined, if possible, to prevent her exposing herself, affected to be extremely moved at this request; and rising from his chair in great seeming agitation, traversed the room for some moments, without speaking a word: then suddenly stopping—

And can you, madam, said he, looking upon Arabella, suppose that I will consent to your visiting my rival; and that I will be mean enough to attend you myself to his house? Do you think that Orontes, you have often reproached me with, would act in such a manner?

I don't know how Orontes would have acted in this case, said Arabella; because it never happened that such a proof of his submission was ever desired of him; but considering that he was of a very fiery and jealous disposition, it is probable he might act as you do.

I always understood, madam, said Glanville, that Orontes was a favourite of yours; but it seems I was mistaken.

You will be very unjust, said Arabella, to draw any unfavourable conclusion from what I have said, to the prejudice of that valiant prince, for whom I confess I have a great esteem; and, truly, whoever reflects upon the great actions he did in the wars between the Amazons and the fierce Naobarzanes king of the Cilicians, must needs conceive a very high idea of his virtue: but if I cannot bring the example of Orontes to influence you in the present case, I can mention those of other persons, no less illustrious for their birth and courage than him. Did not the brave Memnon, when his rival Oxyatres was sick, entreat the beautiful Barsina to favour him with a visit. And the complaisant husband of the divine Parisatis was not contented with barely desiring her to visit Lysimachus, who was dying with despair at their marriage, but would many times bring her himself to the bed-side of this unfortunate lover, and, leaving her there, give him an opportunity of telling her what he suffered for her sake.

I am afraid, madam, said Mr Glanville, I shall never be capable of imitating either the brave Memnon, or the complaisant Lysimachus, in this case; and the humour of Orontes seems to me the most commendable.

Nevertheless, said Arabella, the humour of Orontes cost him an infinite number of pains; and it may happen, you will as near resemble him in his fortune as you do in his disposition: but pray let us end this dispute at present. If you are not generous enough to visit an unfortunate rival, you shall not put a stop to the charity of my intentions; and since Miss Glanville is all of a sudden become so severe, that she will not accompany me in this visit, I shall be contented with the attendance of my women.

Saying this, she rose from her seat, calling Lucy, and ordered her to bid her companions attend.

Mr Glanville seeing her thus determined, was almost mad with vexation.

Upon my soul, madam, said he, seizing her hand, you must not go.

How, sir! said Arabella, sternly.

Not without seeing me die first, resumed he, in a languishing tone.

You must not die, replied Arabella, gravely; nor must you pretend to hinder me from going.

Nay, madam, said Glanville, one of these two things will certainly happen: either you must resolve not to visit Sir George, or else be contented to see me die at your feet.

Was ever any lady in so cruel a dilemma? said Arabella, throwing herself into the chair in a languishing posture: what can I do to prevent the fate of two persons, one of whom I infinitely pity, and the other, obstinate as he is, I cannot hate? Shall I resolve to let the miserable Bellmour die, rather than grant him a favour the most rigid virtue would not refuse him? Or shall I, by opposing the impetuous humour of a lover, to whom I am somewhat obliged, make myself the author of his death? Fatal necessity! which obliges me either to be cruel or unjust; and, with a disposition to neither, makes me, in some degree, guilty of both.

III

In which our heroine is in some little confusion

WHILE ARABELLA WAS UTTERING THIS pathetic complaint, Mr Glanville, with great difficulty, kept himself from smiling; and, by some supplicating looks to his sister, prevented her laughing out: yet she giggled in secret behind her fan; but Arabella was so lost in her melancholy reflections, that she kept her eyes immoveably fixed on the ground for some moments: at last, casting an upbraiding glance at Glanville—

Is it possible, cruel person that you are! said she to him, that you can, without pity, see me suffer so much uneasiness; and knowing the sensibility of my temper, can expose me to the grief of being accessory to the death of an unfortunate man, guilty indeed of a too violent passion, which merits a gentler punishment than that you doom him to?

Do not be uneasy, dear cousin, interrupted Miss Glanville: I dare assure you Sir George won't die.

It is impossible to think that, said Arabella, since he has not so much as received a command from me to live. But tell me truly, pursued she, do you believe it probable, that he will obey me and live?

Indeed, madam, said Miss Glanville, I could swear for him that he will.

Well, replied Arabella, I will content myself with sending him my commands in writing: but it is to be feared they will not have so much efficacy upon his spirit.

Mr Glanville, extremely pleased that she had laid aside her design of visiting Sir George, did not oppose her writing to him, though he was plotting how to prevent the letter reaching his hands: and while she went into her closet to write, he conferred with his sister upon the means he should use; expressing, at the same time, great resentment against Sir George, for endeavouring to supplant him in his cousin's affection.

What then, said Miss Glanville, do you really imagine that Sir George is in love with Lady Bella?

He is either in love with her person or estate, replied Mr Glanville, or perhaps with both: for she is handsome enough to gain a lover of his merit, though she had no fortune; and she has fortune enough to do it, though she had no beauty.

My cousin is well enough, to be sure, said Miss Glanville; but I never could think her a beauty.

If, replied Mr Glanville, a most lovely complexion, regular features, a fine stature, an elegant shape, and an inexpressible grace in all her motions, can form a beauty, Lady Bella may pretend to that character without any dispute.

Though she was all that you say, returned Miss Glanville, I am certain Sir George is not in love with her.

I wish I was certain of that, replied Mr Glanville; for it is very probable you are mistaken.

You may see by this letter, interrupted Miss Glanville, what a jest he makes of her; and if you had heard how he talked to her the other day in the garden, you would have died with laughing; yet my poor cousin thought he was very serious, and was so foolishly pleased.

I assure you, Charlotte, said Mr Glanville, gravely, I shall take it very ill, if you make so free with your cousin's little foibles; and if Sir George presumes to make a jest of her, as you say, I shall teach him better manners.

You are the strangest creature in the world, said Miss Glanville: a minute or two ago, you was wishing to be sure he was not in love with her; and now you are angry, when I assure you he is only in jest.

Arabella, that moment coming out of her closet, broke off their discourse. I have written to Sir George, said she, addressing herself to Mr Glanville; and you are at liberty, if you please, to read my letter, which I propose to send away immediately.

Mr Glanville, taking the letter out of her hand, with a low bow, began to read it to himself; but Arabella, willing his sister should also be acquainted with the contents, obliged him, much against his will, to read it aloud. It was as follows:

Arabella, to Bellmour

Whatever offence your presumptuous declaration may have given me, yet my resentment will be appeased with a less punishment than death: and that grief and submission you have testified in your letter may haply have already procured you pardon for your fault, provided you do not forfeit it by disobedience.

I therefore command you to live, and command you by all that power you have given me over you.

Remember, I require no more of you, than Parisatis did of Lysimachus, in a more cruel and insupportable misfortune. Imitate, then, the obedience and submission of that illustrious prince; and though you should be as unfortunate as he, let your courage also be equal to his; and, like him, be contented with the esteem that is offered you, since it is all that can be bestowed, by

Arabella.

Mr Glanville, finding by this epistle, that Arabella did not design to encourage the addresses of Sir George, would not have been against his receiving it, had he not feared the consequence of his having such a convincing proof of the peculiarity of her temper in his possession: and while he kept the letter in his hand, as if he wanted to consider it a little better, he meditated on the means to prevent its ever being delivered; and had possibly fixed upon some successful contrivance, when a servant coming in, to inform the ladies that Sir George was come to wait on them, put an end to his schemes; and he immediately ran down to receive him, not being willing to increase, by his stay, the astonishment and confusion which appeared in the countenance of Arabella, at hearing a man, whom she had believed and represented to be dying, was come to pay her a visit.

IV

MISS GLANVILLE, NOT HAVING SO much delicacy as her brother, could not help exulting a little upon this occasion.

After the terrible fright you have been in, madam, said she, upon Sir George's account, I wonder you do not rather think it is his ghost than himself that is come to see us.

There is no question but it is himself that is come, said Arabella (who had already reconciled this visit to her first thoughts of him); and it is, haply, to execute his fatal design in my presence, that has brought him here; and, like the unfortunate Agilmond, he means to convince me of his fidelity and love, by falling upon his sword before my eyes.

Bless me, madam, said Miss Glanville, what horrid things come into your head! I vow you terrify me out of my wits, to hear you.

There is no occasion for your fears, interrupted Arabella: since we already suspect his designs, it will be very easy to prevent them. Had the princess of the Sarmrtians known the fatal intentions of her despairing lover, doubtless, she would have used some precautions to hinder him from executing them; for want of which she saw the miserable Agilmond weltering in his blood at her feet; and with reason accused herself of being the cause of so deplorable a spectacle.

The astonishment Miss Glanville was in, to hear her cousin talk in this manner, kept her from giving her any interruption, while she related several other terrible instances of despair.

In the mean time, Sir George, who was impatient to go up to Lady Bella's apartment, having flattered himself into a belief, that his letter was favourably received, and that he should be permitted to hope at least, made a short visit to Sir Charles in his own room, and, accompanied by

Mr Glanville, who was resolved to see in what manner Arabella received him, went to her apartment.

As he had taken care, at his entrance, to accommodate his looks to the character he had assumed of an humble despairing lover, Arabella no sooner saw him, than her countenance changed; and, making a sign to Mr Glanville, who could not comprehend what she meant, to seize upon the guard of his sword, she hastily stept forward to meet him.

I am too well convinced, said she to Sir George, that the intent of your coming hither to-day is to commit some violence against yourself before my eyes: but listen not, I beseech you, to the dictates of your despair. Live, I command you, live; and since you say I have the absolute disposal of your life, do not deprive yourself of it, without the consent of her on whom you profess to have bestowed it.

Sir George, who did not imagine Arabella would communicate his letter to her cousins, and only expected some distant hints from her concerning it, was so confounded at this reception before them, that he was not able to reply. He blushed, and turned pale alternately; and, not daring to look either upon Miss Glanville or her brother, or to meet the eyes of the fair visionary, who with great impatience expected his answer, he hung down his head in a very silly posture; and, by his silence, confirmed Arabella in her opinion.

As he did not want for wit and assurance, during that interval of silence and expectation from all parties, his imagination suggested to him the means of extricating himself out of the ridiculous perplexity he was in; and as it concerned him greatly to avoid any quarrel with the brother and sister, he determined to turn the whole matter into a jest; but, if possible, to manage it so that Arabella should not enter into his meaning.

Raising therefore his eyes, and looking upon Arabella with a melancholy air—

You are not deceived, madam, said he: this criminal with whom you are so justly offended, comes with an intention to die at your feet, and breathe out his miserable life, to expiate those crimes of which you accuse him: but since your severe compassion will oblige me to live, I obey, O most divine, but cruel Arabella! I obey your harsh commands; and, by endeavouring to live, give you a more convincing proof of that respect and submission I shall always have for your will.

I expected no less from your courage and generosity, said Arabella, with a look of great complacency; and, since you so well know how to imitate the great Lysimachus in your obedience, I shall be no less acknowledging than the fair Parisatis; but will have for you an esteem equal to that virtue I have observed in you.

Sir George having received this gracious promise with a most profound bow, turned to Mr Glanville with a kind of chastened smile upon his countenance.

And you, fortunate and deserving knight, said he, happy in the affections of the fairest person in the world! grudge me not this small alleviation of my misfortunes; and envy me not that esteem which alone is able to make me suffer life, while you possess, in the heart of the divine Arabella, a felicity that might be envied by the greatest monarchs in the world.

As diverting as this scene was, Mr Glanville was extremely uneasy; for though Sir George's stratagem took, and he believed he was only indulging the gaiety of his humour by carrying on this farce, yet he could not endure he should divert himself at Arabella's expense. The solemn speech he had made him, did indeed force him to smile; but he soon assumed a graver look, and told Sir George, in a low voice, that when he had finished his visit, he should be glad to take a turn with him in the garden.

Sir George promised to follow him, and Mr Glanville left the room, and went into the gardens, where the baronet, having taken a respectful leave of Arabella, and by a sly glance convinced Miss Glanville he had sacrificed her cousin to her mirth, went to join her brother.

Mr Glanville, as soon as he saw him, walked to meet him with a very reserved air; which Sir George observing, and being resolved to keep up his humour—

What, inhuman but too-happy lover, said he, what am I to understand by that cloud upon your brow? Is it possible that thou canst envy me the small comfort I have received? And, not satisfied with the glorious advantages thou possessest, wilt thou still deny me that esteem which the divine Arabella has been pleased to bestow upon me?

Pray, Sir George, said Mr Glanville, lay aside this pompous style: I am not disposed to be merry at present, and have not all the relish for this kind of wit that you seem to expect. I desired to see you here, that I might tell you, without witnesses, I take it extremely ill you should presume to make my cousin the object of your mirth. Lady Bella, sir, is not the person with whom such liberties ought to be taken: nor will I, in the double character of her lover and relation, suffer it from any one whatever.

Cruel fortune! said Sir George, stepping back a little, and lifting up his eyes, shall I always be exposed to thy persecutions? And must I, without any apparent cause, behold an enemy in the person of my friend; who, though, without murmuring, I resign to him the adorable Arabella, is yet resolved to dispute with me a satisfaction which does not deprive him of any part of that glorious fortune to which he is destined? Since it is so, unjust and cruel friend, pursued he, strike this breast which carries the image of the divine Arabella; but think not that I will offer to defend myself, or lift my sword against a man beloved by her.

This is all very fine, returned Mr Glanville, hardly able to forbear laughing; but it is impossible, with all your gaiety, to hinder me from being serious upon this business.

Then be as serious as thou wilt, dear Charles, interrupted Sir George, provided you will allow me to be gay, and not pretend to infect me with thy unbecoming gravity.

I have but a few words to say to you, then, sir, replied Mr Glanville: either behave with more respect to my cousin, or prepare to give me satisfaction for the insults you offer her.

Oh! I understand you, sir, said Sir George; and because you have taken it into your head to be offended at a trifle of no consequence in the world, I must give you a fair chance to run me through the body! There is something very foolish, faith, in such an extravagant expectation: but since custom has made it necessary that a man must venture his soul and body upon these important occasions, because I will not be out of the fashion you shall command me whenever you think fit; though I shall fight with my school-fellow with a very ill will, I assure you.

There is no necessity for fighting, said Mr Glanville, blushing at the ludicrous light in which the gay baronet had placed his challenge: the concession I have required is very small, and not worth the contesting for on your side. Lady Bella's peculiarity, to which you contribute so much, can afford you at best but an ill-natured diversion, while it gives me a real pain; and sure you must acknowledge you are doing me a very great injury, when you endeavour to confirm a lady, who is to be my wife, in a behaviour that excites your mirth, and makes her a fit object of your ridicule and contempt.

You do Lady Bella a much greater injury than I do, replied Sir George, by supposing she can ever be an object of ridicule and contempt. I think very highly of her understanding; and though the bent of her studies has given her mind a romantic turn, yet the singularity of her manners is far less disagreeable than the lighter follies of most of her sex.

But to be absolutely perfect, interrupted Mr Glanville, I must cure her of that singularity; and therefore I beg you will not persist in assuming a behaviour conformable to her romantic ideas; but rather help me to banish them from her imagination.

Well, replied Sir George, since you no longer threaten, I'll do what I can to content you; but I must quit my heroics by degrees, and sink with decency into my own character, otherwise she will never endure me in her presence.

Arabella and Miss Glanville appearing in the walk broke off the conversation. The baronet and Mr Glanville walked forward to meet them; but Arabella who did not desire company, struck into another walk, whither Mr Glanville following, proposed to join her, when he saw his father, who had been taking a turn there alone, made up to Arabella; and supposing he would take that opportunity to talk to her concerning him, he went back to his sister and Sir George, whose conversation he interrupted, to the great regret of Miss Glanville.

V

In which will be found one of the former mistakes pursued, another cleared up, to the great satisfaction of two persons, among whom the reader, we expect, will make a third

ARABELLA NO SOONER SAW SIR Charles advancing towards her, than, sensible of the consequence of being alone with a person whom she did not doubt would make use of that advantage to talk to her of love, she endeavoured to avoid him, but in vain; for Sir Charles, guessing her intentions, walked hastily up to her; and, taking hold of her hand—

You must not go away, Lady Bella, said he; I have something to say to you.

Arabella, extremely discomposed at this behaviour, struggled to free her hand from her uncle; and giving him a look, on which disdain and fear were visibly painted—

Unhand me, sir, said she, and force me not to forget the respect I owe you as my uncle, by treating you with a severity such uncommon insolence demands.

Sir Charles, letting go her hand in a great surprise at the word insolent, which she had used, asked her if she knew to whom she was speaking.

Questionless, I am speaking to my uncle, replied she; and it is with great regret I see myself obliged to make use of expressions no way conformable to the respect I bear that sacred character.

And pray, madam, said Sir Charles, somewhat softened by this speech, who is it that obliges you to lay aside that respect you seem to acknowledge is due to your uncle?

You do, sir, replied she; and it is with infinite sorrow that I behold you assuming a character unbecoming the brother of my father.

This is pretty plain, indeed, interrupted Sir Charles; but pray, madam, inform me what it is you complain of.

You questionless know much better than I can tell you, replied Arabella, blushing, the offence I accuse you of; nor is it proper for me to mention what it would not become me to suffer.

Zounds! cried Sir Charles, no longer able to suppress his growing anger: this is enough to make a man mad.

Ah! I beseech you, sir, resumed Arabella, suffer not an unfortunate and ill-judged passion to be the bane of all your happiness and virtue. Recall your wandering thoughts: reflect upon the dishonour you will bring upon yourself by persisting in such unjustifiable sentiments.

I do not know how it is possible to avoid it, said Sir Charles; and, notwithstanding all this fine reasoning, there are few people but would fly into greater extremities; but my affection for you makes me—

Hold! hold! I conjure you, sir; interrupted Arabella; force me not to listen to such injurious language: carry that odious affection somewhere else, and do not persecute an unfortunate maid, who has contributed nothing to thy fault, and is only guilty of too much compassion for thy weakness.

Good God! cried Sir Charles, starting back, and looking upon Arabella with astonishment: how I pity my son! What would I not give if he did not love this girl?

Think not, replied Arabella, that the passion your son has for me makes your condition a bit the worse; for I would be such as I am with respect to you, were there no Mr Glanville in the world.

I never thought, niece, said Sir Charles, after a little pause, that any part of my behaviour could give you the offence you complain of, or authorise that hatred and contempt you take the liberty to express for me; but since it is so, I promise you I will quit your house, and leave you to yourself. I have always been solicitous for your welfare; and ungrateful as you are—

Call me not ungrateful, interrupted Arabella again: Heaven is my witness, that had you not forgot I was your niece, I would have always remembered you was my uncle; and not only have regarded you as such, but have looked upon you as another father, under whose direction Providence had placed me, since it had deprived me of my real father, and whose tenderness and care might have in some measure supplied the loss I had of him: but Heaven has decreed it otherwise; and since it is its will that I should be deprived of the comfort and assistance my orphan state requires, I must submit, without murmuring, to my destiny. Go, then, unfortunate and lamented uncle, pursued she, wiping some tears from her fine eyes; go, and endeavour by reason and absence to recover thy repose; and be assured, whenever you can convince me you have triumphed over these sentiments, which now cause both our unhappiness, you shall have no cause to complain of my conduct towards you.

Finishing these words, she left him with so much speed, that it would have been impossible for him to have stopped her, though he had intended it: but indeed he was so lost in wonder and confusion, at a behaviour for which he was not able to assign any other cause than madness, that he remained fixed in the same posture of surprise, in which she had left him; and from which he was first interrupted by the voice of his son, who, seeing Arabella flying towards the house in great seeming emotion, came to know the result of their conversation.

Sir, said Mr Glanville, who had spoken to his father before, but had no answer, will you not inform me what success you have had with my cousin? How did she receive your proposal?

Speak of her no more, said Sir Charles: she is a proud ungrateful girl, and unworthy the affection you have for her.

Mr Glanville, who trembled to hear so unfavourable an answer to his inquiries, was struck dumb with his surprise and grief; when Sir Charles, taking notice of the alteration in his countenance—

I am sorry, said he, to find you have set your heart upon this fantastic girl: if ever she be your wife, which I very much doubt, she will make you very unhappy. But, Charles, pursued he, I would advise you to think no more of her; content yourself with the estate you gain by her refusal of you: with that addition to your own fortune, you may pretend to any lady whatever; and you will find many that are fully as agreeable as your cousin, who will be proud of your addresses.

Indeed, sir, said Mr Glanville, with a sigh, there is no woman upon earth whom I would choose to marry, but Lady Bella. I flattered myself

I had been happy enough to have made some progress in her affection; but it seems I was mistaken: however, I should be glad to know if she gave you any reasons for refusing me.

Reasons! said Sir Charles: there is no making her hear reason, or expecting reason from her. I never knew so strange a woman in my life: she would not allow me to speak what I intended concerning you but interrupted me every moment, with some high-flown stuff or other.

Then I have not lost all hopes of her, cried Mr Glanville, eagerly; for since she did not hear what you had to say, she could not possibly deny you.

But she behaved in a very impertinent manner to me, interrupted Sir Charles; complained of my harsh treatment to her; and said several other things, which, because of her uncommon style, I could not perfectly understand; yet they seemed shocking; and, upon the whole, treated me so rudely, that I am determined to leave her to herself, and trouble my head no more about her.

For God's sake, dear sir, said Mr Glanville, alarmed at this resolution, suspend your anger till I have seen my cousin: there is some mistake, I am persuaded, in all this. I know she has some very odd humours, which you are not so well acquainted with, as I am. I'll go to her, and prevail upon her to explain herself.

You may do so, if you please, replied Sir Charles: but I fear it will be to very little purpose, for I really suspect her head is a little turned. I do not know what to do with her: it is not fit she should have the management of herself; and yet it is impossible to live upon easy terms with her.

Mr Glanville, who did not doubt but Arabella had been guilty of some very ridiculous folly, offered nothing more in her justification; but, having attended his father to his own chamber, went to Arabella's apartment.

He found the pensive fair one in a melancholy posture, her head reclined upon one of her fair hands; and though her eyes were fixed upon a book she held in the other, yet she did not seem to read, but rather to be wholly buried in contemplation.

Mr Glanville having so happily found her alone (for her women were not then in her chamber), seated himself near her, having first asked pardon for the interruption he had given her studies; and Arabella, throwing aside her book, prepared to listen to his discourse; which by the agitation which appeared in his looks, she imagined would he upon some extraordinary subject.

I left my father just now, said he, in a great deal of uneasiness, on account of something you said to him, Lady Bella: he apprehends you are disobliged, and he would willingly know how.

Has your father, then, acquainted you with the subject of our conversation? interrupted Arabella.

I know what would have been the subject of your conversation, replied Mr Glanville, if you had been pleased to listen to what Sir Charles intended to say to you on my behalf.

On your behalf? interrupted Arabella: Ah, poor deceived Glanville! how I pity thy blind sincerity! But it is not for me to undeceive thee: only thus much I may say to you, beware of committing your interests to a person who will be a much better advocate for another than for you.

Mr Glanville, rejoiced to find by these words that her resentment against his father was occasioned by a suspicion so favourable for him, assured her, that Sir Charles wished for nothing more earnestly than that he might be able to merit her esteem; and that it was to dispose her to listen to his addresses, that he wanted to discourse with her this morning.

Mr Glanville being obliged, through his knowledge of his cousin's temper, to speak to her in this distant manner, went on with his assurances of his father's candour in this respect; and Arabella, who would not declare her reasons for doubting it, only replied, that she wished Sir Charles meant all that he had said to him; but that she could not persuade herself to believe him sincere, till his future actions had convinced her he was so.

Mr Glanville, impatient to let his father know how greatly he had been mistaken in the cause of Arabella's behaviour, made his visit shorter than he would otherwise have done, in order to undeceive him.

Is it possible, said Sir Charles, when his son had repeated the conversation he had just had with Arabella, that she should be so foolish as to imagine I had a design to propose any one else to her but you?

What reason have I ever given her, to think I would not be glad to have her for my daughter-in-law? Indeed, she has some odd ways that are very disagreeable; but she is one of the best matches in England for all that. Poor girl! pursued he, she had reason to be angry, if that was the case: and now I remember, she cried, when I told her I would leave the house; yet her spirit was so great, that she told me I might go. Well, I'll go and make it up with her; but who could have imagined she would have been so foolish? Sir Charles, at the repetition of these words, hurried away to Arabella's apartment.

Niece, said he, at his entrance, I am come to ask your pardon, for having led you into a belief, that I meant—

It is enough, sir, interrupted Arabella; I grant you my pardon for what is past; and it does not become me to receive submissions from my uncle, while he remembers he is so. I will dispense with your acknowledgments at present; only to convince me, that this sudden alteration is sincere, avoid, I beseech you, for the future, all occasions of displeasing me.

I protest, cried Sir Charles, that I never intended—

I will not hear you say a word more of your past intentions, interrupted Arabella again; I have forgot them all; and, while you continue to regard me as your niece, I will never remember them to your disadvantage.

Then I may hope—, said Sir Charles.

Oh, heavens! cried Arabella, not suffering him to proceed: do you come to insult me thus, with a mock repentance? And has my easiness in being so ready to forget the injury you would have done me, made you presumptuous to cherish an insolent hope that I will ever change any resolution?

How vexatious is this! replied Sir Charles, fretting to see her continually mistaking him. I swear to you, by all that is sacred, that it is my son for whom I would solicit your consent!

How! said Arabella, astonished, will you then be just at last? And can you resolve to plead for that son, whose interest, but a moment ago, you would have destroyed?

I see, said Sir Charles, it is impossible to convince you.

No, no! interrupted Arabella, hastily; it is not impossible but my own ardent wishes that it may be so, will help to convince me of the truth of what you say: for, in fine, do you think I shall not be as glad as yourself, to find you capable of acting honourably by your son; and to see myself no longer the cause of the most unjustifiable conduct imaginable?

Sir Charles was opening his mouth, to press her in favour of Mr Glanville; whom, notwithstanding her strange behaviour, he was glad to find she loved when Arabella preventing him—

Seek not, I beseech you, said she, to destroy that belief I am willing to give your words, by any more attempts at this time to persuade me; for truly, I shall interpret your solicitude no way in your favour: therefore, if you desire I should be convinced you are sincere, let the silence I require of you be one proof of it.

Sir Charles, who looked excessively out of countenance at such a peremptory command from his niece, was going out of her chamber, in a very ill humour, when the dinner-bell ringing, she gave him her hand with a very gracious air; and permitted him to lead her into the dining-room, where they found Mr Glanville, his sister, and Sir George, who had been detained to dinner by Miss Glanville, expecting their coming.

VI

Containing some account of Thalestris, queen of the Amazons, with other curious anecdotes

LADY BELLA HAVING RECOVERED HER usual cheerfulness, through the satisfaction she felt at her uncle's returning to reason, and the abatement she perceived in Sir George's extreme melancholy, mixed in the conversation with that wit and vivacity which was natural to her, and which so absolutely charmed the whole company, that not one of them remembered any of her former extravagancies.

Mr Glanville gazed on her with a passionate tenderness, Sir George with admiration, and the old baronet with wonder and delight.

But Miss Glanville, who was inwardly vexed at the superiority her cousin's wit gave her over herself, wished for nothing more than an opportunity of interrupting a conversation in which she could have no share; and willing to put them in mind of some of Arabella's strange notions, when she observed them disputing concerning some of the actions of the ancient Romans, she very innocently asked Sir George, whether in former times women went to the wars, and fought like men? For my cousin, added she, talks of one Thaltris, a woman, that was as courageous as any soldier whatever.

Mr Glanville, horribly vexed at a question that was likely to engage Arabella in a discourse very different from that she had been so capable of pleasing in, frowned very intelligibly at his sister; and to prevent any answer being given to her absurd demand, directed some other conversation to Arabella: but she, who saw a favourite subject started, took no notice of what Mr Glanville was saying to her; but directing her looks to Sir George—

Though Miss Glanville, said she, be a little mistaken in the name of that fair queen she has mentioned, yet I am persuaded you know whom she means, and that it is the renowned Thalestris, whose valour staggers her belief; and of whom she wants to be informed.

Aye, aye, Thalestris, said Miss Glanville: it is such a strange name I could not remember it but, pray, was there ever such a person?

Certainly, madam, there was, replied Sir George: she was queen of the Amazons, a warlike nation of women, who possessed great part of Cappadocia, and extended their conquests so far, that they became formidable to all their neighbours.

You find, miss, said Arabella, I did not attempt to impose upon you, when I told you of the admirable valour of that beautiful queen; which indeed was so great, that the united princes, in whose cause she fought, looked upon her assistance to be equal to that of a whole army; and they honoured her accordingly with the most distinguishing marks of their esteem and acknowledgment, and offered her the chief command of their forces.

O shameful! cried Sir Charles: offer a woman the command of an army! Brave fellows, indeed, that would be commanded by a woman! Sure you mistake, niece: there never was such a thing heard of in the world.

What, sir, said Arabella, will you contradict a fact attested by the greatest historians that ever were? You may as well pretend to say, there were never such persons as Oroondates, or Juba, as dispute the existence of the famous Thalestris.

Why, pray, madam, said Sir Charles, who were those?

One of them, replied Arabella, was the great king of Scythia; and the other, prince of the Two Mauritanias.

Odds-heart! interrupted Sir Charles, I believe their kingdoms are in the moon: I never heard of Scythia, or the Two Mauritanias, before.

And yet, sir, replied Arabella, those kingdoms are doubtless as well known as France or England; and there is no question but the descendants of the great Oroondates, and the valiant Juba, sway the sceptres of them to this day.

I must confess, said Sir George, I have a very great admiration for those two renowned princes, and have read their beautiful exploits with infinite pleasure; notwithstanding which, I am more inclined to esteem the great Artaban than either of them.

Though Artaban, replied Arabella, is, without question, a warrior equal to either of them, and haply no person in the world possessed so sublime a courage as his was; yet, it may be, your partiality proceeds from another cause; and you having the honour to resemble him in some little infidelities he was accused of; with less justice than yourself, perhaps, induces you to favour him more than any other.

Arabella blushed when she ended these words: and Sir George replied with a sigh—

I have, indeed, the honour, madam, to resemble the great Artaban, in having dared to raise my thoughts towards a divine person, who, with reason, condemns my adorations.

Hey-day! cried Sir Charles, are you going to speak of divine things, after all the fables you have been talking of? Troth, I love to hear young men enter upon such subjects—but pray, niece, who told you Sir George was an infidel?

Mr Glanville, replied Arabella: and I am inclined to think he spoke truth; for Sir George has never pretended to deny it.

How! interrupted Sir Charles: I am sorry to hear that. I hope you have never, added he, looking at the young baronet, endeavoured to corrupt my son with any of your free-thinking principles. I am for everybody having liberty of conscience; but I cannot endure to hear people of your stamp endeavouring to propagate your mischievous notions; and, because you have no regard for your own future happiness, disturbing other people in the laudable pursuit of theirs.

We will not absolutely condemn Sir George, said Arabella, till we have heard his history from his own mouth, which he promised some time ago to relate when I desired it.

I do not imagine his history is fit to be heard by ladies, said Sir Charles, for your infidels live a strange kind of life.

However that may be, replied Arabella, we must not dispense with Sir George from performing his promise. I dare say there are no ladies here who will think the worse of him for freely confessing his faults.

You may answer for yourself, if you please, madam, said Sir Charles; but I hope my girl there will not say as much.

I dare say my cousin is not so rigid, said Arabella: she has too much the spirit of Julia in her to find fault with a little infidelity.

I am always obliged to you for your comparisons, cousin, said Miss Glanville. I suppose this is greatly to my advantage too.

I assure you, madam, said Sir George, Lady Bella has done you no injury by the comparison she has just now made; for Julia was one of the finest princesses in the world.

Yet she was not free from the suspicion of infidelity, replied Arabella: but though I do not pretend to tax my cousin with that fault, yet it is with a great deal of reason that I say she resembles her in her volatile humour.

I was never thought to be ill-humoured in my life, madam, said Miss Glanville, colouring; and I cannot imagine what reason I have given you for saying I am.

Nay, cousin, said Arabella, I am not condemning your humour; for, to say the truth, there are a great many charms in a volatile disposition; and notwithstanding the admirable beauty of Julia, it is possible she made as many slaves by her light and airy carriage, as she did by her eyes, though they were the fairest in the world, except the divine Cleopatra's.

Cleopatra! cried Sir Charles: why she was a gipsy, was she not?

I never heard her called so, said Arabella gravely; and I am apt to believe you are not at all acquainted with her. But pray, pursued she, let us wave this discourse at present, and prepare to listen to Sir George's relation of his life, which, I dare say, is full of very extraordinary events. However, sir, added she, directing her speech to the young baronet, I am afraid your modesty will induce you to speak with less candour than you ought, of those great actions, which questionless you have performed: therefore we shall hear your history, with greater satisfaction, from the mouth of your faithful squire, who will not have the same reasons that you have for suppressing what is most admirable in the adventures of your life.

Since it is your pleasure, madam, replied Sir George, to hear my adventures, I will recount them as well as I am able myself, to the end that I may have an opportunity of obliging you by doing some violence to my natural modesty, which will not suffer me to relate things the world have been pleased to speak of to my advantage, without some little confusion.

Then, casting down his eyes, he seemed to be recollecting the most material passages in his life. Mr Glanville, though he could have wished he had not indulged Arabella in her ridiculous request, was not able to deny himself the diversion of hearing what kind of history he would invent; and therefore resolved to stay and listen to him.

Miss Glanville was highly delighted with the proposal: but Sir Charles, who could not conceive there could be any thing worth listening to, in a young rake's account of himself, got up with an intention to walk in the garden; when perceiving it rained, he changed his resolution, and, resuming his seat, prepared to listen, as every one else did, to the expected story:

When Sir George, after having paused a quarter of an hour longer, during which all the company observed a profound silence, began his relation in this manner, addressing himself to Arabella.—

END OF THE FIFTH BOOK

BOOK VI

I

Containing the beginning of Sir George's history; in which the ingenious relator has exactly copied the style of romance

THOUGH AT PRESENT, MADAM, YOU behold me in the quality of a private gentleman, in the possession only of a tolerable estate, yet my birth is illustrious enough; my ancestors having formerly won a crown, which, as they won by their valour, so they lost by their misfortune only.

How! interrupted Sir Charles, are you descended from kings? Why, I never heard you say so before: pray, sir, how far are you removed from royal blood? and which of your forefathers was it that wore a crown?

Sir, replied Sir George, it is not much more than eight hundred years since my ancestors, who were Saxons, swayed the sceptre of Kent; and from the first monarch of that mighty kingdom am I lineally descended.

Pray where may that kingdom of Kent lie? said Sir Charles.

Sir, replied Sir George, it is bounded by Sussex on the south-west, Surrey on the west, the English Channel on the south, Dover Straits on the south-east, and the Downs on the east; and it is divided from Middlesex and Essex, on the north, by the Thames.

A mighty kingdom, indeed! said Sir Charles: why, it makes but a very small part of the kingdom of Britain now. Well, if your ancestors were kings of that county, as it is now called, it must be confessed their dominions were very small.

However that may be, said Arabella, it raises Sir George greatly in my esteem, to hear he is descended from kings; for, truly, a royal extraction does infinitely set off noble and valiant actions, and inspires only lofty and generous sentiments: therefore, illustrious prince (for in that light I shall always consider you), be assured, though fortune has despoiled you of your dominions, yet since she cannot deprive you of your courage and virtue, Providence will one day assist your noble endeavours to recover your rights, and place you upon the throne of your ancestors, from whence you have been so inhumanly driven; or, haply, to repair that loss, your valour may procure you other kingdoms, no less considerable than that to which you was born.

For Heaven's sake, niece! said Sir Charles, how come such improbable things into your head? Is it such an easy matter, think you, to conquer kingdoms, that you can flatter a young man, who has neither fleets nor armies, with such strange hopes?

The great Artaban, sir, resumed Arabella, had neither fleets nor armies, and was master only of a single sword; yet he soon saw himself greater than any king, disposing the destinies of monarchs by his will, and deciding the fates of empires by a single word. But pray let this dispute rest where it is, and permit Sir George to continue his relation.

It is not necessary, madam, resumed Sir George, to acquaint you with the misfortunes of my family, or relate the several progressions it made towards the private condition in which it now is; for, besides that reciting the events of so many hundred years may, haply, in some measure, try your patience, I should be glad if you would dispense with me from entering into a detail of accidents that would sensibly afflict me. It shall suffice, therefore, to inform you, that my father, being a peaceable man, fond of retirement and tranquillity, made no attempts to recover the sovereignty from which his ancestors had been unjustly expelled; but quietly beheld the kingdom of Kent in the possession of other masters, while he contented himself with the improvement of that small pittance of ground, which was all that the unhappy Prince Veridomer, my grandfather, was able to bequeath to him.

Hey-day! cried Sir Charles, will you new-christen your grandfather, when he has been in his grave these forty years? I knew honest Sir Edward Bellmour very well, though I was but a youth when he died; but I believe no person in Kent ever gave him the title of Prince Veridomer. Fie! fie! these are idle brags.

Sir George, without taking notice of the old baronet's heat, went on with his narration in this manner:—

Things were in this state, madam, when I was born. I will not trouble you with the relation of what I did in my infancy.

No, pray skip over all that, interrupted Sir Charles; I suppose your infancy was like other people's: what can there be worth hearing in that?

You are deceived, sir, said Arabella: the infancy of illustrious personages has always something very extraordinary in it; and from their childish words and actions there have been often presages drawn of their future greatness and glory.

Not to disoblige Sir Charles, however, said the young prince of Kent, I will not repeat many things which I said and did in the first years of my life, that those about me thought very surprising, and from them prognosticated that very strange accidents would befal me.

I have been a witness of some very unfavourable prognostics of you, said Sir Charles, smiling; for you was the most unlucky bold spark that ever I knew in my life.

It is very certain, pursued Sir George, that the forwardness of my spirit gave great uneasiness to my father; who being, as I said before, inclinable to a peaceable and sedentary life, endeavoured as much as possible to repress that vivacity in my disposition which he feared might involve me in dangerous enterprises. The pains he took in my education, I recompensed by a more than ordinary docility; and before I was thirteen, performed all my exercises with a marvellous grace, and, if I may dare say so, was, at those early years, the admiration and wonder of all that saw me.

Lady Bella had some reason to fear your modesty, I find, said Sir Charles, smiling; for, methinks you really speak too slightly of your excellencies.

However that may be, resumed Sir George, my father saw these early instances of a towering genius in me, with a pleasure, chastened by his fears, that the grandeur of my courage would lead me to attempt something for the recovery of that kingdom, which was my due, and which might haply occasion his losing me.

Possessed with these thoughts, he carefully avoided saying any thing to me concerning the glorious pretences to which my birth gave me a right; and often wished it had been possible for him to conceal from me, that I was the true and lawful heir of the kingdom of Kent; a circumstance he never chose to mention to any person, and would have been glad if it had always remained a secret.

And so it was a secret, interrupted Sir Charles; for, till this day, I never heard of it: and it might still have been a secret if you had pleased; for nobody, I dare say, would suspect such a thing; and very few, I believe, will be inclined to think there is any thing in such an improbable tale.

Notwithstanding all my father's endeavours to the contrary, madam, pursued Sir George, I cherished those towering sentiments the knowledge of my birth inspired me with; and it was not without the utmost impatience that I brooked the private condition to which I found myself reduced.

Cruel fate! would I sometimes cry; was it not enough to deprive me of that kingdom which is my due, and subject me to a mean and inglorious state; but to make that condition infinitely more grievous, must thou give me a soul towering above my abject fortune;—a soul that cannot but disdain the base submission I must pay to those who triumph in the spoils of my ruined house;—a soul which sees nothing above its hopes and expectations;—and, in fine, a soul that excites me daily to attempt things worthy of my birth, and those noble sentiments I inherit from my great forefathers? Ah! pursued I, unhappy Bellmour, what hinders thee from making thyself known and acknowledged for what thou art? What hinders thee from boldly asserting thy just and natural rights, and from defying the usurper who detains them from thee? What hinders thee, I say?

What? interrupted Sir Charles; why the fear of a halter, I suppose: there is nothing more easy than to answer that question.

Such, madam, said Sir George, were the thoughts which continually disturbed my imagination; and, doubtless, they had not failed to push me on to some hazardous enterprise, had not a fatal passion interposed; and, by its sweet but dangerous allurements, stifled for a while that flame which ambition and the love of glory kindled in my soul.

Sir George here pausing, and fixing his eyes with a melancholy air on the ground, as if prest with a tender remembrance—

Mr Glanville asked him, smiling, if the thoughts of poor Dolly disturbed him? Pray, added he, give us the history of your first love, without any mixture of fable; or shall I take the trouble off you? For you know, I am very well acquainted with your affair with the pretty milk-maid, and can tell it very succinctly.

It is true, sir, said Sir George, sighing, I cannot recall the idea of Dorothea into my remembrance without some pain; that fair but unfaithful shepherdess, who first taught me to sigh, and repaid my tenderness with the blackest infidelity; yet I will endeavour to compose myself, and go on with my narration.

Be pleased to know, then, madam, pursued Sir George, that having my thoughts, in this manner, wholly employed with the disasters of my family, I had arrived to my seventeenth year, without being sensible of the power of love; but the moment now arrived, which was to prove fatal to my liberty. Following the chase one day with my father and some other gentlemen, I happened to lag a little behind them; and, being taken up with my ordinary reflections, I lost my way, and wandered a long time without knowing or considering whither I was going. Chance at last conducted me to a pleasant valley, surrounded with trees; and, being tired with riding, I alighted, and, tying my horse to a tree, walked forward with an intention to repose myself a few moments under the shade of one of those trees that had attracted my observation: but while, I was looking for the most convenient place, I spied, at the distance of some few yards from me, a woman lying asleep upon the grass. Curiosity tempted me to go nearer this person; and, advancing softly, that I might not disturb her, I got near enough to have a view of her person; but, ah, heavens! what wonders did my eyes encounter in this view!—The age of this fair sleeper seemed not to exceed sixteen; her shape was formed with the exactest symmetry: one of her hands supported her head; the other, as it lay carelessly stretched at her side, gave me an opportunity of admiring its admirable colour and proportion. The thin covering upon her neck discovered part of its inimitable beauty to my eyes; but her face, her lovely face, fixed all my attention.

Certain it is, madam, that, out of this company, it would be hard to find any thing so perfect as what I now viewed. Her complexion was the purest white imaginable, heightened by the enchanting glow which dyed her fair cheeks with a colour like that of a new-blown rose: her lips, formed with the greatest perfections, and of a deeper red, seemed to receive new beauties from the fragrance of that breath that parted from them. Her auburn hair fell in loose ringlets over her neck; and some straggling curls, that played upon her fair forehead, set off by a charming contrast the whiteness of that skin it partly hid. Her eyes, indeed, were closed; and though I knew not whether their colour and beauty were equal to those other miracles in her face, yet their proportion seemed to be large; and the snowy lids, which covered them, were admirably set off by those long and sable lashes that adorned them.

For some moments I gazed upon this lovely sleeper, wholly lost in wonder and admiration.

Where, whispered I, where has this miracle been concealed, that my eyes were never blessed with the sight of her before? These words, though I uttered them softly, and with the utmost caution, yet by the murmuring noise they made, caused an emotion in the beauteous sleeper, that she started, and presently after opened her eyes: but what words shall I find to express the wonder, the astonishment, and rapture, which the sight of those bright stars inspired me with? The flames which darted from those glorious orbs cast such a dazzling splendour upon a sight too weak to bear a radiance so unusual, that stepping back a few paces, I contemplated at a distance that brightness which began already to kindle a consuming fire in my soul.

Bless me! interrupted Sir Charles, confounded at so pompous a description: who could this be?

The pretty milk-maid, Dolly Acorn, replied Mr Glanville, gravely: did you never see her, sir, when you was at your seat, at ——? She used often to bring cream to my lady.

Aye, aye, replied Sir Charles, I remember her: she was a very pretty girl. And so it was from her eyes that all those splendours and flames

came, that had like to have burnt you up, Sir George? Well, well, I guess
how the story will end: pray let us hear it out.

I have already told you, madam, resumed Sir George, the marvellous
effects the sight of those bright eyes produced upon my spirit. I remained
fixed in a posture of astonishment and delight; and all the faculties of
my soul were so absorbed in the contemplation of the miracles before
me, that I believe, had she still continued before my eyes, I should never
have moved from the place where I then stood; but the fair virgin, who
had spied me at the small distance to which I was retired, turned hastily
about, and flew away with extraordinary swiftness.

When love, now lending me wings, whom admiration had before
made motionless, I pursued her so eagerly, that at last I overtook her;
and, throwing myself upon my knees before her,—

Stay, I conjure you, cried I; and if you be a divinity, as your celestial beauty
makes me believe, do not refuse the adoration I offer you: but if, as I most
ardently wish, you are a mortal, though sure the fairest that ever graced
the earth, stop a moment to look upon a man, whose respects for you as a
mortal fall little short of those adorations he offers you as a goddess.

I can't but think, cried Sir Charles, laughing, how poor Dolly must
be surprised at such a rhodomontade speech!

Oh, sir! replied Mr Glanville, you will find she will make as good a
one.

Will she, by my troth? said Sir Charles: I don't know how to believe it.

This action, pursued Sir George, and the words I uttered, a little
surprised the fair maid, and brought a blush into her lovely cheeks; but
recovering herself, she replied with an admirable grace—

I am no divinity, said she; and therefore your adorations are misplaced:
but if, as you say, my countenance moves you to any respect for me, give
me a proof of it, by not endeavouring to hold any farther discourse with
me, which is not permitted me from one of your sex and appearance.

A very wise answer, indeed! interrupted Sir Charles again. Very few
town-ladies would have disclaimed the title of goddess, if their lovers
had thought proper to bestow it upon them. I am mightily pleased with
the girl for her ingenuity.

The discretion of so young a damsel, resumed Sir George, charmed me no less than her beauty; and I besought her, with the utmost earnestness, to permit me a longer conversation with her.

Fear not, lovely virgin, said I, to listen to the vows of a man, who, till he saw you, never learnt to sigh. My heart, which defended its liberty against the charms of many admirable ladies, yields, without reluctance, to the pleasing violence your beauties lay upon me. Yes, too charming and dangerous stranger, I am no longer my own master; it is in your power to dispose of my destiny: consider, therefore, I beseech you, whether you can consent to see me die; for I swear to you, by the most sacred oaths, unless you promise to have some compassion on me, I will no longer behold the light of day.

You may easily conceive, madam, that, considering this lovely maid in the character of a shepherdess, in which she appeared, I made her a declaration of my passion, without thinking myself obliged to observe those respects, which to a person of equal rank with myself, decorum would not have permitted me to forget.

However, she repelled my boldness with so charming a modesty, that I began to believe she might be a person of illustrious birth, disguised under the mean habit she wore: but, having requested her to inform me who she was, she told me her name was Dorothea; and that she was daughter to a farmer that lived in the neighbouring valley. This knowledge increasing my confidence, I talked to her of my passion, without being the least afraid of offending her.

And therein you was greatly to blame, said Arabella: for, truly, though the fair Dorothea told you she was daughter to a farmer, yet, in all probability, she was of a much higher extraction, if the picture you have drawn of her be true.

The fair Arsinoe, princess of Armenia, was constrained for a while to conceal her true name and quality, and pass for a simple country-woman, under the name of Delia: yet the generous Philadelph, prince of Cilicia, who saw and loved her under that disguise, treated her with all the respect he would have done, had he known she was the daughter of a king. In like manner, Prince Philoxipes, who fell in love with the beautiful Policrete, before he knew she was the daughter of the great Solon, and while he looked upon her as a poor stranger, born of mean parents, nevertheless, his love supplying the want of those advantages of birth and fortune, he wooed her with a passion as full of awe and delicacy as if her extraction had been equal to his own. And, therefore, those admirable qualities the fair Dorothea possessed might also have convinced you she was not what she seemed, but, haply, some great princess in disguise.

To tell you the truth, madam, replied Sir George, notwithstanding the fair Dorothea informed me she was of a mean descent, I could not easily forego the opinion that she was of an illustrious birth; and the histories of those fair princesses you have mentioned coming into my mind, I also thought it very possible, that this divine person might either be the daughter of a great king, or law-giver, like them. But, being wholly engrossed by the violence of my new-born affection, I listened to nothing but what most flattered my hopes; and, addressing my lovely shepherdess with all the freedom of a person who thinks his birth much superior to hers, she listened to my protestations without any seeming reluctance, and condescended to assure me, before we parted, that she did not hate me. So fair a beginning, seemed to promise me the most favourable fortune I could with reason expect. I parted from my fair shepherdess with a thousand vows of fidelity, exacting a promise from her, that she would meet me as often as she conveniently could, and have the goodness to listen to those assurances of inviolable tenderness my passion prompted me to offer her. When she left me, it seemed as if my soul had forsaken my body to go after her: my eyes pursued her steps as long as she was in sight: I envied the ground she prest as she went along, and the breezes that kissed that celestial countenance in their flight.

For some hours I stood in the same posture in which she had left me, contemplating the sudden change I had experienced in my heart, and the beauty of that divine image, which was now engraved in it. Night drawing on, I began to think of going home; and, untying my horse, I returned the way I had come: and at last struck into a road which brought me to the place where I parted from the company; from whence I easily found my way home, so changed both in my looks and carriage, that my father, and all my friends, observed the alteration with some surprise.

II

*In which Sir George, continuing his surprising history, relates a
most stupendous instance of a valour only to be paralleled by that of
the great Oroondates, Caesario, &c., &c., &c.*

FOR SOME MONTHS, CONTINUED SIR George, I prosecuted my addresses
to the admirable Dorothea; and I flattered myself with a hope that I
had made some progress in her heart: but, alas! this deceitful fair one, who
only laughed at the torments she made me endure at the time she vowed
eternal constancy to me, gave her hand to a lover of her father's providing,
and abandoned me, without remorse, to the most cruel despair.

I will not trouble you, madam, with the repetition of those
complaints which this perfidious action drew from me for a long time.
At length, my courage enabling me to overcome the violence of my
grief, I resolved to think of the ungrateful Dorothea no more; and the
sight of another beauty completing my cure, I no longer remembered
the unfaithful shepherdess but with indifference.

Thus, madam, have I faithfully related one of those infidelities
wherewith my enemies slander me; who can support their assertion
with no better proof than that I did not die when Dorothea abandoned
me: but I submit it to your candour, whether an unfaithful mistress
deserved such an instance of affection from a lover she had betrayed?

Why, really, replied Arabella, after a little pause, you had some excuse
to plead for your failure in this point: and though you cannot be called
the most perfect amongst lovers, seeing you neither died nor was in
danger of dying, yet neither ought you to he ranked among those who
are most culpable. But pray proceed in your story: I shall be better able
to form a right judgment of your merit as a lover, when I have heard
all your adventures.

My passion for Dorothea, resumed Sir George, being cured by her
treachery towards me, the love of glory began again to revive in my

soul. I panted after some occasion to signalize my valour, which yet I had met with no opportunity of doing: but hearing that a mighty army was preparing to march upon a secret expedition, I privately quitted my father's seat; and, attended only by my faithful squire, I took the same route the army had taken, and arrived the day before the terrible battle of —— was fought, where, without making myself known, I performed such prodigies of valour as astonished all who beheld me. Without doubt I should have been highly caressed by the commander, who certainly would have given me the honour of a victory my sword alone had procured for him; but having unwittingly engaged myself too far in pursuit of the flying enemy, I found myself alone, encompassed with a party of about five hundred men, who seeing they were pursued only by a single man, faced about, and prepared to kill or take me prisoner.

Pray, sir, interrupted Sir Charles; when did all this happen? And how came it to pass that your friends have been ignorant to this moment of those prodigies of valour you performed at that battle? I never heard you was ever in a battle. Fame has done you great injustice by concealing the part you had in that famous victory.

The great care I took to conceal myself, replied Sir George, was one reason why my friends did not attribute to me the exploits which the knight in black armour, who was no other than myself, performed; and the accident I am going to relate prevented my being discovered, while the memory of those great exploits were yet fresh in the minds of those I had so greatly obliged.

Be pleased to know, therefore, madam, that seeing myself about to be encompassed by this party of the enemy, I disdained to fly; and, though I was alone, resolved to sustain their attack, and sell my life as dear as possible.

Why, if you did so, you was a madman, cried Sir Charles, in a heat: the bravest man that ever lived would not have presumed to fight with so great a number of enemies. What could you expect but to be cut in pieces? Pooh! pooh! don't think any body will credit such a ridiculous tale. I never knew you was so addicted to—

Lying, perhaps, the good knight would have said; but Sir George, who was concerned he was present at his legend, and could not blame him for doubting his veracity, prevented his utterance of a word he would be obliged to take ill, by abruptly going on with his story.

Placing my back therefore against a tree, pursued he, to prevent my being assaulted behind, I presented my shield to the boldest of these assailants; who, having struck an impotent blow upon it, as he was lifting up his arm to renew his attack, I cut it off with one stroke of my sword, and the same instant plunged it to the hilt in the breast of another, and clove the skull of a third, who was making at me, in two parts.

Sir Charles, at this relation, burst into a loud fit of laughter; and being more inclined to divert himself than be offended at the folly and vanity of the young baronet, he permitted him to go on with his surprising story, without giving him any other interruption.

These three executions, madam, pursued Sir George, were the effects only of so many blows, which raised such indignation in my enemies, that they prest forward in great numbers to destroy me; but having, as I before said, posted myself so advantageously, that I could only be assaulted before, not more than three or four could attack me at one time. The desire of lengthening out my life, till happily some succour might come to my relief, so invigorated my arm, and added to my ordinary strength an almost irresistible force, that I dealt death at every blow; and, in less than a quarter of an hour, saw more than fifty of my enemies at my feet, whose bodies served for a bulwark against their fellows' swords.

The commander of this little body, not having generosity enough to be moved with these prodigious effects of valour in my favour, was transported with rage at my resistance; and the sight of so many of his men slain before his face, served only to increase his fury: and that moment, seeing that, with two more blows, I had sent two of his most valiant soldiers to the shades, and that the rest, fearing to come within the length of my sword, had given me a few moments respite—

Ah! cowards! cried he, are you afraid of a single man? And will you suffer him to escape from your vengeance, who has slain so many of your brave comrades before your eyes?

These words inspiring them with a fierceness such as he desired, they advanced towards me with more fury than before. By this time I had received several large wounds, and my blood ran down from many parts of my body; yet was I not sensible of any decay of strength: nor did the settled designs of my enemies to destroy me, daunt me in the least. I still relied upon the assistance I expected Providence would send to my relief, and determined, if possible, to preserve my life till it arrived.

I fought, therefore, with a resolution which astonished my enemies, but did not move them to any regard for my safety: and observing their brutal commander a few paces from me encouraging his men, both with his cries and gestures, indignation against this inhuman wretch so transported me out of my discretion, that I quitted my post, in order to sacrifice him to my revenge.

Seeing me advance furiously towards him, he turned pale with fear, and endeavoured to shelter himself in the midst of his men, who, more valiant than himself, opposed themselves to my rage to favour his retreat; but quickly clearing myself a way with my sword, I pressed towards the barbarous coward, and, ere he could avoid the blow I aimed at him, it struck him senseless at my feet.

My particular revenge thus satisfied, I was sensible of the fault I had committed in quitting my post, by which I exposed myself to be surrounded by the enemy. I endeavoured to regain it, but in vain; I was beset on all sides, and now despaired of any safety; and therefore only sought to die courageously, and make as many of my enemies as I could attend my fall.

Exasperated by the misfortunes of their commander, they pressed upon me with redoubled fury. Faint as I was with the loss of blood, and so fatigued with the past action, and the obstinate fight I had maintained so long with such a considerable number, I could hardly any longer lift up my arm; and, to complete my misfortune, having thrust my sword into the body of one of the forwardest of my enemies, in my endeavouring to regain it, it broke in pieces, and the hilt only remained in my hand.

This accident completed my defeat: deprived of my sword, I was no longer capable of making any defence; several of them pressed upon me at once, and, throwing me down, tied my hands together behind me. Shame and rage at this indignity worked so forcibly upon my spirits; weakened as I then was, that I fell into a swoon. What happened till my recovery I am not able to tell; but at the return of my senses, I found myself laid on a bed in a tolerable chamber, and some persons with me, who kept a profound silence.

III

A love adventure, after the romantic taste

RECOLLECTING IN A FEW MOMENTS all that happened to me, I could not choose but be surprised at finding myself treated with so little severity, considering I was prisoner to persons who had been witnesses of the great quantity of blood I had shed in my own defence. My wounds had been dressed while I continued in my swoon; and the faces of those persons who were about me expressed nothing of unkindness.

After reflecting some time longer on my situation, I called to a young man who sat near my bedside, and entreated him to inform me where I was, and to whom I was a prisoner; but could get no other answer to those questions than a most civil entreaty to compose myself, and not protract the cure of my wounds by talking; which the surgeons had declared would be of a bad consequence, and had therefore ordered me to be as little disturbed as possible.

Notwithstanding this remonstrance, I repeated my request, promising to be entirely governed by them for the future in what regarded my health, provided they would satisfy me in those particulars. But my attendant did not so much as reply to those importunities; but, to prevent the continuance of them, rose from his seat, and retired to the other end of the chamber.

I passed that day, and several others, without being able to learn the truth of my condition. All this time I was diligently waited on by the two persons I had first seen, neither of whom I could prevail upon to inform me of what I desired to know; and judging by this obstinate reserve, and the manner of my treatment, that there was some mystery in the case, I forbore to ask them any more questions, conceiving they had particular orders not to answer them.

The care that was taken to forward my cure, in three weeks entirely restored me to health. I longed impatiently to know what was to be my destiny, and busied myself in conjecturing it in vain; when one morning an elderly lady entered my chamber, at whose appearance my two attendants retired.

After she had saluted me very civilly, and inquired after my health, she seated herself in a chair near my bedside, and spoke to me in this manner—

I make no question, sir, but you are surprised at the manner in which you have been treated, and the care there has been taken to prevent discovering to you the place where you now are; but you will doubtless be more surprised to hear you are in the fortress of ——, and in the house of Prince Marcomire, whose party you fought against alone, and whom you so dangerously wounded before you was taken prisoner by his men.

Is it possible, madam, said I, who from the first moment of her appearance had been in a strange perplexity—is it possible I am in the house of a man whose life I endeavoured so eagerly to destroy'? And is it to him, who oppressed me so basely with numbers, that I am obliged for the succour I have received?

It is not to him, replied the lady, that you are obliged for the favourable treatment you have had; but listen to me patiently, and I will disclose the truth of your adventure.

Prince Marcomire, who was the person that headed that party against which you so valiantly defended yourself, after the loss of the battle, was hastening to throw himself into this place, where his sister, and many ladies of quality, had come for security: your indiscreet pursuit engaged you in the most unequal combat that ever was fought; and—

Nay, sir, interrupted Arabella, though I do not refuse to give you all the praises your gallant defence of yourself against five hundred men deserves: yet I cannot agree with that lady, in saying, it was the most unequal combat that ever was fought: for, do but reflect, I beseech you, upon that which the brave prince of Mauritania sustained against twice that number of men, with no other arms than his sword; and, you having been in battle that day, was, as I conceive, completely armed. The young prince of Egypt, accompanied only by the valiant, but indiscreet,

Cepio his friend, engaged all the king of Armenia's guards, and put them all to flight. The courageous Ariobasanes scorned to turn his back upon a whole army; not to mention the invincible Artaban, whom a thousand armies together could not have made to turn.

Be pleased to observe, madam, said Sir George, that to the end I may faithfully recount my history, I am under the necessity of repeating things which, haply, may seem too advantageous for a man to say of himself: therefore I, indeed, greatly approve of the custom, which, no doubt, this inconveniency introduced, of a squire, who is thoroughly instructed with the secrets of his master's heart, relating his adventures, and giving a proper eulogium of his rare valour, without being in danger of offending the modesty of the renowned knight; who, as you know, madam, upon those occasions, commodiously slips away.

It being, however, this lady's opinion, that no man ever undertook a more hazardous combat, or with greater odds against him, she did not fail to express her admiration of it in very high terms.

The noise of this accident, pursued she, was soon spread over the whole town; and the beautiful Sydimiris, Marcomire's sister, hearing that her brother was wounded, as it was thought, to death, and that the person who killed him was taken prisoner, she flew out to meet her wounded brother, distracted with grief, and vowing to have the severest tortures executed on him who had thus barbarously murdered her brother. Those who bore that unhappy prince, having brought him into the house, his wounds were searched: and the surgeons declared they were very dangerous.

Sydimiris, hearing this, redoubled her complaints and vows of vengeance against you: her brother having then the chief authority in the place, she commanded, in his name, to have you brought hither, and to be most strictly guarded; determined, if her brother died, to sacrifice you to his ghost.

Full of these sanguinary resolutions, she left his chamber, having seen him laid in bed, and his wounds dressed: but, passing along the gallery to her own apartment, she met the persons who were bringing you to the room that was to be your prison. You was not, pursued the lady, yet recovered from your swoon, so that they carried you like one that was dead: they had taken off your helmet to give you air, by which means your face being quite uncovered, pale, languishing, and your eyes closed, as if in death, presented the most moving, and. at the same time, most pleasing object in the world.

Sydimiris, who stopt, and for a moment eagerly gazed upon you, lost all of a sudden the fierceness which before had animated her against you; and, lifting up her eyes to view those men that carried you—

Are you sure, said she to them, that this is the person who wounded my brother?

Yes, madam, replied one of them: this must be he, since there was no other in his company; and he alone sustained the attack of five hundred men; and would probably not have left one of them alive, had not his sword, by breaking, put it into our power to take him prisoner.

Carry him away, said Sydimiris; but let his wounds be dressed, and let him be carefully looked to, that, if my brother dies, he may be punished as he deserves.

Pronouncing these words in a low and faultering voice, she turned her eyes a second time upon you; then, hastily averting her looks, she hurried to her own chamber, and threw herself into a chair, with all the marks of a very great disturbance.

The affection I have for her, being the person who had brought her up, and most favoured with her confidence, made me behold her in this condition with great concern; and, supposing it was her brother that disquieted her, I besought her not to give way to the violence of her grief, but to hope that Heaven would restore him to her prayers.

Alas! my dear Urinoe, said she, I am more culpable than you can imagine; and I grieve less for the condition to which I see Marcomire reduced, than for that moderation wherewith I am constrained, spite of myself, to behold his enemy.

Yes, dear Urinoe, pursued she, blushing, and casting down her eyes, the actions of this unknown appear to me in quite another light since I have seen him: and, instead of looking upon him as the murderer of my brother, I cannot help admiring that rare valour with which he defended himself against so great a number of his enemies; and am even ready to condemn the furious Marcomire for oppressing so brave a man.

As I had never approved of those violent transports of grief and rage which she had expressed upon the first news of her brother's misfortune, and as I looked upon your glorious defence with the utmost admiration, so far from condemning the change of her thoughts, I confirmed her in the favourable opinion she began to entertain of you; and, continuing to make remarks upon all the particulars of the combat, which had come to our knowledge, we found nothing in your behaviour but what increased our admiration.

Sydimiris, therefore, following the dictates of her own generosity, as well as my advice, placed two persons about you, whose fidelity we could rely on, and gave them orders to treat you with all imaginable care and respect, but not to inform you of the place in which you was, or to whom you was prisoner.

In the mean time, Marcomire, whose wounds had been again examined, was declared out of danger by the surgeons: and he having understood the excess of his sister's grief, and the revenge she had vowed against you, gave her thanks for those expressions of her tenderness; and also uttered some threats, which intimated a violent hatred against you, and a design of prosecuting his revenge upon you as soon as he was in a condition to leave his chamber.

Sydimiris, who heard him, could with difficulty dissemble her concern.

Ah! Urinoe, said she to me, when we were alone: it is now that I more than ever repent of that excess of rage which transported me against the brave unknown. I have thereby put him entirely into my brother's power, and shall be haply accessary to that death he is meditating for him, or else a perpetual imprisonment.

This reflection gave her so much pain, that I could not choose but pity her; and considering that the only way to preserve you was for her to dissemble a rage equal to Marcomire's against you, in order to prevent being suspected of any design in your favour, I persuaded her to join with him in everything he said; while, in the mean time, we would endeavour to get you cured of your wounds, that you might at least be in a condition once more to defend yourself with that miraculous valour Heaven has bestowed on you.

Sydimiris, perceiving her brother would soon be in a condition to execute his threats, resolved to hazard everything rather than to expose you to his rage: she therefore communicated to me her design of giving you liberty, and, by presenting a sufficient reward to your guard, induce them to favour your escape.

I undertook to manage this business in her name, and have done it so effectually, that you will this night be at liberty, and may depart the town immediately; in which it will be dangerous to stay any time, for fear of being discovered.

Sydimiris forbade me to let you know the person to whom you would be obliged for your freedom; but I could not endure that you should unjustly involve the sister of Marcomire in that resentment you will questionless always preserve against him: and to keep you from being innocently guilty of ingratitude, I resolved to acquaint you with the nature of those obligations you owe to her.

IV

The adventure continued

AH, MADAM! SAID I, OBSERVING she had finished her discourse, doubt not but I shall most gratefully preserve the remembrance of what the generous Sydimiris has done for me; and shall always be ready to lose that life in her defence, which she has had the superlative goodness to take so much care of. But, madam, pursued I, with an earnest look, do not, I beseech you, refuse me one favour, without which I shall depart with inconceivable sorrow.

Depend upon it, valiant sir, replied she, that if what you will require of me, be in my power, and fit for me to grant, I shall very willingly oblige you.

It is then, resumed I, trembling at the boldness of my request, that you would condescend to entreat the most generous Sydimiris to favour me with an interview, and give me an opportunity of throwing myself at her feet, to thank her for all those favours I have received from her compassion.

I cannot promise you, replied the lady, rising, to prevail upon Sydimiris to grant you an audience; but I assure you, that I will endeavour to dispose her to do you this favour; and it shall not be my fault if you are not satisfied.

Saying this, she went out of my chamber, I having followed her to the door, with protestations that I would never forget her kindness upon this occasion.

I past the rest of that day in an anxious impatience for night, divided between fear and hope, and more taken up with the thoughts of seeing Sydimiris, than with my expected liberty.

Night came at last, and the door of my apartment opening, I saw the lady who had been with me in the morning enter.

I have prevailed upon Sydimiris to see you, said she; and she is willing, at my entreaty, to give that favour to a person who, she with reason thinks, has been inhumanly treated by her brother.

Then giving me her hand, she conducted me along a large gallery, to a stately apartment: and after traversing several rooms, she led me into one where Sydimiris herself was; who, as soon as she perceived me, rose from her seat, and received me with great civility.

In the transport I then was, I know not how I returned the graceful salute the incomparable Sydimiris gave me; for most certain it is, that I was so lost in wonder, at the sight of the many charms I beheld in her person, that I could not unlock my tongue, or remove my eyes from her enchanting face, but remained fixed in a posture which at once expressed my admiration and delight.

To give you a description of that beauty which I then contemplated, I must inform you, madam, that Sydimiris is tall, of a handsome stature, and admirably proportioned: her hair was of the finest black in the world; her complexion marvellously fair: all the lineaments of her visage were perfectly beautiful; and her eyes, which were large and black, sparkled with so quick and piercing a fire, that no heart was able to resist their powerful glances. Moreover, Sydimiris is admirably shaped; her port is high and noble; and her air so free, yet so commanding, that there are few persons in the world with whom she may not dispute the priority of beauty. In fine, madam, Sydimiris appeared with so many advantages to a spirit prepossessed already with the most grateful sense of her favours, that I could not resist the sweet violence wherewith her charms took possession of my heart: I yielded, therefore, without reluctance, to my destiny, and resigned myself, in an instant, to those fetters which the sight of the divine Sydimiris prepared for me. Recovering, therefore, a little from that admiration which had so totally engrossed all my faculties, I threw myself at her feet with an action wholly composed of transport.

Divine Sydimiris! said I, beholding her with eyes in which the letters of my new-born passion might very plainly be read, see at your feet a man devoted to your service by all the ties of gratitude and respect. I come, madam, to declare to you, that from the first moment you gave me liberty, I had devoted that and my life to you; and at your feet I confirm the gift, protesting by all that is most dear and sacred to me, that since I hold my life from the divine Sydimiris, she alone shall have the absolute disposal of it for the future; and should she please again to demand it, either to appease her brother's fury or to sacrifice it to her own security, I will most faithfully perform her will, and shed the last drop of that blood at her command which I would with transport lose in her defence!

A fine high-flown speech, indeed! said Sir Charles, laughing. But I hope you did not intend to keep your word.

Sure, sir, replied Arabella, you do not imagine that Sir George would have failed in executing all he had promised to the beautiful and generous Sydimiris: what could he possibly have said less? And indeed what less could she have expected from a man, whom, at the hazard of her own life and happiness, she had given freedom to?

I accompanied these words, madam, pursued Sir George, with so passionate a look and accent that the fair Sydimiris blushed, and for a moment cast down her eyes with a visible confusion. At last,—

Sir, replied she, I am too well satisfied with what I have done with respect to your safety, to require any proofs of your gratitude that might be dangerous to it; and shall remain extremely well satisfied, if the obligations you think you owe me may induce you to moderate your resentment against my brother, for the cruel treatment you received from him.

Doubt not, madam, interrupted I, eagerly, but I shall, in the person of Marcomire, regard the brother of the divine Sydimiris; and that consideration will be sufficient not only to make me forget all the violences he committed against me, but even to defend his life, if need be, with the hazard of my own.

Excessively generous indeed! said Sir Charles: I never heard any thing like it.

Oh! dear sir, replied Arabella, there are numberless instances of equal and even superior generosity to be met with in the lives of the heroes of antiquity. You will there see a lover, whose mistress has been taken from him either by treachery or force, venture his life in defence of the injurious husband who possesses her; and though all his felicity depends upon his death, yet he will rescue him from it at the expence of the greater part of his blood.

Another, who, after a long and bloody war, has, by taking his enemy prisoner, an opportunity of terminating it honourably; yet, through an heroic principle of generosity, he gives his captive liberty without making any conditions, and has all his work to do over again.

A third, having contracted a violent friendship for the enemies of his country, through the same generous sentiments, draws his sword in their defence, and makes no scruple to fight against an army where the king his father is in person.

I must confess, said Sir Charles, that generosity seems to me very peculiar that will make a man fight for his enemies against his own father.

It is in that peculiarity, sir, said Arabella, that his generosity consists; for certainly there is nothing extraordinary in fighting for one's father and one's country; but when a man has arrived to such a pitch of greatness of soul as to neglect those mean and selfish considerations, and, loving virtue in the persons of his enemies, can prefer their glory before his own particular interest, he is then a perfect hero indeed. Such an one was Oroondates, Artaxerxes, and many others I could name, who all gave eminent proofs of their disinterestedness and greatness of soul upon the like occasions: therefore, not to detract from Sir George's merit, I must still insist, that in the resolutions he had taken to defend his enemy's life at the expence of his own, he did no more than what any man of ordinary generosity ought to do, and what he was particularly obliged to, by what the amiable Sydimiris had done for him.

I was happy, however, madam, continued Sir George, to find that those expressions of my gratitude wrought somewhat upon the heart of the lovely Sydimiris in my favour: her words discovered as much, and her eyes spoke yet more intelligibly; but our conversation was interrupted by the discreet Urinoe, who, fearing the consequence of so long a stay in her chamber, represented to me that it was time to take my leave.

I turned pale at this cruel sound; and, beholding Sydimiris with a languishing look,—

Would to Heaven, madam, said I, that instead of giving me liberty, you would keep me eternally your prisoner! for though a dungeon was to be the place of my confinement, yet, if it was near you, it would seem a palace to me; for indeed I am no longer in a condition to relish that freedom you bestow upon me, since it must remove me farther from you. But I beseech you, madam, to believe that in delivering me from your brother's fetters, you have cast me into your own, and that I am more a prisoner than ever; but a prisoner to so lovely a conqueror, that I do not wish to break my chains, and prefer the sweet and glorious captivity I am in to all the crowns in the world.

You are very bold, said Sydimiris, blushing, to entertain me with such discourse; yet I pardon this offence, in consideration of what you have suffered from my brother, and on condition that you will depart immediately without speaking another word.

Sydimiris spoke this so earnestly, that I durst not disobey her; and kissing the hem of her robe with a passionate air, I left her chamber, conducted by Urinoe, who having brought me to a private door, which carried us into the street, I there found a man waiting for me, whom I knew to be the same that had attended me during my stay in that house.

Urinoe having recommended to him to see me safe out of the town, I took leave of her with the most grateful acknowledgments for her kindness, and followed my conductor, so oppressed with grief at the thoughts of leaving the place where Sydimiris was, that I had hardly strength to walk.

V

An extraordinary instance of generosity in a lover, somewhat resembling that of the great Artaxerxes in Cassandraia

THE FARTHER I WENT, CONTINUED Sir George, the more my regret increased; and finding it would be impossible to live and quit the divine Sydimiris, I all at once took a resolution to remain in the town concealed; and, communicating my design to my guide, I engaged him to assist me in it by a present of a considerable sum, which he could not resist.

Accordingly, he left me in a remote part of the town, and went to find out a convenient lodging for me; which he soon procured, and also a suit of clothes to disguise me, my own being very rich and magnificent.

Having recommended me as a relation of his, who was newly arrived, I was received very civilly by the people with whom he placed me; and finding this young man to he very witty and discreet, and also very capable of serving me, I communicated to him my intentions by staying, which were only to be near the divine Sydimiris, and to have the happiness of sometimes seeing her when she went abroad.

This man, entering into my meaning, assured me he would faithfully keep my secret, and that he would not fail to bring me intelligence of all that passed in the palace of Marcomire.

I could with difficulty keep myself from falling at his feet to express my sense of his kind and generous offers; but I contented myself with presenting him with another sum of money larger than the first, and assured him of my future gratitude.

He then took leave, and left me to my reflections, which were wholly upon the image of the divine Sydimiris, and the happiness of being so near the object I adored.

My confidant came to me the next day, but brought me no other news than that my escape was not yet known to Marcomire. I inquired if he had seen Sydimiris: but he replied he had not, and that Urinoe had only asked if he had conducted me safe out of town; to which he had answered, as we had agreed, that I had got out safe and undiscovered.

A day or two after he brought me news more pleasing: for he told me that Sydimiris had sent for him into her chamber, and asked him several questions concerning me; that she appeared very melancholy, and even blushed whenever she mentioned my name.

This account gave sufficient matter for my thoughts to work upon for several days. I interpreted Sydimiris's blush a thousand different ways: I reflected upon all the different causes to which it might be owing, and busied myself with all those innumerable conjectures, which, as you know, madam, such an incident always gives rise to in a lover's imagination. At length I explained it to my own advantage, and felt thereby a considerable increase of my affection.

A whole week having elapsed without another sight of my confidant, I began to be greatly alarmed; when on the eighth day of this cruel suspense, I saw him appear, but with so many marks of disturbance in his face, that I trembled to hear what he had to acquaint me with.

Oh! sir, said he, as soon as his concern suffered him to speak, Marcomire has discovered your escape; and the means by which it was procured. One of those in whom Urinoe confided, has betrayed it to him, and the beauteous Sydimiris is likely to feel the most terrible effects of his displeasure. He has confined her to her chamber, and vows to sacrifice her life to the honour of his family, which he says she has stained; and he loads that admirable lady with so many reproaches, that it is thought her grief for such undeserved calumnies will occasion her death.

Scarce had he finished these cruel words, when I, who, all the time he had been speaking, beheld him with a dying eye, sunk down at his feet in a swoon, which continued so long that he began to think me quite dead: however, I at last opened my eyes; but it was only to pour forth a river of tears, and to utter complaints which might have moved the most obdurate heart. After having a long time tormented myself in weeping and complaining, I at last took a resolution which offered me some alleviation of my grief, and the faithful Toxares, seeing me a little composed, left me to myself, with a promise to return soon, and acquaint me with what passed farther in the palace of Marcomire.

As soon as he was gone, I rose from my bed and, dressing myself in those clothes I wore when I was taken prisoner, I went to the palace of Marcomire, and, demanding to see him, I was told he was in the apartment of Sydimiris, and at my earnest desire they conducted me thither.

When I entered the room, I beheld that incomparable beauty stretched upon a couch dissolved in tears, and Urinoe upon her knees before her, accompanying with her own those precious drops which fell from the bright eyes of her mistress.

Marcomire, who was walking furiously about the room, exclaiming with the utmost violence against that fair sufferer, did not observe my entrance; so that I had an opportunity of going towards Sydimiris, who lifting up her eyes to look upon me, gave a loud shriek, and, by a look of extreme anguish, let me understand how great her apprehensions were upon my account.

I am come, madam, said I, to perform part of the promise I made you, and, by dying, to prove your innocence; and, freeing you from the reproaches you suffer on my account, I shall have the happiness to convince you that my life is infinitely less dear to me than your tranquillity. Sydimiris, who hearkened to me with great emotion, was going to make some answer, when Marcomire, alarmed by his sister's shriek, came towards us, and, viewing me at first with astonishment, and then with a smile of cruelty and revenge,—Is it possible, said he, that I behold my designed murderer again in my power?

I am in thy power, said I, because I am willing to be so, and come voluntarily to put myself into your hands, to free that excellent lady from the imputation you have laid on her. Know, Marcomire, that it is to myself alone I owed my liberty, which I would still preserve against all the forces thou couldst bring to deprive me of it; and this sword, which left thee life enough to threaten mine, would haply once more put yours in danger, were I not restrained by a powerful consideration, which leaves me not the liberty of even wishing you ill.

Ah, dissembler! said Marcomire, in a rage, think not to impose upon me by thy counterfeit mildness: thou art my prisoner once more, and I shall take care to prevent your escaping a second time.

I am not your prisoner, replied I, while I possess this sword, which has already defended me against greater numbers than you have here to oppose me. But, continued I, throwing down my sword at Sydimiris's feet, I resign my liberty to restore that lady to your good opinion, and to free her from those base aspersions thou hast unjustly loaded her with upon my account.

It matters not, said the brutal brother, taking up my sword, whether thou hast resigned, or I have deprived thee of liberty; but since thou art in my power, thou shalt feel all the effects of my resentment. Take him away, pursued he, to some of his people: put him into the worst dungeon you can find; and let him be guarded carefully, upon pain of death if he again escapes.

With these words several men offered to lead me out of the room, but I repulsed them with disdain; and making a low reverence to Sydimiris, whose countenance expressed the extremes of fear and anguish, I followed my conductors to the prison allotted for me, which, hideous as it was, I contemplated with a secret pleasure, since I had, by that action which had brought me into it, given a testimony of my love for the adorable Sydimiris.

VI

In which it will be seen, that the lady is as generous as her lover

I PASSED SOME DAYS IN THIS confinement, melancholy enough: my ignorance of the destiny of Sydimiris gave me more pain than the sense of my own misfortunes; and one evening, when I was more than usually disquieted, one of my guard entered my prison, and, giving me a letter, retired without speaking a word. I opened this letter with precipitation, and, by the light of a lamp which was allowed me, I read the following words

Sydimiris to the Most Generous Bellmour

It is not enough to tell you, that the method you took to free me from my brother's severity has filled me with the utmost esteem and admiration. So generous an action merits a greater acknowledgment and I will make no scruple to confess, that my heart is most sensibly touched by it. Yes, Bellmour, I have received this glorious testimony of your affection with such a gratitude as you yourself could have wished to inspire me with; and it shall not be long before you will have a convincing proof of the effect it has had upon the spirit of

Sydimiris.

This letter, madam, pursued Sir George, being wholly calculated to make me hope that I was not hated by the divine Sydimiris, and that she meditated something in my favour, I resigned myself up to the most delightful expectations.

What! cried I, transported with the excess of my joy, does the most admirable Sydimiris condescend to assure me that I have touched her heart? And does she promise me that I shall receive some convincing proof of her acknowledgment!

Ah! too happy and too fortunate Bellmour, to what a glorious destiny hast thou been reserved! And how oughtest thou to adore these fetters that have procured thee the esteem of the divine Sydimiris!

Such, madam, were the apprehensions which the billet I had received inspired me with. I continually flattered myself with the most pleasing hopes; and during three weeks longer, in which I heard no more from Sydimiris, my imagination was wholly filled with those sweet thoughts which her letter had made me entertain.

At length, on the evening of a day which I had wholly spent in reading over Sydimiris's letter, and interpreting the sense of it a thousand different ways, but all agreeable to my ardent wishes; I saw the sage Urinoe enter my prison, accompanied by Toxares, whom I had not seen during my last confinement. Wholly transported at the sight of these two friends, and not doubting but they had brought me the most agreeable news, I ran towards them; and throwing myself at Urinoe's feet, I begged her, in an ecstacy of joy, to acquaint me with Sydimiris's commands.

Urinoe, in some confusion at this action, entreated me to rise. It is fit, cried I, in a transport I could not master, that in this posture I should receive the knowledge of that felicity Sydirniris has had the goodness to promise me. Urinoe sighed at these words; and beholding me with a look of compassion and tenderness—

Would to God, said she, that all I have to say were as agreeable as the first news I have to tell you; which is, that you are free, and at liberty to leave the town this moment! Sydimiris, continued she, has bought your freedom, at the expense of her own; and, to deliver you from her brother's chains, she has put on others, haply more cruel than those you have worn. In fine, she has married a man whom she detested, to procure your liberty, her brother having granted it to her upon that condition alone.

Scarce had Urinoe finished these words, when I fell without sense or motion at her feet. Toxares and she, who had foreseen what might happen, having provided themselves with cordials necessary to restore me, brought me to myself with infinite trouble.

Cruel! said I to them, with a tone and look which witnessed the excess of my despair, why have you hindered me from dying, at once to prevent the thousand deaths I shall suffer from my grief? Is this the confirmation of those glorious hopes Sydimiris had permitted me to entertain? Is this that proof of the acknowledgments I was to expect? And is it by throwing herself into the arms of my rival, that she repays those obligations she thinks she owes me?

Ah, inhuman Sydimiris! was it to make my despair more poignant, that thou flatteredst me with such a prospect of happiness? And was it necessary to the grandeur of thy nuptials, that my life should be the sacrifice?

But how unjust am I, cried I, repenting in an instant of those injurious suspicions; how unjust am I, to accuse the divine Sydimiris of inhumanity? Was it not to give me freedom, that she bestowed herself on a man she hates? And has she not made herself miserable for ever, to procure me a fancied happiness?

Ah! if it be so, what a wretch am I! I, who have been the only cause of that misery to which she has doomed herself! Ah, Liberty! pursued I, how I detest thee, since purchased by the misfortune of Sydimiris! And how far more sweet and glorious were those chains which I wore for her sake!

My sighs and tears leaving me no longer the power of speech, I sunk down on my bed, oppressed with a mortal grief.

Urinoe and Toxares drew near to comfort me, and said all that sensible and discreet persons could think of to alleviate my despair.

Though I have heard that Sydimiris is married, replied I, without dying immediately; yet do not imagine that I will suffer this odious life to continue long. If sorrow do not quickly dispatch me I will seek death by other means; for since Sydimiris is lost, I have no more business in the world.

The charitable Urinoe and Toxares endeavoured in vain to divert me from this sad resolution, when Urinoe, finding all their reasonings ineffectual, drew a letter out of her pocket, and presenting it to me, I had orders, said she, not to let this letter be delivered to you till you had left the town; but the despair to which I see you reduced, does, I conceive, dispense with my rigorous observation of those directions. While Urinoe was speaking, I opened this letter, trembling, and found it as follows.

VII

Containing an incident full as probable as any in Scudery's Romances

S YDIMIRIS TO BELLMOUR.

If that proof of my gratitude, which I promise to give you, fall short of your expectations, blame not the defect of my will, but the rigour of my destiny; it was by this only way I could give you liberty: nor is it too dearly bought by the loss of all my happiness, if you receive it as you ought. Had I been allowed to follow my own inclinations, there is no man in the world I would have preferred to yourself. I owe this confession to the remembrance of your affection, of which you gave me so generous an instance; and the use I expect you will make of it, is to console yourself under a misfortune, which is common to us both; though I haply have most reason to complain, since I could not be just to you, without being cruel at the same time, or confer a benefit, without loading you with a misfortune. If the sacrifice I have made of myself for your sake, gives me any claim to the continuance of your love, I command you, by the power it gives me over you, to live, and not to add to the miseries of my condition the grief of being the cause of your death. Remember, I will look upon your disobedience as an act of the most cruel ingratitude; and your compliance with this request shall ever be esteemed as the dearest mark you can give of that passion you have borne to the unfortunate

Sydimiris.

Ah, Sydimiris! cried I, having read this letter, more cruel in your kindness than severity! after having deprived me of yourself; do you forbid me to die, and expose me by so rigorous a command to ills infinitely more hard and painful than death?

Yes, pursued I, after a little pause; yes, Sydimiris, thou shalt be obeyed: we will not die, since thou least commanded us to live; and, notwithstanding the tortures to which thou condemnest us, we will obey this command, and give thee a glorious proof of our present submission, by enduring that life which the loss of thee has rendered truly wretched.

Urinoe and Toxares, somewhat re-assured by the resolution I had taken, exhorted me by all the persuasions friendship could put in their mouths, to persevere in it; and, Urinoe bidding me farewell, I endeavoured to prevail upon her to procure me a sight of Sydimiris once more, or at least to bear a letter from me to her; but she refused both these requests so obstinately, telling me, Sydimiris would neither consent to the one nor the other, that I was obliged to be contented with the promise she made me, to represent my affliction in a true light to her mistress, and to assure her, that nothing but her absolute commands could have hindered me from dying. Then, taking leave of me with much tenderness, she went out of the prison, leaving Toxares with me, who assisted me to dress, and conducted me out of that miserable place, where I had passed so many sad, and also joyful hours. At a gate to which he brought me I found a horse waiting; and having embraced this faithful confidant with many expressions of gratitude, I bestowed a ring of some value upon him to remember me by; and, mounting my horse, with a breaking heart, I took the first road which presented itself to my eyes, and galloped away, without knowing whither I went. I rode the whole night, so totally engrossed by my despair, that I did not perceive my horse was so tired, it could hardly carry me a step farther. At last the poor beast fell down under me, so that I was obliged to dismount; and, looking about me, perceived that I was in a forest, without seeing the least appearance of any habitation.

The wildness and solitude of the place flattered my despair; and while my horse was feeding upon what grass he could find, I wandered about: the morning just breaking, gave me light enough to direct my steps. Chance at last conducted me to a cave, which seemed to have been the residence of some hermit, or unfortunate lover like myself. It was dug at the side of a rock; the entrance to it thick set with bushes, which hid it from view. I descended by a few steps cut rudely enough, and was convinced it had formerly served for a habitation for some religious or melancholy person; for there were seats of turf raised on each side of it, a kind of bed composed of dried leaves and rushes, and a hole made artificially at the top, to admit the light.

While I considered this place attentively, I all at once took up a resolution, inspired by my despair; which was, to continue there, and indulge my melancholy in a retirement so fitted for my purpose.

Giving my horse, therefore, liberty to go where he pleased, and hanging up my arms upon a tree near my cave, I took possession of this solitary mansion, with a gloomy kind of satisfaction, and devoted all my hours to the contemplation of my misfortunes.

I lived in this manner, madam, for ten months, without feeling the least desire to change my habitation; and, during all that time, no mortal approached my solitude, so that I lived perfectly secure and undiscovered.—Sir George pausing here to take breath, the old baronet said what will be found in the following chapter.

VIII

A single combat fought with prodigious valour, and described with amazing accuracy

Give me leave, sir, said Sir Charles, to ask if you ate in all this time?

Alas, sir, replied Sir George, sighs and tears were all my sustenance.

Sir Charles, Mr Glanville, and Miss, laughing at this answer, Arabella seemed greatly confused.

It is not to be imagined, said she, that Sir George, or, to say better, Prince Veridomer, lived ten months without eating any thing to support nature: but such trifling circumstances are always left out in the relations of histories; and truly an audience must be very dull and unapprehensive, that cannot conceive, without being told, that a man must necessarily eat in the space of ten months.

But the food Sir George lived on, replied the baronet, was very unsubstantial, and would not afford him much nourishment.

I suppose, resumed Arabella, he lived much upon such provisions as the forest afforded him; such as wild fruit, herbs, bitter sallads, and the like; which, considering the melancholy that possessed him, would appear a voluptuous repast; and which the unfortunate Orontes, when he was in the same situation, thought infinitely too good for him.

Sir Charles, finding Arabella took no notice of the historian's hyperbole of living upon his sighs and tears, passed it over for fear of offending her; and Sir George, who had been in some anxiety how to bring himself off, when he perceived Arabella was reasonable enough to suppose he must have eat during his abode in the forest, went on with his relation in this manner.—

I lived, as I before observed to you, madam, in this cave for ten months; and truly I was so reconciled to that solitary way of life, and found so much sweetness in it, that I believe I should have remained there till this day, but for the adventure which I am going to recount.

It being my custom to walk out every evening in the forest, returning to my cave, something later than usual, I heard the cries of a woman at some distance, who seemed to be in distress. I stopped to listen from what side those cries proceeded; and, perceiving they seemed to approach nearer to me, I took down my armour from the tree where I had hung it; and hastily arming myself, shaped my course towards the place from whence those complaints seemed to come, resolving to assist that unknown person with all the strength that was left me.

Having gone some paces, I spied through the branches of the trees a man on horseback, with a lady, who struggled to get loose, and at times called aloud for succour.

This sight inflaming me with rage against that impious ravisher, I flew towards him; and when I came within hearing—

Hold, wretch! cried I, and cease to offer violence to that lady, whom thou bearest away by force; or prepare to defend thyself against one who will die before he will suffer thee to prosecute thy unjust designs.

The man, without answering me, clapped spurs to his horse; and it would have been impossible to have overtaken him, had not my own horse, which had never quitted the forest, appeared in my view. I quickly mounted him, and followed the track the ravisher had taken, with such speed, that I came up with him in a moment.

Caitiff! said I, release the lady, and defend thyself. These words, which I accompanied with a thundering blow upon his head-piece, obliged him to set down the lady, who implored Heaven, with the utmost ardour, to grant me the victory; and, recoiling back a few paces, to take a view of me—

I know not, said he, for what reason thou settest thyself to oppose my designs; but I well know that thou shalt clearly repent of thy temerity.

Saying this, he advanced furiously towards me, and aimed so heavy a blow at my head, that, had I not received it on my shield, I might haply have no longer been in a condition to defend the distressed lady: but having, with the greatest dexterity imaginable, avoided this blow, I made at him with so much fierceness, and directed my aims so well, that in a few moments I wounded him in several places; and his arms were all dyed with his blood.

This good success redoubled my vigour; and having, by a lucky stroke of my sword, cut the strings of his head-piece, it fell off; and his head being bare, I was going to let fall a dreadful blow upon it, which doubtless would have shivered it in a thousand pieces, when he cried out for quarter, and, letting fall his sword, by that action assured me my victory was entire.

Live, wretch, cried I, since thou art base enough to value life after being vanquished: but swear upon my sword, that thou wilt never more attempt the liberty of that lady.

While I was speaking, I perceived he was no longer able to sit his horse; but, staggering a moment, he fell off, and lay extended without motion upon the ground. Touched with compassion at this sight, I alighted, and, supposing him to be in a swoon, was preparing to give him some assistance; but, upon my nearer approach, I found he was quite dead.

Leaving therefore this mournful object, I turned about, with an intention to go and offer the distressed lady my farther help; but I perceived her already at my feet.—Valiant knight, said she, with a tone of voice so bewitching, that all my faculties were suspended, as by enchantment, suffer me, on my knees, to thank you for the deliverance you have procured me from that base man; since to your admirable valour I owe not only the preservation of my life, but, what is infinitely dearer to me, my honour.

The astonishment wherewith I beheld the miraculous beauty that appeared before me, kept me a moment in such an attentive gaze, that I forgot she was at my feet: recollecting myself, however, with some confusion at my neglect—

Oh, rise, madam! cried I, helping her up with infinite respect, and debase not such perfection to a posture in which all the monarchs of the earth might glory to appear before it.

That you may the better conceive the alteration which the sight of this fair unknown produced in my soul, I will endeavour to give you a description of her beauty, which was altogether miraculous.

IX

In which the reader will find a description of a beauty, in a style truly sublime

THE NEW-FALLEN SNOW, PURSUED SIR George, was tanned, in comparison of the refined purity of that white which made up the ground of her complexion; and though fear had a little gathered the carnations of her cheeks, yet her joy at being delivered seemed to plant them there with such fresh advantages, that any eye might shrink at the brightness of that mingled lustre. Her mouth, as well for shape as colour, might shame the imitation of the best pencils, and the liveliest tints; and though, through some petty intervals of joy, it wanted the smiles which grief and terror sequestered, yet she never opened it, but like the east, at the birth of a beautiful day, and then discovered treasures, whose excelling whiteness made the price inestimable. All the features of her face had so near a kindred to proportion and symmetry, that the several masters of Apelles's art might have called it his glory to have copied beauties from her, as the best of models: the circumference of her visage sheaved the extremes of an imperfect circle, and almost formed it to a perfect oval; and this abridgement of marvels was tapered by a pair of the brightest stars that ever were lighted up by the hand of Nature. As their colour was the same with the heavens, there was a spherical harmony in their motion, and that mingled with a vivacity so penetrating, as neither the firmest eye, nor the strongest soul, could arm themselves with a resistance of proof against those pointed glories. Her head was crowned with a prodigious quantity of fair long hair, which colour as fitly suited the beauty of her eyes, as imagination could make it. To these marvels of face were joined the rest of her neck, hands, and shape; and there seemed a contest between the form and whiteness of the two former, which had the largest commission from Nature to work wonders.

In fine, her beauty was miraculous, and could not fail of producing a sudden effect upon a heart like mine.

Having passed in an instant from the extremest admiration to something yet more tender, I reiterated my offers of service to the fair unknown; who told me she feared her father had occasion for some assistance, her ravisher having left his men to engage him, and keep off his pursuit, while he rode off with his prize. Hereupon I begged her to direct me to the place where she left her father, assuring her I would gladly venture my life a second time to preserve his; and she desiring to go with me, I placed her before me on my horse, and had the exquisite pleasure of supporting with my arms the fairest and most admirable creature in the world.

In less than half an hour, which had appeared to me but a moment, we got to the place where she had been torn from her father; whom we beheld, with three of his servants, maintaining a fight against twice as many of their enemies.

Having gently set down the beauteous unknown upon the grass, I flew to the relief of her father; and, throwing myself furiously among his assailants, dispatched two of them with as many blows: the others seeing so unexpected an assistance, gave back a little; and I took advantage of their consternation, to redouble my blows, and brought two more of them at my feet.

There remained now but four to overcome; and my arrival having given new vigour to those whose part I had taken, they seconded me so well that we soon had nothing more left to do; for the rest, seeing their comrades slain, sought their safety in flight. We were too generous to pursue them, the blood of such wretches being unworthy to be shed by our swords.

The fair unknown, seeing us conquerors, flew to embrace her father; who, holding her pressed between his arms, turned his eyes upon me; then quitting her, came towards me, and, in the most obliging terms imaginable, returned me thanks for the assistance I had brought him. And being informed by his daughter, of what I had done for her preservation, this old gentleman renewed his acknowledgments, calling me the preserver of his life, the valiant defender of his daughter's honour, his tutelary angel, and the guardian of his house.

In fine, he loaded me with so many thanks and praises, that I could not choose but be in some confusion; and to put an end to them, I begged he would inform me by what means he came into that misfortune.

He told me, that, residing in a castle at the extremity of this forest, the charms of his daughter had captivated a neighbouring lord, whose character and person being disagreeable both to her and himself, he had absolutely refused to give her to him: thereupon he had set upon them as they were going to visit a relation at some distance, and, dragging Philonice out of the coach, put her before him on his horse, and carried her away, leaving eight of his men to engage him and his servants; who, being but four in number, must inevitably have perished, had I not cone to his relief, and, by my miraculous valour, vanquished all his enemies.

Saying this, he desired me to go home with him to the castle; and having led his daughter to the coach, insisted upon my placing myself next her; and, getting in himself, ordered them to return home.

This accident having altered his design of making the visit which had been the occasion of this journey,—

The baron, for that I found was his title, entertained me all the way with repeated expressions of acknowledgments and tenderness; and the incomparable Philonice condescended also to assure me of her gratitude for the service I had done her.

At our arrival at the castle, I perceived it was very large and magnificent. The baron conducted me to one of the best apartments, and would stay in the room till my armour was taken off; that he might be assured I had received no hurts. Having rendered him the like civility in his own chamber, and satisfied myself he was not wounded, we returned to the beautiful Philonice; and this second sight having finished my defeat, I remained so absolutely her slave, that neither Dorothea nor Sydimiris were more passionately beloved.

At the earnest entreaty of the baron, I staid some weeks in the castle; during which, the daily sight of Philonice so augmented my flames, that I was no longer in a condition to conceal them. But, fearing to displease that divine beauty by a confession of my passion, I languished in secret; and the constraint I laid upon myself gave me such torments, that I fell into a profound melancholy, and looked so pale and dejected that the baron was sensible of the alteration, and conjured me, in the most pressing terms, to acquaint him with the cause of my uneasiness: but though I continued obstinately silent with my tongue, yet my eyes spoke intelligibly enough; and the blushes which appeared in the fair cheeks of Philonice, whenever she spoke to me on the subject of my grief, convinced me she was not ignorant of my passion.

At length the agitation of my mind throwing me into a fever, the baron, who was firmly persuaded that my illness proceeded from some concealed vexation, pressed me continually to declare myself; and, finding all his entreaties ineffectual, he commanded his daughter to endeavour to find out the cause of that grief which had put me into such a condition.

For that purpose, therefore, having brought the fair Philonice into my chamber, he staid a few minutes; and leaving the room under pretence of business, Philonice remained alone by my bed-side, her women, out of respect, staying at the other end of the chamber.

This divine person, seeing herself alone with me, and remembering her father's command, blushed, and cast down her eyes in such apparent confusion, that I could not help observing it: and interpreting it to the displeasure she took in being so near me—

Whatever joy I take in the honour your visit does me, madam, said I, in a weak voice; yet, since nothing is so dear to me as your satisfaction, I would rather dispense with this mark of your goodness to an unfortunate wretch, than see you in the least constraint.

And why, replied she, with a tone full of sweetness, do you suppose that I am here by constraint, when it would be more just to believe, that in visiting the valiant defender of my honour, and the life of my father, I only follow my own inclinations?

Ah, madam! said I, transported with joy at so favourable a speech, the little service I had the happiness to do you, does not merit so infinite a favour; and though I had lost the best part of my blood in your defence, I should have been well rewarded with your safety.

Since you do not repent of what you have done, replied she, I am willing to be obliged to you for another favour; and ask it with the greater hope of obtaining it, as I must acquaint you, it is by my father's command I take that liberty, who is much interested in my success.

There is no occasion, madam, returned I, to make use of any interest but your own, to engage me to obey you, since that is, and ever will be, all-powerful with me. Speak then, madam, and let me know what it is you desire of me, that I may, once in my life, have the glory of obeying you.

It is, said she, blushing still more than before, that you will acquaint us with the cause of that melancholy, which has, as we imagine, occasioned your present illness.

At these words I trembled, turned pale; and, not daring to discover the true cause of my affliction, I remained in a profound silence.

I see, said the beautiful Philonice, that you have no inclination to obey me; and since my request has, as I perceive, given you some disturbance, I will prevail upon my father to press you no farther upon this subject.

No, madam, said I, eagerly: the baron shall be satisfied, and you shall be obeyed; though after the knowledge of my crime, you doom me to that death I so justly merit.

Yes, madam, this unfortunate man, who has had the glory to acquire your esteem, by the little service he did you, has cancelled the merit of that service by daring to adore you.

I love you, divine Philonice; and not being able either to repent, or cease to be guilty of loving you, I am resolved to die, and spare you the trouble of pronouncing my sentence. I beseech you therefore to believe, that I would have died in silence, but for your command to declare myself; and you should never have known the excess of my love and despair, had not my obedience to your will obliged me to confess it.

I finished these words with so much fear and confusion, that I durst not lift my eyes up to the fair face of Philonice, to observe how she received this discourse. I waited therefore, trembling, for her answer; but finding that in several minutes she spoke not a word, I ventured at last to cast a languishing glance upon the visage I adored, and saw so many marks of disorder upon it, that I was almost dead with the apprehensions of having offended her beyond even the hope of procuring her pardon by my death.

X

Wherein Sir George concludes his history; which produces an unexpected effect

THE SILENCE OF PHILONICE, CONTINUED Sir George, pierced me to the heart: and when I saw her rise from her seat, and prepare to go away without speaking, grief took such possession of my spirits, that, uttering a cry, I fell into a swoon, which, as I afterwards was informed, greatly alarmed the beautiful Philonice; who, resuming her seat, had the goodness to assist her women in bringing me to myself; and, when I opened my eyes, I had the satisfaction to behold her still by me, and all the signs of compassion in her face.

This sight a little re-assuring me, I ask your pardon, madam, said I, for the condition in which I have appeared before you, and also for that I am not yet dead, as is doubtless your wish. But I will make haste, pursued I, sighing, to fulfil your desires; and you shall soon be freed from the sight of a miserable wretch, who to his last moment will not cease to adore you.

It is not your death that I desire, said the fair Philonice; and after having preserved both my father and me from death, it is not reasonable that we should suffer you to die if we can help it.

Live, therefore, Bellmour, pursued she, blushing; and live if possible, without continuing in that weakness I cannot choose but condemn: yet whatever are your thoughts for the future, remember that your death will be a fault I cannot resolve to pardon.

Speaking these words without giving me time to answer, she left my chamber; and I found something so sweet and favourable in them, that I resolved to obey her, and forward my cure as much as I was able. However, the agitation of spirits increased my fever so much, that my life was despaired of.

The baron hardly ever left my bed-side. Philonice came every day to see me, and seemed extremely moved at the danger I was in. One day, when I was worse than usual, she came close to the bed-side, and, opening the curtain—

What, Bellmour! said she, do you pay so little obedience to my commands that you resolve to die? Heaven is my witness, madam, said I, faintly, that nothing is so dear and sacred to me as your commands; and since, out of your superlative goodness, you are pleased to have some care for my life, I would preserve it to obey you, were it in my power; but, alas! madam, I strive in vain to repel the violence of my distemper.

In a few days more, I was reduced to the last extremity. It was then that the fair Philonice discovered that she did not hate me; for she made no scruple to weep before me; and those tears she so liberally shed had so powerful an effect upon my mind, that the contentment I felt communicated itself to my body, and gave such a turn to my distemper, that my recovery was not only hoped but expected. The baron expressed his satisfaction at this alteration, by the most affectionate expressions; and though the fair Philonice said very little, yet I perceived, by the joy that appeared in her fair eyes, that she was not less interested in my recovery than her father.

The physicians having declared me out of danger, the baron, who had taken his resolution long before, came one day into my chamber, and ordering those who attended me to leave us alone—Prince, said he, for in recounting my history to him I had disclosed my true quality, I am not ignorant of that affection you bear my daughter, and am sensible it has occasioned the extremity to which we have seen you reduced. Had you been pleased to acquaint me with your sentiments, you would have avoided those displeasures you have suffered; for though your birth were not so illustrious as it is, yet, preferring virtue to all other advantages, I should have esteemed my daughter honoured by your love, and have freely bestowed her on you: but since to those rare qualities wherewith Heaven has so liberally endowed you, you add also that of a birth so noble, doubt not but I shall think myself highly favoured by your alliance. If therefore, your thoughts of my daughter be not changed, and you esteem her worthy to be your bride, I here solemnly promise you to bestow her upon you as soon as you are perfectly recovered.

I leave you to guess, madam, the joy which I felt at this discourse. It was so great, that it would not permit me to thank him, as I should have done, for the inestimable blessing he bestowed on me. I saw Philonice a few minutes after; and, being commanded by her father to give me her hand, she did so without any marks of reluctance: and having respectfully kissed it, I vowed to be her slave for ever.

Who would have imagined, continued Sir George, with a profound sigh, that fortune, while she thus seemed to flatter me, was preparing to make me suffer the severest torments? I began now to leave my bed, and was able to walk about my chamber. The baron was making great preparations for our nuptials; when one night I was alarmed with the cries of Philonice's women, and a few moments after the baron came into my chamber with a distracted air. O son! cried he, for so he always called me, now Philonice is lost both to you and me. She is carried off by force, and I am preparing to follow and rescue her, if possible; but I fear my endeavours will be fruitless, since I know not which way her ravishers have taken.

Oh, sir! cried I, transported both with grief and rage, you shall not go alone: her rescue belongs to me; and I will effect it, or perish in the attempt!

The baron having earnestly conjured me not to expose myself to the danger of a relapse by so imprudent a resolution, was obliged to quit me, word being brought him that his horse was ready; and as soon as he was gone out of the room, in spite of all that could be said to prevent me, by my attendants, I made them put on my armour; and mounting a horse I had caused to be made ready, sallied furiously out of the castle, breathing out vows of vengeance against the wretch who had robbed me of Philonice.—I rode the whole night without stopping. Day appeared, when I found myself near a small village. I entered it, and made strict inquiry after the ravisher of Philonice, describing that fair creature, and offering vast rewards to any who could bring me the least intelligence of her: but all was in vain; I could make no discovery.

After travelling several days to no purpose, I returned to the castle, in order to know if the baron had been more successful in his pursuit than myself; but I found him oppressed with grief: he had heard no tidings of his daughter, and had suffered no small apprehensions upon my account. Having assured him I found myself very able to travel, I took an affectionate leave of him, promising him never to give over my search, till I had found the divine Philonice. But Heaven has not permitted me that happiness; and though I have spent several years in search for her, I have never been able to discover where she is. Time has not cured me of my grief for her loss; and, though by an effect of my destiny, another object possesses my soul, yet I do not cease to deplore her misfortune, and to offer up vows for her happiness.

And is this all you have to say? said Arabella, whom the latter part of his history had extremely surprised; or are we to expect a continuance of your adventures?—I have faithfully related all my adventures that are worth your hearing, madam, returned Sir George: and I flatter myself, you will do me the justice to own, that I have been rather unfortunate than faithless; and that Mr Glanville had little reason to tax me with inconstancy.

In my opinion, resumed Arabella, Mr Glanville spoke too favourably of you, when he called you only inconstant; and if he had added the epithet of ungrateful and unjust, he would have marked your character better. For, in fine, sir, pursued she, you will never persuade any reasonable person, that your being able to lose the remembrance of the fair and generous Sydimiris, in your new passion for Philonice, was not an excess of levity; but your suffering so tamely the loss of this last beauty, and allowing her to remain in the hands of her ravisher, while you permit another affection to take possession of your soul, is such an outrage to all truth and constancy, that you deserve to be ranked among the falsest of mankind.

Alas! madam, replied Sir George (who had not foreseen the inference Arabella would draw from this last adventure), what would you have an unfortunate man, whose hopes have been so often and so cruelly disappointed, do? I have bewailed the loss of Philonice with a deluge of tears; I have taken infinite pains to find her, but to no purpose; and when Heaven, compassionating my sufferings, presented to my eyes an object to whom the whole world ought to pay adoration, how could I resist that powerful impulse, which forced me to love what appeared so worthy of my affection?

Call not, interrupted Arabella, that an irresistible impulse, which was only the effect of thy own changing humour. The same excuse might be pleaded for all the faults we see committed in the world; and men would no longer be answerable for their own crimes. Had you imitated the illustrious heroes of antiquity, as well in the constancy of their affections, as, it must be confessed, you have done in their admirable valour, you would now be either sighing in your cave for the loss of the generous Sydimiris, or wandering through the world in search of the beautiful Philonice. Had you persevered in your affection, and continued your pursuit of that fair one, you would, perhaps, ere this, have found her sleeping under the shade of a tree in some lone forest, as Philodaspes did his admirable Delia, or disguised in a slave's habit, as Ariobarsanes saw his divine Olympia; or bound haply in a chariot, and have had the glory of freeing her, as Ambriomer did the beauteous Agione; or in a ship in the hands of pirates, like the incomporable Eliza; or—

Enough, dear niece, interrupted Sir Charles; you have quoted examples sufficient, if this inconstant man would have the grace to follow them.

True, sir, replied Arabella; and I would recommend to his consideration the conduct of those illustrious persons I have named, to the end that, pursuing their steps, he may arrive at their glory and happiness; that is, the reputation of being perfectly constant, and the possession of his mistress. And be assured, sir, pursued Arabella, looking at Sir George, that Heaven will never restore you the crown of your ancestors, and place you upon the throne to which you pretend, while you make yourself unworthy of its protection, by so shameful an inconstancy.—I perhaps speak with too much freedom to a great prince; who, though fortune has despoiled him of his dominions, is entitled to a certain degree of respect: but, I conceive, it belongs to me, in a particular manner, to resent the baseness of that crime to which you are pleased to make me the excuse, and looking upon myself as dishonoured by those often prostituted vows you have offered me, I am to tell you, that I am highly disobliged; and forbid you to appear in my presence again, till you have resumed those thoughts which are worthy your noble extraction; and are capable of treating me with that respect which is my due. Saying this, she rose from her seat, and walked very majestically out of the room, leaving Sir George overwhelmed with shame and vexation at having conducted the latter part of his narration so ill, and drawn upon himself a sentence which deprived him of all his hopes.

XI

Containing only a few inferences, drawn from the foregoing chapters

Mr Glanville, excessively delighted at this event, could not help laughing at the unfortunate baronet; who seemed, by his silence and down-cast looks, to expect it.

Who would have imagined, said he, that so renowned a hero would have tarnished the glory of his laurels, as my cousin says, by so base an ingratitude? Indeed, prince, pursued he, laughing, you must resolve to recover your reputation, either by retiring again to your cave, and living upon bitter herbs, for the generous Sydimiris; or else wander through the world in search of the divine Philonice.

Don't triumph, dear Charles, replied Sir George, laughing in his turn. Have a little compassion upon me, and confess, that nothing could be more unfortunate than that damn'd slip I made at the latter end of my history: but for that, my reputation for courage and constancy had been as high as the great Oroondates or Juba.

Since you have so fertile an invention, said Sir Charles, you may easily repair this mistake. Odsheart! it is pity you are not poor enough to be an author; you would occupy a garret in Grub-street, with great fame to yourself and diversion to the public.

Oh! sir, cried Sir George, I have stock enough by me to set up for an author to-morrow, if I please: I have no less than five tragedies, some quite, others almost finished; three or four essays on virtue, happiness, &c.; three thousand lines of an epic poem; half a dozen epitaphs; a few acrostics; and a long string of puns, that would serve to embellish a daily paper, if I was disposed to write one.

Nay, then, interrupted Mr Glanville, you are qualified for a critic at the Bedford Coffee-house; where, with the rest of your brothers, demi-wits, you may sit in judgment upon the productions of a Young, a Richardson, or a Johnson; rail with premeditated malice at the Rambler; and, for the want of faults, turn even its inimitable beauties into ridicule. The language, because it reaches to perfection, may be called stiff, laboured, and pedantic; the criticisms, when they let in more light than your weak judgment can bear, superficial and ostentatious glitter: and because those papers contain the finest system of ethics yet extant, damn the queer fellow, for over propping virtue;—an excellent new phrase! which those who can find no meaning in, may accommodate with one of their own. Then give shrewd hints, that some persons, though they do not publish their performances, may have more merit than those that do.

Upon my soul, Charles, said Sir George, thou art such an ill-natured fellow, that I am afraid thou wilt be sneering at me when I am gone; and wilt endeavour to persuade Lady Bella, that not a syllable of my story is true. Speak, pursued he, wilt thou have the cruelty to deprive me of my lawful claim to the great kingdom of Kent, and rob me of the glory of fighting singly against five hundred men?

I do not know, said Sir Charles, whether my niece be really imposed upon, by the gravity with which you told your surprising history; but I protest I thought you were in earnest at first, and that you meant to make us believe it all to be fact.

You are so fitly punished, said Mr Glanville, for that ill-judged adventure you related last, by the bad opinion Lady Bella entertains of you, that I need not add to your misfortune: and, therefore, you shall be Prince Veridomer, if you please, since, under that character, you are obliged not to pretend to any lady but the incomparable Philonice.

Sir George, who understood his meaning, went home to think of some means by which he might draw himself out of the embarrassment he was in; and Mr Glanville, as he had promised, did not endeavour to undeceive Lady Bella with regard to the history he had feigned, being very well satisfied with his having put it out of his power to make his addresses to her, since she now looked upon him as the lover of Philonice.

As for Sir Charles, he did not penetrate into the meaning of Sir George's story; and only imagined, that, by relating such a heap of adventures, he had a design to entertain the company, and give a proof of the facility of his invention; and Miss Glanville, who supposed he had been ridiculing her cousin's strange notions, was better pleased with him than ever.

Arabella, however, was less satisfied than any of them. She could not endure to see so brave a knight, who drew his birth from a race of kings, tarnish the glory of his gallant actions by so base a perfidy.

Alas! said she to herself, how much reason has the beautiful Philonice to accuse me for all the anguish she suffers! since I am the cause that the ungrateful prince, on whom she bestows her affections, suffers her to remain quietly in the hands of her ravisher, without endeavouring to rescue her. But, oh! too lovely and unfortunate fair one, said she, as if she had been present, and listening to her, distinguish, I beseech you, between those faults which the will and those which necessity makes us commit. I am the cause, it is true, of thy lover's infidelity; but I am the innocent cause, and would repair the evils my fatal beauty gives rise to, by any sacrifice in my power to make.

While Arabella, by her romantic generosity, bewailed the imaginary afflictions of the full as imaginary Philonice, Mr Glanville, who thought the solitudes he lived in confirmed her in her absurd and ridiculous notions, desired his father to press her to go to London.

Sir Charles complied with his request, and earnestly entreated her to leave the castle, and spend a few months in town. Her year of mourning being now expired, she consented to go: but Sir Charles, who did not think his son's health absolutely confirmed, proposed to spend a few weeks at Bath; which was readily complied with by Arabella.

END OF THE SIXTH BOOK

BOOK VII

I

For the shortness of which the length of the next shall make some amends

Sɪʀ Gᴇᴏʀɢᴇ, ᴛᴏ ɢʀᴀᴛɪFʏ Aʀᴀʙᴇʟʟᴀ's humour, had not presumed to come to the castle for several days; but hearing that they were preparing to leave the country, he wrote a short billet to her; and, in the style of romance, most humbly entreated her to grant him a moment's audience.—Arabella being informed by Lucy, to whom Sir George's gentleman had addressed himself, that he had brought a letter from his master, she ordered her to bring him to her apartment, and as soon as he appeared—

How comes it, said she, that the prince, your master has had the presumption to importune me again, after my absolute commands to the contrary?

The prince my master, madam! said the man, excessively surprised.

Aye! said Arabella, are you not Sir George's squire? And does he not trust you, with his most secret thoughts?

I belong to Sir George Bellmour, madam, replied the man, who did not understand what she meant. I have not the honour to be a squire.

No! interrupted Arabella: it is strange then that he should have honoured you with his commission.—Pray, what is it you come to request for him?

My master, madam, said he, ordered me to get this letter delivered to your ladyship, and to stay for your commands.

You would persuade me, said she, sternly, being provoked that he did not deliver the letter upon his knees, as was the custom in romances, that you are not acquainted with the purport of this audacious billet, since you express so little fear of my displeasure. But know, presumptuous, that I am mortally offended with your master, for his daring to suppose I would read this proof at once of his insolence and infidelity; and were you worth my resentment, I would haply make you suffer for your want of respect to me.

The poor man, surprised and confounded at her anger, and puzzled extremely to understand what she meant, was opening his mouth to say something, it is probable, in his own defence, when Arabella preventing him,

I know what thou wouldst say, said she: thou wouldst abuse my patience by a false detail of thy master's sighs, tears, exclamations, and despair.

Indeed, madam, I don't intend to say any such thing, replied the man.

No! repeated Arabella, a little disappointed, Bear back this presumptuous billet, then, which I suppose contains the melancholy account; and tell him, he that could so soon forget the generous Sydimiris for Philonice, and could afterwards be false to that incomparable beauty, is not a person worthy to adore Arabella.—The man, who could not tell what to make of this message, and feared he should forget these two hard names, humbly entreated her to be pleased to acquaint his master by a line with her intentions.

Arabella, supposing he meant to importune her still more, made a sign with her hand, very majestically, for him to be gone; but he, not able to comprehend her meaning, stood still with an air of perplexity, not daring to beg her to explain herself, supposing she, by that sign, required something of him.

Why dost thou not obey my commands? said Arabella, finding he did not go.

I will, to be sure, madam, replied he; wishing at the same time secretly she would let him know what they were.

And yet, said she, hastily, thou art disobeying me this moment: did I not bid you get out of my presence, and speak no more of your inconstant master, whose crimes have rendered him the detestation of all generous persons whatever?

Sir George's messenger, extremely surprised at so harsh a character of his master, and the rage with which the lady seemed to be actuated, made haste to get out of her apartment; and, at his return, informed his master, very exactly, of the reception he had met with, repeating all Lady Bella's words; which, notwithstanding the blunders he made in the names of Sydimiris and Philonice, Sir George understood well enough; and found new occasion of wondering at the excess of Arabella's extravagance, who he never imagined would have explained herself in that manner to his servant.

Without endeavouring, therefore, to see Arabella, he went to pay his compliments to Sir Charles, Mr Glanville, and Miss Glanville; to the last of whom he said some soft things, that made her extremely regret his staying behind them in the country.

II

Not so long as was first intended; but contains, however, a surprising adventure on the road

THE DAY OF THEIR DEPARTURE being come, they set out in a coach and six, attended by several servants on horseback. The first day's journey passed off without any accident worthy relating; but, towards the close of the second, they were alarmed by the appearance of three highwaymen, well mounted, at a small distance.

One of the servants, who had first spied them, immediately rode up to the coach; and, for fear of alarming the ladies, whispered Mr Glanville in the ear.

Sir Charles, who was sitting next his son, and had heard it, cried out, with too little caution, How's this? Are we in any danger of being attacked, say you?

Mr Glanville, without replying, jumped out of the coach; at which Miss Glanville screamed out; and, lest her father should follow, sprung into her brother's seat, and held him fast by the coat.

Arabella, being in a strange consternation at all this, put her head out of the coach, to see what was the matter; and, observing three or four men of a genteel appearance, on horseback, who seemed to halt and gaze on them without offering to advance—

Sir, said she to her uncle, are yonder knights the persons whom you suppose will attack us?

Aye, aye, said Sir Charles, they are knights of the road indeed. I suppose we shall have a bout with them; for it will be scandalous to deliver, since we have the odds of our side, and are more than a match for them.

Arabella, interpreting these words in her own way, looked out again; and, seeing the robbers, who had by this time taken their resolution, galloping towards them, her cousin and the servants ranging themselves of each side of the coach, as if to defend them—

Hold, hold, valiant men! said she, as loud as she could speak, addressing herself to the highwaymen, Do not, by a mistaken generosity, hazard your lives in a combat, to which the laws of honour do not oblige you. We are not violently carried away, as you falsely suppose: we go willingly along with these persons, who are our friends and relations.

Hey-day! cried Sir Charles, staring at her with great surprise: what's the meaning of all this? Do you think these fellows will mind your fine speeches, niece?—I hope they will, sir, said she: then pulling her cousin—Shew yourself, for Heaven's sake, miss, pursued she, and second my assurances, that we are not forced away. These generous men come to fight for our deliverance.

The highwaymen, who were near enough to hear Arabella's voice, though they could not distinguish her words, gazed on her with great surprise; and, finding they would be very well received, thought fit to abandon their enterprize, and galloped away as fast as they were able. Some of the servants made a motion to pursue them; but Mr Glanville forbade it; and, entering again into the coach, congratulated the ladies upon the escape they had had.

Since these men, said Arabella, did not come to deliver us, out of a mistaken notion, that we were carried away by force, it must necessarily follow, they had some bad design; and I protest I know not who to suspect is the author of it, unless the person you vanquished, said she, to Mr Glanville, the other day in a single combat; for the disguised Edward, you assured me, was dead. But, perhaps, continued she, it was some lover of Miss Glanville's who designed to make an attempt to carry her away. Methinks he was too slenderly attended for such an hazardous undertaking.

I'll assure you, madam, said Miss Glanville, I have no lovers among highwaymen.

Highwaymen! repeated Arabella,

Why, aye, to be sure, madam, rejoined Sir Charles: what do you take them for?

For persons of quality, sir, resumed Arabella and though they came, questionless, either upon a good or bad design, yet it cannot be doubted but that their birth is illustrious; otherwise they would never pretend either to fight in our defence or to carry us away.

I vow, niece, said Sir Charles, I can't possibly understand you.

My cousin, sir, interrupted Mr Glanville, has been mistaken in these persons; and has not yet, possibly, believed them to be highwaymen who came to rob us.

There is no question, sir, said Arabella, smiling, that if they did not come to defend us, they came to rob you: but it is hard to guess, which of us it was of whom they designed to deprive you; for it may very possibly be for my cousin's sake, as well as mine, that this enterprize was undertaken.

Pardon me, madam, said Mr Glanville, who was willing to prevent his father from answering her absurdities: these men had no other design than to rob us of our money,

How! said Arabella: were these cavaliers, who appeared to be in so handsome a garb that I took them for persons of prime quality—were they robbers? I have been strangely mistaken, it seems. However, apprehend there is no certainty that your suspicions are true; and it may still be as I say, that they either came to rescue or carry us away.

Mr Glanville, to avoid a longer dispute, changed the discourse; having observed, with confusion, that Sir Charles and his sister seemed to look upon his beloved cousin as one that was out of her senses.

III

Which concludes with an authentic piece of history

ARABELLA, DURING THE REST OF this journey, was so wholly taken up in contemplating upon the last adventure, that she mixed but little in the conversation. Upon their drawing near Bath, the situation of that city afforded her the means of making a comparison between the valley in which it was placed (with the amphitheatrical view of the hills around it), and the valley of Tempe.

It was in such a place as this, said she, pursuing her comparison, that the fair Andronice delivered the valiant Hortensius: and really I could wish our entrance into that city might he preceded by an act of equal humanity with that of that fair princess.

For the gratification of that wish, madam, said Mr Glanville, it is necessary some person should meet with a misfortune, out of which you might be able to relieve him: but I suppose the benevolence of your disposition may be equally satisfied with not finding any occasion of exercising it when it is found.

Though it be not my fortune to meet with those occasions, replied Arabella, there is no reason to doubt but others do, who possibly have less inclination to afford their assistance than myself: and it is possible, if any other than the princess of Messina had happened to pass by when Hortensius was in the hands of the Thessalians, he would not have been rescued from the ignominious death he was destined to, merely for killing a stork.

How! interrupted Sir Charles: put a man to death for killing a stork! Ridiculous! Pray in what part of the world did that happen? Among the Indians of America, I suppose.

No, sir, said Arabella, in Thessaly; the fairest part in all Macedonia, famous for the beautiful valley of Tempe, which excited the curiosity of all travellers whatever.

No, not all, madam, returned Sir Charles; for I am acquainted with several travellers, who never saw it, nor even mentioned it; and if it is so famous as you say, I am surprised I never heard of it before.

I don't know, said Arabella, what those travellers thought worthy of their notice; but I am certain, that if any chance should conduct me into Macedonia, I would not leave it till I saw the valley of Tempe, so celebrated by all the poets and historians.

Dear cousin, cried Glanville, who could hardly forbear smiling, what chance, in the name of wonder, should take you into Turkey, at so great a distance from your own country?—And so, said Sir Charles, this famous valley of Tempe is in Turkey? Why, you must be very fond of travelling, indeed, Lady Bella, if you would go into the Great Mogul's country, where the people are all Pagans, they say, and worship the devil.

The country my cousin speaks of, said Mr Glanville, is in the Grand Signior's dominions: the Great Mogul, you know, sir—

Well, interrupted Sir Charles, the Great Mogul, or the Grand Signior, I know not what you call him: but I hope my niece does not propose to go thither.

Not unless I am forcibly carried thither, said Arabella; but I do determine, if that misfortune should ever happen to me, that I would, if possible, visit the valley of Tempe, which is in that part of Greece they call Macedonia.—Then I am persuaded, replied Sir Charles, you'll never see that famous vale you talk of; for it is not very likely you should be forcibly carried away into Turkey.—And why do you think it unlikely that I should be carried thither? interrupted Arabella. Do not the same things happen now, that did formerly? And is any thing more common, than ladies being carried, by their ravishers, into countries far distant from their own? May not the same accidents happen to me, that have happened to so many illustrious ladies before me? And may I not be carried into Macedonia by a similitude of destiny with that of a great many beautiful princesses, who, though, born in the most distant quarters of the world, chanced to meet at one time in the city of Alexandria, and related their miraculous adventures to each other.

And it was for that very purpose they met, madam, said Mr Glanville, smiling.—Why, truly, said Arabella, it happened very luckily for each of them, that they were brought into a place where they found so many illustrious companions in misfortune, to whom they might freely communicate their adventures, which otherwise might, haply, have been concealed, or, at least, have been imperfectly delivered down to us. However, added she, smiling, if I am carried into Macedonia, and by that means have an opportunity of visiting the famous vale of Tempe, I shall take care not to draw the resentment of the Thessalians upon me, by an indiscretion like that of Hortensius.

For be pleased to know, sir, said she, addressing herself to her uncle, that his killing a stork, however inconsiderable a matter it may appear to us, was yet looked upon as a crime of a very atrocious nature among the Thessalians; for they have a law, which forbids, upon pain of death, the killing of storks; the reason for which is, that Thessaly being subject to be infested with a prodigious multitude of serpents, which are a delightful food to these sort of fowls, they look upon them as sacred birds, sent by the gods to deliver them from these serpents and vipers: and though Hortensius, being a stranger, was pardoned through the intercession of the princess Andronice, they made him promise to send another stork into Thessaly, to the end that he might be reputed innocent.

IV

In which one of our heroine's whims is justified, by some others full as whimsical

THIS PIECE OF HISTORY, WITH Sir Charles's remarks upon it, brought them into Bath. Their lodgings being provided beforehand, the ladies retired to their different chambers, to repose themselves after the fatigue of their journey, and did not meet again till supper was on table; when Miss Glanville, who had eagerly inquired what company was then in the place, and heard there were a great many persons of fashion just arrived, prest Arabella to go to the Pump-room the next morning, assuring her she would find a very agreeable amusement.

Arabella accordingly consented to accompany her; and being told the ladies went in an undress of a morning, she accommodated herself to the custom, and went in a negligent dress: but instead of a capuchin, she wore something like a veil, of black gauze, which covered almost all her face, and part of her waist, and gave her a very singular appearance.

Miss Glanville was too envious of her cousin's superiority in point of beauty, to inform her of any oddity in her dress, which she thought might expose her to the ridicule of those that saw her; and Mr Glanville was too little a critic in ladies' apparel, to be sensible that Arabella was not in the fashion: and, since every thing she wore became her extremely, he could not choose but think she drest admirably well: he handed her, therefore, with a great deal of satisfaction into the Pump-room, which happened to be greatly crowded that morning.

The attention of most part of the company was immediately engaged by the appearance Lady Bella made. Strangers are here most strictly criticised, and every new object affords a delicious feast of raillery and scandal.

The ladies, alarmed at the singularity of her dress, crowded together in parties; and the words, Who can she be? Strange creature!

Ridiculous! and other exclamations of the same kind, were whispered very intelligibly. The men were struck with her figure, veiled as she was. Her fine stature, the beautiful turn of her person, the grace and elegance of her motion, attracted all their notice. The phaenomenon of the veil, however, gave them great disturbance. So lovely a person seemed to promise the owner had a face not unworthy of it; but that was totally hid from their view: for Arabella, at her entrance into the room, had pulled the gauze quite over her face, following therein the custom of the ladies in Clelia, and the Grand Cyrus, who, in mixed companies, always hid their faces with great care.

The wits and pretty fellows railed at the envious covering, and compared her to the sun obscured by a cloud; while the beaux *dem'd* the horrid innovation, and expressed a fear, lest it should grow into a fashion.

Some of the wiser sort took her for a foreigner: others, of still more sagacity, supposed her a Scotch lady, covered with her plaid; and a third sort, infinitely wiser than either, concluded she was a Spanish nun, that had escaped from a convent, and had not yet quitted her veil.— Arabella, ignorant of the diversity of opinions to which her appearance gave rise, was taken up in discoursing with Mr Glanville upon the medicinal virtue of the springs, the economy of the baths, the nature of the diversions, and such other topics as the objects around them furnished her with.—In the mean time, Miss Glanville was got amidst a crowd of her acquaintance, who had hardly paid the civilities of a first meeting, before they eagerly inquired who that lady she brought with her was.—Miss Glanville informed them, that she was her cousin, and daughter to the deceased Marquis of ——; adding, with a sneer, that she had been brought up in the country, knew nothing of the world and had some very peculiar notions, As you may see, said she, by that odd kind of covering she wears.

Her name and quality were presently whispered all over the room. The men, hearing she was a great heiress, found greater beauties to admire in her person: the ladies, awed by the sanction of quality, dropt their ridicule on her dress, and began to quote examples of whims full as inexcusable.—One remembered that Lady J— F— always wore her ruffles reversed; that the Countess of —— went to court in a farthingale; that the Duchess of —— sat astride upon a horse; and a certain lady of great fortune, and nearly allied to quality, because she was not dignified with a title invented a new one for herself; and directed her servants to say in speaking to her, Your honoress; which afterwards became a custom among all her acquaintance; who mortally offended her if they omitted that instance of respect.

V

Containing some historical anecdotes, the truth of which may possibly be doubted, as they are not to be found in any of the historians

AFTER A SHORT STAY IN the room, Arabella expressing a desire to return home, Mr Granville conducted her out. The gentlemen of his acquaintance attending Miss Glanville, Sir Charles detained them to breakfast, by which means they had an opportunity of satisfying their curiousity; and beheld Arabella divested of that veil which had, as they said (and it is possible they said no more than they thought) concealed one of the finest faces in the world.

Miss Glanville had the mortification to see both the gentlemen so charmed with the sight of her cousin's face, that for a long time she sat wholly neglected; but the seriousness of her behaviour giving some little disgust to the youngest of them, who was what the ladies call a pretty fellow, a dear creature, and the most diverting man in the world; he applied himself wholly to Miss Glanville, and soon engaged her in a particular conversation. Mr Selvin, so was the other gentleman called, was of a much graver cast; he affected to be thought deep-read in history, and never failed to take all opportunities of displaying his knowledge of antiquity, which was indeed but very superficial: but having some few anecdotes by heart, which he would take occasion to introduce as often as he could, he passed among many persons for one who, by application and study, had acquired an universal knowledge of ancient history.—Speaking of any particular circumstance, he would fix the time, by computing the year with the number of the Olympiads. It happened, he would say, in the 141st Olympiad.

Such an amazing exactness had a suitable effect on his audience, and always procured him a great degree of attention.—This gentleman hitherto had no opportunity of displaying his knowledge of history;

the discourse having wholly turned upon news and other trifles; when Arabella, after some more inquiries concerning the place, remarked, that there was a very great difference between the medicinal waters at Bath, and the fine springs at the foot of the mountain Thermopylae, in Greece, as well in their qualities as manner of using them: And I am of opinion, added she, that Bath, famous as it is for restoring health, is less frequented by infirm persons, than the famous springs of Thermopylae were by the beauties of Greece, to whom those waters have the reputation of giving new lustre. Mr Selvin, who, with all his reading, had never met with any account of these celebrated Grecian springs, was extremely disconcerted at not being able to continue a conversation, which the silence of the rest of the company made him imagine was directed wholly to him.

The shame he conceived at seeing himself opposed by a girl, in a matter which so immediately belonged to him, made him resolve to draw himself out of this dilemma at any rate; and, though he was far from being convinced, that there was no such springs at Thermopylae as Arabella mentioned, yet he resolutely maintained that she must be mistaken in their situation; for to his certain knowledge there was no medicinal waters at the foot of that mountain. Arabella, who could not endure to be contradicted in what she took to be so incontestible a fact, reddened with vexation at his unexpected denial.—It should seem, said she, by your discourse, that you are unacquainted with many material passages that passed among very illustrious persons there; and if you knew any thing of Pisistratus the Athenian, you would know, that an adventure he had at those baths laid the foundation of all those great designs, which he afterwards effected, to the total subversion of the Athenian government.

Mr Selvin, surprised that this piece of history had likewise escaped his observation, resolved, however, not to give up his point.—I think, madam, replied he, with great self sufficiency, that I am pretty well acquainted with every thing which relates to the affairs of the Athenian Commonwealth; and know by what steps Pisistratus advanced himself to the sovereignty.—It was, indeed, a great stroke of policy in him, said he, turning to Mr Glanville, to wound himself, in order to get a guard assigned him.

You are mistaken, sir, said Arabella, if you believe there was any truth in the report of his having wounded himself: it was done either by his rival Lycurgus, or Theocrites; who, believing him still to be in love with the fair Cerinthe, whom he courted, took that way to get rid of him. Neither is it true, that ambition alone inspired Pisistratus with a design of enslaving his country: those authors who say so, must know little of the springs and motives of his conduct. It was neither ambition nor revenge that made him act as he did: it was the violent affection he conceived for the beautiful Cleorante, whom he first saw at the famous baths of Thermopylae, which put him upon those designs; for, seeing that Lycurgus, who was not his rival in ambition, but love, would certainly become the possessor of Cleorante, unless he made himself tyrant of Athens, he had recourse to that violent method, in order to preserve her for himself.

I protest, madam, said Mr Selvin, casting down his eyes in great confusion, at her superior knowledge in history, these particulars have all escaped my notice: and this is the first time I ever understood that Pisistratus was violently in love, and that it was not ambition which made him aspire to sovereignty.

I do not remember any mention of this in Plutarch, continued he, rubbing his forehead, or any of the authors who have treated on the affairs of Greece.

Very likely, sir, replied Arabella; but you will see the whole story of Pisistratus's love for Cleorante, with the effects it produced, related at large in Scudery.—Scudery, madam! said the sage Mr Selvin, I never read that historian.—No, sir! replied Arabella: then your reading has been very confined.—I know, madam, said he, that Herodotus, Thucydides, and Plutarch, have indeed quoted him frequently.—I am surprised, sir, said Mr Glanville, who was excessively diverted at this discovery of his great ignorance and affectation, that you have not read that famous historian; especially as the writers you have mentioned quote him so often.

Why, to tell you the truth, sir, said he, though he was a Roman, yet it is objected to him, that he wrote but indifferent Latin; with no purity or elegance; and you are quite mistaken, sir, interrupted Arabella: the great Scudery was a Frenchman; and both his Clelia and Artamanes were written in French.—A Frenchman was he? said Mr Selvin, with a lofty air. Oh, then! it is not surprising that I have not read him. I read no authors but the ancients, madam, added he, with a look of self-applause: I cannot relish the moderns at all; I have no taste for their way of writing. But Scudery must needs be more ancient than Thucydides, and the rest of those Greek historians you mentioned, said Mr Glanville: how else could they quote him?

Mr Selvin was here so utterly at a loss, that he could not conceal his confusion. He held down his head, and continued silent: while the beau, who had listened to the latter part of their discourse, exerted his supposed talent of raillery against the unhappy admirer of the ancient authors; and increased his confusion by a thousand sarcasms, which gave more diversion to himself than any body else.

VI

Which contains some excellent rules for raillery

Mr Glanville, who had too much politeness and good nature to insist too long upon the ridicule in the character of his acquaintance, changed the discourse; and Arabella, who had observed, with some concern, the ill-judged raillery of the young beau, took occasion to decry that species of wit; and gave it, as her opinion, that it was very dangerous and unpleasing.

For, truly, said she, it is almost impossible to use it without being hated or feared; and whoever gets a habit of it, is in danger of wronging all the laws of friendship and humanity.

Certainly, pursued she, looking at the beau, it is extremely unjust to rally one's friends and particular acquaintance: first, choose them well, and be as nice as you please in the choice; but when you have chosen them, by no means play upon them. It is cruel and malicious to divert one's self at the expense of one's friend.

However, madam, said Mr Glanville, who was charmed to hear her talk so rationally, you may give people leave to rally their enemies.

Truly, resumed Arabella, I cannot allow that, any more than upon friends; for raillery is the poorest kind of revenge that can be taken. Methinks it is mean to rally persons who have a small share of merit; since, haply, their defects were born with them, and not of their own acquiring; and it is great injustice to descant upon one slight fault in men of parts, to the prejudice of a thousand good qualities.

For aught I see, madam, said the beau, you will not allow one to rally any body.

I am of opinion, sir, said Arabella, that there are very few proper objects for raillery; and still fewer who can rally well. The talent of raillery ought to be born with the person: no art can infuse it; and those who endeavour to rally, in spite of nature, will be so far from diverting others that they will become the objects of ridicule themselves. Many other pleasing qualities of wit may be acquired by pains and study, but raillery must be the gift of nature. It is not enough to have many lively and agreeable thoughts; but there must be such an expression, as must convey their full force and meaning: the air, the aspect, the tone of the voice, and every part in general, must contribute to its perfection.

There ought also to be a great distance between raillery and satire, so that one may never be mistaken for the other. Raillery ought indeed to surprise, and sensibly touch, those to whom it is directed; but I would not have the wounds it makes either deep or lasting. Let those who feel it, be hurt like persons who, gathering roses, are pricked by the thorns, and find a sweet smell to make amends.

I would have raillery raise the fancy, and quicken the imagination: the fire of its wit should only enable us to trace its original, and shine as the stars do, but not burn. Yet, after all, I cannot greatly approve of raillery, or cease to think it dangerous and, to pursue my comparisons, said she, with an enchanting smile, persons who possess the true talent of raillery are like comets; they are seldom seen, and are at once admired and feared.

I protest, Lady Bella, said Sir Charles, who had listened to her with many signs of admiration, you speak like an orator.

One would not imagine, interrupted Mr Glanville, who saw Arabella in some confusion at the coarse praise her uncle gave her, that my cousin could speak so accurately of a quality she never practises: and it is easy to judge, by what she has said, that nobody can rally finer than herself, if she pleases.

Mr Selvin, though he bore her a grudge for knowing more history than he did, yet assured her that she had given the best rules imaginable for rallying well. But the beau, whom she had silenced by her reproof, was extremely angry; and supposing it would mortify her to see him pay court to her cousin, he redoubled his assiduities to Miss Glanville, who was highly delighted at seeing Arabella less taken notice of by this gay gentleman than herself.

VII

In which the author condescends to be very minute in the description of our heroine's dress

THE INDIFFERENCE OF MR TINSEL convincing Miss Glanville that Arabella was less to be dreaded than she imagined, she had no reluctance at seeing her prepare for her public appearance the next ball-night.

Having consulted her fancy in a rich silver stuff she had bought for that purpose, a person was sent for to make it; and Arabella, who followed no fashion but her own taste, which was formed on the manners of the heroines, ordered the woman to make her a robe after the same model as the princess Julia's.

The mantua-maker, who thought it might do her great prejudice with her new customer, to acknowledge she knew nothing of the princess Julia, or the fashion of her gown, replied at random, and with great pertness, That that taste was quite out, and she would advise her ladyship to have her clothes made in the present mode, which was far more becoming.

You can never persuade me, said Arabella, that any fashion can be more becoming than that of the princess Julia's, who was the most gallant princess upon earth, and knew better than any other how to set off her charms. It may indeed be a little obsolete now, pursued she, for the fashion could not but alter a little in the compass of near two thousand years.

Two thousand years, madam! said the woman, in a great surprise: Lord help us trades-people, if they did not alter a thousand times in as many days! I thought your ladyship was speaking of the last month's taste, which, as I said before, is quite out now.—Well, replied Arabella, let the present mode be what it will, I insist upon having my clothes made after the pattern of the beautiful daughter of Augustus; being convinced that none other can be half so becoming.—What fashion was that, pray, madam? said the woman: I never saw it.—How! replied Arabella, have you already forgot the fashion of the princess Julia's robe, which you said was worn but last month? Or, are you ignorant that the princess Julia and the daughter of Augustus is the same person?—I protest, madam, said the woman, extremely confused, I had forgot that till you called it to my mind.—Well, said Arabella, make me a robe in the same taste.

The mantua-maker was now wholly at a loss in what manner to behave; for, being conscious that she knew nothing of the princess Julia's fashion, she could not undertake to make it without directions, and she was afraid of discovering her ignorance by asking for any; so that her silence and embarrassment persuading Arabella she knew nothing of the matter, she dismissed her with a small present for the trouble she had given her, and had recourse to her usual expedient, which was to make one of her women, who understood a little of the mantua-making business, make a robe for her after her own directions. Miss Glanville, who imagined she had sent for work-women in order to have clothes made in the modern taste, was surprised, at her entrance into her chamber, to see her dressing for the ball in a habit singular to the last degree.

She wore no hoop, and the blue and silver stuff of her robe was only kept by its own richness from hanging close about her. It was quite open round her breast, which was shaded with a rich border of lace; and clasping close to her waist by small knots of diamonds, descended in a sweeping train on the ground. The sleeves were short, wide, and slashed, fastened in different places with diamonds, and her arms were partly hid by half a dozen falls of ruffles. Her hair, which fell in very easy ringlets on her neck, was placed with great care and exactness round her lovely face; and the jewels and ribands, which were all her head-dress, were disposed to the greatest advantage. Upon the whole, nothing could be more singularly becoming than her dress; or set off with greater advantage the striking beauties of her person.

Miss Glanville, though she was not displeased to see her persist in her singularity of dress, yet could not behold her look so lovely in it, without feeling a secret uneasiness; but consoling herself with the hopes of the ridicule she would occasion, she assumed a cheerful air, approved her taste in the choice of her colours, and went with her at the usual hour to the rooms, attended by Mr Glanville, Mr Selvin, and the young beau we have formerly mentioned.

The surprise Arabella's unusual appearance gave to the whole company, was very visible to every one but herself. The moment she entered the room, every one whispered the person next to them; and for some moments nothing was heard but the words, the princess Julia; which was echoed at every corner, and at last attracted her observation.

Mr Glanville, and the rest of the company with her, were in some confusion at the universal exclamation, which they imagined was occasioned by the singularity of her habit; though they could not conceive why they gave her that title. Had they known the adventure of the mantua-maker, it would doubtless have easily occurred to them; for the woman had no sooner left Arabella, than she related the conference she had with a lady newly arrived, who had required her to make a robe in the manner of the princess Julia's, and dismissed her because she did not understand the fashions that prevailed two thousand years. ago.

This story was quickly dispersed, and, for its novelty, afforded a great deal of diversion: every one longed to see a fashion of such antiquity, and expected the appearance of the princess Julia with great impatience. It is not to be doubted but much mirth was treasured up for her appearance; and the occasional humourist had already prepared his accustomed jest, when the sight of the devoted fair one repelled his vivacity, and the designed ridicule of the whole assembly.—Scarce had the tumultuous whisper escaped the lips of each individual, when they found themselves awed to respect by that irresistible charm in the person of Arabella which commanded reverence and love from all who beheld her.

Her noble air, the native dignity in her looks, the inexpressible grace which accompanied all her motions, and the consummate loveliness of her form, drew the admiration of the whole assembly.—A respectful silence succeeded; and the astonishment her beauty occasioned left them no room to descant on the absurdity of her dress.

Miss Glanville, who felt a malicious joy at the sneers she expected would be cast on her cousin, was greatly disappointed at the deference which seemed to be paid to her; and, to vent some part of her spleen, took occasion to mention her surprise at the behaviour of the company on their entrance, wondering what they could mean by whispering, The princess Julia, to one another.

I assure you, said Arabella, smiling, I am not less surprised than you at it; and since they directed their looks to me at the same time, I fancy they either took me for some princess of the name of Julia, who is expected here to-night, or else flatter me with some resemblance to the beautiful daughter of Augustus.

The comparison, madam, said Mr Selvin, who took all occasions to shew his reading, is too injurious to you; for I am of opinion you as much excel that licentious lady in the beauties of your person, as you do in the qualities of your mind.

I never heard licentiousness imputed to the daughter of Augustus Caesar, said Arabella; and the most her enemies can say of her, is, that she loved admiration, and would permit herself to be beloved, and to be told so, without shewing any signs of displeasure.—Bless me, madam! interrupted Mr Selvin, how strangely do you mistake the character of Julia! Though the daughter of an emperor, she was (pardon the expression) the most abandoned prostitute in Rome. Many of her intrigues are recorded in history; but, to mention only one, was not her infamous commerce with Ovid the cause of his banishment?

VIII

Some reflections very fit, and others very unfit, for an assembly-room

YOU SPEAK IN STRANGE TERMS, replied Arabella, blushing, of a princess, who, if she was not the most reserved and severe person in the world, was yet, nevertheless, absolutely chaste. I know there were people who represented her partiality for Ovid in a very unfavourable light; but that ingenious poet, when he related his history to the great Agrippa, told him in confidence all that had passed between him and the princess Julia, than which nothing could be more innocent, though a little indiscreet. For it is certain that she permitted him to love her, and did not condemn him to any rigorous punishment for daring to tell her so; yet, for all this, as I said before, though she was not altogether so austere as she ought to have been, yet she was, nevertheless, a most virtuous princess.

Mr Selvin, not daring to contradict a lady, whose extensive reading had furnished her with anecdotes unknown almost to any body else, by his silence confessed her superiority: but Mr Glanville, who knew all these anecdotes were drawn from romances, which he found contradicted the known facts in history, and assigned the most ridiculous causes for things of the greatest importance, could not help smiling at the facility with which Mr Selvin gave in to those idle absurdities. For, notwithstanding his affectation of great reading, his superficial knowledge of history made it extremely easy to deceive him; and as it was his custom to mark in his pocket-book all the scraps of history he heard introduced into conversation, and retail them again in other company, he did not doubt but he would make a figure with the curious circumstances Arabella had furnished him with.

Arabella observing Mr Tinsel, by his familiar bows, significant smiles, and easy salutations, was acquainted with the greatest part of the assembly, told him, that she did not doubt but he knew the adventures of many persons whom they were viewing; and that he would do her a pleasure, if he would relate some of them.—Mr Tinsel was charmed with a request which afforded him an opportunity of gratifying a favourite inclination; and, seating himself near her immediately, was beginning to obey her injunctions, when she gracefully entreated him to stay a moment; and calling to Mr Glanville, and his sister, who were talking to Mr Selvin, asked them if they chose to partake of a more rational amusement than dancing, and listen to the adventures of some illustrious persons, which Mr Tinsel had promised to relate.

I assure you, madam, said Mr Glanville, smiling, you will find that a less innocent amusement than dancing.—Why so, sir, replied Arabella; since it is not an indiscreet curiosity which prompts me to a desire of hearing the histories Mr Tinsel has promised to entertain me with; but rather a hope of hearing something which may at once improve and delight me; something which may excite my admiration, engage my esteem, or influence my practice?

It was, doubtless, with such motives as these, that we find princesses and ladies of the most illustrious rank, in Clelia and the Grand Cyrus, listening to the adventures of persons in whom they were probably as little interested as we are in these around us. Kings, princes, and commanders of armies, thought it was no waste of their time, in the midst of the hurry and clamour of a camp, to listen many hours to the relation of one single history, and not filled with any extraordinary events, but haply a simple recital of common occurrences. The great Cyrus, while he was busy in reducing all Asia to his yoke, heard, nevertheless, the histories of all the considerable persons in the camp, besides those of strangers, and even his enemies. If there was, therefore, any thing either criminal or mean in hearing the adventures of others, do you imagine so many great and illustrious persons would have given in to such an amusement?

After this Arabella turned gravely about to Mr Tinsel, and told him, he was at liberty to begin his recital.

The beau, a little disconcerted by the solemnity with which she requested his information, knew not how to begin with the formality that he saw was required of him, and therefore sat silent for a few moments; which Arabella supposed was to recall to his memory all the passages he proposed to relate. His perplexity would probably have increased instead of lessening by the profound silence which she observed, had not Miss Glanville seated herself with a sprightly air on the other side of him, and directing his eyes to a tall handsome woman that had just entered, asked him, pleasantly, to tell her history, if he knew it. Mr Tinsel, brought into his usual track by this question, answered, smiling, that the history of that lady was yet a secret, or known but to a very few; but my intelligence, added he, is generally the earliest, and may always be depended on.

Perhaps, said Arabella, the lady is one of your acquaintances, and favoured you with the recital of her adventures from her own mouth.—No, really, madam, answered Mr Tinsel, surprised at the great simplicity of Arabella, for so he understood it: the lady, I believe, is not so communicative: and, to say the truth, I should not choose to hear her adventures from herself, since she certainly would suppress the most material circumstances.

In a word, said he, lowering his voice, that lady was for many years the mistress of a young military nobleman, whom she was so complaisant as to follow in all his campaigns, marches, sieges, and every inconveniency of war. He married her in Gibraltar, from whence he is lately arrived, and introduced his new lady to his noble brother, by whom she was not unfavourably received. It is worth remarking, that this same haughty peer thought fit to resent with implacable obstinacy the marriage of another of his brothers, with the widow of a brave officer, of considerable rank in the army. It is true, she was several years older than the young lord, and had no fortune; but the duke assigned other reasons for his displeasure: he complained loudly, that his brother had dishonoured the nobility of his birth by this alliance, and continued his resentment till the death of the young hero, who gave many remarkable proofs of his courage and fortitude upon several occasions, and died gloriously before the walls of Carthegena; leaving his disconsolate lady a widow a second time, with the acquisition of a title indeed, but a very small addition to her fortune.

Observe that gay, splendid lady, I beseech you, madam, pursued he, turning to Arabella. How affectedly she looks and talks, and throws her eyes around the room, with a haughty self-sufficiency in her aspect, and insolent contempt for every thing but herself! Her habit, her speech, her motions, are all French: nothing in England is able to please her; the people so dull, so awkwardly polite; the manner so gross; no delicacy, no elegance, no magnificence in their persons, houses, or diversions; every thing is so distasteful, there is no living in such a place. One may crawl about, indeed, she says, and make a shift to breathe in the odious country, but one cannot be said to live; and with all the requisites to render life delightful, here, one can only suffer, not enjoy it.

Would one not imagine, pursued he, this fine lady was a person of very exalted rank, who has the sanction of birth, riches, and grandeur, for her extraordinary pride? And yet she is no other than the daughter of an innkeeper at Spa, and had the exalted post assigned her of attending new lodgers to their apartments, acquainting them with all the conveniences of the place, answering an humble question or two concerning what company was in the town, what scandal was stirring, and the like.

One of our great sea-commanders going thither for his health, happened to lodge at this inn; and was so struck with her charms that he married her in a few weeks, and soon after brought her to England.

Such was the origin of this fantastic lady, whose insupportable pride and ridiculous affectation draw contempt and aversion wherever she appears.

Did I not tell you, madam, interrupted Mr Glanville, that the amusement you had chosen was not so innocent as dancing? What a deal of scandal has Mr Tinsel uttered in the compass of a few minutes?

I assure you, replied Arabella, I know not what to make of the histories he has been relating. I think they do not deserve that name, and are rather detached pieces of satire on particular persons, than a serious relation of facts. I confess my expectations from this gentleman have not been answered.

I think, however, madam, said Mr Glanville, we may allow that there is a negative merit in the relations Mr Tinsel has made; for, if he has not shewn us any thing to approve, he has not at least shewn us what to condemn.

The ugliness of vice, replied Arabella, ought only to be represented to the vicious; to whom satire, like a magnifying glass, may aggravate every defect, in order to make its deformity appear more hideous; but since its end is only to reprove and amend, it should never be addressed to any but those who come within its correction, and may be the better for it: a virtuous mind need not be shewn the deformity of vice, to make it be hated and avoided; the more pure and uncorrupted our ideas are, the less shall we be influenced by example. A natural propensity to virtue or vice often determines the choice: it is sufficient, therefore, to shew a good mind what it ought to pursue, though a bad one must be told what to avoid. In a word, one ought to be always incited, the other always restrained.

I vow, Lady Bella, said Miss Glanville, you'd make one think one came here to hear a sermon; you are so very grave, and talk upon such high-flown subjects. What harm was there in what Mr Tinsel was telling us? It would be hard indeed if one might not divert one's self with other people's faults.

I am afraid, miss, said Arabella, those who can divert themselves with the faults of others are not behind in affording diversion. And that very inclination, added she, smilingly, to hear other people's faults, may, by those very people, be condemned as one, and afford them the same kind of ill-natured pleasure your are so desirous of.

Nay, madam, returned Miss Glanville, your ladyship was the first who introduced the discourse you condemn so much. Did not you desire Mr Tinsel to tell you histories about the company; and asked my brother and me to come and hear them?

It is true, replied Arabella, that I did desire you to partake with me of a pleasing and rational amusement, for such I imagined Mr Tinsel's histories might afford. Far from a detail of vices, follies, and irregularities, I expected to have heard the adventures of some illustrious personages related; between whose actions, and those of the heroes and heroines of antiquity, I might have found some resemblance.

For instance, I hoped to have heard imitated the sublime courage of a Clelia; who, to save her honour from the attempts of the impious Tarquin, leapt into the river Tyber, and swam to the other side; or the noble resolution of the incomparable Candace, who to escape out of the hands of her ravisher, the pirate Zenadorus, set fire to his vessel with her own hands, and committed herself to the mercy of the waves; or the constancy and affection of a Mandane, who, for the sake of a Cyrus, refused the richest crowns in the world, and braved the terrors of death to preserve herself for him.

As for the men, I hoped to have heard of some who might have almost equalled the great Oroondates, the invincible Artaban, the valiant Juba, the renowned Alcamenes, and many thousand heroes of antiquity; whose glorious exploits in war, and unshaken constancy in love, have given them immortal fame.

While Arabella was uttering this long speech, with great emotion, Miss Glanville, with a sly look at the beau, gave him to understand, that was her cousin's foible.

Mr Tinsel, however, not able to comprehend the meaning of what she said, listened to her with many signs of perplexity and wonder.

Mr Selvin, in secret, repined at her prodigious knowledge of history; and Mr Glanville, with his eyes fixed on the ground, bit his lips almost through with madness.

In the mean time, several among the company, desirous of hearing what the strange lady was saying so loud, and with so much eagerness and emotion, gathered round them; which Mr Glanville observing, and fearing Arabella would expose herself still farther, whispered his sister to get her away, if possible.

Miss Glanville, though very unwilling, obeyed his injunctions; and complaining of a sudden headache, Arabella immediately proposed retiring, which was joyfully complied with by Mr Glanville, who, with the other gentlemen attended them home.

IX

Being a chapter of the satirical kind

At their return, Sir Charles told his niece, that she had now had a specimen of the world, and some of the fashionable amusements; and asked her how she had been entertained.

Why, truly, sir, replied she, smiling, I have brought away no great relish for a renewal of the amusement I have partaken of to-night. If the world, in which you seem to think I am but newly initiated, affords only these kinds of pleasures, I shall very soon regret the solitude and books I have quitted.

Why, pray? said Miss Glanville: what kind of amusements did your ladyship expect to find in the world? And what was there disagreeable in your entertainment to-night? I am sure there is no place in England, except London, where there is so much good company to be met with as here. The assembly was very numerous and brilliant, and one can be at no loss for amusements: the Pump-room in the morning; the parade, and the rooms, in the evening; with little occasional parties of pleasure, will find one sufficient employment, and leave none of one's time to lie useless upon one's hand.

I am of opinion, replied Arabella, that one's time is far from being well employed in the manner you portion it out; and people who spend theirs in such trifling amusements must certainly live to very little purpose.

What room, I pray you, does a lady give for high and noble adventures, who consumes her days in dressing, dancing, listening to songs, and ranging the walks with people as thoughtless as herself? How mean and contemptible a figure must a life spent in such idle amusements make in history? Or rather, are not such persons always buried in oblivion; and can any pen be found who would condescend to record such inconsiderable actions? Nor can I persuade myself, added she, that any of those men whom I saw at the assembly, with figures so feminine, voices so soft, such tripping steps and unmeaning gestures, have ever signalized either their courage or constancy; but might be overcome by their enemy in battle, or be false to their mistress in love.

Lau! cousin, replied Miss Glanville, you are always talking of battles and fighting. Do you expect that persons of quality and fine gentleman will go to the wars? What business have they to fight? That belongs to the officers.

Then every fine gentleman is an officer, said Arabella; and some other title ought to be found out for men who do nothing but dance and dress.

I could never have imagined, interrupted Mr Tinsel, surveying Arabella, that a lady so elegant and gay in her own appearance, should have an aversion to pleasure and magnificence.

I assure you, sir, replied Arabella, I have an aversion to neither: on the contrary, I am a great admirer of both. But my ideas of amusements and grandeur are probably different from yours.

I will allow the ladies to be solicitous about their habits and dress with all the care and elegance they are capable of: but such trifles are below the consideration of a man; who ought not to owe the dignity of his appearance to the embroidery on his coat, but to his high and noble air, the grandeur of his courage, the elevation of his sentiments, and the many heroic actions he has performed.

Such a man will dress his person with a graceful simplicity, and lavish all his gold and embroidery upon his armour, to render him conspicuous in the day of battle. The plumes in his helmet will look more graceful in the field, than the feather in his hat at a ball; and jewels blaze with more propriety on his shield and cuirass in battle, than glittering on his finger in a dance.

Do not imagine, however, pursued she, that I absolutely condemn dancing, and think it a diversion wholly unworthy of a hero.

History has recorded some very famous balls, at which the most illustrious persons in the world have appeared. Cyrus the Great, we are informed, opened a ball with the divine Mandane at Sardis. The renowned king of Scythia danced with the princess Cleopatra at Alexandria; the brave Cleomedon with the fair Candace at Ethiopia. But these diversions were taken but seldom, and considered indeed as an amusement, not as a part of the business of life.

How would so many glorious battles have been fought, cities taken, ladies rescued, and other great and noble adventures been achieved, if the men, sunk in sloth and effeminacy, had continually followed the sound of a fiddle, sauntered in public walks, or tattled over a tea-table?

I vow, cousin, said Miss Glanville, you are infinitely more severe in your censures than Mr Tinsel was at the assembly. You had little reason, methinks, to be angry with him.

All I have said, replied Arabella, was the natural inference from your own account of the manner in which people live here. When actions are a censure upon themselves, the reciter will always be considered as a satirist.

X

In which our heroine justifies her own notions by some very illustrious examples

MR SELVIN AND MR TINSEL, who had listened attentively to this discourse of Arabella, took leave as soon as it was ended, and went away with very different opinions of her;—

Mr Tinsel declaring she was a fool, and had no knowledge of the world; and Mr Selvin convinced she was a wit, and very learned in antiquity.

Certainly, said Mr Selvin, in support of his opinion, the lady has great judgment; has been capable of prodigious application, as is apparent by her extensive reading: then her memory is quite miraculous. I protest I am quite charmed with her. I never met with such a woman in all my life.

Her cousin, in my opinion, replied Mr Tinsel, is infinitely beyond her in every merit, but beauty. How sprightly and free her conversation! What a thorough knowledge of the world! So true a taste for polite amusements, and a fund of spirits that sets vapours and spleen at defiance!

This speech bringing on a comparison between the ladies, the champions for each grew so warm in the dispute, that they had like to have quarrelled. However, by the interposition of some other gentlemen who were with them, they parted tolerable friends that night, and renewed their visits to Sir Charles in the morning.

They found only Miss Glanville with her father and brother. Arabella generally spent the mornings in her own chamber, where reading and the labours of the toilet employed her time till dinner: though it must be confessed, to her honour, that the latter engrossed but a very small part of it. Miss Glanville, with whom the beau had a long conversation at one of the windows, in which he recounted his dispute with Mr

Selvin, and the danger he ran of being pinked in a duel (that was his phrase) for her sake, at last proposed a walk; to which she consented, and engaged to prevail upon Arabella to accompany them. That lady at first positively refused, alleging in excuse, that she was so extremely interested in the fate of the princess Melisintha, whose story she was reading, that she could not stir till she had finished it.

That poor princess, continued she, is at present in a most terrible situation. She has just set fire to the palace, in order to avoid the embraces of a king who forced her to marry him. I am in pain to know how she escapes the flarnes.—Pshaw! interrupted Miss Glanville, let her perish there if she will: don't let her hinder our walk.—Who is it you doom with so much cruelty to perish? said Arabella, closing the book, and looking stedfastly on her cousin. Is it the beautiful Melisintha; that princess whose fortitude and patience have justly rendered her the admiration of the whole world; that princess, descended from a race of heroes, whose heroic virtues all glowed in her own beauteous breast; that princess, who, when taken captive, with the king her father, bore her imprisonment and chains with a marvellous constancy; and who, when she had enslaved her conqueror, and given fetters to the prince who held her father and herself in bonds, nobly refused the diadem he proffered her, and devoted herself to destruction, in order to punish the enemy of her house? I am not able to relate the rest of her history, seeing I have read no farther myself; but if you will be pleased to sit down and listen to me while I read what remains, I am persuaded you will find new cause to love and admire this amiable princess.

Pardon me, madam, said Miss Glanville, I have heard enough; and I could have been very well satisfied not to have heard so much. I think we waste a great deal of time talking about people we know nothing of. The morning will be quite lost, if we don't make haste. Come, added she, you must go. You have a new lover below, who waits to go with us: he'll die if I don't bring you.—A new lover! returned Arabella, surprised.—Aye, aye, said Miss Glanville, the learned Mr Selvin, I assure you, he had almost quarrelled with Mr Tinsel last night about your ladyship.

Arabella, at this intelligence, casting down her eyes, discovered many signs of anger and confusion; and after a silence of some moments, during which Miss Glanville had been employed in adjusting her dress at the glass, addressing herself to her cousin with an accent somewhat less sweet than before.

Had any other than yourself, miss, said she, acquainted me with the presumption of that unfortunate person, I should haply have discovered my resentment in other terms: but, as it is, I most inform you, that I take it extremely ill you should be accessary to giving me this offence.—Hey-dey! said Miss Glanville, turning about hastily: how have I offended your ladyship, pray?—I am willing to hope, cousin, replied Arabella, that it was only to divert yourself with the trouble and confusion in which you see me, that you have indiscreetly told things which ought to have been buried in silence.

And what is all this mighty trouble and confusion about, then, madam? said Miss Glanville, smiling. Is it because I told you Mr Selvin was a lover of your ladyship?—Certainly, said Arabella: such an information is sufficient to give one a great deal of perplexity. Is it such a little matter, think you, to be told that a man has the presumption to love one?

A mere trifle, replied Miss Glanville, laughing. A hundred lovers are not worth a moment's thought, when one's sure of them; for then the trouble is all over: and as for this unfortunate person, as your ladyship called him, let him die at his leisure, while we go to the parade.—Your levity, cousin, said Arabella, forces me to smile, notwithstanding the cause I have to be incensed. However, I have charity enough to make me not desire the death of Mr Selvin, who may repair the crime he has been guilty of by repentance and discontinuation.—Well, then, said Miss Glanville, you are resolved to go to the parade: shall I reach you your odd kind of capuchin?—How, said Arabella, can I with any propriety see a man who has discovered himself to have a passion for me? Will he not construe such a favour into a permission for him to hope?

Oh, no! interrupted Miss Glanville: he does not imagine I have told your ladyship he loves you; for indeed he don't know that I am acquainted with his passion.—Then he is less culpable than I thought him, replied Arabella; and if you think I am in no danger of hearing a confession of his fault from his own mouth, I'll comply with your request, and go with you to the parade. But, added she, I must first engage you to promise not to leave me alone a moment, lest he should take advantage of such an opportunity to give some hint of his passion, that would force me to treat him very rigorously.—Miss Glanville answered, laughing, that she would be sure to mind her directions. However, said she, your ladyship need not be apprehensive he will say any fine things to you; for I knew a young lady he was formerly in love with, and the odious creature visited her a twelvemonth before he found courage enough to tell her she was handsome.

Doubtless, replied Arabella, he was much to be commended for his respect. A lover should never have the presumption to declare his passion to his mistress, unless in certain circumstances, which may at the same time in part disarm her anger. For instance, he must struggle with the violence of his passion, till it has cast him into a fever. His physicians must give him over, pronouncing his distemper incurable; since the cause of it being in his mind, all their art is incapable of removing it. Thus he must suffer, rejoicing at the approach of death, which will free him from all his torments, without violating the respect he owes to the divine object of his flame. At length, when he has but a few hours to live, his mistress, with many signs of compassion, conjures him to tell her the cause of his despair. The lover, conscious of his crime, evades all her inquiries; but the lady laying at last a peremptory command upon him to disclose the secret, he dares not disobey her, and acknowledges his passion with the utmost contrition, for having offended her; bidding her take the small remainder of his life to expiate his crime, and finishes his discourse by falling into a swoon. The lady is touched at his condition, commands him to live, and, if necessary, permits him to hope.

This is the most common way in which such declarations are, and ought to be, brought about. However, there are others, which are as well calculated for sparing a lady's confusion, and deprecating her wrath.

The lover, for example, like the prince of the Massagetes, after having buried his passion in silence for many years, may chance to be walking with his confidant in a retired place; to whom, with a deluge of tears, he relates the excess of his passion and despair. And while he is thus unbosoming his griefs, not in the least suspecting he is overheard, his princess, who had been listening to him in much trouble and confusion, by some little rustling she makes, unawares discovers herself. The surprised lover throws himself at her feet, begs pardon for his rashness, observes that he had never presumed to discover his passion to her, and implores her leave to die before her, as a punishment for his undesigned offence. The method which the great Artamenes took to let the princess of Media know he adored her was not less respectful. This valiant prince, who had long loved her, being to fight a great battle, in which he had some secret presages he should fall, which however deceived him, wrote a long letter to the divine Mandane, wherein he discovered his passion, and the resolution his respect had inspired him with, to consume in silence, and never presume to disclose his love while he lived; acquainted her that he had ordered that letter not to be delivered to her, till it was certainly known that he was dead.

Accordingly, he received several wounds in the fight, which brought him to the ground; and his body not being found, they concluded it was in the enemy's possession. His faithful squire, who had received his instructions before the battle, hastens to the princess, who, with all the court, is mightily affected at his death. He presents her the letter, which she makes no scruple to receive, since the writer is no more. She reads it, and her whole soul is melted with compassion; she bewails his fate with the most tender and affectionate marks of grief.

Her confidante asks why she is so much affected, since, in all probability, she would not have pardoned him for loving her, had he been alive?

She acknowledges the truth of her observation, takes notice that his death having cancelled his crime, his respectful passion alone employs her thoughts: she is resolved to bewail, as innocent and worthy of compassion when dead, him whom living she would treat as a criminal; and insinuates, that her heart had entertained an affection for him.

Her confidante treasures up this hint, and endeavours to console her, but in vain, till news is brought that Artamenes, who had been carried for dead out of the field, and, by a very surprising adventure, concealed all this time, is returned.

The princess is covered with confusion; and, though glad he is alive, resolves to banish him for his crime.

Her confidante pleads his cause so well, that she consents to see him: and, since he can no longer conceal his passion, he confirms the confession in his letter, humbly begging pardon for being still alive. The princess, who cannot plead ignorance of his passion, nor deny the sorrow she testified for his death, condescends to pardon him, and he is also permitted to hope. In like manner the great prince of Persia—Does your ladyship consider how late it is? interrupted Miss Glanville, who had hitherto very impatiently listened to her. Don't let us keep the gentlemen waiting any longer for us.

I must inform you how the prince of Persia declared his love for the incomparable Berenice, said Arabella.

Another time, dear cousin, said Miss Glanville; methinks we have talked long enough upon this subject.—I am sorry the time has seemed so tedious to you, said Arabella, smiling; and therefore I'll trespass no longer upon your patience. Then, ordering Lucy to bring her hat and gloves, she went down stairs, followed by Miss Glanville, who was greatly disappointed at her not putting on her veil.

XI

In which our heroine, being mistaken herself, gives occasion for a great many other mistakes

As soon as the ladies entered the room, Mr Selvin, with more gaiety than usual, advanced toward Arabella, who put on so cold and severe a countenance at his approach, that the poor man, extremely confused, drew back, and remained in great perplexity, fearing he had offended her.

Mr Tinsel, seeing Mr Selvin's reception, and awed by the becoming majesty in her person, notwithstanding all his assurance, accosted her with less confidence than was his custom; but Arabella, softening her looks with the most engaging smiles, made an apology for detaining them so long from the parade, gave her hand to the beau, as being not a suspected person, and permitted him to lead her out; Mr Glanville, to whom she always allowed the preference on those occasions, being a little indisposed, and not able to attend her.

Mr Tinsel, whose vanity was greatly flattered by the preference Arabella gave him to his companion, proceeded, according to his usual custom, to examine her looks and behaviour with more care, conceiving such a preference must proceed from a latent motive which was not unfavourable for him. His discernment on these occasions being very surprising, he soon discovered in the bright eyes of Arabella a secret approbation of his person, which he endeavoured to increase by displaying it, with all the address he was master of, and did not fail to talk her into an opinion of his wit, by ridiculing every body that passed them, and directing several studied compliments to herself.

Miss Glanville, who was not so agreeably entertained by the grave Mr Selvin, saw these advances to a gallantry with her cousin with great disturbance. She was resolved to interrupt it, if possible; and, being convinced Mr Selvin preferred Arabella's conversation to hers, she plotted how to pair them together, and have the beau to herself. As they walked a few paces behind her cousin and Mr Tinsel, she was in no danger of being overheard; and taking occasion to put Mr Selvin in mind of Arabella's behaviour to him, when he accosted her, she asked him if he was conscious of having done any thing to offend her.

I protest, madam, replied Mr Selvin, I know not of any thing I have done to displease her. I never failed, to my knowledge, in my respects towards her ladyship, for whom indeed I have a most profound veneration.—I know so much of her temper, resumed Miss Glanville, as to be certain, if she has taken it into her head to be angry with you, she will be ten times more so at your indifference; and if you hope for her favour, you must ask her pardon with the most earnest submission imaginable.

If I knew I had offended her, replied Mr Selvin, I would very willingly ask her pardon: but really, since I have not been guilty of any fault towards her ladyship, I don't know how to acknowledge it.

Well, said Miss Glanville coldly, I only took the liberty to give you some friendly advice, which you may follow, or not, as you please. I know my cousin is angry at something, and I wish you were friends again; that's all.—I am mightily obliged to you, madam, said Mr Selvin; and since you assure me her ladyship is angry, I'll ask her pardon, though, really, as I said before, I don't know for what.

Well, interrupted Miss Glanville, we'll join them at the end of the parade; and to give you an opportunity of speaking to my cousin, I'll engage Mr Tinsel myself.

Mr Selvin, who thought himself greatly obliged to Miss Glanville for her good intentions, though in reality she had a view of exposing her cousin, as well as an inclination to engage Mr Tinsel, took courage, as they turned, to get on the other side of Arabella, whom he had not dared before to approach; while Miss Glanville, addressing a whisper of no great importance to her cousin, parted her from the beau, and slackening her pace a little, fell into a particular discourse with him, which Arabella being too polite to interrupt, remained in a very perplexing situation, dreading every moment that Mr Selvin would explain himself; alarmed at his silence, yet resolved to interrupt him if he began to speak, and afraid of beginning a conversation first lest he should construe it to his advantage. Mr Selvin being naturally timid in the company of ladies, the circumstance of disgrace which he was in with Arabella, her silence and reserve, so added to his accustomed diffidence, that though he endeavoured several times to speak, he was not able to bring out any thing but a preluding hem; which he observed, to his extreme confusion, seemed always to increase Arabella's constraint. Indeed, that lady, upon any suspicion that he was going to break his mysterious silence, always contracted her brow into a frown, cast down her eyes with an air of perplexity, endeavoured to hide her blushes with her fan; and to shew her inattention, directed her looks to the contrary side. The lady and gentleman being in equal confusion, no advances were made on either side towards a conversation; and they had reached almost the end of the parade in an uninterrupted silence, when Mr Selvin, fearing he should never again have so good an opportunity of making his peace, collected all his resolution, and with an accent trembling under the importance of the speech he was going to make, began—

Madam, since I have had the honour of walking with your ladyship, I have observed so many signs of constraint in your manner, that I hardly dare entreat you to grant me a moment's hearing, while I—

Sir, interrupted Arabella, before you go any farther, I must inform you, that what you are going to say will mortally offend me. Take heed then how you commit any indiscretion which will force me to treat you very rigorously.—If your ladyship will not allow me to speak in my own justification, said Mr Selvin, yet I hope you will not refuse to tell me my offence: since I—You are very confident, indeed, interrupted Arabella again, to suppose I will repeat what would be infinitely grievous for me to hear.—Against my will, pursued she, I must give you the satisfaction to know, that I am not ignorant of your crime: but I also assure you, that I am highly incensed; and that not only with the thoughts you have dared to entertain of me, but likewise with your presumption in going about to disclose them.

Mr Selvin, whom the seeming contradictions in this speech astonished, yet imagined in general it hinted at the dispute between him and Mr Tinsel; and supposing the story had been told to his disadvantage, which was the cause of her anger, replied in great emotion at the injustice done him—

Since somebody has been so officious to acquaint your ladyship with an affair which ought to have been kept from your knowledge, it is a pity they did not inform you that Mr Tinsel was the person that had the least respect for your ladyship, and is more worthy of your resentment.—If Mr Tinsel, replied Arabella, is guilty of an offence like yours, yet since he has concealed it better, he is less culpable than you; and you have done that for him, which, haply, he would never have had courage enough to do for himself as long as he lived.—Poor Selvin, quite confounded at these intricate words, would have begged her to explain herself, had she not silenced him with a dreadful frown; and making a stop till Miss Glanville and Mr Tinsel came up to them, she told her cousin with a peevish accent, that she had performed her promise very ill; and whispered her, that she was to blame for all the mortifications she had suffered. Mr Tinsel, supposing the alteration in Arabella's humour proceeded from being so long deprived of his company, endeavoured to make her amends by a profusion of compliments; which she received with such an air of displeasure, that the beau, vexed at the ill success of his gallantry, told her, he was afraid Mr Selvin's gravity had infected her ladyship.

Say, rather, replied Arabella, that his indiscretion has offended me. Mr Tinsel, charmed with this beginning confidence, which confirmed his hopes of having made some impression on her heart, conjured her very earnestly to tell him how Mr Selvin had offended her. It is sufficient, resumed she, that I tell you he has offended me, without declaring the nature of his crime; since, doubtless, it has not escaped your observation, which, if I may believe him, is not wholly disinterested. To confess yet more, it is true that he hath told me something concerning you, which—

Let me perish, madam, interrupted the beau, if one syllable he has said be true.—How! said Arabella, a little disconcerted: will you always persist in a denial then?—Deny it, madam! returned Mr Tinsel: I'll deny what he has said with my last breath. It is all a scandalous forgery: no man living is less likely to think of your ladyship in that manner. If you knew my thoughts, madam, you would be convinced nothing is more impossible, and—

Sir, interrupted Arabella, extremely mortified, methinks you are very eager in your justification. I promise you, I do not think you guilty of the offence he charged you with. If I did, you would haply experience my resentment in such a manner as would make you repent of your presumption. Arabella, in finishing these words, interrupted Miss Glanville's discourse with Mr Selvin, to tell her she desired to return home; to which that young lady, who had not been at all pleased with the morning's walk, consented.

XII

In which our heroine reconciles herself to a mortifying incident, by recollecting an adventure in a romance, similar to her own

As soon as the ladies were come to their lodgings, Arabella went up to her own apartment to meditate upon what had passed, and Miss Glanville retired to dress for dinner; while the two gentlemen, who thought they had great reason to be dissatisfied with each other, on account of Lady Bella's behaviour, went to a coffee-house, in order to come to some explanation about it.

Well, sir, said the beau, with a sarcastic air, I am greatly obliged to you for the endeavours you have used to ruin me in Lady Bella's opinion. Rat me! if it is not the greatest misfortune in the world to give occasion for envy.—Envy, sir! interrupted Mr Selvin: I protest I do really admire your great skill in stratagems, but I do not envy you the possession of it. You have indeed very wittily contrived to put your own sentiments of that lady, which you delivered so freely the other night, into my mouth. It was a master-piece of cunning, indeed; and, as I said before, I admire your skill prodigiously.—I don't know what you mean, replied Tinsel: you talk in riddles. Did you not yourself acquaint Lady Bella with the preference I gave Miss Glanville to her? What would you propose by such a piece of treachery? You have ruined all my hopes by it. The lady resents it excessively: and it is no wonder, faith; it must certainly mortify her. Upon my soul, I can never forgive thee for so *mal à propos* a discovery.—Forgive me, sir! replied Selvin, in a rage: I don't want your forgiveness. I have done nothing unbecoming a man of honour. The lady was so prejudiced by your insinuations, that she would not give me leave to speak; otherwise I would have fully informed her of her mistake, that she might have known how much she was obliged to you.—So she would not hear thee? interrupted Tinsel, laughing: dear soul! how very kind was that! Faith, I don't know how it is, but I am very lucky without deserving to be so. Thou art a witness for me, Frank, I took no great pains to gain this fine creature's heart: but it was damn'd malicious though to attempt to make discoveries. I see she is a little piqued; but I'll set all to rights again with a *billet-doux*. I've an excellent hand, though I say it, at a *billet-doux*. I never knew one of mine fail in my life.—Harkee, sir, said Selvin, whispering: any more attempts to shift your sentiments upon me, and you shall hear of it. In the mean time, be assured, I'll clear myself, and put the saddle upon the right horse!—Demme, if thou art not a queer fellow, said Tinsel, endeavouring to hide his discomposure at this threat under a forced laugh. Selvin, without making any reply, retired to write to Arabella; which Tinsel suspecting, resolved to be before-hand with him: and, without leaving the coffee-house, called for paper, and wrote a billet to her, which he dispatched away immediately. The messenger had just got admittance to Lucy, when another arrived from Selvin.

They both presented their letters; but Lucy refused them, saying, her lady would turn her away, if she received such sort of letters.—Such sort of letters! returned Tinsel's man. Why, do you know what they contain, then?—To be sure I do, replied Lucy: they are love-letters; and my lady has charged me never to receive any more.—Well, replied Selvin's servant, you may take my letter; for my master desired me to tell you it was about business of consequence, which your lady must be acquainted with.

Since you assure me it is not a love-letter, I'll take it, said Lucy.—And pray take mine too, said Tinsel's Mercury; for, I assure you, it is not a love-letter neither; it is only a *billet-doux*.—Are you sure of that? replied Lucy: because I may venture to take it, I fancy, if it is what you say.—I'll swear it, said the man, delivering it to her.—Well, said she, receiving it, I'll take them both up. But what did you call this? pursued she. I must not forget it, or else my lady will think it a love-letter.

A *billet-doux*, said the man. Lucy, for fear she should forget it, repeated the words *billet-doux* several times as she went up stairs; but entering her lady's apartment, she, perceiving the letters in her hand, asked her so sternly how she durst presume to bring them into her presence, that the poor girl in her fright forgot the lesson she had been conning; and endeavouring to recal it into her memory, took no notice of her lady's question, which she repeated several times, but to no purpose.

Arabella, surprised at her inattention, reiterated her commands in a tone somewhat louder than usual; asking her, at the same time, why she did not obey her imediately. Indeed, madam, replied Lucy, your ladyship would not order me to take back the letters, if you knew what they were. They are not love-letters: I was resolved to be sure of that before I took them. This, madam, is a letter about business of consequence; and the other—Oh dear, I can't think what the man called it; but it is not a love-letter, indeed, madam.

You are a simple wench, said Arabella, smiling. You may depend upon it, all letters directed to me must contain matters of love and gallantry; and those I am not permitted to receive. Take them away then immediately.—But stay, pursued she, seeing she was about to obey her: one of them, you say, was delivered to you as a letter of consequence.

Perhaps it is so: indeed, it may contain an advertisement of some design to carry me away. How do I know but Mr Selvin, incited by his love and despair, may intend to make such an attempt? Give me that letter, Lucy: I am resolved to open it. As for the other—yet, who knows but the other may also bring me warning of the same danger from another quarter! The pains Mr Tinsel took to conceal his passion, nay, almost, as I think, to deny it, amounts to a proof that he is meditating some way to make sure of me. 'Tis certainly so. Give me that letter, Lucy: I should be accessary to their intended violence, if I neglected this timely discovery.

Well, cried she, taking one of the letters, this is exactly like what happened to the beautiful princess of Cappadocia, who, like me, in one and the same day, received advice that two of her lovers intended to carry her off.—As she pronounced these words, Miss Glanville entered the room, to whom Arabella immediately recounted the adventure of the letters; telling her she did not doubt but that they contained a discovery of some conspiracy to carry her away.—And whom does your ladyship suspect of such a strange design, pray? said Miss Glanville, smiling.—At present, replied Arabella, the two cavaliers who walked with us to-day are the persons who seem the most likely to attempt that violence.

I dare answer for Mr Tinsel, replied Miss Glanville: he thinks of no such thing.—Well, said Arabella, to convince you of your mistake, I must inform you, that Mr Selvin, having the presumption to begin a declaration of love to me on the parade this morning, I reproved him severely for his want of respect, and threatened him with my displeasure. In the rage of his jealousy, at seeing me treat Mr Tinsel well, he discovered to me that he also was as criminal as himself, in order to oblige me to a severer usage of him.

So he told you Mr Tinsel was in love with you? interrupted Miss Glanville.—He told it me in other words, replied Arabella; for he said Mr Tinsel was guilty of that offence which I resented so severely to him.—Miss Glanville, beginning to comprehend the mystery, with great difficulty forbore laughing at her cousin's mistake; for she well knew the offence of which Mr Selvin hinted at, and desirous of knowing what those letters contained, she begged her to delay opening them no longer. Arabella, pleased at her solicitude, opened one of the letters; but glancing her eye to the bottom, and seeing the name of Selvin, she threw it hastily upon the table, and averting her eyes, What a mortification have I avoided! said she: that letter is from Selvin, and, questionless, contains an avowal of his crime. Nay, you must read it, cried Miss Glanville, taking it up: since you have opened it, it is the same thing. You can never persuade him but you have seen it. However, to spare your nicety, I'll read it to you. Which accordingly she did, and found it as follows:

Madam,

I know not what insinuations have been made use of to persuade you I was guilty of the offence which, with justice, occasioned your resentment this morning; but I assure you, nothing was ever more false. My thoughts of your ladyship are very different, and full of the profoundest respect and, veneration. I have reason to suspect Mr Tinsel is the person who has thus endeavoured to prejudice me with your ladyship: therefore I am excusable if I tell you, that those very sentiments, too disrespectful to be named, which he would persuade you are mine, he discovered himself. He then, madam, is the person guilty of that offence he so falsely lays to the charge of him who is, with the utmost respect and esteem, madam, your ladyship's most obedient, and most humble servant,

F. Selvin.

How's this? cried Miss Glanville. Why, madam, you are certainly mistaken. You see Mr Selvin utterly denies the crime of loving you. He has suffered very innocently in your opinion. Indeed, your ladyship was too hasty in condemning him.—if what he says be true, replied Arabella, who had been in extreme confusion while a letter so different from what she expected was reading, I have indeed unjustly condemned him. Nevertheless, I am still inclined to believe this is all artifice; and that he is really guilty of entertaining a passion for me.—But why should he take so much pains to deny it, madam? said Miss Glanville. Methinks that looks very odd.—Not at all, interrupted Arabella, whose spirits were raised by recollecting an adventure in a romance similar to this: Mr Selvin has fallen upon the same stratagem with Seramenes, who, being in love with the beautiful Cleobuline, princess of Corinth, took all imaginable pains to conceal his passion, in order to be near that fair princess, who would have banished him from her presence, had she known he was in love with her. Nay, he went so far in his dissimulation, as to pretend love to one of the ladies of her court, that his passion for the princess might be the less taken notice of. In these cases, therefore, the more resolutely a man denies his passion, the more pure and violent it is.

Then Mr Selvin's passion is certainly very violent, replied Miss Glanville, for he denies it very resolutely; and I believe none but your ladyship would have discovered his artifice. But shall we not open the other letter? I have a strong notion it comes from Tinsel.

For that very reason I would not be acquainted with the contents, replied Arabella. You see Mr Selvin accuses him of being guilty of that offence which he denies. I shall doubtless meet with a confirmation of his love in that letter.—Do not, I beseech you, added she, seeing her cousin preparing to open the letter, expose me to the pain of hearing a presumptuous declaration of love. Nay, pursued she, rising in great emotion, if you are resolved to persecute me by reading it, I'll endeavour to get out of the hearing of it.

You shan't, I declare, said Miss Glanville, laughing, and holding her: I'll oblige you to hear it.

I vow, cousin, said Arabella, smiling, you use me just as the princess Cleopatra did the fair and wise Antonia. However, if by this you mean to do any kindness to the unfortunate person who wrote that billet, you are greatly mistaken; since, if you oblige me to listen to a declaration of his crime, you will lay me under a necessity to banish him, A sentence he would have avoided, while I remained ignorant of it.

To this Miss Glanville made no other reply than by opening the billet, the contents of which may be found in the following chapter.

XIII

In which our heroine's extravagance will be thought, perhaps, to be carried to an extravagant length

M ADAM,

I had the honour to assure you this morning on the parade, that the insinuations Mr Selvin made use of to rob me of the superlative happiness of your esteem, were entirely false and groundless. May the beams of your bright eyes never shine on me more, if there is any truth in what he said to prejudice me with your ladyship! If I am permitted to attend you to the rooms this evening, I hope to convince you, that it was absolutely impossible I could have been capable of such a crime; who am, with the most profound respect, your ladyship's most devoted, &c.

D. Tinsel

Well, madam, said Miss Glanville, when she had read this epistle, I fancy you need not pronounce a sentence of banishment upon poor Mr Tinsel: he seems to be quite innocent of the offence your ladyship suspects him of.—Why, really, returned Arabella, blushing with extreme confusion at this second disappointment, I am greatly perplexed to know how I ought to act on this occasion. I am much in the same situation with the princess Serena. For, you must know, this princess—Here Lucy entering, informed the ladies dinner was served. I shall defer till another opportunity, said Arabella, upon this interruption, the relation of the princess Serena's adventures; which you will find, added she, in a low voice, bear a very great resemblance to mine. Miss Glanville replied, she would hear it whenever she pleased and then followed Arabella to the dining-room.

The cloth was scarce removed, when Mr Selvin came in. Arabella blushed at his appearance, and discovered so much perplexity in her behaviour, that Mr Selvin was apprehensive he had not yet sufficiently justified himself; and therefore took the first opportunity to approach her.

I shall think myself very unhappy, madam, said he, bowing, if the letter I did myself the honour to write to you this morning—

Sir, interrupted Arabella, I perceive you are going to forget the contents of that letter, and preparing again to offend me by a presumptuous declaration of love.—Who, I, madam! replied he, in great astonishment and confusion. I-I-I protest—though I have a very great respect for your ladyship, yet—yet I never presumed to—to—to—You have presumed too much, replied Arabella; and I should forget what I owed to my own glory, if I furnished you with any more occasions of offending me. Know, then, I absolutely forbid you to appear before me again, at least till I am convinced you have changed your sentiments.

Saying this, she rose from her seat, and making a sign to him not to follow her, which, indeed, he had no intention to do, she quitted the room, highly satisfied with her own conduct upon this occasion, which was exactly conformable to the laws of romance.

Mr Tinsel, who had just alighted from his chair, having a glimpse of her, as she passed to her own apartment, resolved, if possible, to procure a private interview; for he did not doubt but his billet had done wonders in his favour. For that purpose he ventured up to her anti-chamber, where he found Lucy in waiting, whom he desired to acquaint her lady, that he entreated a moment's speech with her. Lucy, after hesitating a moment, and looking earnestly at him, replied, Sir, if you'll promise me faithfully you are not in love with my lady, I'll go and deliver your message.—Deuce take me, said Tinsel, if that is not a very whimsical condition truly—Pray, my dear, how came it into thy little brain, to suspect I was in love with thy lady? But, suppose I should be in love with her, what then?—Why then, it is likely you would die, that's all, said Lucy, without my lady would be so kind to command you to live.—I vow thou hast pretty notions, child, said Tinsel, smiling. Hast thou been reading any play-book lately? But pray, dost think thy lady would have compassion on me, if I was in love with her? Come, I know thou art in her confidence: hast thou ever heard her talk of me? Does she not tell thee all her secrets?

Here Arabella's bell ringing, the beau slipped half-a-guinea into her hand, which Lucy not willing to refuse, went immediately to her lady; to whom, with a trembling accent, she repeated Mr Tinsel's request.

Imprudent girl! cried Arabella, (for I am loth to suspect thee of disloyalty to thy mistress), dost thou know the nature and extent of the request thou hast delivered? Art thou ignorant that the presumptuous man whom thou solicitest this favour for, has mortally offended me?—Indeed, madam, said Lucy, frightened out of her wits, I don't solicit for him: I scorn to do any such thing. I would not offend your ladyship for the world; for, before I would deliver his message to your ladyship, I made him assure me, that he was not in love with your ladyship.

That was very wisely done indeed, replied Arabella, smiling: and do you believe he spoke the truth? Yes, indeed, I am sure of it, said Lucy, eagerly. If your ladyship will but be pleased to see him; he is only in the next room; I dare promise—How! interrupted Arabella. What have you done? Have you brought him into my apartment, then? I protest this adventure is exactly like what befel the beautiful Statira, when, by a stratagem of the same kind, Oroondates was introduced into her presence. Lucy, thou art another Barsina, I think; but I hope thy intentions are not less innocent than hers were.—Indeed, madam, replied Lucy, almost weeping, I am very innocent. I am no Barsina, as your ladyship calls me.—I dare answer for thee, said Arabella, smiling at the turn she gave to her words, thou art no Barsina: and I should wrong thee very much to compare thee with that wise princess; for thou art certainly one of the most simple wenches in the world. But since thou hast gone so far, let me know what the unfortunate person desires of me; for, since I am neither more rigid nor pretend to more virtue than Statira, I may do at least as much for him as that great queen did for Oroondates.He desires, madam, said Lucy, that your ladyship would be pleased to let him speak with you.—Or, in his words, I suppose, replied Arabella, he humbly implored a moment's audience.

I told your ladyship his very words, indeed, madam, said Lucy.—I tell thee, girl, thou art mistaken, said Arabella: it is impossible he should sue for such a favour in terms like those: therefore, go back, and let him know that I consent to grant him a short audience upon these conditions:—First, Provided he does not abuse my indulgence by offending me with any protestations of his passion; secondly, That he engages to fulfil the injunctions I shall lay upon him, however cruel and terrible they may appear;—lastly, That his despair must not prompt him to any act of desperation against himself. Lucy, having received this message, quitted the room hastily, for fear she should forget it.

Well, my pretty ambassadress, said Tinsel, when he saw her enter the anti-chamber, will your lady see me?

No, sir, replied Lucy.   No! interrupted Tinsel, that's kind, 'faith, after waiting so long.

Pray, sir, said Lucy, don't put me out so: I shall forget what my lady ordered me to tell you.—Oh! I ask your pardon, child, said Tinsel: come, let me hear your message.—Sir, said Lucy, adopting the solemnity of her lady's accent, my lady bade me say that she will grant—No, that she consents to grant you a short dience.—Audience, you would say, child, said Tinsel: but how came you to tell me before she would not see me?—I vow and protest, sir, said Lucy, you have put all my lady's words clean out of my head: I don't know what comes next.—Oh, no matter, said Tinsel: you have told me enough: I'll wait upon her directly.—Lucy, who saw him making towards the door, pressed between it and him; and having all her lady's whims in her head, supposed he was going to carry her away. Possessed with this thought, she screamed out, Help! help! for Heaven's sake! My lady will be carried away!—Arabella hearing this exclamation of her woman's, echoed her screams, though with a voice infinitely more delicate; and seeing Tinsel, who, confounded to the last degree at the cries of both the lady and her woman, had got into her chamber he knew not how, she gave herself over for lost, and fell back in her chair in a swoon, or something she took for a swoon; for she was persuaded it could happen no otherwise, since all ladies in the same circumstances are terrified into a fainting fit, and seldom recover till they are conveniently carried away; and when they awake, find themselves many miles off, in the power of their ravisher. Arabella's other women, alarmed by her cries, came running into the room; and seeing Mr Tinsel there, and their lady in a swoon, concluded some very extraordinary accident had happened.—What is your business here? cried they all at a time. Is it you that has frighted her ladyship?— Devil take me! said Tinsel, amazed, if I can tell what all this means.

By this time, Sir Charles, Mr Glanville, and his sister, came running astonished up stairs. Arabella still continued motionless in her chair, her eyes closed, and her head reclined upon Lucy, who, with her other women, was endeavouring to recover her. Mr Glanville eagerly ran to her assistance, while Sir Charles and his daughter as eagerly interrogated Mr Tinsel, who stood motionless with surprise, concerning the cause of her disorder. Arabella, then first discovering some signs of life, half opened her eyes. Inhuman wretch! cried she, with a faint voice, supposing herself in the hands of her ravisher, think not thy cruel violence shall procure thee what thy submissions could not obtain; and if when thou hadst only my indifference to surmount, thou didst find it so difficult to overcome my resolution, now that, by this unjust attempt, thou hast added aversion to that indifference, never hope for any thing but the most bitter reproaches from me.—Why, niece, said Sir Charles, approaching her, what is the matter? Look up, I beseech you: nobody is attempting to do you any hurt: here's none but friends about you. Arabella, raising her head at the sound of her uncle's voice, and casting a confused look on the persons about her.

May I believe my senses? Am I rescued, and in my own chamber? To whose valour is my deliverance owing? Without doubt, it is to my cousin's: but where is he? Let me assure him of my gratitude.

Mr Glanville, who had retired to a window in great confusion, as soon as he heard her call for him, came towards her, and in a whisper begged her to be composed; that she was in no danger. And pray, niece, said Sir Charles, now you are a little recovered, be so good to inform us of the cause of your fright. What has happened to occasion all this confusion?—How, sir! said Arabella, don't you know, then, what has happened? Pray, how was I brought again into my chamber, and by what means was I rescued? I protest, said Sir Charles, I don't know that you have been out of it.

Alas! replied Arabella, I perceive you are quite ignorant of what has befallen me: nor am I able to give you any information. All I can tell you is, that alarmed by my woman's cries, and the sight of my ravisher, who came into my chamber, I fainted away, and so facilitated his enterprise; since, doubtless, it was very easy for him to carry me away while I remained in that senseless condition. How I was rescued, or by whom, one of my women can haply inform you; since, it is probable, one of them was also forced away with me—Oh, Heavens! cried she, seeing Tinsel, who all this while stood gazing like one distracted: what makes that impious man appear in my presence! What am I to think of this? Am I really delivered, or no?

What can this mean? cried Sir Charles, turning to Tinsel. Have you, sir, had any hand in frighting my niece?—I, sir! said Tinsel: let me perish, if ever I was so confounded in my life. The lady's brain is disordered, I believe.—Mr Glanville, who was convinced all this confusion was caused by some of Arabella's whims, dreaded lest an explanation would the more expose her; and therefore told his father that it would be best to retire, and leave his cousin to the care of his sister and her women; adding, that she was not yet quite recovered, and their presence did but discompose her. Then addressing himself to Tinsel, he told him he would wait upon him down stairs.—Arabella, seeing them going away together, and supposing they intended to dispute the possession of her with their swords, called out to them to stay.

Mr Glanville, however, without minding her, pressed Mr Tinsel to walk down. Nay, pray, sir, said the beau, let us go in again: she may grow outrageous, if we disoblige her.—Outrageous, sir! said Glanville: do you suppose my cousin is mad? Upon my soul, sir, replied Tinsel, if she is not mad, she is certainly a little out of her senses, or so. Arabella, having reiterated her commands for her lovers to return, and finding they did not obey her, ran to her chamber-door, where they were holding a surly sort of conference, especially on Glanville's side, who was horridly out of humour.

I perceive by your looks, said Arabella to her cousin, the design you are meditating; but know, that I absolutely forbid you, by all the power I have over you, not to engage in combat with my ravisher here.

Madam, interrupted Glanville, I beseech you, do not——. I know, said she, you will object to me the examples of Artamenes, Aronces, and many others, who were so generous as to promise their rivals not to refuse them that satisfaction whenever they demanded it; but consider, you have not the same obligations to Mr Tinsel that Artamenes had to the king of Assyria, or that Aronces had to——

For God's sake, cousin, said Glanville, what's all this to the purpose? Curse on Aronces and the king of Assyria, I say!—The astonishment of Arabella at this intemperate speech of her cousin, kept her for a moment immoveable; when Sir Charles, who, during this discourse, had been collecting all the information he could from Lucy concerning this perplexed affair, came towards Tinsel, and, giving him an angry look, told him, he should take it well if he forbore visiting any of his family for the future.—Oh, your most obedient servant, sir, said Tinsel. You expect, I suppose, I should be excessively chagrined at this prohibition; but upon my soul, I am greatly obliged to you. Agad! I have no great mind to a halter: and since this lady is so apt to think people have a design to ravish her, the wisest thing a man can do is to keep out of her way.

Sir, replied Glanville, who had followed him to the door, I believe there has been some little mistake in what has happened to-day. However, I expect you'll take no unbecoming liberties with the character of Lady Bella. —Oh, sir! said Tinsel, I give you my honour I shall always speak of the lady with the most profound veneration. She is a most accomplished, incomprehensible lady: and the devil take me, if I think there is her fellow in the world—And so, sir, I am your most obedient——A word with you before you go, said Glanville, stopping him. No more of these sneers, as you value that smooth face of yours, or I'll despoil it of a nose.—Oh! your humble servant, said the beau, retiring in great confusion, with something betwixt a smile and a grin upon his countenance, which he took care, however, Mr

Glanville should not see; who, as soon as he quitted him, went again to Arabella's apartment, in order to prevail upon his father and sister to leave her a little to herself: for he dreaded lest some more instances of her extravagance would put it into his father's head that she was really out of her senses.—Well, sir, said Arabella, upon his entrance, you have, I suppose, given your rival his liberty. I assure you this generosity is highly agreeable to me. And herein you imitate the noble Artamenes, who, upon a like occasion, acted as you have done: for when Fortune had put the ravisher of Mandane in his power, and he became the vanquisher of his rival, who endeavoured by violence to possess that divine princess, this truly generous hero relinquished the right he had of disposing of his prisoner, and, instead of sacrificing his life to his just and reasonable vengeance, he gave a proof of his admirable virtue and clemency by dismissing him in safety, as you have done.—However, added she, I hope you have made him swear upon your sword that he will never make a second attempt upon my liberty.—I perceive, pursued she, seeing Mr Glanville continued silent, with his eyes bent on the ground, for indeed he was ashamed to look up, that you would willingly avoid the praise due to the heroic action you have just performed: nay, I suppose you are resolved to keep it secret, if possible: yet I must tell you, that you will not escape the glory due to it. Glory is as necessarily the result of a virtuous action, as light is an effect of the sun which causeth it, and has no dependence on any other cause; since a virtuous action continues still the same, though it be done without testimony: and glory, which is, as one may say, born with it, constantly attends it, though the action be not known.

I protest, niece, said Sir Charles, that's very prettily said.

In my opinion, sir, pursued Arabella, if any thing can weaken the glory of a good action, it is the care a person takes to make it known; as if one did not do good for the sake of good, but for the praise that generally follows it. Those, then, that are governed by so interested a motive, ought to be considered as sordid rather than generous persons; who, making a kind of traffic between virtue and glory, barter just so much of the one for the other, and expect, like other merchants, to make advantage by the exchange.—Mr Glanville, who was charmed into an ecstasy at this sensible speech of Arabella's, forgot in an instant all her absurdities. He did not fail to express his admiration of her understanding, in terms that brought a blush into her fair face, and obliged her to lay her commands upon him to cease his excessive commendations. Then making a sign to them to leave her alone, Mr Glanville, who understood her, took his father and sister down stairs, leaving Arabella with her faithful Lucy, whom she immediately commanded to give her a relation of what had happened to her from the time of her swooning till she recovered.

XIV

A dialogue between Arabella and Lucy, in which the latter seems to have the advantage

WHY, MADAM, SAID LUCY, ALL I can tell your ladyship is, that we were all excessively frightened, to be sure, when you fainted, especially myself; and that we did what we could to recover you. And so accordingly your ladyship did recover.

What's this to the purpose? Said Arabella, perceiving she stopped here. I know that I fainted, and it is also very plain that I recovered again, I ask you what happened to me in the intermediate time between my fainting and recovery? Give me a faithful relation of all the accidents to which by my fainting I am quite a stranger, and which, no doubt, are very considerable.—Indeed, madam, replied Lucy, I have given your ladyship a faithful relation of all I can remember.—When? resumed Arabella, surprised.

This moment, madam, said Lucy.—Why, sure thou dreamest, wench! replied she. Hast thou told me how I was seized and carried off? how I was rescued again? And—No, indeed, madam, interrupted Lucy, I don't dream: I never told your ladyship that you was carried off.—Well, said Arabella., and why dost thou not satisfy my curiosity? Is it not fit I should be acquainted with such a momentous part of my history?—I can't, indeed, and please your ladyship, said Lucy.—What canst thou not? said Arabella, enraged at her stupidity.—Why, madam, said Lucy, sobbing, I can't make a history of nothing!—Of nothing, wench! resumed Arabella, in a greater rage than before. Dost thou call an adventure to which thou wast a witness, and borest haply so great a share in, nothing? An adventure which hereafter will make a considerable figure in the relation of my life, dost thou look upon as trifling and of no consequence?—No, indeed I don't, madam, said Lucy.

Why, then, pursued Arabella, dost thou wilfully neglect to relate it? Suppose, as there is nothing more likely, thou wert commanded by some persons of considerable quality, or haply some great princes and princesses, to recount the adventures of my life, wouldest thou omit a circumstance of so much moment?

No, indeed, madam! said Lucy.—I am glad to hear thou art so discreet, said Arabella: and pray do me the favour to relate this adventure to me, as thou wouldest do to those princes and princesses, if thou went commanded.—Here Arabella, making a full stop, fixed her eyes upon her woman, expecting every moment she would begin the desired narrative; but, finding she continued silent longer than she thought was necessary for recalling the several circumstances of the story into her mind—I find, said she, it will be necessary to caution you against making your audience wait too long for your relation. It looks as if you was to make a studied speech, not a simple relation of facts, which ought to be free from all affectation of labour and art, and be told with that graceful negligence which is so becoming to truth. This I thought proper to tell you, added she, that you may not fall into that mistake when you are called upon to relate my adventures. Well, now if you please to begin.—What, pray madam? said Lucy.—What! repeated Arabella: why the adventures which happened to me so lately. Relate to me every circumstance of my being carried away, and how my deliverance was affected by my cousin.

Indeed, madam, said Lucy, I know nothing about your ladyship's being carried away.

Be gone, cried Arabella, losing all patience at her obstinacy: get out of my presence this moment: Wretch! unworthy of my confidence and favour: thy treason is too manifest: thou art bribed by that presumptuous man to conceal all the circumstances of his attempt from my knowledge, to the end that I may not have a full conviction of his guilt.—Lucy, who never saw her lady so much offended before, and knew not the occasion of it, burst into tears; which so affected the tender heart of Arabella, that, losing insensibly all her anger, she told her, with a voice softened to a tone of the utmost sweetness and condescension, that provided she would confess how far she had been prevailed upon by his rich presents to forget her duty, she would pardon and receive her again into favour.

Speak, added she, and be not afraid, after this promise, to let me know what Mr Tinsel required of thee, and what were the gifts with which he purchased thy services. Doubtless, he presented thee with jewels of a considerable value.

Since your ladyship, said Lucy, sobbing, has promised not to be angry, I don't care if I do tell your ladyship what he gave me. He gave me this half-guinea, madam: indeed he did: but for all that, when he would come into your chamber, I struggled with him, and cried out, for fear he should carry your ladyship away. Arabella, lost in astonishment and shame at hearing of so inconsiderable a present made to her woman, the like of which not one of her romances could furnish her, ordered her immediately to withdraw, not being willing she should observe the confusion this strange bribe had given her. After she had been gone some time, she endeavoured to compose her looks, and went down to the dining-room, where Sir Charles and his son and daughter had been engaged in a conversation concerning her; the particulars of which may be found in the first chapter of the next book.

END OF THE SEVENTH BOOK

BOOK VIII

I

Contains the conversation referred to in the last chapter of the preceding book

MISS GLANVILLE, WHO WITH A malicious pleasure had secretly triumphed in the extravagancies her beautiful cousin had been guilty of, was now sensibly disappointed to find they had so little effect on her father and brother; for instead of reflecting upon the absurdities to which they had been a witness, Mr Glanville artfully pursued the subject Arabella had just before been expatiating upon, taking notice frequently of some observations of hers, and by a well-contrived repetition of her words, obliged his father a second time to declare that his niece had spoken extremely well. Mr Glanville, taking the word, launched out into such praises of her wit, that Miss Glanville, no longer able to listen patiently, replied—It was true Lady Bella sometimes said very sensible things; that it was a great pity she was not always in a reasonable way of thinking, or that her intervals were not longer.—Her intervals, miss! said Glanville: pray what do you mean by that expression?—Why, pray, said Miss Glanville, don't you think my cousin is sometimes a little wrong in the head?

Mr Glanville, at these words starting from his chair, took a turn across the room in great discomposure: then stopping all of a sudden, and giving his sister a furious look—Charlotte, said he, don't give me cause to think you are envious of your cousin's superior excellencies.—Envious! repeated Miss Glanville: I envious of my cousin! I vow I should never have thought of that. Indeed, brother, you are much mistaken: my cousin's superior excellencies never gave me a moment's disturbance; though, I must confess, her unaccountable whims have often excited my pity.

No more of this, Charlotte, interrupted Mr Glanville, as you value my friendship: no more of it. Why, really, son, said Sir Charles, my niece has very strange whimsies sometimes. How it came into her head to think Mr Tinsel would attempt to carry her away, I can't imagine. For, after all, he only pressed rather too rudely into her chamber for which, as you see, I have forbidden his visits. That was of a piece, said Miss Glanville, sneeringly, to her brother, with her asking you if you had made Mr Tinsel swear upon your sword that be would never again attempt to carry her away; and applauding you for having given him his liberty, as the generous Atermens did on the same occasion.—I would advise you, Charlotte, said Mr Glanville, not to aim at repeating your cousin's words, till you know how to pronounce them properly.—Oh! that's one of her superior excellencies! said Miss Glanville.—Indeed, miss, said Glanville, very provokingly, she is superior to you in many things and as much so in the goodness of her heart as in the beauty of her person!

Come, come, Charles, said the baronet, who observed his daughter sat swelling and biting her lips at this reproach, personal reflections are better avoided. Your sister is very well, and not to be disparaged; though, to be sure, Lady Bella is the finest woman I ever saw in my life.—Miss Glanville was, if possible, more disgusted at her father's palliation than her brother's reproaches; and, in order to give a loose to her passion, accused Mr Glanville of a decrease in his affection for her, since he had been in love with her cousin; and, having found this excuse for her tears, very freely gave vent to them. Mr Glanville, being softened by this sight, sacrificed a few compliments to her vanity, which soon restored her to her usual tranquillity; then, turning the discourse on his beloved Arabella, pronounced a panegyric on her virtues and accomplishments of an hour long; which, if it did not absolutely persuade his sister to change her opinion, certainly convinced his father that his niece was not only perfectly well in her understanding, but even better than most others of her sex. Mr Glanville had just finished her eulogium when Arabella appeared. Joy danced in his eyes at her approach: he gazed upon her with a kind of conscious triumph in his looks; her consummate loveliness justifying his passion, and being in his opinion more than an excuse for all her extravagancies.

II

In which our heroine, as we presume, shews herself in two very different lights

ARABELLA, WHO AT HER ENTRANCE had perceived some traces of uneasiness upon Miss Glanville's countenance, tenderly asked her the cause; to which that young lady answering in a cold and reserved manner, Mr Glanville, to divert her reflections on it, very freely accused himself of having given his sister some offence.—To be sure, brother, said Miss Glanville, you are very vehement in your temper, and are as violently carried away about things of little importance as of the greatest; and then, whatever you have a fancy for, you love so obstinately.—I am obliged to you, miss, interrupted Mr Glanville, for endeavouring to give Lady Bella so unfavourable as opinion of me.—I assure you, said Arabella, Miss Glanville has said nothing to your disadvantage; for, in my opinion, the temperament of great minds ought to be such as she represents yours to be. For there is nothing at so great a distance from true and heroic virtue, as that indifference which obliges some people to be pleased with all things or nothing: whence it comes to pass, that they neither entertain great desires of glory, nor fear of infamy; that they neither love nor hate; that they are wholly influenced by custom, and are sensible only of the afflictions of the body, their minds being in a manner insensible.

To say the truth, I am inclined to conceive a greater hope of a man, who in the beginning of his life is hurried away by some evil habit, than one that fastens on nothing. The mind that cannot be brought to detest vice, will never be persuaded to love virtue; but one who is capable of loving or hating irreconcilably, by having, when young, his passions directed to proper objects, will remain fixed in his choice of what is good. But with him who is incapable of any violent attraction, and whose heart is chilled by a general indifference, precept or example will have no force; and philosophy itself, which boasts it hath remedies for all indispositions of the soul, never had any that could cure an indifferent mind. Nay, added she, I am persuaded that indifference is generally the inseparable companion of a weak and imperfect judgment; for it is so natural to a person to be carried towards that which he believes to be good, that if indifferent people were able to judge of things, they would fasten on something. But certain it is, that this lukewarmness of soul, which sends forth but feeble desires, sends also but feeble lights; so that those who are guilty of it, not knowing any thing clearly, cannot fasten on any thing with perseverance.—Mr Glanville, when Arabella had finished this speech, cast a triumphing glance at his sister, who had affected great inattention all the while she had been speaking. Sir Charles, in his way, expressed much admiration of her wit; telling her, if she had been a man, she would have made a great figure in parliament, and that her speeches might have come, perhaps, to be printed, in time.—This compliment, odd as it was, gave great joy to Glanville; when the conversation was interrupted by the arrival of Mr Selvin, who had slipt away unobserved at the time that Arabella's indisposition had alarmed them, and now came to inquire after her health; and also, if an opportunity offered, to set her right with regard to the suspicions she had entertained of his designing to pay his addresses to her.

Arabella, as soon as he had sent in his name, appeared to be in great disturbance; and upon his entrance, offered immediately to withdraw, telling Mr Glanville, who would have detained her, that she found no place was likely to secure her from the persecutions of that gentleman.—Glanville stared, and looked strangely perplexed at this speech: Miss Glanville smiled; and poor Selvin, with a very silly look, hemm'd two or three times, and then, with a faultering accent, said, Madam, I am very much concerned to find your ladyship resolved to persist in—Sir, interrupted Arabella, my resolutions are unalterable. I told you so before, and am surprised, after the knowledge of my intentions, you presume to appear in my presence again, from whence I had so positively banished you.—Pray, niece, said Sir Charles, what has Mr Selvin done to disoblige you?—Sir, replied Arabella, Mr Selvin's offence can admit of no other reparation than that which I required of him, which was a voluntary banishment from my presence; and in this, pursued she, I am guilty of no more severity to you than the princess Udosia was to the unfortunate Thrasimedes. For the passion of this prince having come to her knowledge, notwithstanding the pains he took to conceal it, this fair and wise princess thought it not enough to forbid his speaking to her, but also banished him from her presence; laying a peremptory command upon him, never to appear before her again till he was perfectly cured of that unhappy love he had entertained for her. Imitate, therefore, the meritorious obedience of this poor prince: and if that passion you profess for me—

How, sir! interrupted Sir Charles: do you make love to my niece, then?—Sir, replied Mr Selvin, who was strangely confounded at Arabella's speech, though I really admire the perfections this lady is possessed of, yet I assure you, upon my honour, I never had a thought of making any addresses to her; and I cannot imagine why her ladyship persists in accusing me of such presumption.—So formal a denial, after what Arabella had said, extremely perplexed Sir Charles, and filled Mr Glanville with inconceivable shame.—Miss Glanville enjoyed their disturbance, and, full of an ill-natured triumph, endeavoured to look Arabella into confusion; but that lady not being at all discomposed by this declaration of Mr Selvin's, having accounted for it already, replied with great calmness—

Sir, it is easy to see through the artifice of your disclaiming any passion for me. Upon any other occasion, questionless, you would rather sacrifice your life, than consent to disavow the sentiments which, unhappily for your peace, you have entertained. At present the desire of continuing near me obliges you to lay this constraint upon yourself. However, you know Thrasimedes fell upon the same stratagem to no purpose. The rigid Udosia saw through the disguise, and would not dispense with herself from banishing him from Rome, as I do you from England.

How, madam! interrupted Selvin, amazed.

Yes, sir, replied Arabella, hastily: nothing less can satisfy what I owe to the consideration of my own glory.—Upon my word, madam, said

Selvin, half angry, and yet strongly inclined to laugh, I don't see the necessity of my quitting my native country, to satisfy what you owe to the consideration of your own glory. Pray, how does my staying in England affect your ladyship's glory?—To answer your question with another, said Arabella, pray how did the stay of Thrasimedes in Rome affect the glory of the empress Udosia?—Mr Selvin was struck dumb with this speech, for he was not willing to be thought so deficient in the knowledge of history, as not to be acquainted with the reasons why Thrasimedes should not stay in Rome. His silence therefore seeming to Arabella to be a tacit confession of the justness of her commands, a sentiment of compassion for this unfortunate lover intruded itself into her mind; and turning her bright eyes, full of a soft complacency, upon Selvin, who stared at her as if he had lost his wits—I will not, said she, wrong the sublimity of your passion for me so much as to doubt your being ready to sacrifice the repose of your own life to the satisfaction of mine: nor will I do so much injustice to your generosity, as to suppose the glory of obeying my commands will not in some measure soften the rigour of your destiny. I know not whether it may be lawful for me to tell you that your misfortune does really cause me some affliction; but I am willing to give you this consolation, and also to assure you, that to whatever part of the world your despair will carry you, the good wishes and compassion of Arabella shall follow you.—Having said this, with one of her fair hands she covered her face, to hide the blushes which so compassionate a speech had caused; holding the other extended with a careless air, supposing he would kneel to kiss it, and bathe it with his tears, as was the custom on such melancholy occasions, her head at the same time turned another way, as if reluctantly and with confusion she granted this favour. But after standing a moment in this posture, and finding her hand untouched, she concluded grief had deprived him of his sense and that he would shortly fall into a swoon as Thrasimedes did; and to prevent being a witness of so doleful a sight, she hurried out of the room, without once turning about; and having reached her own apartment, sunk into a chair, not a little affected with the deplorable condition in which she had left her supposed miserable lover.

III

The contrast continued

THE COMPANY SHE HAD LEFT behind her being all, except Mr
Glanville, to the last degree surprised at her strange words and
actions, continued mute for several minutes after she was gone, staring
upon one another, as if each wished to know the other's opinion of
such an unaccountable behaviour. At last Miss Glanville, who observed
her brother's back towards her, told Mr Selvin, in a low voice, that she
hoped he would call and take his leave of them before he set out for
the place where his despair would carry him—Mr Selvin, in spite of
his natural gravity, could not forbear laughing at this speech of Miss
Glanville's, which shocked her brother; and not being able to stay where
Arabella was ridiculed, nor entitled to resent it, which would have been
a manifest injustice on that occasion, he retired to his own apartment,
to give vent to that spleen which in those moments made him out of
humour with all the world.—Sir Charles, when he was gone, indulged
himself in a little mirth on his niece's extravagance, protesting he did
not know what to do with her. Upon which Miss Glanville observed,
that it was a pity there were not such things as Protestant nunneries;
giving it as her opinion, that her cousin ought to be confined in one
of those places, and never suffered to see any company, by which means
she would avoid exposing herself in the manner she did now. Mr Selvin,
who possibly thought this a reasonable scheme of Miss Glanville's,
seemed by his silence to assent to her opinion; but Sir Charles was
greatly displeased with his daughter for expressing herself so freely;
alleging that Arabella, when she was out of those whims, was a very
sensible young lady, and sometimes talked as learnedly as a divine. To
which Mr Selvin also added, that she had a great knowledge of history,
and had a most surprising memory; and after some more discourse to
the same purpose, he took his leave, earnestly entreating Sir Charles to

believe that he never entertained any design of making his addresses to Lady Bella.

In the mean time, that lady, after having given near half an hour to those reflections which occur to heroines in the same situation with herself, called for Lucy, and ordered her to go to the dining-room, and see in what condition Mr Selvin was, telling her she had certainly left him in a swoon, as also the occasion of it; and bade her give him all the consolation in her power.—Lucy, with tears in her eyes at this recital, went down as she was ordered; and entering the room without any ceremony, her thoughts being wholly fixed on the melancholy circumstance her lady had been telling her, she looked eagerly round the room without speaking a word, till Sir Charles and Miss Glanville, who thought she had been sent with some message from Ararbella, asked her, both at the same instant, what she wanted.—I came, sir, said Lucy, repeating her lady's words, to see in what condition Mr Selvin is in, and to give him all the solation in my power.—Sir Charles, laughing heartily at this speech, asked her what she could do for Mr Selvin? To which she replied she did not know, but her lady had told her to give him all the solation in her power.

Consolation thou wouldst say, I suppose, said Sir Charles.—Yes, sir, said Lucy, curtseying.—Well, child, added he, go up and tell your lady, Mr Selvin does not need any consolation.—Lucy accordingly returned with this message, and was met at the chamber-door by Arabella, who hastily asked her if Mr Selvin was recovered from his swoon: to which Lucy replied, that she did not know; but that Sir Charles bade her tell her ladyship, Mr Selvin did not need any consolation. Oh, Heavens! cried Arabella, throwing herself into a chair as pale as death: he is dead! He has fallen upon his sword, and put an end to his life and miseries at once. Oh! how unhappy am I, cried she, bursting into tears, to be the cause of so cruel an accident! Was ever any fate so terrible as mine? Was ever beauty so fatal? Was ever rigour so unfortunate? How will the quiet of my future days be disturbed by the sad remembrance of a man whose death was caused by my disdain!—But why, resumed she, after a little pause, why do I thus afflict myself for what has happened by an unavoidable necessity?

Nor am I singular in the misfortune which has befallen me. Did not
the sad Perinthus die for the beautiful Panthea? Did not the rigour of
Barsina bring the miserable Oxyatres to the grave? and the severity of
Statira make Oroondates fall upon his sword in her presence, though
happily he escaped being killed by it? Let us, then, not afflict ourselves
unreasonably at this sad accident: let us lament, as we ought, the fatal
effects of our charms. But let us comfort ourselves with the thought
that we have only acted conformably to our duty.—Arabella having
pronounced these last words with a solemn and lofty accent, ordered
Lucy, who listened to her with eyes drowned in tears, to go down and
ask if the body was removed. For, added she, all my constancy will not
be sufficient to support me against that pitiful sight. Lucy accordingly
delivered her message to Sir Clarles and Miss Glanville, who were still
together, discoursing on the fantastical turn of Arabella; when the knight,
who could not possibly comprehand what she meant by asking if the
body was removed, bid her tell her lady he desired to speak with her.

Arabella, upon receiving this summons, set herself to consider what
could be the intent of it. If Mr Selvin be dead, said she, what good can
my presence do among them? Surely it cannot be to upbraid me with
my severity, that my uncle desires to see me. No, it would be unjust to
suppose it, Questionless, my unhappy lover is still struggling with the
pangs of death, and, for a consolation in his last moments, implores the
favour of resigning up his life in my sight. Pausing a little at these words,
she rose from her seat with a resolution to give the unhappy Selvin her
pardon before he died. Meeting Mr Glanville as he was returning from
his chamber to the dining-room, she told him, she hoped the charity
she was going to discover towards his rival, would not give him any
uneasiness; and preventing his reply, by going hastily into the room,
he followed her, dreading some new extravagance, yet not able to
prevent it, endeavoured to conceal his confusion from her observation.
Arabella, after breathing a gentle sigh, told Sir Charles, that she was
come to grant Mr Selvin her pardon for the offence he had been
guilty of, that he might depart in peace.—Well, well, said Sir Charles,
he is departed in peace without it.—How, sir! interrupted Arabella: is

he dead then already? Alas! why had he not the satisfaction of seeing me before he expired, that his soul might have departed in peace? He would have been assured not only of my pardon, but pity also; and that assurance would have made him happy in his last moments.—Why, niece, interrupted Sir Charles, staring, you surprise me prodigiously. Are you in earnest?—Questionless I am, sir, said she: nor ought you to be surprised at the concern I expressed for the fate of this unhappy man, nor at the pardon I proposed to have granted him; since herein I am justified by the example of many great and virtuous princesses, who have done as much, nay, haply, more than I intended to have done, for persons whose offences were greater than Mr Selvin's.

I am very sorry, madam, said Sir Charles, to hear you talk in this manner. It is really enough to make one suspect you are—You do me great injustice, sir, interrupted Arabella, if you suspect me to be guilty of any unbecoming weakness for this man. If barely expressing my compassion for his misfortunes be esteemed so great a favour, what would you have thought if I had supported his head on my knees while he was dying, shed tears over him, and discovered all the tokens of a sincere affliction for him?—Good God! said Sir Charles, lifting up his eyes: did any body ever hear of any thing like this? —What, sir, said Arabella, with as great an appearance of surprise in her countenance as his had discovered, do you say you never heard of any thing like this? Then you never heard of the princess of Media, I suppose?—No, not I, madam, said Sir Charles, peevishly.—Then, sir, resumed Arabella, permit me to tell you, that this fair and virtuous princess condescended to do all I have mentioned for the fierce Labynet, prince of Assyria: who, though he had mortally offended her by stealing her away out of the court of the king her father, nevertheless, when he was wounded to death in her presence, and humbly implored her pardon before he died, she condescended, as I have said, to support him on her knees, and shed tears for his disaster. I could produce many more instances of the like compassion in ladies; almost as highly born as herself, though, perhaps, their quality was not quite so illustrious, she being the heiress of two powerful kingdoms. Yet to mention only these—

Good Heavens! cried Mr Glanville here, being quite out of patience, I shall go distracted! Arabella, surprised at this exclamation, looked earnestly at him for a moment, and then asked him, whether any thing she had said had given him uneasiness.—Yes, upon my soul, madam! said Glanville, so vexed and confused that he hardly knew what he said.—I am sorry for it, replied Arabella, gravely; and also am greatly concerned to find that in generosity you are so much exceeded by the illustrious Cyrus; who was so far from taking umbrage at Mandane's behaviour to the dying prince, that he commended her for the compassion she had shown him. So also did the brave and generous Oroondates, when the fair Statira—By Heavens! cried Glanville, rising in a passion, there's no hearing this. Pardon me, madam, but upon my soul you'll make me hang myself!—Haug yourself! repeated Arabella: sure you know not what you say! You meant, I suppose, that you'll fall upon your sword. What hero ever threatened to give himself so vulgar a death? But pray, let me know the cause of your despair, so sudden and so violent. Mr Glanville continuing in a sort of sullen silence, Arabella, raising her voice, went on—Though I do not conceive myself obliged to give you an account of my conduct, seeing that I have only permitted you yet to hope for my favour; yet I owe to myself, and my own honour, the justification I am going to make. Know then, that, however suspicious my compassion for Mr Selvin may appear to your mistaken judgment, yet it has its foundation only in the generosity of my disposition, which inclines me to pardon the fault when the unhappy criminal repents; and to afford him my pity when his circumstances require it. Let not, therefore, the charity I have discovered towards your rival, be the cause of your despair, since my sentiments for him, were he living, would be what they were before; that is, full of indifference, nay, haply, disdain. And suffer not yourself to be so carried away by a violent and unjust jealousy, as to threaten your own death, which, if you really had any grounds for your suspicions, and truly loved me, would come unsought for, though not undesired—for, indeed, were your despair reasonable, death would necessarily follow it; for what lover can live under so desperate a misfortune? In that case you may meet death undauntedly when it comes, nay, embrace it with joy. But truly the killing one's self is but a false picture of true courage, proceeding rather from fear of a farther evil, than contempt of that you fly to: for if it were a contempt of pain, the same principle would make you resolve to bear patiently and fearlessly all kinds of pains; and hope being, of all other, the most contrary thing to fear, this, being an utter banishment of hope, seems to have its ground in fear.

IV

In which Mr Glanville makes an unsuccessful attempt upon Arabella

ARABELLA, WHEN SHE HAD FINISHED these words, which banished in part Mr Glanville's confusion, went to her own apartment, followed by Miss Glanville, to whom she had made a sign for that purpose: and throwing herself into a chair, burst into tears, which greatly surprising Miss Glanville, she pressed her to tell her the cause. Alas! replied Arabella, have I not cause to think myself extremely unhappy? The deplorable death of Mr Selvin, the despair to which I see your brother reduced, with the fatal consequences which may attend it, fill me with a mortal uneasiness.

Well, said Miss Glanville, your ladyship may make yourself quite easy as to both these matters; for Mr Selvin is not dead, nor is my brother in despair, that I know of—What do you say, miss? interrupted Arabella: is not Mr Selvin dead? Was the wound he gave himself not mortal, then?—I know of no wound that he gave himself, not I, said Miss Glanville. What makes your ladyship suppose he gave himself a wound? Lord bless me, what strange thoughts come into your head!—Truly I am rejoiced to hear it, replied Arabella; and in order to prevent the effects of his despair, I'll instantly dispatch my commands to him to live.—I'll dare answer for his obedience, madam, said Miss Glanville, smiling. Arabella then gave orders for paper and pens to be brought her; and seeing Mr Glanville enter the room, very formally acquainted him with her intention, telling him that he ought to be satisfied with the banishment to which she had doomed his unhappy rival, and not require his death, since he had nothing to fear from his pretensions.—I assure you, madam, said Mr Glanville, I am perfectly easy upon that account: and in order to spare you the trouble of sending to Mr Selvin, I may venture to assure you that he is in no danger of dying.—It is impossible, sir, replied Arabella: according to the nature of things, it is impossible but he must already be very near death. You know the rigour of my sentence, you know—I know, madam, said Mr Glanville, that Mr Selvin does not think himself under a necessity of obeying your sentence; and has the impudence to question your authority for banishing him from his native country.—My authority, sir, said Arabella, strangely surprised, is founded upon the absolute power he has given me over him.—He denies that, madam, said Glanville, and says that he neither can give, nor you exercise, an absolute power over him; since you are both accountable to the King, whose subjects you are, and both restrained by the laws under whose sanction you live.—Arabella's apparent confusion at these words giving Mr Glanville hopes that he had fallen upon a proper method to cure her of some of her strange notions, he was going to pursue his arguments, when Arabella, looking a little sternly upon him—The empire of love, said she, like the empire of honour, is governed by laws of its own, which have no dependence upon, or relation to, any other.—Pardon me, madam, said Glanville, if I presume to differ from you. Our laws have fixed the boundaries of honour as well as those of love.—How is that possible, replied Arabella, when they differ so widely, that a man may be justified by the one, and yet condemned by the other? For instance, pursued she, you are not permitted by the laws of the land to take away the life of any person whatever: yet the laws of honour oblige you to hunt your enemy through the world, in order to sacrifice him to your vengeance. Since it is impossible, then, for the same actions to be at once just and unjust, it must necessarily follow, that the law which condemns it, and that which justifies it, is not the same, but directly opposite. And now, added she, after a little pause, I hope I have entirely cleared up that point to you.—You have indeed, madam, replied Mr Glanville, proved to a demonstration, that what is called honour is something distinct from justice, since they command things absolutely opposite to each other.

Arabella, without reflecting on this inference, went on to prove the independent sovereignty of love, Which, said she, may be collected from all the words and actions of those heroes who were inspired by this passion. We see it in them, pursued she, triumphing not only over all natural and avowed allegiance, but superior even to friendship, duty, and honour itself. This the actions of Oroondates, Artaxerxes, Spitridates, and many other illustrious princes, sufficiently testify. Love requires a more unlimited obedience from its slaves, than any other monarch can expect from his subjects; an obedience which is circumscribed by no laws whatever, and dependent upon nothing but itself. I shall live, madam, says the renowned prince of Scythia to the divine Statira; I shall live, since it is your command I should do so; and death can have no power over a life which you are pleased to take care of. Say only that you wish I should conquer, said the great Juba to the incomparable Cleopatra, and my enemies will be already vanquished: victory will come over to the side you favour; and an army of an hundred thousand men will not be able to overcome the man who has your commands to conquer. How mean and insignificant, pursued she, are the titles bestowed on other monarchs compared with those which dignify the sovereigns of hearts, such as Divine Arbitress of my Fate, Visible Divinity, Earthly Goddess, and many others equally sublime!—Mr Glanville, losing all patience at her obstinate folly, interrupted her here with a question quite foreign to the subject she was discussing: and soon after, quitting her chamber, retired to his own, more than ever despairing of her recovery.

V

In which is introduced a very singular character

MISS GLANVILLE, WHOSE ENVY AND dislike of her lovely cousin were heightened by her suspicions that she disputed with her the possession of Sir George's heart, she having been long in reality a great admirer of that gay gentleman, was extremely delighted with the ridicule her absurd behaviour had drawn upon her at Bath, which she found by inquiry, was, through Mr Tinsel's representation, grown almost general. In order, therefore, to be at liberty to go to the public places uneclipsed by the superior beauty of Arabella, she acquainted her father and brother with part of what she had heard, which determined them to prevent that young lady's appearance in public while they stayed at Bath; this being no difficult matter to bring about, since Arabella only went to the rooms or parade in compliance with the invitation of her cousins. Miss Glanville being by these means rid of a rival too powerful even to contend with, went with more than usual gaiety to the assembly, where the extravagances of Arabella afforded a perpetual fund for diversion. Her more than passive behaviour upon this occasion, banishing all restraint among those she conversed with, the jest circulated very freely at Arabella's expense. Nor did Miss Glanville fail to give new poignancy to their sarcasms, by artfully deploring the bent of her cousin's studies, and enumerating the many absurdities they made her guilty of. Arabella's uncommon beauty had gained her so many enemies among the ladies that composed this assembly, that they seemed to contend with each other who should ridicule her most. The celebrated Countess of ——, being then at Bath, approached a circle of these fair defamers, and, listening a few moments to the contemptuous jests they threw out against the absent beauty, declared herself in her favour; which in a moment (such was the force of her universally acknowledged merit, and the deference always paid to her opinion) silenced every pretty impertinent around her. This lady, who among her own sex had no superior in wit, elegance, and ease, was inferior to very few of the other in sense, learning, and judgment. Her skill in poetry, painting, and music, though incontestably great, was numbered among the least of her accomplishments. Her candour, her sweetness, her modesty, and benevolence, while they secured her from the darts of envy, rendered her superior to praise, and made the one as unnecessary as the other was ineffectual. She had been a witness of the surprise Arabella's extraordinary appearance had occasioned; and struck with that as well as the uncommon charms of her person, had pressed near her, with several others of the company, when she was discoursing in the manner we have related. A person of the countess's nice discernment could not fail of observing the wit and spirit, which, though obscured, was not absolutely hid under the absurdity of her notions; and this discovery adding esteem to the compassion she felt for the fair visionary, she resolved to rescue her from the ill-natured raillery of her sex. Praising, therefore, her understanding, and the beauty of her person, with a sweetness and generosity peculiar to herself, she accounted in the most delicate manner imaginable for the singularity of her notions, from her studies, her retirement, her ignorance of the world, and her lively imagination. And to abate the keenness of their sarcasms, she acknowledged that she herself had, when very young, been deep read in romances; and but for an early acquaintance with the world, and being directed to other studies, was likely to have been as much a heroine as Lady Bella.

Miss Glanville, though she was secretly vexed at this defence of her cousin, was however under a necessity of seeming obliged to the countess for it: and that lady expressing a desire to be acquainted with Lady Bella, Miss Glanville respectfully offered to attend her cousin to her lodgings; which the countess as respectfully declined, saying, as Lady Bella was a stranger, she would make her the first visit. Miss Glanville, at her return, gave her brother an account of what had happened at the assembly, and filled him with an inconceivable joy at the countess's intention. He had always been a zealous admirer of that lady's character, and flattered himself that the conversation of so admirable a woman would be of the utmost use to Arabella. That very night he mentioned her to his beloved cousin; and after enumerating all her fine qualities, declared that she had already conceived a friendship for her, and was solicitous of her acquaintance. I think myself extremely fortunate, replied Arabella, in that I have (though questionless undeservedly) acquired the amity of this lovely person—and I beg you, pursued she, to Miss Glanville, to tell her, that I long with impatience to embrace her, and to give her that share in my heart which her transcendent merit deserves. Miss Glanville only bowed her head in answer to this request, giving her brother at the same time a significant leer; who, though used to Arabella's particularities, could not help being a little confounded at the heroic speech she had made.

VI

Containing something which at first sight may possibly puzzle the reader

THE COUNTESS WAS AS GOOD as her word, and two days after sent a card to Arabella, importing her design to wait on her that afternoon.—Our heroine expected her with great impatience; and, the moment she entered the room, flew towards her with a graceful eagerness, and, straining her in her arms, embraced her with all the fervour of a long absent friend.

Sir Charles and Mr Glanville were equally embarrassed at the familiarity of this address; but observing that the countess seemed not to be surprised at it, but rather to receive it with pleasure, they were soon composed.

You cannot imagine, lovely stranger, said Arabella to the countess, as soon as they were seated, with what impatience I have longed to behold you, since the knowledge I have received of your rare qualities, and the friendship you have been pleased to honour me with. And I may truly protest to you, that such is my admiration of your virtues, that I would have gone to the farthest part of the world to render you that which you with so much generosity have condescended to bestow upon me.—Sir Charles stared at this extraordinary speech, and not being able to comprehend a word of it, was concerned to think how the lady to whom it was addressed would understand it. Mr Glanville looked down, and bit his nails in extreme confusion: but the countess, who had not forgot the language of romance, returned the compliment in a strain as heroic as hers.—The favour I have received from Fortune, said she, in bringing me to the happiness of your acquaintance, charming Arabella, is so great, that I may rationally expect some terrible misfortune will befal me; seeing that in this life our pleasures are so constantly succeeded by pains; that we hardly ever enjoy the one without suffering the other soon after.

Arabella was quite transported to hear the countess express herself in language so conformable to her own; but Mr Glanville was greatly confounded, and began to suspect she was diverting herself with his cousin's singularities: and Sir Charles was within a little of thinking her as much out of the way as his niece.

Misfortunes, madam, said Arabella, are too often the lot of excellent persons like yourself. The sublimest among mortals both for beauty and virtue have experienced the frowns of Fate. The sufferings of the divine Statira, or Cassandra, for she bore both names, the persecutions of the incomparable Cleopatra, the distresses of the beautiful Candace, and the afflictions of the fair and generous Mandane, are proofs that the most illustrious persons in the world have felt the rage of calamity.—It must be confessed, said the countess, that all those fair princesses you have named, were for a while extremely unfortunate; yet in the catalogue of these lovely and afflicted persons, you have forgot one who might with justice dispute the priority of sufferings with them all—I mean the beautiful Elisa, princess of Parthia.—Pardon me, madam, replied Arabella, I cannot be of your opinion. The princess of Parthia may indeed justly be ranked among the number of unfortunate persons, but she can by no means dispute the melancholy precedence with the divine Cleopatra. For, in fine, madam, what evils did the princess of Parthia suffer which the fair Cleopatra did not likewise endure, and some of them haply in a greater degree? If Elisa, by the tyrannical authority of the king her father, saw herself upon the point of becoming the wife of a prince she detested, was not the beautiful daughter of Antony, by the more unjustifiable tyranny of Augustus likely to be forced into the arms of Tiberius, a proud and cruel prince, who was odious to the whole world as well as to her? If Elisa was for some time in the power of pirates, was not Cleopatra captive to an inhuman king, who presented his sword to the fair breast of that divine princess, worthy the admiration of the whole earth? And in fine, if Elisa had the grief to see her dear Artaban imprisoned by the order of Augustus, Cleopatra beheld with mortal agonies her beloved Coriolanus inclosed amidst the guards of that enraged prince, and doomed to a cruel death.—It is certain, madam, replied the countess, that the misfortunes of both these princesses were very great, though, as you have shewn me, with some inequality: and when one reflects upon the dangerous adventures to which persons of their quality were exposed in those times, one cannot help rejoicing that we live in an age in which the customs, manners, habits, and inclinations, differ so widely from theirs, that it is impossible such adventures should ever happen. Such is the strange alteration of things, that some people, I dare say, at present cannot be persuaded to believe there ever were princesses wandering through the world by land and sea in mean disguises, carried away violently out of their fathers' dominions by insolent lovers; some discovered sleeping in forests, others shipwrecked on desolate islands, confined in castles, bound in chariots, and even struggling amidst the tempestuous waves of the sea, into which they had cast themselves to avoid the brutal force of their ravishers. Not one of these things having happened within the compass of several thousand years, people unlearned in antiquity would be apt to deem them idle tales, so improbable do they appear at present.

Arabella, though greatly surprised at this discourse, did not think proper to express her thoughts of it. She was unwilling to appear absolutely ignorant of the present customs of the world before a lady, whose good opinion she was ardently desirous of improving. Her prepossessions in favour of the countess made her receive the new lights she held out to her with respect, though not without doubt and irresolution. Her blushes, her silence, and down-cast eyes, gave the countess to understand part of her thoughts; who, for fear of alarming her too much for that time, dropped the subject, and, turning the conversation on others more general, gave Arabella an opportunity of mingling in it with that wit and vivacity which was natural to her when romances were out of the question.

VII

*In which, if the reader has not anticipated it, he will find an
explanation of some seeming inconsistencies in the foregoing chapter*

THE COUNTESS, CHARMED WITH THE wit and good sense of Arabella,
could not conceal her admiration, but expressed it in terms the most
obliging imaginable and Arabella, who was excessively delighted with
her, returned the compliments she made her with the most respectful
tenderness. In the midst of these mutual civilities, Arabella, in the style
of romance, entreated the countess to favour her with the recital of her
adventures. At the mention of this request, that lady conveyed so much
confusion into her countenance, that Arabella, extremely embarrassed
by it, though she knew not why, thought it necessary to apologise for
the disturbance she seemed to have occasioned in her.—Pardon me,
madam, replied the countess, recovering herself; if the uncommonness
of your request made a moment's reflection necessary to convince me
that a young lady of your sense and delicacy could mean no offence
to decorum by making it. The word adventures carries in it so free
and licentious a sound in the apprehensions of people at this period
of time, that it can hardly with propriety be applied to those few and
natural incidents which compose the history of a woman of honour.
And when I tell you, pursued she, with a smile, that I was born and
christened, had a useful and proper education, received the addresses
of my Lord ——, through the recommendation of my parents, and
married him with their consents and my own inclination, and that
since we have lived in great harmony together, I have told you all the
material passages of my life; which, upon inquiry, you will find differ
very little from those of other women of the same rank, who have a
moderate share of sense, prudence, and virtue.—Since you have already,
madam, replied Arabella, blushing, excused me for the liberty I took
with you, it will be unnecessary to tell you it was grounded upon the

customs of ancient times, when ladies of the highest rank and sublimest virtue were often exposed to a variety of cruel adventures, which they imparted in confidence to each other when chance brought them together.—Custom, said the countess, smiling, changes the very nature of things; and what was honourable a thousand years ago, may probably be looked upon as infamous now. A lady in the heroic age you speak of, would not be thought to possess any great share of merit, if she had not been many times carried away by one or other of her insolent lovers: whereas a beauty in this could not pass through the hands of several different ravishers, without bringing an imputation on her chastity. The same actions which made a man a hero in those times would constitute him a murderer in these; and the same steps which led him to a throne then, would infallibly conduct him to a scaffold now.

But custom, madam, said Arabella, cannot possibly change the nature of virtue or vice: and since virtue is the chief characteristic of a hero, a hero in the last age will be a hero in this.—Though the natures of virtue or vice cannot be changed, replied the countess, yet they may be mistaken; and different principles, customs, and education, may probably change their names if not their natures. Sure, madam, said Arabella, a little moved, you do not intend by this inference to prove Oroondates, Artaxerxes, Juba, Artaban, and the other heroes of antiquity bad men?

Judging them by the rules of Christianity, and our present notions of honour, justice, and humanity, they certainly are, replied the countess.—Did they not possess all the necessary qualifications of heroes, madam, said Arabella; and each in a superlative degree? Was not their valour invincible, their generosity unbounded, and their fidelity inviolable?—It cannot be denied, said the countess, but that their valour was invincible; and many thousand men, less courageous than themselves, felt the fatal effects of that invincible valour, which was perpetually seeking after occasions to exert itself. Oroondates gave many extraordinary proofs of that unbounded generosity so natural to the heroes of his time. This prince being sent by the king his father, at the head of an army, to oppose the Persian monarch, who had unjustly invaded his dominions, and was destroying the lives and properties of his subjects, having taken the wives and daughters of his enemy prisoners, had by these means an opportunity to put a period to a war so destructive to his country: yet, out of a generosity truly heroic, he released them immediately, without any conditions; and falling in love with one of those princesses, secretly quitted his father's court, resided several years in that of the enemy of his father and country, engaged himself to his daughter, and, when the war broke out again between the two kings, fought furiously against an army in which the king his father was in person, and shed the blood of his future subjects without remorse; though each of those subjects, we are told, would have sacrificed his life to save that of their prince, so much was he beloved. Such are the actions which immortalize the heroes of romance, and are by the authors of those books styled glorious, godlike, and divine: yet, judging of them as Christians, we shall find them impious and base, and directly opposite to our present notions of moral and relative duties.

It is certain, therefore, madam, added the countess, with a smile, that what was virtue in those days, is vice in ours: and to form a hero according to our notions of them at present, it is necessary to give him qualities very different from Oroondates.

The secret charm in the countenance, voice, and manner of the countess, joined to the force of her reasoning, could not fail of making some impression on the mind of Arabella; but it was such an impression as came far short of conviction. She was surprised, embarrassed, perplexed, but, not convinced. Heroism, romantic heroism, was deeply rooted in her heart: it was her habit of thinking, a principle imbibed from education. She could not separate her ideas of glory, virtue, courage, generosity, and honour, from the false representations of them in the actions of Oroondates, Juba, Artaxerxes, and the rest of the imaginary heroes. The countess's discourse had raised a kind of tumult in her thoughts, which gave an air of perplexity to her lovely face, and made that lady apprehensive she had gone too far, and lost that ground in her esteem, which she had endeavoured to acquire by a conformity to some of her notions and language. In this, however, she was mistaken; Arabella felt a tenderness for her that had already the force of a long contracted friendship, and an esteem little less than veneration. When the countess took leave, the professions of Arabella, though delivered in the language of romance, were very sincere and affecting, and were returned with an equal degree of tenderness by the countess, who had conceived a more than ordinary affection for her. Mr Glanville, who could have almost worshipped the countess for the generous design he saw she had entertained, took an opportunity, as he handed her to her chair, to entreat, in a manner as earnest as polite, that she would continue the happiness of her acquaintance to his cousin; which, with a smile of mingled dignity and sweetness, she assured him of.

VIII

Which concludes book the eighth

M R GLANVILLE, AT HIS RETURN to the dining-room, finding Arabella retired, told his father, in a rapture of joy, that the charming countess would certainly make a convert of Lady Bella. Methinks, said the baronet, she has as strange whims in her head as my niece. Ad's-heart, what a deal of stuff did she talk about! A parcel of heroes, as she calls them, with confounded hard names. In my mind, she is more likely to make Lady Bella worse than better.—Mr Glanville, a little vexed at his father's misapprehension, endeavoured, with as much delicacy as he could, to set him right with regard to the countess; so that he brought him at last to confess she managed the thing very well. The countess, who had resolved to take Arabella openly into her protection, was thinking on means to engage her to appear at the assembly, whither she proposed to accompany her in a modern dress. But her good intentions towards our lovely heroine were suspended by the account she received of her mother's indisposition, which commanded her immediate attendance on her at her seat in ———. Her sudden departure gave Arabella an extreme uneasiness, and proved a cruel disappointment to Mr Glanville, who had founded all his hopes of her recovery on the conversation of that lady. Sir Charles having affairs that required his presence in London, proposed to his niece the leaving Bath in a few days, to which she consented; and accordingly they set out for London in Arabella's coach and six, attended by several servants on horseback, her women having been sent away before in the stage.

Nothing very remarkable happened during this journey; so we shall not trouble our readers with several small mistakes of Arabella's, such as her supposing a neat country girl, who was riding behind a man, to be some lady or princess in disguise, forced away by a lover she hated, and entreating Mr Glanville to attempt her rescue; which occasioned some little debate between her and Sir Charles, who could not be persuaded to believe it was as she said, and forbade his son to meddle in other people's affairs. Several of these sorts of mistakes, as we said before, we omit; and will therefore, if our reader pleases, bring our heroine, without further delay, to London.

END OF THE EIGHTH BOOK

BOOK IX

I

In which is related an admirable adventure

MISS GLANVILLE, WHOSE SPIRITS WERE greatly exhilarated at their entrance into London, that seat of magnificence and pleasure, congratulated her cousin upon the entertainment she would receive from the new and surprising objects which every day for a considerable time would furnish her with; and ran over the catalogue of diversions with such a volubility of tongue, as drew a gentle reprimand from her father, and made her keep a sullen silence till they were set down in St James's square, the place of their residence in town. Sir Charles having ordered his late lady's apartment to be prepared for the accommodation of his niece, as soon as the first civilities were over, she retired to her chamber where she employed herself in giving her women directions for placing her books, of which she had brought a moderate quantity to London, in her closet. Miss Glanville, as soon as she had dispatched away some hundred cards to her acquaintance, to give them notice she was in town, attended Arabella in her own apartment; and as they sat at the tea, she began to regulate the diversions of the week, naming the Drawing-room, Park, Concert, Ranelagh, Lady ———'s Assembly, the Duchess of ———'s Rout, Vauxhall, and a long &c. of visits; at which Arabella, with an accent that expressed her surprise, asked her, if she supposed she intended to stay in town three or four years. Lau, cousin, said Miss Glanville, all this is but the amusement of a few days.—Amusement, do you say? replied Arabella: methinks it seems to be the sole employment of those days; and what you call the amusement, must of necessity be the business of life.—You are always so grave, cousin, said Miss Glanville, one does not know what to say to you. However, I shan't press you to go to public places against your inclination; yet you'll condescend to receive a few visits, I suppose?—Yes, replied Arabella, and if, among the ladies whom I shall see, I find any like the amiable Countess of ———, I shall not scruple to enter into the most tender amity with them.—The Countess of —— is very well, to be sure, said Miss Glanville; yet, I don't know how it is, she does not suit my taste. She is very particular in a great many things, and knows too much for a lady, as I heard my Lord Trifle say one day. Then she is quite unfashionable: she hates cards, keeps no assembly, is seen but seldom at public places; and, in my opinion, as well as in a great many others, is the dullest company in the world. I'm sure I met her at a visit a little before I went down to your seat; and she had not been a quarter of an hour in the room, before she set a whole circle of ladies a-yawning. Arabella, though she had a sincere contempt for her cousin's manner of thinking, yet always politely concealed it; and, vexed as she was at her sneers upon the countess, she contented herself with gently defending her, telling her, at the same time, that till she met a lady who had more merit than the countess, she should always possess the first place in her esteem.

Arabella, who had from her youth adopted the resentments of her father, refused to make her appearance at court, which Sir Charles gently intimated to her; yet, being not wholly divested of the curiosity natural to her sex, she condescended to go *incog.* to the gallery on a ball night, accompanied by Mr Glanville and his sister, in order to behold the splendour of the British Court. As her romances had long familiarised her thoughts to objects of grandeur and magnificence, she was not so much struck as might have been expected with those that now presented themselves to her view. Nor was she a little disappointed to find, that among the men, she saw none whose appearance came up with her ideas of the air and port of an Artaban, Oroondates, or Juba; nor any of the ladies, who did not, in her opinion, fall short of the perfections of Elisa, Mandane, Statira, &c. It was remarkable, too, that she never inquired how often the princesses had been carried away by love-captivated monarchs, or how many victories the king's sons had gained; but seemed the whole time she was there to have suspended all her romantic ideas of glory, beauty, gallantry, and love.

Mr Glanville was highly pleased with her composed behaviour, and a day or two after entreated her to allow him the honour of shewing her what was remarkable and worthy of her observation in this great metropolis. To this she also consented, and for the greater privacy began their travels in a hired coach. Part of several days was taken up in this employment; but Mr Glanville had the mortification to find she was full of allusions to her romances upon every occasion; such as her asking the person who shews the armoury at the Tower, the names of the knights to whom each suit belonged, and wondering there were no devices on the shields or plumes of feathers in the helmets. She observed, that the lion Lysimachus killed, was, according to the history of that prince, much larger than any of those she was shown in the Tower, and also much fiercer; took notice that St Paul's was less magnificent in the inside, than the temple in which Cyrus, when he went to Mandane, heard her return thanks for his supposed death; inquired if it was not customary for the king and his whole court to sail in barges upon the Thames, as Augustus used to do upon the Tyber; whether they had not music and collations in the Park; and where they celebrated the justs and tournaments. The season for Vauxhall being not yet over, she was desirous of once seeing a place, which, by the description she had heard of it, greatly resembled the gardens of Lucullus at Rome, in which the emperor, with all the princes and princesses of his court, were so nobly entertained and where so many gallant conversations had passed among those admirable persons.

The singularity of her dress (for she was covered with her veil) drew a number of gazers after her, who pressed round her with so little respect, that she was greatly embarrassed, and had thoughts of quitting the place, delightful as she owned it, immediately, when her attention was wholly engrossed by an adventure in which she soon interested herself very deeply. An officer of rank in the sea-service had brought his mistress, disguised in a suit of man's or rather boy's clothes, and a hat and feather, into the gardens. The young creature being a little intoxicated with the wine she had taken too freely, was thrown so much off her guard, as to give occasion to some of the company to suspect her sex; and a gay fellow, in order to give them some diversion at her expense, pretending to be affronted at something she had said, drew his sword upon the disguised fair one, which so alarmed her, that she shrieked out she was a woman, and ran for protection to her lover; who was so disordered with liquor, that he was not able to defend her.

Miss Glanville, ever curious and inquisitive, demanded the cause why the company ran in crowds to that particular spot: and received for answer, that a gentleman had drawn his sword upon a lady disguised in a man's habit.—Oh, heavens! cried Arabella, this must certainly be a very notable adventure. The lady has doubtless some extraordinary circumstances in her story, and haply, upon inquiry, her misfortunes will be found to resemble those which obliged the beautiful Aspasia to put on the same disguise, who was by that means murdered by the cruel Zenodorus in a fit of jealousy at the amity his wife expressed for her. But can I not see this unfortunate fair one? added she, pressing, in spite of Mr Glanville's entreaties, through the crowd: I may haply be able to afford her some consolation. Mr Glanville, finding his persuasions were not regarded, followed her with very little difficulty: for her veil falling back in her hurry, she did not mind to replace it; and the charms of her face, joined to the majesty of her person, and singularity of her dress, attracted every person's attention and respect: they made way for her to pass, not a little surprised at the extreme earnestness and solemnity that appeared in her countenance upon an event so diverting to every one else.—The disguised lady, whom she was endeavouring to approach, had thrown herself upon a bench in one of the boxes, trembling still with the apprehension of the sword, though her antagonist was kneeling at her feet, making love to her in mock-heroics, for the diversion of the company. Her hat and peruke had fallen off in a fright; and her hair, which had been turned up under it hung now loosely about her neck, and gave such an appearance of woe to a face, which, notwithstanding the paleness that terror had overspread it with, was really extremely pretty, that Arabella was equally struck with compassion and admiration of her.

Lovely unknown, said she to her, with an air of extreme tenderness, though I am a stranger both to your name and history, yet your aspect persuadeth me your quality is not mean; and the condition and disguise in which I behold you, showing that you are unfortunate, permit me to offer you all the assistance in my power, seeing that I am moved thereto by my compassion for your distress, and that esteem which the sight of you must necessarily inspire.—Mr Glanville was struck dumb with confusion at this strange speech, and at the whispers and scoffs it occasioned among the spectators. He attempted to take hold of her hand, in order to lead her away, but she disengaged herself from him with a frown of displeasure; and taking no notice of Miss Glanville, who whispered with great emotion, Lord, cousin, how you expose yourself! pressed nearer to the beautiful disguised, and again repeated her offers of service.—The girl, being perfectly recovered from her intoxication, by the fright she had been in, gazed upon Arabella with a look of extreme surprise: yet being moved to respect by the dignity of her appearance, and, strange as her words seemed to be, by the obliging purport of them, and the affecting earnestness with which they were delivered, she rose from her seat, and thanked her, with an accent full of regard and submission.

Fair maid, said Arabella, taking her hand, let us quit this place, where your discovery may probably subject you to more dangers. If you will be pleased to put yourself into my protection, and acquaint me with the history of your misfortunes, I have interest enough with a valiant person, who shall undertake to free you from your persecutions, and re-establish the repose of your life.—The kneeling hero, who, as well as every one else that were present, had gazed with astonishment at Arabella during all this passage, perceiving she was about to rob him of the disguised fair, seized hold of the hand she had at liberty, and swore he would not part with her.—Mr Glanville, almost mad with vexation, endeavoured to get Arabella away.—Are you mad, madam, said he, in a whisper, to make all this rout about a prostitute? Do you see how every body stares at you? What will they think? For Heaven's sake, let us be gone!—What, sir! replied Arabella, in a rage, are you base enough to leave this admirable creature in the power of that man, who is, questionless, her ravisher? And will you not draw your sword in her defence?—Hey-day! cried the sea officer, waked out of his stupid dose by the clamour about him: what's the matter here? What are you doing? Where's my Lucy? Zounds, sir! said he, to the young fellow who held her, what business have you with my Lucy? And, uttering a dreadful oath, drew out his sword, and staggered towards his gay rival, who, observing the weakness of his antagonist, flourished with his sword to shew his courage, and frighten the ladies, who all ran away screaming. Arabella, taking Miss Glanville under the arm, cried out to Mr Glanville, as she left the place, to take care of the distressed lady, and, while the two combatants were disputing for her, to carry her away in safety. But Mr Glanville, without regarding this injunction, hastened after her; and, to pacify her, told her the lady was rescued by her favourite lover, and carried off in triumph.—But are you sure, said Arabella, it was not some other of her ravishers who carried her away, and not the person whom she has haply favoured with her affection? May not the same thing have happened to her, as did to the beautiful Candace, queen of Ethiopia, who, while two of her ravishers were fighting for her, a third, whom she took for her deliverer, came and carried her away?—But she went away willingly, I assure you, madam, said Mr Glanville. Pray, don't he in any concern about her.—If she went away willingly with him, replied Arabella, it is probable it may not be another ravisher; and yet if this person that rescued her happened to he in armour, and the vizor of his helmet down, she might be mistaken as well as Queen Candace.—Well, well, he was not in armour, madam, said Glanville, almost beside himself with vexation at her folly.—You seem to be disturbed, sir, said Arabella, a little surprised at his peevish tone. Is there any thing in this adventure which concerns you? Nay, now I remember, you did not offer to defend the beautiful unknown. I am not willing to impute your inaction upon such an occasion to want of courage or generosity. Perhaps you are acquainted with her history, and from this knowledge refused to engage in her defence.

Mr Glanville, perceiving the company gather from all parts to the walk they were in, told her he would acquaint her with all he knew concerning the disguised lady when they were in the coach on their return home; and Arabella, impatient for the promised story, proposed to leave the gardens immediately, which was gladly complied with by Mr Glanville, who heartily repented his having carried her thither.

II

Which ends with a very favourable prediction for our heroine

As soon as they were seated in the coach, she did not fail to call upon him to perform his promise; but Mr Glanville excessively out of humour at her exposing herself in the gardens, replied, without considering whether he should not offend her, that he knew no more of the disguised lady than any body else in the place.

How, sir! replied Arabella, did you not promise to relate her adventures to me? And would you have me believe you knew no more of them than the rest of the cavaliers and ladies in the place?—Upon my soul, I don't, madam! said Glanville: yet what I know of her is sufficient to let me understand she was not worth the consideration you seemed to have for her.—She cannot, sure, be more indiscreet than the fair and unfortunate Hermione, replied Arabella; who, like her, put on man's apparel, through despair at the ill success of her passion for Alexander. And certain it is, that though the beautiful Hermione was guilty of one great error, which lost her the esteem of Alexander, yet she had a high and noble soul, as was manifest by her behaviour and words when she was murdered by the sword of Demetrius. Oh, Death! cried she, as she was falling, how sweet do I find thee, and how much and how earnestly have I desired thee!

O Lord! O Lord! cried Mr Glanville, hardly sensible of what he said. Was there ever any thing so intolerable!—You pity the unhappy Hermione, sir, said Arabella, interpreting his exclamation her own way. Indeed, she is well worthy of your compassion; and if the bare recital of the words she uttered at receiving her death's wound, affects you so much, you may guess what would have been your agonies, had you been Demetrius that gave it her! Here Mr Glanville groaning aloud through impatience at her absurdities—

This subject affects you deeply, I perceive, said Arabella. There is no question but you would have acted in the same circumstance as

Demetrius did yet, let me tell you, the extravagancy of his rage and despair for what he had innocently committed, was imputed to him as a great imbecility, as was also the violent passion he conceived soon after for the fair Deidamia. You know the accident which brought that fair princess into his way.—Indeed I do not, madam, said Glanville, peevishly.—Well, then, I'll tell you, said Arabella; but, pausing a little—The recital I have engaged myself to make, added she, will necessarily take up some hours' time, as upon reflection I have found: so, if you will dispense with my beginning it at present, I will satisfy your curiosity to-morrow, when I may be able to pursue it without interruption.

To this, Mr Glanville made no other answer than a bow with his head; and the coach a few moments after arriving at their own house, he led her to her apartment, firmly resolved never to attend her to any more public places, while she continued in the same ridiculous folly.

Sir Charles, who had several times been in doubt whether Arabella was not really disordered in her senses, upon Miss Glanville's account of her behaviour at the gardens, concluded she was absolutely mad, and held a short debate with himself, whether he ought not to bring a commission of lunacy against her, rather than marry her to his son, who, he was persuaded, could never be happy with a wife so unaccountably absurd.

Though he only hinted at this to Mr Glanville, in a conversation he had with him while his dissatisfaction was at its height, concerning Arabella, yet the bare supposition that his father ever thought of such a thing, threw the young gentleman into such agonies, that Sir Charles, to compose him, protested he would do nothing in relation to his niece that he would not approve of. Yet he expostulated with him on the absurdity of her behaviour, and the ridicule to which she exposed herself wherever she went; appealing to him, whether, in a wife, he could think those follies supportable, which in a mistress occasioned him so much confusion. Mr Glanville, as much in love as he was, felt all the force of this inference, and acknowledged to his father that he could not think of marrying Arabella, till the whims her romances had put into her head, were erased by a better knowledge of life and manners. But he added, with a sigh, that he knew not how this reformation would be effected; for she had such a strange facility in reconciling every incident to her own fantastic ideas, that every new object added strength to the fatal deception she laboured under.

III

In which Arabella meets with another admirable adventure

OUR LOVELY HEROINE HAD NOT been above a fortnight in London, before the gross air of that smoky town affected her health so much, that Sir Charles proposed to her to go for a few weeks to Richmond, where he hired a house elegantly furnished for her reception.

Miss Glanville had been too long out of that darling city to pay her the compliment of attending her constantly at Richmond; yet she promised to be as often as possible with her: and Sir Charles, having affairs that could not dispense with his absence from town, placed his steward in her house, being a person whose prudence and fidelity he could rely upon; and he, with her women, and some other menial servants, made up her equipage. As it was not consistent with decorum for Mr Glanville to reside in her house, he contented himself with riding to Richmond generally every day; and as long as Arabella was pleased with that retirement, he resolved not to press her return to town till the Countess of —— arrived, in whose conversation he grounded all his hopes of her cure. At that season of the year, Richmond not being quite deserted by company, Arabella was visited by several ladies of fashion; who, charmed with her affability, politeness, and good sense, were strangely perplexed how to account for some peculiarities in her dress and manner of thinking. Some of the younger sort, from whom Arabella's extraordinary beauty took away all pretensions to equality on that score, made themselves extremely merry with her oddnesses, as they called them, and gave broad intimations that her head was not right. As for Arabella, whose taste was as delicate, sentiments as refined, and judgment as clear as any person's could be who believed the authenticity of Scudery's romances, she was strangely disappointed to find no lady with whom she could converse with any tolerable pleasure; and that instead of Clelias, Statiras, Mandanes, &c. she found only Miss Glanvilles among all she knew. The comparison she drew between such as these and the charming Countess of ——, whom she had just began to be acquainted with at Bath, increased her regret for the interruption that was given to so agreeable a friendship; and it was with infinite pleasure Mr Glanville heard her repeatedly wish for the arrival of that admirable lady (as she always called her) in town.

Not being able to relish the insipid conversation of the young ladies that visited her at Richmond, her chief amusement was to walk in the park there; which, because of its rural privacy, was extremely agreeable to her inclination. Here she indulged contemplation, leaning on the arm of her faithful Lucy, while her other women walked at some distance behind her, and two men-servants kept her always in sight. One evening when she was returning from her usual walk, she heard the sound of a woman's voice, which seemed to proceed from a tuft of trees that hid her from her view; and, stopping a moment, distinguished some plaintive accents, which increasing her curiosity, she advanced towards the place, telling Lucy she was resolved, if possible, to discover who the distressed lady was, and what was the subject of her affliction. As she drew near with softly treading steps, she could distinguish through the branches of the trees, now despoiled of great part of their leaves, two women seated on the ground, their backs towards her, and one of them, with her head gently reclined on the other's shoulder, seemed, by her mournful action, to be weeping; for she often put her handkerchief to her eyes, breathing every time a sigh, which, as Arabella phrased it, seemed to proceed from the deepest recesses of her heart. This adventure, more worthy indeed to be styled an adventure than all our fair heroine had ever yet met with, and so conformable to what she had read in romances, filled her heart with eager expectation. She made a sign to Lucy to make no noise, and creeping still closer towards the place where this afflicted person sat, she heard her distinctly mutter these words, which, however, were often interrupted with her sighs—Ah, Ariamenes! whom I, to my misfortune, have too much loved, and whom, to my misfortune, I fear I shall never sufficiently hate, since that Heaven, and thy cruel ingratitude, have ordained that thou shalt never be mine, and that so many sweet and dear hopes are for ever taken from me, return me at least, ungrateful man! return me those testimonies of my innocent affection, which were sometimes so dear and precious to thee. Return me those favours, which, all innocent as they were, are become criminal by thy crime. Return me, cruel man! return me those relics of my heart which thou detainest in despite of me, and which, notwithstanding thy infidelity, I cannot recover.

Here her tears interrupting her speech, Arabella, being impatient to know the history of this afflicted person, came softly round to the other side, and, shewing herself, occasioned some disturbance to the sad unknown; who, rising from her seat, with her face averted, as if ashamed of having so far disclosed her sorrows in a stranger's hearing, endeavoured to pass by her unnoticed. Arabella, perceiving her design, stopped her with a very graceful action, and, with a voice all composed of sweetness, earnestly conjured her to relate her history. Think not, lovely unknown, said she, (for she was really very pretty,) that my endeavours to detain you proceed from an indiscreet curiosity. It is true, some complaints which have fallen from your fair mouth, have raised in me a desire to be acquainted with your adventures; but this desire has its foundation in that compassion your complaints have filled me with: and if I wish to know your misfortunes, it is only with a view of affording you some consolation.—Pardon me, madam, said the fair afflicted, gazing on Arabella with many signs of admiration, if my confusion at being overheard in a place I had chosen to bewail my misfortunes, made me be guilty of some appearance of rudeness, not seeing the admirable person I wanted to avoid. But, pursued she, hesitating a little, those characters of beauty I behold in your face, and the gracefulness of your deportment, convincing me you can be of no ordinary rank, I will the less scruple to acquaint you with my adventures, and the cause of those complaints you have heard proceed from my mouth.

Arabella assuring her, that, whatever her misfortunes were, she might depend upon all the assistance in her power, seated herself near her at the foot of the tree where she had been sitting; and giving Lucy orders to join the rest of her women, and stay at a distance till she made a sign to them to advance, she prepared to listen to the adventures of the fair unknown; who, after some little pause, began to relate them in this manner.—

IV

In which is related the history of the princess of Gaul

MY NAME, MADAM, IS CYNECIA; my birth illustrious enough, seeing that I am the daughter of a sovereign prince, who possesses a large and spacious territory in what is now called ancient Gaul.—What, madam! interrupted Arabella, are you a princess, then?—Questionless I am, madam, replied the lady; and a princess happy and prosperous, till the felicity of my life was interrupted by the perfidious Ariamenes.— Pardon me, madam, interrupted Arabella again, that my ignorance of your quality made me be deficient in those respects which are due to your high birth, and which, notwithstanding those characters of greatness I might read in the lineaments of your visage, I yet neglected to pay.—Alas, madam! said the stranger, that little beauty which the heavens bestowed on me only to make me wretched, as by the event it has proved, has long since taken its flight, and, together with my happiness, I have lost that which made me unhappy. And certain it is, grief has made such ravages among what might once have been thought tolerable in my face, that I should not be surprised if my being no longer fair, should make you, with difficulty, believe I ever was so. Arabella, after a proper compliment in answer to this speech, entreated the princess to go on with her history; who, hesitating a little, complied with her request. Be pleased to know then, madam, said she, that being bred up with all imaginable tenderness in my father's court, I had no sooner arrived to my sixteenth year than I saw myself surrounded with lovers; who, nevertheless, such was the severity with which I behaved myself, concealed their passions under a respectful silence, well knowing banishment from my presence was the least punishment they had to expect, if they presumed to declare their sentiments to me. I lived in this fashion, madam, for two years longer, rejoicing in the insensibility of my own heart, and triumphing in the sufferings of others, when my tranquillity was all at once interrupted by an accident which I am going to relate to you, The princess stopped here to give vent to some sighs which a cruel remembrance forced from her; and continuing in a deep muse for five or six minutes, resumed her story in this manner—It being my custom to walk in a forest adjoining to one of my father's summer residences, attended only by my women, one day when I was taking this amusement, I perceived at some distance a man lying on the ground: and, impelled by a sudden curiosity, I advanced towards this person, whom, upon a nearer view, I perceived to have been wounded very much, and fainted away through loss of blood. His habit being very rich, I concluded by that he was of no mean quality: but when I had looked upon his countenance, pale and languishing as it was, methought there appeared so many marks of greatness, accompanied with a sweetness so happily blended, that my attention was engaged in an extraordinary manner, and interested me so powerfully in his safety, that I commanded some of my women to run immediately for proper assistance, and convey him to the castle, while I directed others to throw some water in his face, and to apply some linen to his wounds, to stop the bleeding.

These charitable cares restored the wounded stranger to his senses. He opened his eyes, and turning them slowly to the objects around him, fixed at last their languishing looks on me: when moved, as it should seem, to some respect by what he saw in my countenance, he rose with some difficulty from the ground, and bowing almost down to it again, by that action, seemed to pay me his acknowledgments for what he supposed I had done for his preservation. His extreme weakness having obliged him to creep towards a tree, against the back of which he supported himself, I went nearer to him, and having told him the condition in which I found him, and the orders I had dispatched for assistance, requested him to acquaint me with his name and quality, and the adventure which had brought him into that condition. My name, madam, answered he, is Ariamenes. My birth is noble enough. I have spent some years in my travels, and was returning to my native country; when, passing through this forest, I was seized with an inclination to sleep. I had tied my horse to a tree, and retiring some few paces off, stretched myself at the foot of a large oak, whose branches promised me an agreeable shade. I had not yet closed my eyes, when the slumber I invited was dissipated by the sound of some voices near me. A curiosity, not natural to me, made me listen to the discourse of these persons, whom, by the tone of their voices, though I could not see them, I knew to be men. In short, madam, I was a witness to a most horrible scheme, which they concerted together. My weakness will not permit me to enter into an exact detail of all I heard: the result of their conference was, to seize the princess of this country, and carry her off.—Here, pursued Cynecia, I interrupted the stranger with a loud cry, which giving him to understand who I was, he apologized in the most graceful manner imaginable for the little respect he had hitherto paid me, I then entreated him to tell me, if he had any opportunity of hearing the name of my designed ravisher: to which he replied, that he understood it to be Taxander.

This man, madam, was one of my father's favourites, and had been long secretly in love with me.—Ariamenes then informed me, that being inflamed with rage against these impious villains, he rose from the ground, remounted his horse, and defied the two traitors aloud, threatening them with death, unless they abandoned their impious design, Taxander made no answer, but rushed furiously upon him, and had the baseness to suffer his wicked associate to assist him: but the valiant Ariamenes, though he spoke modestly of his victory, yet gave me to understand that he had made both the villains abandon their wicked enterprise, with their lives; and that dismounting, in order to see if they were quite dead, he found himself so faint with the wounds he had received from them both, that he had not strength to remount his horse; but crawling on, in hopes of meeting with some assistance, fainted away at last through weariness and loss of blood. While he was giving me this account, the chariot I had sent for arrived, and having made him such acknowledgments as the obligation I had received from him demanded, I caused him to get into the chariot; and sending one with him to acquaint the prince, my father, with all that had happened, and the merit of the valiant stranger, I returned the same way I came with my women, my thoughts being wholly engrossed by this unknown. The service he had done me filled me with a gratitude and esteem for him, which prepared my heart for those tender sentiments I afterwards entertained, to the ruin of my repose. I will not tire your patience, madam, with a minute detail of all the succeeding passages of my story: it shall suffice to tell you that Ariamenes was received with extraordinary marks of esteem by my father; that his cure was soon completed; and that, having vowed himself to my service, and declared an unalterable passion for me, I permitted him to love me, and gave him that share in my heart, which, I fear, not all his infidelities will ever deprive me of. His attachment to me was soon suspected by Taxander's relations, who having secretly vowed his ruin, endeavoured to discover if I had admitted his addresses; and having made themselves masters of our secrets, by means of the treachery of one of my women, procured information to be given to my father of our mutual passion.—Alas! what mischiefs did not this fatal discovery produce! My father, enraged to the last degree at this intelligence, confined me to my apartment, and ordered Ariamenes to leave his dominions within three days.

Spare me, madam, the repetition of what passed at our last sad interview, which, by large bribes to my guards, he obtained. His tears, his agonies, his vows of everlasting fidelity, so soothed my melancholy at parting with him, and persuaded me of his constancy, that I waited for several months, with perfect tranquillity, for the performance of the promise he had made me, to do my father such considerable services in the war he was engaged in with one of his neighbours, as should oblige him to give me to him for his reward. But, alas! two years rolled on without bringing back the unfaithful Ariamenes. My father died, and my brother, who succeeded him, being about to force me to marry a prince whom I detested, I secretly quitted the court, and, attended only by this faithful confidante whom you behold with me, and some few of my trusty domestics, I came hither in search of Ariamenes; he having told me this country was the place of his birth. Polenor, the most prudent and faithful of my servants, undertook to find out the ungrateful Ariamenes, whom yet I was willing to find excuses for: but all his inquiries were to no effect; the name of Ariamenes was not known in this part of the world. Tired out with unsuccessful inquiries, I resolved to seek out some obscure place, where I might in secret lament my misfortunes, and expect the end of them in death. My attendants found me out such a retreat as I wanted, in a neighbouring village, which they call Twickenham, I think; from whence I often make excursions to this park, attended only as you see, and here indulge myself in complaints upon the cruelty of my destiny.

The sorrowful Cynecia here ended her story, to which, in the course of her relation, she had given a great many interruptions through the violence of her grief: and Arabella, after having said every thing she could think on to alleviate her affliction, earnestly entreated her to accept of an asylum at her house; where she should be treated with all the respect due to her illustrious birth. The afflicted lady, though she respectfully declined this offer, yet expressed a great desire of commencing a strict amity with our fair heroine, who, on her part, made her the most tender protestations of friendship. The evening being almost closed, they parted with great reluctancy on both sides; mutually promising to meet in the same place the next day. Cynecia, having enjoined her new friend to absolute secrecy, Arabella was under a necessity of keeping this adventure to herself. And, though she longed to tell Mr Glanville, who came to visit her the next day, that the countess was extremely mistaken, when she maintained there were no more wandering princesses in the world, yet the engagement she had submitted to kept her silent.

V

A very mysterious chapter

ARABELLA, WHO IMPATIENTLY LONGED FOR the hour of meeting the fair princess, with whom she was extremely delighted, consulted her watch so often, and discovered so much restlessness and anxiety, that Mr Glanville began to be surprised: and the more, as she peremptorily commanded him not to attend her in her evening walk. This prohibition, which, though he durst not dispute, he secretly resolved to disobey; and as soon as she set out for the park with her usual attendants, he slipped out by a back-door, and, keeping her in his sight, himself unseen, he ventured to watch her motions.

As he had expected to unravel some great mystery, he was agreeably disappointed to find she continued her walk in the park with great composure; and though she was soon joined by the imaginary princess, yet conceiving her to be some young lady with whom she had commenced an acquaintance at Richmond, his heart was at rest; and, for fear of displeasing her, he took a contrary path from that she was in, that he might not meet her, yet resolved to stay till he thought she would be inclined to return, and then show himself, and conduct her home;—a solicitude for which he did not imagine she need be offended.

The two ladies being met, after reciprocal compliments, the princess entreated Arabella to relate her adventures; who not being willing to violate the laws of romance, which require an unbounded confidence upon these occasions, began very succinctly to recount the history of her life; which, as she managed it, contained events almost as romantic and incredible as any in her romances; winding them up with a confession that she did not hate Mr Glanville, whom she acknowledged to be one of the most faithful and zealous of lovers.—Cynecia, with a sigh, congratulated her upon the fidelity of a lover, who, by her description, was worthy the place he possessed in her esteem; and expressing a wish that she could see, unobserved by him, this gallant and generous person, Arabella, who that moment espied him at a distance, yet advancing towards them, told her, with a blush that overspread all her face, that her curiosity might be satisfied in the manner she wished, For yonder, added she, is the person we have been talking of. Cynecia, at these words, looking towards the place where her fair friend had directed, no sooner cast her eyes upon Mr Glanville, than, giving a loud cry, she sunk into the arms of Arabella, who, astonished and perplexed as she was, eagerly held them out to support her. Finding her in a swoon, she dispatched Lucy, who was near her, to look for some water to throw in her face; but that lady, breathing a deep sigh, opened her languishing eyes, and fixed a melancholy look upon Arabella. Ah! madam, said she, wonder not at my affliction and surprise, since in the person of your lover I behold the ungrateful Ariamenes.

Oh, Heavens! my fair princess, replied Arabella, what is it you say? Is it possible Glanville can he Ariamenes?—He, cried the afflicted princess, with a disordered accent, he whom I now behold, and whom you call Glanville, was once Ariamenes, the perjured, the ungrateful Ariamenes! Adieu! madam; I cannot bear his sight: I will hide myself from the world for ever; nor need you fear a rival, or an enemy, in the unfortunate Cynecia, who, if possible, will cease to love the unfaithful Ariamenes, and will never hate the beautiful Arabella. Saying this, without giving her time to answer, she took hold of her confidante by the arm, and went away with so much swiftness, that she was out of sight before Arabella was enough recovered from her astonishment to be able to entreat her stay.—Our charming heroine, ignorant till now of the true state of her heart, was surprised to find it assaulted at once by all the passions which attend disappointed love. Grief, rage, jealousy, and despair, made so cruel a war in her gentle bosom, that, unable either to express or conceal the strong emotions with which she was agitated, she gave way to a violent burst of tears, leaning her head upon Lucy's shoulder, who wept as heartily as her lady, though ignorant of the cause of her affliction. Mr Glanville, who was now near enough to take notice of her posture, came running with eager haste to see what was the matter; when Arabella, roused from her ecstacy of grief by the sound of his steps, lifted up her head, and seeing him approach—Lucy, cried she, trembling with the violence of her resentment, tell that traitor to keep out of my sight. Tell him, I forbid him ever to appear before me again. And, tell him, added she, with a sigh that shook her whole tender frame, all the blood in his body is too little to wash away his guilt, or to pacify my indignation. Then hastily turning away, she ran towards her other attendants, who were at some distance; and, joining her women, proceeded directly home. Mr Glanville, amazed at this action, was making after her as fast as he could, when Lucy, crossing in his way, cried out to him to stop. My lady, said she, bid me tell you, traitor—Hey-day! interrupted Glanville, what the devil does the girl mean?

Pray, sir, said she, let me deliver my message: I shall forget, if you speak to me till I have said it all. Stay, let me see, what comes next?—No more traitor, I hope, said Glanville.—No, sir, said Lucy; but there was something about washing in blood, and you must keep out of her sight, and not appear before the nation. Oh, dear! I have forgot it half: my lady was in such a piteous taking, I forgot it, I believe, as soon as she said it. What shall I do?—No matter, said Glanville, I'll overtake her, and ask.—No, no, sir, said Lucy; pray don't do that, sir! my lady will be very angry. I'll venture to ask her to tell me over again, and come back and let you know it.—But tell me, replied Glanville, was any thing the matter with your lady? She was in a piteous taking, you say?—Oh dear! yes, sir; said Lucy; but I was not bid to say any thing about that. To be sure, my lady did cry sadly, and sighed as if her heart would break; but I don't know what was the matter with her.—Well, said Glanville, excessively shocked at this intelligence, go to your lady: I am going home: you may bring me her message to my own apartment. Lucy did as she was desired; and Mr Glanville, impatient as he was to unravel the mystery, yet dreading lest his presence should make Arabella be guilty of some extravagance before the servants who were with her, he followed slowly after her, resolving, if possible, to procure a private interview with the lovely visionary, for whose sorrow, though he suspected it was owing to some ridiculous cause, he could not help being affected.

VI

Not much plainer than the former

ARABELLA, WHO HAD WALKED AS fast as her legs would carry her, got home before Lucy could overtake her, and, retiring to her chamber, gave way to a fresh burst of grief, and bewailed the infidelity of Glanville in terms befitting a Clelia or Mandane. As soon as she saw Lucy enter, she started from her chair with great emotion. Thou comest, said she, I know, to intercede for that ungrateful man, whose infidelity I am weak enough to lament: but open not thy mouth, I charge thee, in his defence.—No, indeed, madam! said Lucy.—Nor bring me any account of his tears, his desperation, or his despair, said Arabella; since, questionless, he will feign them all to deceive me.—Here Glanville, who had watched Lucy's coming, and had followed her into Arabella's apartment, appeared at the door. Oh, Heavens! cried Arabella, lifting up her fine eyes, can it be that this disloyal man, unawed by the discovery of his guilt, again presumes to approach me?—Dearest cousin, said Glanville, what is the meaning of all this? How have I disobliged you? What is my offence? I beseech you, tell me.—Ask the inconstant Ariamenes, replied Arabella, the offence of the ungrateful Glanville. The betrayer of Cynecia can best answer that question to the deceiver of Arabella; and the guilt of the one can only be compared to the crimes of the other.—Good God! interrupted Mr Glanville, fretting excessively, what am I to understand by all this? On my soul, madam, I don't know the meaning of one word you say.—Oh, dissembler! said Arabella, is it thus that thou wouldest impose upon my incredulity? Does not the name of Ariamenes make thee tremble, then? And, canst thou hear that of Cynecia without confusion?

Dear Lady Bella, said Glanville, smiling, what are these names to me?—False man! interrupted Arabella, dost thou presume to sport with thy crimes, then? Are not the treacheries of Ariamenes the crimes of

Glanville? Could Ariamenes be false to the princess of Gaul, and can Glanville be innocent towards Arabella?

Mr Glanville, who had never heard her, in his opinion, talk so ridiculously before, was so amazed at the incomprehensible stuff she uttered with so much emotion, that he began to fear her intellects were really touched. This thought gave him a concern that spread itself in a moment over his countenance. He gazed on her with a fixed attention, dreading, yet wishing she would speak again; equally divided between his hopes that her next speech would remove his suspicion and his fears, or that it might more confirm them. Arabella, taking notice of his pensive posture, turned away her head, lest, by beholding him, she should relent, and treat him with less severity than she had intended, making at the same time a sign to him to be gone.—Indeed, Lady Bella, said Glanville, who understood her perfectly well, I cannot leave you in this temper. I must know how I have been so unfortunate as to offend you. Arabella, no longer able to contain herself, burst into tears at this question: with one hand she made repeated signs to him to be gone; with the other she held her handkerchief to her eyes, vexed and ashamed of her weakness. But Mr Glanville, excessively shocked at this sight, instead of leaving her, threw himself on his knees before her, and taking her hand, which he tenderly pressed to his lips—Good God! My dearest cousin, said he, how you distract me by this behaviour! Sure something extraordinary must be the matter. What can it be that thus afflicts you? Am I the cause of these tears? Can I have offended you so much? Speak, dear madam! let me know my crime. Yet, may I perish if I am conscious of any towards you!—Disloyal man! said Arabella, disengaging her hand from his, does then the crime of Ariamenes seem so light in thy apprehension, that thou canst hope to be thought innocent by Arabella? No, no, ungrateful man! the unfortunate Cynecia shall have no cause to say that I will triumph in her spoils. I myself will be the minister of her revenge; and Glanville shall suffer for the crime of Ariamenes.—Who the devil is this Ariamenes? cried Glanville, rising in a passion: and why am I to suffer for his crime, pray? For Heaven's sake, dear cousin, don't let your imagination wander thus. Upon my

soul, I don't believe there is any such person as Ariamenes in the world.
—Vile equivocator! said Arabella; Ariamenes, though dead to Cynecia,
is alive to the deluded Arabella. The crimes of Ariamenes are the guilt
of Glanville: and if the one has made himself unworthy of the princess
of Gaul, by his perfidy and ingratitude, the other, by his baseness and
deceit, merits nothing but contempt and detestation from Arabella.

Frenzy, by my soul! cried Glanville, mutteringly between his teeth:
this is downright frenzy. What shall I do?—Hence from my presence,
resumed Arabella, false and ungrateful man! Persecute me no more
with the hateful offers of thy love. From this moment I banish thee
from my thoughts for ever; and neither as Glanville nor as Ariamenes
will I ever behold thee more.—Stay, dear cousin, said Glanville,
holding her, (for she was endeavouring to rush by him, unwilling he
should see the tears that had overspread her face as she pronounced
those words): hear me, I beg you, but one word. Who is it you mean
by Ariamenes? Is it me? Tell me, madam, I beseech you. This is some
horrid mistake. You have been imposed upon by some villainous
artifice. Speak, dear Lady Bella! Is it me you mean by Ariamenes?
for so your last words seemed to hint.—Arabella, without regarding
what he said, struggled violently to force her hand from his; and,
finding him still earnest to detain her, told him, with an enraged
voice, that she would call for help, if he did not unhand her directly.
Poor Glanville, at this menace, submissively dropt her hand; and the
moment she was free, she flew out of the room, and locking herself ap
in her closet, sent her commands to him by one of her women, whom
she called to her, to leave her apartment immediately.

VII

Containing indeed no great matters, but being a prelude to greater

M R GLANVILLE, WHO HAD STOOD fixed like a statue in the place where Arabella had left him, was roused by this message, which, though palliated a little by the girl that delivered it, who was not quite so punctual as Lucy, nevertheless filled him with extreme confusion. He obeyed, however, immediately, and retiring to his own apartment, endeavoured to recal to his memory all Lady Bella had said. The ambiguity of her style, which had led him into a suspicion he had never entertained before, her last words had partly explained, if, as he understood she did, she meant him by Ariamenes. Taking this for granted, he easily conceived some plot, grounded on her romantic notions, had been laid, to prepossess her against him.

Sir George's behaviour to her rushed that moment into his thoughts. He instantly recollected all his fooleries, his history, his letter, his conversation, all apparently copied from those books she was so fond of, and probably done with a view to some other design upon her. These reflections, joined to his new awakened suspicions that he was in love with her, convinced him he was the author of their present misunderstanding; and that he had imposed some new fallacy upon Arabella, in order to promote a quarrel between them. Fired almost to madness at this thought, he stamped about his room, vowing revenge upon Sir George, execrating romances, and cursing his own stupidity, for not discovering Sir George was his rival, and, knowing his plotting talent, not providing against his artifices. His first resolutions were, to set out immediately for Sir George's seat, and force him to confess the part he had acted against him: but a moment's consideration convinced him, that was not the most probable place to find him in, since it was much more likely he was waiting the success of his schemes in London, or perhaps at Richmond. Next to satiating his vengeance, the pleasure of detecting him in such a manner, that he could not possibly deny or palliate his guilt, was nearest his heart.

He resolved, therefore, to give it out that he was gone to London, to make Lady Bella believe it was in obedience to her commands that he had left her, with a purpose not to return till he had cleared his innocence; but, in reality, to conceal himself in his own apartment, and see what effects his reputed absence would produce. Having thus taken his resolution, he sent for Mr Roberts, his father's steward, to whose care he had entrusted Lady Bella in her retirement, and acquainting him with part of his apprehensions with regard to Sir George's attempt upon his cousin, he imparted to him his design of staying concealed there, in order to discover more effectually those attempts, and to preserve Lady Bella from any consequence of them. Mr Roberts approved of his design, and assured him of his vigilance and care, both in concealing his stay, and also in giving him notice of every thing that passed. Mr Glanville then wrote a short billet to Arabella, expressing his grief for her displeasure, his departure in obedience to her orders, and his resolution not to appear in her presence till he could give her convincing proofs of his innocence. This letter he sent by Roberts, which Arabella condescended to read, but would return no answer. Mr Glanville then mounting his horse, which Roberts had ordered to be got ready, rode away, and leaving him at a house he sometimes put up at, returned on foot, and was let in by Mr Roberts at the garden-door, and conducted unseen to his chamber. While he passed that night, and great part of the next day, meditating on the treachery of Sir George, and soothing his uneasiness with the hopes of revenge; Arabella, not less disquieted, musing on the infidelity of her lover, the despair of Cynecia, and the impossibility of her ever being happy: then ransacking her memory for instances in her romances of ladies equally unfortunate with herself, she would sometimes compare herself to one lady, sometimes to another, adapting their sentiments, and making use of their language in her complaints. Great part of the day being spent in this manner, the uneasy restlessness of her mind made her wish to see Cynecia again. She longed to ask her a hundred questions about the unfaithful Ariamenes, which the suddenness of her departure, and her own astonishment, prevented her from doing, when she made that fatal discovery, which had cost her so much uneasiness.

Sometimes a faint hope would arise in her mind, that Cynecia might be mistaken, through the great resemblance that possibly was between Ariamenes and Glanville. She remembered that Mandane had been deceived by the likeness of Cyrus to Spitridates: and concluded that illustrious prince inconstant, because Spitridates, whom she took for Cyrus, saw her carried away without offering to rescue her. Dwelling with eagerness upon this thought, because it afforded her a temporary relief from others more tormenting, she resolved to go to the park, though she had but little hopes of finding Cynecia there; supposing it but too probable that the disturbance which the sight, or fancied sight, of Ariamenes had given her, would confine her for some days to her chamber. Yet, however small the probability was of meeting with her, she could not resist the impatient desire she felt of going to seek her. Dispensing, therefore, with the attendance of any other servant but Lucy, she left her apartment, with a design of resuming her usual walk, when she was met, at her stepping out of the door, by Lady L ———'s three daughters (who had visited her during her residence at Richmond), and another young lady. These ladies, who, to vary the scene of their rural diversions, were going to cross over to Twickenham, and walk there, pressed Lady Bella to accompany them. Our melancholy heroine refused them at first; but, upon their repeated importunity, recollecting that the princess of Gaul had informed her she resided there, she consented to go, in hopes some favourable chance might bring her in their way, or discover the place of her retreat, when she could easily find some excuse for leaving her companions and going to her. Mr Roberts, who, according to his instructions, narrowly watched Arabella's motions, finding she did not command his attendance as usual, resolved however to be privately of this party. He had but just time to run up and acquaint Mr Glanville, and then followed the ladies at a distance, who, taking boat, passed over to Twickenham, which he also did as soon as he saw them landed.

VIII

Which acquaints the reader with two very extraordinary accidents

Mr Glanville, who did not doubt but Roberts would bring him some intelligence, sat waiting with anxious impatience for his return. The evening drew on a pace, he numbered the hours, and began to grow uneasy at Arabella's long stay. His chamber-window looking into the garden, he thought he saw his cousin, covered with her veil as usual, hasten down one of the walks. His heart leaped at this transient view: he threw up the sash, and, looking out, saw her very plainly strike into a cross-walk, and a moment after saw Sir George, who came out of a little summer-house, at her feet. Transported with rage at this sight, he snatched up his sword, flew down the stairs into the garden, and came running like a madman up the walk in which the lovers were. The lady observing him first, for Sir George's back was towards him, shrieked aloud, and not knowing what she did, ran towards the house, crying for help, and came back as fast, yet not time enough to prevent mischief: for Mr Glanville, actuated by an irresistible fury, cried out to Sir George to defend himself, who had but just time to draw his sword, and make an ineffectual pass at Mr Glanville, when he received his into his body, and fell to the ground.

Mr Glanville losing his resentment, insensibly, at the sight of his rival's blood, threw down his sword, and endeavoured to support him; while the lady, who had lost her veil in running, and, to the great astonishment of Mr Glanville, proved to be his sister, came up to them with tears and exclamations, blaming herself for all that had happened. Mr Glanville, with a heart throbbing with remorse for what he had done, gazed on his sister with an accusing look, as she hung over the wounded baronet with streaming eyes, sometimes wringing her hands, then clasping them together in an agony of grief. Sir George, having strength enough left to observe her disorder, and the generous concern of Glanville, who, holding him in his arms, entreated his sister to send for proper assistance, Dear Charles, said he, you are too kind: I have used you very ill: I have deserved my death from your hand. You know not what I have been base enough to practise against you. If I can but live to clear you innocence to Lady Bella, and free you from the consequence of this action, I shall die satisfied.—His strength failing him at these words, he fainted away in Mr Glanville's arms; who, though now convinced of his treachery, was extremely shocked at the condition he saw him in. Miss Glanville renewing her tears and exclamations at this sight, he was obliged to lay Sir George gently upon the ground, and ran to find out somebody to send for a surgeon, and to help him to convey him into the house. In his way he was met by Mr Roberts, who was coming to seek him; and, with a look of terror and confusion, told him Lady Bella was brought home extremely ill—that her life had been in danger, and that she was but just recovered from a terrible fainting fit.

Mr Glanville, though greatly alarmed at this news, forgot not to take all possible care of Sir George; directing Roberts to get some person to carry him into the house, and giving him orders to procure proper assistance, flew to Lady Bella's apartment. Her women had just put her to bed, raving as in a strong delirium. Mr Glanville approached her, and finding she was in a violent fever, dispatched a man and horse immediately to town, to get physicians, and to acquaint his father with what had happened. Mr Roberts, upon the surgeon's report, that Sir George was not mortally wounded, came to inform him of this good news; but he found him incapable of listening to him, and in agonies not to be expressed. It was with difficulty they forced him out of Arabella's chamber into his own; where, throwing himself upon his bed, he refused to see or speak to any body, till he was told Sir Charles and the physicians were arrived. He then ran eagerly to hear their opinions of his beloved cousin, which he soon discovered, by their significant gestures and half-pronounced words, to be very bad. They comforted him, however, with hopes that she might recover; and, insisting upon her being kept very quiet, obliged him to quit the room. While all the necessary methods were taken to abate the violence of the disease, Sir

Charles, who had been informed by his steward of his son's duel with
Sir George, was amazed to the last degree at two such terrible accidents.
Having seen his son to his chamber, and recommended him to be
patient and composed, he went to visit the young baronet; and was not
a little surprised to find his daughter sitting at his bed's head, with all
the appearance of a violent affliction. Indeed, Miss Glanville's cares were
so wholly engrossed by Sir George, that she hardly ever thought of her
cousin Arabella, and had just stept into her chamber while the surgeons
were dressing Sir George's wound, and renewed her attendance upon
him as soon as that was over.

Miss Glanville, however, thought proper to make some trifling
excuses to her father for her solicitude about Sir George. And the
young baronet, on whom the fear of death produced its usual effects,
and made him extremely concerned for the errors of his past life, and
very desirous of atoning for them, if possible, assured Sir Charles, that
if he lived, he would offer himself to his acceptance for a son-in-law;
declaring that he had basely trifled with the esteem of his daughter,
but that she had wholly subdued him to herself by her forgiving
tenderness. Sir Charles was very desirous of knowing the occasion of his
quarrel with his son; but Sir George was too weak to hold any farther
conversation; upon which, Sir Charles, after a short visit, retired, taking
Miss Glanville along with him.

That the reader, whose imagination is no doubt upon the stretch to
conceive the meaning of these two extraordinary incidents, may be left
no longer in suspense, we think proper to explain them both in the
following chapter, that we may in the next pursue our history without
interruption.

IX

Which will be found to contain information absolutely necessary for the right understanding of this history

OUR FAIR AND AFFLICTED HEROINE, accompanied by the ladies we have mentioned, having crossed the river, pursued their walk upon its winding banks, entertaining themselves with the usual topics of conversation among young ladies, such as their winnings and losings at brag, the prices of silks, the newest fashions, the best hair-cutter, the scandal at the last assembly, etc. Arabella was so disgusted with this (as she thought) insipid discourse, which gave no relief to the anxiety of her mind, but added a kind of fretfulness and impatience to her grief, that she resolved to quit them, and with Lucy to go in quest of the princess of Gaul's retreat. The ladies, however, insisted upon her not leaving them; and her excuse that she was going in search of an unfortunate unknown, for whom she had vowed a friendship, made them all immediately resolve to accompany her, extremely diverted with the oddity of the design, and sacrificing her to their mirth by sly leers, whispers, stifled laughs, and a thousand little sprightly sallies, of which the disconsolate Arabella took no notice, so deeply were her thoughts engaged. Though she knew not which way to direct her steps, yet concluding the melancholy Cynecia would certainly choose some very solitary place for her residence, she rambled about among the least frequented paths, followed by the young ladies, who ardently desired to see this unfortunate unknown; though, at Arabella's earnest request, they promised not to shew themselves to the lady, who, she informed them, for very urgent reasons, was obliged to keep herself concealed. Fatiguing as this ramble was to the delicate spirits of Arabella's companions, they were enabled to support it by the diversion her behaviour afforded them. Every peasant she met, she inquired if a beautiful lady, disguised, did not dwell somewhere thereabout. To some she gave a description of her person, to others an account of the domestics that were with her; not forgetting her dress, her melancholy, and the great care she took to keep herself concealed. These strange inquiries, with the strange language in which they were made, not a little surprised the good people to whom she addressed herself; yet, moved to respect by the majestic loveliness of her person, they answered her in the negative, without any mixture of scoff and impertinence.

How unfavourable is chance, said Arabella, fretting at the disappointment, to persons who have any reliance upon it! This lady that I have been in search of so long without success, may probably be found by others who do not seek her, whose presence she may wish to avoid, yet not be able.—The young ladies, finding it grow late, expressed their apprehensions of being without any attendants, and desired Arabella to give over her search for that day. Arabella, at this hint of danger, inquired very earnestly if they apprehended any attempts to carry them away; and, without staying for an answer, urged them to walk home as fast as possible, apologizing for the danger into which she had so indiscreetly drawn both them and herself; yet added her hopes, that, if any attempts should be made upon their liberty, some generous cavalier would pass by who would rescue them: a thing so common, that they had no reason to despair of it.

Arabella, construing the silence with which her companions heard these assurances into a doubt of their being so favoured by fortune, proceeded to inform them of several instances wherein ladies met with unexpected relief and deliverance from ravishers. She mentioned particularly the rescue of Statira by her own brother, whom she imagined for many years dead; that of the princess Berenice, by an absolute stranger; and many others, whose names, characters, and adventures, she occasionally ran over;—all which the young ladies heard with inconceivable astonishment: and the detail had such an effect upon Arabella's imagination, bewildered as it was in the follies of romances, that, espying three or four horsemen riding along the road towards them, she immediately concluded they would be all seized and carried off. Possessed with this belief, she uttered a loud cry, and flew to the water-

side; which alarming the ladies, who could not imagine what was the
matter, they ran after her as fast as possible. Arabella stopped when she
came to the water-side, and looking round about, and not perceiving any
boat to waft them over to Richmond, a thought suddenly darted into
her mind, worthy those ingenious books which gave it birth. Turning
therefore to the ladies, who all at once were inquiring the cause of her
fright—It is now, my fair companions, said she, with a solemn accent,
that the Destinies have furnished you with an opportunity of displaying,
in a manner truly heroic, the sublimity of your virtue, and the grandeur
of your courage, to the world. The action we have it in our power to
perform will immortalize our fame, and raise us to a pitch of glory equal
to that of the renowned Clelia herself. Like her, we may expect statues
erected to our honour; like her, be proposed as patterns to heroines in
ensuing ages; and like her, perhaps, meet with sceptres and crowns for our
reward. What that beauteous Roman lady performed to preserve herself
from violation by the impious Sextus, let us imitate, to avoid the violence
our intended ravishers yonder come to offer us. Fortune, who has thrown
us into this exigence, presents us the means of gloriously escaping; and
the admiration and esteem of all ages to come, will be the recompence
of our noble daring. Once more, my fair companions, if your honour
be dear to you, if an immortal glory be worth your seeking, follow the
example I shall set you, and equal, with me, the Roman Clelia.

Saying this, she plunged into the Thames, intending to swim over it,
as Clelia did the Tyber. The young ladies, who had listened with silent
astonishment at the long speech she had made them, the purport of
which not one of them understood, screamed out aloud at this horrid
spectacle, and wringing their hands, ran backwards and forwards, like
distracted persons, crying for help. Lucy tore her hair, and was in the
utmost agony of grief; when Mr Roberts, who, as we have said before,
kept them always in sight, having observed Arabella running towards
the water-side, followed them as fast as he could, and came up time
enough to see her frantic action. Jumping into the river immediately
after her, he caught hold of her gown, and drew her after him to the
shore. A boat that instant appearing, he put her into it, senseless, and to

all appearance dead. He and Lucy supporting her, they were wafted over in a few moments to the other side. Her house being near the river, Mr Roberts carried her in his arms to it; and as soon as he saw her shew signs of returning life, left her to the care of the women, who made haste to put her into a warm bed, and ran to find out Mr Glanville, as we have related.—There remains now only to account for Sir George and Miss Glanville's sudden appearance, which happened, gentle reader, exactly as follows. Miss Glanville having set out pretty late in the afternoon, with a design of staying all night at Richmond, as her chaise drove up Kew-lane, saw one of her cousin's women, Deborah by name, talking to a gentleman, whom, notwithstanding the disguise of a horse-man's coat, and a hat slouched over his face, she knew to be Sir George Bellmour. This sight alarmed her jealousy, and renewed all her former suspicions that her cousin's charms rivalled hers in his heart. As soon as she alighted, finding Arabella was not at home, she retired in great anguish of mind to her chamber, revolving in her mind every particular of Sir George's behaviour to her cousin in the country; and finding new cause for suspicion in every thing she recollected, and reflecting upon the disguise in which she saw him, and his conference with her woman, she concluded that herself had all along been the dupe of his artifice, and her cousin the real object of his love. This thought throwing her into an extremity of rage, all her tenderest emotions were lost in the desire of revenge. She imagined to herself so much pleasure from exposing his treachery, and putting it out of his power to deny it, that she resolved, whatever it cost her, to have that satisfaction. Supposing, therefore, Deborah was now returned, she rung her bell, and commanded her attendance on her in her chamber. The stern brow with which she received her, frightened the girl, conscious of her guilt, into a disposition to confess all, even before she was taxed with any thing.

Miss Glanville saw her terror, and endeavoured to heighten it, by entering at once into complaints and exclamations against her, threatening to acquaint her father with her plots to betray her lady, and assuring her of a very severe punishment for her treachery. The girl, terrified extremely at these menaces, begged Miss Glanville, with tears, to forgive her, and not to acquaint Sir Charles or her lady with her fault; adding, that she would confess all, and never while she lived do such a thing again.

Miss Glanville would make her no promises, but urged her to confess; upon which Deborah, sobbing, owned, that for the sake of the present Sir George had made her, she consented to meet him privately, from time to time, and give him an account of every thing that passed with regard to her lady, not thinking there was any harm in it; that, according to his desires, she had constantly acquainted him with all her lady's motions, when and where she went, how she and Mr Glanville agreed, and a hundred other things which he inquired about;—that that day, in particular, he had entreated her to procure him the means of an interview with her lady, if possible; and understanding Mr Glanville was not at Richmond, she had let him privately into the garden, where she hoped to prevail upon her lady to go.—What! said Miss Glanville, surprised, is Sir George waiting for my cousin in the garden, then?—Yes, indeed, madam, said Deborah; but I'll go and tell him to wait no longer; and never speak to him again, if your ladyship will but be pleased to forgive me. Miss Glanville, having taken her resolution, not only promised Deborah her pardon, but also a reward, provided she would contrive it so, that she might meet Sir George instead of her cousin. The girl, having the true chambermaid spirit of intrigue in her, immediately proposed her putting on one of her lady's veils, which, as it was now the close of the evening, would disguise her sufficiently, to which Miss Glanville, transported with the thoughts of thus having an opportunity of convincing Sir George of his perfidy, and reproaching him for it, consented, and bid her bring it without being observed into her chamber. Deborah informing her that Sir George was concealed in the summer-house, as soon as she had equipped herself with Arabella's veil, she went into the walk that led to it; and Sir George, believing her to be that lady, hastened to throw himself at her feet, and had scarce got through half a speech he had studied for the purpose, when Mr Glanville gave a fatal interruption to his heroics, in the manner we have already related.

X

A short chapter indeed, but full of matter

RICHMOND WAS NOW A SCENE of the utmost confusion and distress. Arabella's fever was risen to such a height, that she was given over by the physicians; and Sir George's wounds, though not judged mortal at first, yet, by the great effusion of blood, had left him in so weak a condition, that he was thought to be in great danger. Sir Charles, almost distracted with the fears of the death of Sir George, entreated his son to quit the kingdom: but Mr Glanville, protesting he would rather die than leave Arabella in that illness, he was obliged to give bail for his apearance, in case Sir George died; this affair, notwithstanding all endeavours to prevent it, having made a great noise. Poor Sir Charles, oppressed as he was with the weight of all these calamities, was yet obliged to labour incessantly to keep up the spirits of his son and daughter. The settled despair of the one, and the silent grief of the other, cut him to the heart. He omitted no arguments his paternal affection suggested to him, to moderate their affliction. Mr Glanville often endeavoured to assume a composure he was very far from feeling, in order to satisfy his father. But Miss Glanville, looking upon herself to be the cause of Sir George's misfortune, declared she should be miserable all her life, if he died.

Arabella, in her lucid intervals, being sensible of her danger, prepared for death with great piety and constancy of mind, having solemnly assured Mr Glanville of her forgiveness, who would not at that time enter into an explanation of the affair which had given her offence, for fear of perplexing her. She permitted his presence often in her chamber, and desired, with great earnestness, the assistance of some worthy divine in her preparations for death. The pious and learned Doctor ——, at Sir Charles's intimation of his niece's desire, came twice a day to attend her. Her fever, by a favourable crisis, and the great skill of her physicians, left her in a fortnight; but this violent distemper had made such a ravage in her delicate constitution, and reduced her so low, that there seemed very little probability of her recovery. Doctor ———, in whom her unfeigned piety, her uncommon firmness of mind, had created a great esteem and tenderness for her, took all opportunities of comforting, exhorting, and praying by her. The occasion of her illness being the subject of every body's conversation at Richmond, he gently hinted it to her, and urged her to explain her reasons for so extravagant an action. In the divine frame Arabella was then in, this action appeared to her rash and vain-glorious, and she acknowledged it to be so to her pious monitor; yet she related the motives which induced her to it, the danger she was in of being carried away, the parity of her circumstances then with Clelia, and her emulous desire of doing as much to preserve her honour as that renowned Roman lady did for hers. The good doctor was extremely surprised at this discourse; he was beginning to think her again delirious: but Arabella added to this account such sensible reasoning on the nature of that fondness for fame which prompted her to so rash an undertaking, the doctor left her in strange embarrassment, not knowing how to account for a mind at once so enlightened and so ridiculous. Mr Glanville meeting him as he came out of her chamber, the doctor took this opportunity to acknowledge the difficulties Arabella's inconsistent discourse had thrown him into. Mr Glanville taking him into his own apartment, explained the nature of that seeming inconsistency, and expatiated at large upon the disorders romances had occasioned in her imagination; several instances of which he recounted and filled the doctor with the greatest astonishment and concern. He lamented pathetically the ruin such a ridiculous study had brought on so noble a mind; and assured Mr Glanville he would spare no endeavours to rescue it from so shocking a delusion. Mr Glanville thanked him for his good design, with a transport which his fears for his cousin's danger almost mingled with tears; and the doctor and he agreed to expect, for some few days longer, an alteration for the better, in the health of her body, before he attempted the cure of her mind. Mr Glanville's extreme anxiety had made him in appearance neglect the repentant Sir George, contenting himself with constantly sending twice a day to inquire after his health, but had not yet visited him. No sooner had the physicians declared that Arabella was no longer in danger, than his mind, being freed from that tormenting load of suspense, under which it had laboured while her recovery was yet doubtful, he went to Sir George's chamber, who, by reason of his weakness, though he was also upon the recovery, still kept his bed. Sir George, though he ardently wished to see him, yet, conscious of the injuries he had both done and designed him, could not receive his visit without extreme confusion: but entering into the cause of their quarrel, as soon as he was able to speak, he freely acknowledged his fault, and all the steps he had taken to supplant him in Arabella's affection. Mr Glanville, understanding, by this means, that he had bribed a young actress to personate a princess forsaken by him, and had taught her all that heap of absurdity with which she had imposed upon Arabella, as has been related, desired only, by way of reparation, that when his cousin was in a condition to be spoken to upon the subject, he would condescend to own the fraud to her; which Sir George faithfully promising, an act of oblivion passed on Mr Glanville's side for all former injuries, and a solemn assurance from Sir George of inviolable friendship for the future;—an assurance, however, which Mr Glanville would willingly have dispensed with; for though not of a vindictive temper, it was one of his maxims, that a man who had once betrayed him, it would be an error in policy ever to trust again.

XI

Being, in the author's opinion, the best chapter in this history

THE GOOD DIVINE, WHO HAD the cure of Arabella's mind greatly at heart, no sooner perceived that the health of her body was almost restored, and that he might talk to her without the fear of any inconvenience, than he introduced the subject of her throwing herself into the river, which he had before lightly touched upon, and still declared himself dissatisfied with. Arabella, now more disposed to defend this point, than when languishing under the pressure of pain, and dejection of mind, endeavoured, by arguments founded upon romantic heroism, to prove, that it was not only reasonable and just, but also great and glorious, and exactly conformable to the rules of heroic virtue. The doctor listened to her with a mixed emotion, between pity, reverence, and amazement: and though in the performance of his offices he had been accustomed to accommodate his notions to every understanding, and had, therefore, accumulated a great variety of topics and illustrations; yet he found himself now engaged in a controversy for which he was not so well prepared as he imagined, and was at a loss for some leading principle, by which he might introduce his reasonings, and begin his confutation. Though he saw much to praise in her discourse, he was afraid of confirming her obstinacy by commendation; and though he also found much to blame, he dreaded to give pain to a delicacy he revered. Perceiving, however, that Arabella was silent, as if expecting his reply, he resolved not to bring upon himself the guilt of abandoning her to her mistake, and the necessity of speaking, forced him to find something to say.

Though it is not easy, madam, said he, for anyone that has the honour of conversing with your ladyship, to preserve his attention free from any other idea than such as your discourse tends immediately to impress, yet I have not been able, while you was speaking, to refrain from some very mortifying reflections on the imperfection of all human happiness, and the uncertain consequences of all those advantages which we think ourselves not only at liberty to desire, but obliged to cultivate. Though I have known some dangers and distresses, replied Arabella, gravely, yet I did not imagine myself such a mirror of calamity as could not be seen without concern. If my life has not been eminently fortunate, it has yet escaped the great evils of persecution, captivity, shipwrecks, and dangers. to which many ladies, far more illustrious, both by birth and merit than myself, have been exposed. And, indeed, though I have sometimes raised envy, or possibly incurred hatred, yet I have no reason to believe I was ever beheld with pity before.—The doctor saw he had not introduced his discourse in the most acceptable manner; but it was too late to repent. Let me not, madam, said he, be censured before I have fully explained my sentiments. That you have been envied I can readily believe; for who that gives way to natural passions, has not reason to envy the Lady Arabella? But that you have been hated, I am indeed less willing to think, though I know how easily the greater part of mankind hate those by whom they are excelled.—If the misery of my condition, replied Arabella, has been able to excite that melancholy your first words seem to imply, flattery will contribute very little towards the improvement of it. Nor did I expect, from the severity of the sacerdotal character, any of those praises which I hear, perhaps with too much pleasure, from the rest of the world. Having been so lately on the brink of that state, in which all distinctions but that of goodness are destroyed, I have not recovered so much levity but that I would yet rather hear instructions than compliments. If, therefore, you have observed in me any dangerous tenets, corrupt passions, or criminal desires, I conjure you to discover me to myself. Let no false civility restrain your admonitions. Let me know this evil which can strike a good man with horror, and which I dread the more, as I do not feel it. I cannot suppose that a man of your order would be alarmed at any other misery than guilt: nor will I think so meanly of him whose direction I have entreated, as to imagine he can think virtue unhappy, however overwhelmed by disasters or oppression.

The good man was now completely embarrassed: he saw his meaning mistaken, but was afraid to explain it, lest he should seem to pay court by a cowardly retraction: he therefore paused a little, and Arabella supposed he was studying for such expressions as might convey censure without offence. Sir, said she, if you are not yet satisfied of my willingness to hear your reproofs, let me evince my docility, by entreating you to consider yourself as dispensed from all ceremony upon this occasion. Your imaginations, madam, replied the doctor, are too quick for language: you conjecture too soon what you do not wait to hear, and reason upon suppositions which cannot be allowed you. When I mentioned my reflections upon human misery, I was far from concluding your ladyship miserable, compared with the rest of mankind; and though contemplating the abstracted idea of possible felicity, I thought that even you might be produced as an instance that it is not attainable in this world. I did not impute the imperfection of your state to wickedness, but intended to observe, that though even virtue be added to external advantages, there will yet be something wanting to happiness. Whoever sees you, madam, will immediately say, that nothing can hinder you from being the happiest of mortals, but want of power to understand your own advantages. And whoever is admitted to your conversation, will be convinced that you enjoy all that intellectual excellence can confer; yet I see you harassed with innumerable terrors and perplexities, which never disturb the peace of poverty or ignorance.

I cannot discover, said Arabella, how poverty or ignorance can be privileged from casualty or violence; from the ravisher, the robber, or the enemy, I should hope, rather, that if wealth and knowledge can give nothing else, they at least confer judgment to foresee danger, and power to oppose it. They are not, indeed, returned the doctor, secured against real misfortunes, but they are happily defended from wild imaginations: they do not suspect what cannot happen, nor figure ravishers at a distance, and leap into rivers to escape them.

Do you suppose, then, said Arabella, that I was frighted without cause?—It is certain, madam, replied he, that no injury was intended you.—Disingenuity, sir, said Arabella, does not become a clergyman. I think too well of your understanding, to imagine your fallacy deceives yourself: why, then, should you hope that it will deceive me? The laws of conference require, that the terms of the question and answer be the same. I ask, if I had not cause to he frighted? Why, then, am I answered, that no injury was intended? Human beings cannot penetrate intentions, nor regulate their conduct but by exterior appearances. And surely there was sufficient appearance of intended injury, and that the greatest which my sex can suffer.—Why, madam, said the doctor, should you still persist in so wild an assertion?—A coarse epithet, said Arabella, is no confutation. It rests upon you to shew, that, in giving way to my fears, even supposing them groundless, I departed from the character of a reasonable person.

I am afraid, replied the doctor, of a dispute with your ladyship; not because I think myself in danger of defeat, but because, being accustomed to speak to scholars with scholastic ruggedness, I may perhaps depart, in the heat of argument, from that respect to which you have so great a right, and give offence to a person I am really afraid to displease. But if you will promise to excuse my ardour, I will endeavour to prove that you have been frighted without reason—I should be content, replied Arabella, to obtain truth upon harder terms, and therefore entreat you to begin.—The apprehension of any future evil, madam, said the divine, which is called terror, when the danger is from natural causes, and suspicion, when it proceeds from a moral agent, must always arise from comparison. We can judge of the future only by the past, and have therefore only reason to fear or suspect, when we see the same causes in motion which have formerly produced mischief, or the same measures taken as have before been preparatory to a crime. Thus, when the sailor, in certain latitudes, sees the clouds rise, experience bids him expect a storm. When any monarch levies armies, his neighbours prepare to repel an invasion. This power of prognostication may, by reading and conversation, be extended beyond our own knowledge: and the great use of books is, that of participating, without labour or hazard, the experience of others. But, upon this principle, how can you find any reason for your late fright? Has it ever been known that a lady of your rank was attacked with such intentions, in a place so public, without any preparations made by the violator for defence or escape? Can it be imagined that any man would so rashly expose himself to infamy by failure, and to the gibbet by success? Does there, in the records of the world, appear a single instance of such hopeless villany?

It is now time, sir, said Arabella, to answer your questions, before they are too many to be remembered. The dignity of my birth can very little defend me against an insult to which the heiresses of great and powerful empires, the daughters of valiant princes, and the wives of renowned monarchs, have been a thousand times exposed. The danger which you think so great, would hardly repel a determined mind; for, in effect, who would have attempted my rescue, seeing that no knight, or valiant cavalier, was within view? What then should have hindered him from placing me in a chariot, driving it into the pathless desert, and immuring me in a castle among woods and mountains; or hiding me perhaps in the caverns of a rock; or confining me in some island of an immense lake?

From all this, madam, interrupted the clergyman, he is hindered by impossibility. He cannot carry you to any of these dreadful places, because there is no such castle, desert, cavern, or lake.

You will pardon me, sir, said Arabella, if I recur to your own principles. You allow that experience may be gained by books, and certainly there is no part of knowledge in which we are obliged to trust them more than in descriptive geography. The most restless activity in the longest life can survey but a small part of the inhabitable globe: and the rest can only be known from the report of others. Universal negatives are seldom safe, and are least to be allowed when the disputes are about objects of sense; where one position cannot be inferred from another. That there is a castle, any man who has seen it may safely affirm. But you cannot, with equal reason, maintain that there is no castle, because you have not seen it. Why should I imagine that the face of the earth is altered since the time of those heroines who experienced so many changes of uncouth captivity? Castles, indeed, are the works of art, and are therefore subject to decay. But lakes, and caverns, and deserts, must always remain. And why, since you call for instances, should I not dread the misfortunes which happened to the divine Clelia, who was carried to one of the isles of the Thrasymenian lake? Or those which befel the beautiful Candace, queen of Ethiopia, whom the pirate Zenedorus wandered with on the seas? Or the accidents which embittered the life of the incomparable Cleopatra? Or the persecutions which made that of the fair Elisa miserable? Or, in tine, the various distresses of many other fair and virtuous princesses; such as those which happened to Olympia, Bellamira, Parisatis, Berenice, Amalazontha, Agione, Albysinda, Placida, Arsinoe, Deidamia, and a thousand others I could mention.

To the names of many of these illustrious sufferers, I am an absolute stranger, replied the doctor: the rest I faintly remember some mention of in those contemptible volumes with which children are sometimes injudiciously suffered to amuse their imaginations, but which I little expected to hear quoted by your ladyship in a serious discourse. And though I am very far from catching occasions of resentment, yet I think myself at liberty to observe, that if I merited your censure for one indelicate epithet, we have engaged on very unequal terns, if I may not likewise complain of such contemptuous ridicule as you are pleased to exercise upon my opinions, by opposing them with the authority of scribblers, not only of fictions but of senseless fictions; which at once vitiate the mind and pervert the understanding, and which, if they are at any time read with safety, owe their innocence only to their absurdity.— From these books, sir, said Arabella, which you condemn with so much ardour, though you acknowledge yourself little acquainted with them, I have learnt not to recede from the conditions I have granted, and shall not therefore censure the licence of your language, which glances from the books upon the readers. These books, sir, thus incorrect, thus absurd, thus dangerous, alike to the intellect and morals, I have read, and that, I hope, without injury to my judgment or my virtue.—The doctor, whose vehemence had hindered him from discovering all the consequences of his position, now found himself entangled, and replied, in a submissive tone—I confess, madam, my words imply an accusation very remote from my intention. It has always been the rule of my life, not to justify any words or actions because they are mine. I am ashamed of my negligence; I am sorry for my warmth, and entreat your ladyship to pardon a fault which I hope never to repeat.—The reparation, sir, said Arabella, smiling, over-balances the offence, and by thus daring to own you have been in the wrong, you have raised in me a much higher esteem for you. Yet I will not pardon you, added she, without enjoining you a penance for the fault you own you have committed; and this penance shall be to prove—First, That these histories you condemn are fictions; next, That they are absurd; and, lastly, That they are criminal. The doctor was pleased to find a reconciliation offered upon so very easy terms, with a person whom he beheld at once with reverence and affection, and could not offend without extreme regret. He therefore answered with a very cheerful composure—To prove those narratives to be fictions, madam, is only difficult, because the position is almost too evident for proof. Your ladyship knows, I suppose, to what authors these writings are ascribed?—To the French wits of the last century, said Arabella.—And at what distance, madam, are the facts related in them from the age of the writer?—I was never exact in my computation, replied Arabella; but I think most of the events happened about two thousand years ago.   How then, madam, resumed the doctor, could these events be so minutely known to writers so far remote from the time in which they happened?—By records, monuments, memoirs, and histories, answered the lady.—But by what accident, then, said the doctor, smiling, did it happen these records and monuments were kept universally secret to mankind till the last century? What brought all the memoirs of the remotest nations and earliest ages only to France? Where were they hidden that none could consult them but a few obscure authors? And whither are they now vanished again, that they can be found no more?—Arabella having sat silent a while, told him, that she found his questions very difficult to be answered; and that, though perhaps the authors themselves could have told from whence they borrowed their materials, she should not at present require any other evidence of the first assertion, but allowed him to suppose them

fictions, and required now that he should show them to be absurd.—
Your ladyship, returned he, has, I find, too much understanding to
struggle against demonstration, and too much veracity to deny your
convictions: therefore, some of the arguments by which I intended
to show the falsehood of these narratives, may be now used to prove
their absurdity. You grant them, madam, to be fictions—Sir, interrupted
Arabella, eagerly, you are again infringing the laws of disputation. You
are not to confound a supposition of which I allow you only the
present use, with an unlimited and irrevocable concession. I am too well
acquainted with my own weakness to conclude an opinion false, merely
because I find myself unable to defend it. But I am in haste to hear the
proof of the other positions, not only because they may perhaps supply
what is deficient in your evidence of the first, but because I think it of
more importance to detect corruption than fiction. Though, indeed,
falsehood is a species of corruption, and what falsehood is more hateful
than the falsehood of history?—Since you have drawn me back, madam,
to the first question, returned the doctor, let me know what arguments
your ladyship can produce for the veracity of these books. That there are
many objections against it, you yourself have allowed; and the highest
moral evidence of falsehood appears when there are many arguments
against an assertion, and none for it. Sir, replied Arabella, I shall never
think that any narrative, which is not confuted by its own absurdity, is
without one argument at least on its side. There is a love of truth in
the human mind, if not naturally implanted, so easily obtained from
reason and experience, that I should expect it universally to prevail
where there is no strong temptation to deceit: we hate to be deceived;
we therefore hate those that deceive us: we desire not to be hated,
and therefore know that we are not to deceive. Shew me an equal
motive to falsehood, or confess that every relation has some right to
credit.—This may be allowed, madam, said the doctor, when we claim
to be credited; but that seems not to be the hope or intention of these
writers.—Surely, sir, replied Arabella, you must mistake their design:
he that writes without intention to be credited, must write to little
purpose; for what pleasure or advantage can arise from facts that never

happened? What examples can be afforded by the patience of those who never suffered, or the chastity of those who were never solicited? The great end of history is to shew how much human nature can endure or perform. When we hear a story in common life that raises our wonder or compassion, the first confutation stills our emotions; and however we were touched before, we then chase it from the memory with contempt as a trifle, or with indignation as an imposture. Prove, therefore, that the books which I have hitherto read, as copies of life, and models of conduct, are empty fictions, and from this hour I deliver them to moths and mould; from this time forward consider their authors as wretches who cheated me of those hours I ought to have dedicated to application and improvement.

Shakspeare, said the doctor, calls just resentment the child of integrity; and therefore I do not wonder, that what vehemence the gentleness of your ladyship's temper allows should be exerted upon this occasion. Yet though I cannot forgive these authors for having destroyed so much valuable time, I cannot think them intentionally culpable, because I cannot believe they expected to be credited. Truth is not always injured by fiction. An admirable writer[1] of our own time, has found the way to convey the most solid instructions, the noblest sentiments, and the most exulted piety in the pleasing dress of a novel,[2] and, to use the words of the greatest genius[3] in the present age, 'has taught the passions to move at the command of virtue.' The fables of Æsop, though never, I suppose, believed, yet have been long continued as lectures of moral and domestic wisdom, so well adapted to the faculties of man that they have been received by all civilized nations; and the Arabs themselves have honoured his translator with the appellation of Locman the Wise.—The fables of Æsop, said Arabella, are among those of which the absurdity discovers itself, and the truth is comprised in the application; but what can be said of those

---

1 Richardson

2 *Clarissa*

3 Author of *The Rambler*, Issue 97

tales which are told with the solemn air of historical truth, and, if false, convey no instruction?

That they cannot he defended, madam, said the doctor, it is my purpose to prove; and if to evince their falsehood be sufficient to procure their banishment from your ladyship's closet, their day of grace is near an end. How is any oral or written testimony confuted or confirmed?—By comparing it, says the lady, with the testimony of others, or with the natural effects, and standing evidence of the facts related, and sometimes by comparing it with itself.—If then your ladyship will abide by the last, returned he, and compare these books with ancient histories, you will not only find innumerable names, of which no mention was ever made before, but persons who lived in different ages, engaged as the friends or rivals of each other. You will perceive that your authors have parcelled out the world at discretion, erected palaces, and established monarchies wherever the conveniency of their narrative required them, and set kings and queens over imaginary nations. Nor have they considered themselves as invested with less authority over the works of nature, than the institutions of men: for they have distributed mountains and deserts, gulphs and rocks, wherever they wanted them; and whenever the course of their story required an expedient, raised a gloomy forest, or overflowed the regions with a rapid stream.—I suppose, said Arabella, you have no intention to deceive me; and since, what you have asserted being true, the cause is undefensible, I shall trouble you no longer to argue on this topic, but desire now to hear why, supposing them fictions, and intended to be received as fictions, you censure them as absurd?—The only excellence of falsehood, answered he, is its resemblance to truth: as therefore any narrative is more liable to be confuted by its inconsistency with known facts, it is at a greater distance from the perfection of fiction; for there can be no difficulty in framing a tale, if we are left at liberty to invert all history and nature for our own conveniency. When a crime is to be concealed, it is easy to cover it with an imaginary wood. When virtue is to be rewarded, a nation with a new name may, without any expence of invention, raise her to the throne. When Ariosto was told of the magnificence of his palaces, he answered, that the cost of poetical architecture was very little; and still less is the cost of building without art, than without materials. But their historical failures may be easily passed over, when we consider their physical or philosophical absurdities; to bring men together from different countries, does not shock with every inherent or demonstrable absurdity; and therefore when we read only for amusement, such improprieties may be borne: but who can forbear to throw away the story that gives one again the strength of thousands; that puts life or death in a smile or a frown; that, recounts labours and sufferings to which the powers of humanity are utterly unequal; that disfigures the whole appearance of the world, and represents every thing in a form different from that which experience has shown? It is the fault of the best fictions, that they teach young minds to expect strange adventures and sudden vicissitudes, and therefore encourage them often to trust to chance. A long life may be passed without a single occurrence that can cause much surprise, or produce any unexpected consequence of great importance; the order of the world is so established, that all human affairs proceed in a regular method, and very little opportunity is left for sallies or hazards, for assault or rescue; but the brave and the coward, the sprightly and the dull, suffer themselves to be carried alike down the stream of custom.— Arabella, who had for some time listened with a wish to interrupt him, now took advantage of a short pause. I cannot imagine, sir, said she, that you intended to deceive me, and therefore I am inclined to believe that you are yourself mistaken, and that your application to learning has hindered you from that acquaintance with the world in which these authors excelled. I have not long conversed in public, yet I have found that life is subject to many accidents. Do you count my late escape for nothing? Is it to be numbered among daily and cursory transactions, that a woman flies from a ravisher into a rapid stream?—You must not, madam, said the doctor, urge as an argument the fact which is at present the subject of dispute.—Arabella, blushing at the absurdity she had been guilty of, and not attempting any subterfuge or excuse, the doctor found himself at liberty to proceed.—You must not imagine, madam,

continued he, that I intend to arrogate any superiority, when I observe
that your ladyship must suffer me to decide, in some measure authori-
tatively, whether life is truly described in those books: the likeness of a
picture can only be determined by a knowledge of the original. You
have yet had little opportunity of knowing the ways of mankind, which
cannot be learned but from experience, and of which the highest
understanding, and the lowest, must enter the world in equal ignorance.
I have lived long in a public character, and have thought it my duty to
study those whom I have undertaken to admonish or instruct. I have
never been so rich as to affright men into disguise and concealment, nor
so poor as to be kept at a distance too great for accurate observation. I
therefore presume to tell your ladyship, with great confidence, that your
writers have instituted a world of their own, and that nothing is more
different from a human being, than heroes or heroines.—I am afraid, sir,
said Arabella, that the difference is not in favour of the present world.—
That, madam, answered he, your own penetration will enable you to
judge when it shall have made you equally acquainted with both: I have
no desire to determine a question, the solution of which will give so
little pleasure to purity and benevolence. The silence of a man who
loves to praise, is a censure sufficiently severe, said the lady. May it never
happen that you should be unwilling to mention the name of Arabella!
I hope, wherever corruption prevails in the world, to live in it with
virtue; or, if I find myself too much endangered, to retire from it with
innocence. But if you can say so little in commendation of mankind,
how will you prove these histories to he vicious, which, if they do not
describe real life, give us an idea of a better race of beings than now
inhabit the world.—It is of little importance, madam, replied the doctor,
to decide whether in real or fictitious life most wickedness is to be
found. Books ought to supply an antidote to example; and if we retire
to a contemplation of crimes, and continue in our closets to inflame our
passions, at what time must we rectify our words, or purify our hearts?
The immediate tendency of these books, which your ladyship must
allow me to mention with some severity, is to give new fire to the
passions of revenge and love; two passions which, even without such

powerful auxiliaries, it is one of the severest labours of reason and piety to suppress, and which yet must be suppressed if we hope to be approved in the sight of the only Being, whose approbation can make us happy. I am afraid your ladyship will think me too serious.—I have already learned too much from you, said Arabella, to presume to instruct you; yet suffer me to caution you never to dishonour your sacred office by the lowliness of apologies.—Then, let me again observe, resumed he, that these books soften the heart to love, and harden it to murder;—that they teach women to exact vengeance, and men to execute it; teach women to expect not only worship, but the dreadful worship of human sacrifices. Every page of these volumes is filled with such extravagance of praise, and expressions of obedience, as one human being ought not to hear from another; or with accounts of battles, in which thousands are slaughtered, for no other purpose than to gain a smile from the haughty beauty, who sits a calm spectatress of the ruin and desolation, bloodshed and misery, incited by herself. It is impossible to read these tales without lessening part of that humility, which, by preserving in us a sense of our alliance with all human nature, keeps us awake to tenderness and sympathy, or without impairing that compassion which is implanted in us as an incentive of acts of kindness. If there be any preserved by natural softness, or early education, from learning pride and cruelty, they are yet in danger of being betrayed to the vanity of beauty, and taught the arts of intrigue. Love, madam, is, you know, the business, the sole business of ladies in romances.

Arabella's blushes now hindered him from proceeding as he had intended.—I perceive, continued he, that my arguments begin to be less agreeable to your ladyship's delicacy: I shall therefore insist no longer upon false tenderness of sentiment, but proceed to those outrages of the violent passions which, though not more dangerous, are more generally hateful.—It is not necessary, sir, interrupted Arabella, that you strengthen by any new proof a position which, when calmly considered, cannot be denied. My heart yields to the force of truth; and I now wonder how the blaze of enthusiastic bravery could hinder me from remarking, with abhorrence, the crime of deliberate unnecessary bloodshed. I begin to perceive that I have hitherto at least trifled away my time, and fear that I have already made some approaches to the crime of encouraging violence and revenge.—I hope, madam, said the good man, with horror in his looks, that no life was ever lost by your incitement? Arabella, seeing him, thus moved, burst into tears, and could not immediately answer. Is it possible, cried the doctor, that such gentleness and elegance should be stained with blood?—Be not too hasty in your censure, said Arabella, recovering herself: I tremble, indeed, to think how nearly I have approached the brink of murder, when I thought myself only consulting my own glory; but, whatever I suffer, I will never more demand or instigate vengeance, nor consider my punctilios as important enough to be balanced against life.—The doctor confirmed her in her new resolutions, and thinking solitude was necessary to compose her spirits, after the fatigue of so long a conversation, he retired, to acquaint Mr Glanville, with his success; who, in the transport of his joy, was almost ready to throw himself at his feet, to thank him for the miracle, as he called it, that he had performed.

XII

In which the history is concluded

Mr GLANVILLE, WHO FANCIED TO himself the most ravishing delight from conversing with his lovely cousin, now recovered to the free use of all her noble powers of reason, would have paid her a visit that afternoon, had not a moment's reflection convinced him that now was the time, when her mind was labouring under the force of conviction, to introduce the repentant Sir George to her; who, by confessing the ridiculous farce he had invented to deceive her, might restore him to her good opinion, and add to the doctor's solid arguments, the poignant sting of ridicule which she would then perceive she had incurred. Sir George being now able to leave his chamber, and Arabella well enough recovered to admit a visit into hers, Mr Glanville entreated his father to wait on her, and get permission for Sir George to attend her upon a business of some consequence. Sir Charles no sooner mentioned this request, than Arabella, after a little hesitation, complied with it. As she had been kept a stranger to all the particulars of Mr Glanville's quarrels with the young baronet, her thoughts were a little perplexed concerning the occasion of this visit, and her embarrassment was considerably increased by the confusion which she perceived in the countenance of Sir George. It was not without some tokens of a painfully suppressed reluctance, that Sir George consented to perform his promise, when Mr Glanville claimed it; but the disadvantages that would attend his breach of it, dejected and humbled as he now was, presenting themselves in a forcible manner to his imagination, confirmed his wavering resolutions. And since he found himself obliged to be his own accuser, he endeavoured to do it with the best grace he could. Acknowledging, therefore, to Lady Bella, all the artifices her deception by romances had given him encouragement to use upon her, and explaining, very explicitly, the last with relation to the pretended princess of Gaul, he submissively asked her pardon for the offence it would now give her, as well as for the trouble it had formerly. Arabella, struck with inconceivable confusion, having only bowed her head to his apology, desired to be left alone, and continued, for near two hours afterwards, wholly absorbed in the most disagreeable reflections on the absurdity of her past behaviour, and the contempt and ridicule to which she now saw plainly she had exposed herself. The violence of these first emotions having at length subsided, she sent for Sir Charles and Mr Glanville; and having, with a noble ingenuity, expatiated upon the follies her vitiated judgment had led her into, she apologized to the first, for the frequent causes she had given him of uneasiness; and, turning to Mr Glanville, whom she beheld with a look of mingled tenderness and modesty, To give you myself, said she, with all my remaining imperfections, is making you but a poor present in return for the obligations your generous affection has laid me under to you; yet, since I am so happy as to be desired for a partner for life by a man of your sense and honour, I will endeavour to make myself as worthy as I am able of such a favourable distinction. Mr Glanville kissed the hand she gave him with an emphatic silence; while Sir Charles, in the most obliging manner imaginable, thanked her for the honour she conferred both on himself and son by this alliance.—Sir George, entangled in his own artifices, saw himself under a necessity of confirming the promises he had made to Miss Glanville, during his fit of penitence; and was accordingly married to that young lady, at the same time that Mr Glanville and Arabella were united.

We choose, reader, to express this circumstance, though the same, in different words, as well to avoid repetition as to intimate that the first-mentioned pair were indeed only married in the common acceptation of the word: that is, they were privileged to join fortunes, equipages, titles, and expence; while Mr Glanville and Arabella were united, as well in these, as in every virtue and laudable affection of the mind.

HUGH BAIRD COLLEGE
LIBRARY AND LEARNING CENTRES

END OF THE NINTH BOOK

ALSO AVAILABLE IN THE NONSUCH CLASSICS SERIES

For forthcoming titles and sales information see
www.nonsuch-publishing.com